The story embraces slavery, the emancipation movement, military action, and a daring escape from the infamous Libby Prison and across the Union lines.

I0612820

From Wig to Sword

Howard Giffard

www.newgeneration-publishing

 New Generation Publishing

Characters
England – Present Day – Ficitonal

Roger – University Lecturer who finds the diaries and letters in the attic of a house belonging to his deceased uncle.

1860's

England – Ficitional
Richard Clarke- law student who goes to America – initially to join the Union Army but becomes involved in espionage.
Laura Clarke – his sister.
George Clarke – their domineering father.
Harry Harper-   A school contemporary of Richard's who also goes to America to join the Union Army.
Victor – a loyal friend to Richard.

The South /The Confederacy/ The Rebels / The Secessionists/Secesh

Fictional
Beaumont Plantation
Colonel William Turner – the owner.
Solange   - his wife.
Kate   - his strong –willed and enterprising daughter.

His sons   - Jeff, Harry, Frank (Kate's twin) and Custis (ten years old at the opening of the novel) .

The slaves - Matthew (head groom), Sam (butler) , Nathaniel, an intelligent old man who had run away in his youth and had been returned to the plantation and punished, Cuffy (the young groom).
Susie (Kate's maid) , Mammy (old housekeeper and former nursemaid) .Rachel a beautiful young woman of mixed race whose grandfather was a member of the Turner family .

Noah Harrison - The Overseer.
Tyler Lloyd - A bumptious young man visiting the plantation.
Mr Scheider - A cotton dealer.

The Miller Family
Preston Miller (the brother of Solange) an effective businessman and entrepreneur;his daughters - Millie, Sarah and Helen and his second wife Henrietta .

The Smythe Household in Richmond Virginia
Susan Smythe – an attractive woman whose husband is away in the Confederate Army.
Walter and Martin- her Schoolboy sons.   .
Gabriel - her slave and Manager of her household.
.

Miscellaneous
Clara and Amelia - Southern Belles engaged in espionage activity for the North.

Philip/ Phillipe DuFresne- An adventurer and blockade – runner of dubious repute.

Lord Bullingdon - An arrogant English aristocrat.
John - A farmer outside Richmond.
Michael Wilson - A young acquaintance of Kate's.

True Historical Characters ,
General Robert E . Lee – Commander of the Confederate Army of Northern Virginia .
General Winder – Brigadier General and Provost Marshall of the Confederacy.
General Bonham- briefly appears in the novel prior to the Battle of Bull Run.
Jefferson Davis – President of the Confederacy.
Varina Davis - His wife.
Rose O'Neal Greenhow - A 'femme fatale' and former doyenne of social and ambassadorial circles who spied for the South.
Little Rose - Her daughter – (eight years old at the opening of the novel).
Betty Duval – A young woman involved in an espionage mission.
Mary Chesnut - A celebrated diarist who gave a good view of the social effects of the War on Southern Society .
Elizabeth Van Lew -A wealthy , committed abolitionist living in Richmond who was involved in very effective espionage for the North and who was instrumental in the escape of a number of Federal prisoners of war from the infamous prisons in and around Richmond back across the Union lines.
Eliza Van Lew - her mother.

Dr Hauptmann - A German Doctor who proves useful to Elizabeth.

Mary Bowser - Elizabeth's freed slave who was sent North to be educated and now forms an essential part of her spy ring.

The North / The Federals / The Yankees / The Union .

True Historical Characters
President Abraham Lincoln –
Mary Todd Lincoln - His wife who was liable to violent swings of mood . She was the daughter of a slave- owner .

Allan Pinkerton - The founder of ' Pinkerton's Dectective Agency' .

.

Fictional Characters .
The Matthews Family – In New York.

Foster Matthews – a young doctor whom Richard meets on the voyage out to New York. Dr John Matthews his father and Mary his mother. His sisters – Susannah and Ann.

Colonel Wilmer – An officer who along with Pinkerton interviews Richard for espionage work.

Dick Jenkins - A successful lawyer in New York.

Sam Parker - A youth Richard meets in Washington.

Duncan and his brother Fergus Maclean - Young Scottish engineers whom Richard meets In Liverpool and who accompany him on the voyage.

Hal - An obnoxious acquaintance of Foster Matthews.

Colonel Brent -Imprisoned by the Confederates.

Note – Washington the capital of the Union is a mere 100 miles from Richmond the capital of the Confederacy.

Chapter One

England – Present Day

Roger stepped from the rickety ladder into the loft. His tolerance of practical matters such as cleaning cars and sorting out houses was low.

He was anxious to return to his students. Those in the third year had their exams in three weeks. This was the most stressful time of year for them and they needed Roger's support.

However, he mustn't complain.. At the start of the autumn term he had received a letter from a firm of solicitors informing him that an uncle, whom he had met infrequently had left him his entire estate.

It was not possible to give an exact figure at this early stage, but the firm stated a conservative estimate would be approximately three quarters of a million pounds. Although Roger was unmarried and had always been careful with money, his salary as a lecturer was not brilliant. He now had total financial independence. He was also to discover that when solicitors use the word 'conservative' they mean 'ultra-conservative'. When the price had been agreed for the sale of the house, he would receive just over a million pounds.

Contracts had been exchanged with a far earlier date for completion than Roger had expected. He had been told that everything must be cleared from the house-including the loft-prior to the sale. Roger had decided not to use a firm of house clearers. They would probably charge the earth and if there happened to be anything of great value or interest he may never know about it. No, although the timing was very inconvenient he would have to do the job himself.

When Roger arrived at the house he quailed at the size of the task. Uncle Arthur had been an eccentric bachelor who had hoarded everything. However, Roger would never regret his decision.

Amongst the mass of clutter were some valuable pieces of furniture and interesting paintings. These had already been placed in storage. He had made an arrangement to have the hundreds of books delivered to the college library where he would sort them out later. The same had happened to the boxes of papers. He had glanced at just a few of them.

Many of the papers appeared to relate to Arthur's work as an archaeologist, which would be of interest to the Archaeology Department at the college. Roger would certainly look through the other papers and letters himself which dated back to the nineteen thirties. He saw that some of them were addressed from Bletchley Park which had the official stamp on them after they had been passed for censorship.

Roger had no idea that Arthur was there! Although, thinking about it, Arthur was just the sort of eccentric academic oddball to be selected and his first degree was in Maths. He would have been in his element in decoding. Due to the Official Secrets Act he could not have told anybody and was not the type to mention it inadvertently and certainly not to his garrulous extrovert sister (Roger's mother) who had little in common with her secretive, scholarly loner of a brother.

"You're just like your Uncle Arthur. He always had his nose in a book! Why don't you go out and play football?" She would say to Roger when she thought that the bookish youngster had been reading for too long.

Roger flashed his torch and heaved a sigh of relief

that the loft was almost empty. Judging by the rest of the house, he had been frightened that it would be full of junk. He fumbled with a light switch . A weak light guttered from the solitary bulb hanging from the centre of the rafters.

Roger heaved himself up onto the grime–impregnated floor and peered around. He was a man who did things thoroughly. The dim light did not reveal the dark recesses so he methodically walked round the roof, shining his torch and taking care to keep his head low. He glimpsed a heap of what looked like cloth. He gave it a kick. His foot struck something hard. He stepped back quickly. He crouched down and started to pull away the filthy material which he rolled up in a loose ball. He saw that it covered a large metal trunk. He tried to move it without success.

Roger then knelt down and managed to work the trunk free from its entrenched position flush with the roof and, still kneeling, shoved it with difficulty in short bursts until it lay under the dim light.

He then rested back on his heels. He fiddled with the lid and was not surprised that it did not open although he could see that the lock was up so it would be a mere matter of leverage to open the lid. He was glad that he had brought his tools which were wrapped in a leather roll.

Gradually Roger inched the blade of his screwdriver under the lid until the gap widened to enable his fingers to gain sufficient purchase to wiggle it further. Eventually he threw the lid open. It hit the floor with a resounding slap sending up a cloud of dust.

Holding the torch in his right hand Roger peered down to examine the contents. With his left hand he picked up some newspapers – yellow with age – taking care that they did not crumble. 'The Times'of 1925 peered at him though the grime. Had not the trunk been opened since then?

Interest now fully awakened, Roger laid the papers carefully inside the lid. They would make fascinating reading. He groped a number of items which were individually wrapped in cloth. He took out one which felt small and hard. He slowly opened the cloth to find brown paper. The beam of the torch revealed that it was heavily impregnated with oil. He opened the paper. It was a revolver.

Roger examined it carefully turning it over and caressing it with his fingers whilst, at the same time keeping the torch trained on it. His lifelong interest in firearms told him that it was a Colt made sometime around the eighteen fifties or sixties.

Intrigued, he set to work on the remainder of the contents. He piled them up inside the lid. He did not have time to examine them properly now, nor, save for a sword, could he identify most of them as they were all encrusted with grunge. Roger could tell that the bottom of the trunk contained just papers.

Roger's knees were now sore and he could feel the cramp in the backs of his thighs from kneeling for too long. With one hand resting on the edge of the trunk he struggled painfully to his feet and searched for a space between the rafters where he could stretch to his full height.

Roger looked at his watch. He had been up here for nearly half an hour! The removal men were coming in the morning when the house would be finally cleared and the keys handed to the agent. There was still a lot to do. Regrettably he could spend no more time examining this treasure trove. He clambered down the ladder to fetch black bin-liners so that he could take the contents home to examine them at leisure. The trunk was too heavy and cumbersome to move by himself. In this one small instance he would just be inconsiderate to the new owners and leave it where it was.

Two evenings later Roger sat at his kitchen table over which he had methodically spread newspapers. He was tired and ready for bed but just had to examine the articles found in the loft. He had left Uncle Arthur's house early the previous afternoon and had decided he couldn't be bothered to cook for himself at home but would have a meal in the college refectory.

As soon as he walked in he realised that this had been a mistake.Three days is a long time in the life of an angst-ridden student in the weeks prior to exams and he had to spend the evening listening to woes and giving whatever reassurance he could.It was past ten o'clock before he reached home. By the time he had unloaded the car and dumped everything in the hall he was exhausted and flopped into bed.

Roger was now able to examine the objects properly. There was a soldier's drinking canteen; a small heap of decayed cloth but with a small hard piece which could have been the peak to a cap formed by the cloth then, a hinged frame containing two photographs which were so filthy that the subjects were indecipherable.

Roger set to work on the photographs with a damp cloth soaked in hot water and detergent, slowly rubbing the glass set in a silver frame. Eventually he could see two individual, spotted, sepia daguerreotypes. The first was of a young man in military uniform which from Roger's detailed knowledge of military history, he identified as being American – from the mid-nineteenth century.

The second picture was of a young woman in the usual sort of formal dress which is associated with the few people of that era who were wealthy enough to have their photographs taken. Both subjects were looking slightly to the left in the stiff, unsmiling, and expressionless manner worn for the new strange science of photography. Who were they and what bound them together to have their pictures in hinged frames? Brother and sister, husband and wife, star-crossed lovers....?

The next article was a heavy watch and chain. The metal was so dull Roger could not distinguish it but he thought that it could be silver, or an alloy of silver. After some fiddling the watch flew open. The metal on the inside was much cleaner than that on the outside and he could detect an inscription. He held it up to the light. It read 'To Richard from Kate with love. 1865 '.

1865! That was the year the American Civil War ended. The man in the photograph must have served in the Federal Army judging by his uniform. He was presumably Richard and the woman must be Kate. They were probably sweethearts or husband and wife. Sisters didn't usually give their brothers inscribed watches. Did Richard survive the war? Or did Kate live a long and lonely life mourning her dead husband or lover, taking these mementos out from time to time and caressing them sadly and lovingly?

Now for the sword. After trying to tug it from its scabbard Roger jiggled it gently and with the aid of W.D.40. managed to pull it free. He held the blade up to the light and just under the hilt he glimpsed an inscription which would be far more difficult to read than that on the watch. With the aid of steel wool, water, detergent and a magnifying glass he eventually managed to decipher. 'Prstd. Lt .R. Clarke. Jne 1865'. Gen Sherman'.

Sherman! The scourge of the South. One of Roger's specialised papers in his finals had been Sherman's campaign through Georgia and the Carolinas. When he was doing his doctorate he had spent a year at the University of Atlanta and the name of Sherman still

16

caused people to spit.

Lieutenant R. Clarke must be the young man in the photograph and the Richard who was the recipient of the watch from Kate. The war finished in April and the sword was presented in June so Richard survived the war. An unreasonable and unexpected wave of gladness surged through Roger that a young love had not been destroyed before it had time to mature and flourish. Roger was now burning with curiosity to find out more about the lives of Kate and Richard. Could the huge packet of papers provide some clues?

For the first time Roger now noticed that the ends of the brown paper were sealed together by big blobs of red sealing wax. The parcel couldn't have been opened for at least fifty years.The only time he had ever seen sealing wax was on old legal documents which he had seen once whilst doing research in the British Museum on the Tolpuddle Martyrs.

There was no room on the kitchen table so Roger took the package into the dining room. He cut the string and levered the bladed of his Swiss Army penknife under the hard old wax which broke off in small lumps. He carefully opened up the brown paper to find bundles of papers tied round in ancient ribbons. His eyes lighted on some newspaper articles. Although the paper was old he could read the print easily. The first one was 'The New York Times 'of April 1865.

April 1865.This was one of the most momentous months in American History which marked the end of the Civil War and the Assassination of Lincoln. Roger was used to reading old newspaper articles but still never failed to be surprised at the muted form of reporting. Today photographs would proliferate and headlines would scream ' Death of Lincoln Shock' or 'Nation Heaves A Sigh of Relief as War Ends in Country Court House, or'Union Merciful to South

Beaten Into Submission'. The articles were written in the detached formal style of the period. The standard of English dwarfed that of today's broadsheets to say nothing of the tabloids.

Most of the other papers seemed to be letters and diaries. The paper was now fairly dark with age but was, for the most part thick, and of good quality and it opened without tearing.Roger saw that there were several different types of handwriting but the common denominators were that they were all sloping and closely packed and legible . People were taught to write properly in those days.

Some letters were addressed to 'Father 'and signed 'Your dutiful son Richard'. Some were addressed to 'My dearest Laura' and signed by 'Your ever-loving brother Richard'. The other correspondence included many letters to and from Kate,and various military personnel.

Roger raised his head from his arms and looked at his watch. It was nearly seven-fifteen a.m. He had fallen asleep at the table. He must have been reading until after four because that was when he last remembered looking at the time and he still had only read a fraction of the contents.

Roger could see from what he had read was that Richard Clarke had been a meticulous diarist as well as a prolific writer of letters to correspondents who replied to him, and each other, with enthusiasm. The quality of the prose of the writers would put his students to shame and indeed many of the lecturers. It did not 'get dark 'for Richard but he became 'cloaked in the dark mantle of the night '.

Roger had to leave for college now but he could not wait to return to the world of Lieutenant Richard Clarke and Kate Turner.

Chapter Two

South Carolina - April 1861

Kate thundered along the bank of the Wateree River. Jack's head stretched out in front of her crouched body. The scenery bumped past her. She reached the huge pine tree well before Frank and reined in patting the animal's heaving, sweating flanks, allowing him to dip his head and drink. Frank had slowed his pace when he knew there was no chance of beating his sister. He cantered up, grinning.

"I guess I should have known there was no chance of beating a horse bred by the Worthingtons.He's a fine animal."

Kate turned round in the saddle. "Isn't he beautiful? I'm so glad Father bought him. I know you were annoyed that I did not wait for you to come home but I knew somebody else would have him if we weren't quick. I was so certain you would love him .We've never disagreed about horseflesh yet". Nor, about much else, she thought to herself.

"We'd better wait for Custis." Their youngest brother galloped up on his first horse. He had just graduated from a pony. "You shouldn't race each other when I'm with you. It's not fair."

He took off his hat and wiped his red shining face with the back of his hand. Frank laughed and reached out from his saddle and rumpled his hair.

"Life ain't fair, Junior. Hey, you got nothing to worry about. You won the five mile race for your age at the Worthingtons' picnic, and the way you took those hedges and swam your horse through the river at the hunt last fall was brilliant. You are only ten! You're a

19

better rider than any other kids your age in the county and plenty of adults besides."

Jack suddenly jerked his head up from the water. Kate controlled him expertly until he was quiet.

"You're certainly a better rider than Greg Morrison. He always looks as though he's following a funeral." Custis laughed. His good humour restored. The three of them sat forward with the reins extended, their hands resting on the horses' necks whilst the animals drank thirstily.

"Do you think I could outride most Yankees?"

"Sure, you could. And outshoot them as well. You got that squirrel right between the eyes yesterday." Frank assured him.

"I hope the war won't start until I'm old enough to fight the Yankees."

"Stop it, the pair of you! I'm sick of all this talk of war. Let's just enjoy this beautiful sunshine and this lovely ride. There's no war yet and there might still not be one." Kate looked at Frank for reassurance but it was not forthcoming.

"I wish you were right but somehow I don't think so."

"Neither do I but we can still hope."

Frank sighed. Both knew that war was inevitable. Unlike many other young Southern people of their background, they did not revel in the prospect. Although Frank was a first-class horseman and shot he was similar to his sister in that there was a thoughtful academic side to him. He loved reading, was a good pianist and was the best student in his college in Charleston which he regarded as a great comedown after Harvard where he had also excelled but was eclipsed inevitably by some students who were drawn from the elite of America. He was upset when his father withdrew him in the fall due to the increasing tension between the States.

"Boston will not be the place for a Southerner – particularly the son of a slave-owner if war comes. The situation is becoming increasingly serious now. It is a question of 'when.' war comes not 'if.' Finish college near home. Transfer to Charleston."

Although he had been annoyed, Frank knew that his father was right. He had not mentioned to his father that things were becoming increasingly difficult at Harvard. Had he done so he would have been withdrawn earlier.

Boston in general, and Harvard in particular had always been in the forefront of political and social thought and discussion. Southerners had always been in the minority and now the abolitionist movement which had always been strong was becoming increasingly more vociferous and debates both in and out of the debating society were escalating.

Robert Gould Shaw, the son of leading Boston abolitionists ,was particularly prominent in these debates.

"Frank how can you justify that one human being can own another?" Shaw had put to him on more than one occasion. "You know it's wrong."

"I know we cannot justify it morally or intellectually. The trouble is we have it whether it's right or wrong, and the whole Southern society and economy is based on it."

"That's no justification for keeping something that's indefensible: the fact that the society that it shores up will crumble if it is kicked away! Better that the society collapse and starts again. And it will collapse." Frank knew that there was no intellectual counter-argument to Shaw. The young men formed part of a circle where sloppy reasoning was immediately challenged. Shaw knew this and warmed to his theme.

"Frank. The world will not stand for it. Nobody has

it now in the civilised world other than us and Brazil (if you can call Brazil civilised!). The British abolished it in their colonies nearly thirty years ago. The British Government did compensate the owners to a certain extent although they are not nearly as well off as they were – Elizabeth Barrett Browning's father was among them but the family still manages to live in Wimpole Street which is not exactly the workhouse. And she could still write her poems whilst waited on by servants. I daresay our Government might have to compensate people like you although you will be worse off but still a good deal better off than most of the population and no doubt you will be able to more than survive. Families like yours always do. It's just a price which has to be paid for humanity and one which I can equally see that you Southerners just don't want to pay."

"Judge Taney doesn't agree," countered Frank without great conviction. This argument didn't deserve any serious recognition from Shaw neither did it receive any.

"What can you expect from lawyers? They get so tangled up in their own legal complexities and arguments that it's surprising they don't strangle themselves. Anyway he doesn't agree with slavery. Not only has he freed his own slaves but he has bought the freedom of others. That judgement won't last".

Frank did not pursue what he knew was a lame argument. Taney's judgement in the Dredd Scott case had delighted the slave owning fraternity and appalled the abolitionists in equal degrees.

Dredd Scott was a slave who had sued for his freedom on the basis that he had lived on free soil for a number of years. After various hearings,the case eventually reached the Supreme Court when Chief Justice Taney held that according to the Constitution

22

Scott was still a slave and that neither slaves nor any of their descendants could not only not have any rights of hearing in court but they could never be American citizens .The founders of the republic had considered them as "beings of an inferior order and unfit to associate with the white race – so far inferior that they had no rights which the white man was bound to respect ."

Frank at this stage of the arguments could say nothing. He had always admitted to himself that the Taney judgement was wrong and it would not be long before it would be overturned in some respect – probably by an amendment in the Constitution.

Frank knew that Shaw was right but could not force himself to denounce a way of life in which he had grown up nor could he be disloyal to his state of South Carolina or the South in general. Frank had dutifully enrolled at the college in Charleston and had joined the local militia .When the time came he would do his duty but he detested the fervour of many of his contemporaries who declared that they ' could not wait to shoot that stove-pipe hat off ole Abe Lincoln' head .' He knew that war would be disastrous for the South and finish for ever the way of life that he had known.

Kate's feelings were similar to those of her brother. She had been a keen student at home and her father had suggested that when Frank leave for Harvard that she also go north to one of the new colleges for women that were quickly sprouting up. Her mother wouldn't hear of it.

"No girl round here has ever been. She'll never get a husband." The Colonel sighed. He knew that most Southern men did not like clever, well-informed women who would argue on politics and world affairs preferring women who fluttered their eye-lashes and pouted – until they married them of course when they were expected to run the household efficiently, produce many babies and care for children and slaves who were sick. However, in this respect he did not bother to argue with his wife. He just continued to educate Kate in his own way.

Kate sat upright in her saddle. "Come on. We'd better get back. I want to spend a few minutes in our favourite spot." They hoisted their horses' heads from the water and with dripping muzzles the animals slowly ambled along the bank. Custis was fidgety. Kate looked at him reprovingly. Younger brothers can be very irritating. Nothing was going to spoil her precious moments with Frank – there probably wouldn't be opportunities for many more."Go on .We'll follow you. And don't ride that horse too hard! You've given him a good enough gallop already. Horses are not machines! And mind you are careful near the house and stables! There are lots of visitors and some of their horses may have uncertain tempers so don't get too close to them!"

Custis raised his eyes to Heaven: he had heard these warnings many times but he knew one couldn't be too careful with horses. The Turner children had been very well- trained in horsemanship, taking care of horses and how to behave when near them. The slightest inconsiderate movement could cause a nervous or bad – tempered horse to kick, rear or even bolt. Custis whooped and cantered off.

Frank laughed. "You should have told him to rush back and he would have gone slowly! No need to go on at him about the house and stables. He knows all that. He's not stupid".

"I know. I am beginning to sound like a nagging mother! It must be all this uncertainty in the air!"

Kate's red hair glinted in the April sunlight. With her fair skin and blue eyes and Frank's brown eyes, dark hair and general swarthy appearance, nobody would have thought they were twins. Frank had inherited his mother's French looks whilst Kate resembled her father's family which was a mixture of Scottish, Irish and English stock..

Beaumont covered an area of some five square miles and was bisected by the Wateree River which had been the means of transporting cotton to Charleston before the coming of the railway. In the 1740's George Turner, an English boy of fifteen, had become orphaned when his widowed mother and two younger brothers died of smallpox. Seeing no future for himself in rural Gloucestershire, he made his way to Bristol and obtained a passage as an indentured slave to Charleston and began his period of indentured servitude with the owner of a small plantation.

George was an intelligent and willing worker and quickly gained the confidence of the owner, and more importantly, of his young wife who was not immune to the good looks and pleasing personality of this indentured slave who had received a sound, if basic education ,and was literate and numerate. Shortly before George's indentures expired the owner died suddenly. The new widow realised that she could not run the plantation on her own. She offered to marry George and Beaumont would be theirs. Apart from the obvious commercial sense of the idea, the prospect was not physically or emotionally repugnant to either of them. The marriage worked well. So did the plantation although there were a few disturbances during the War of Independence.

The plantation and the number of slaves grew, but not spectacularly.

Slavery was dying out in the North for economic as well as altruistic reasons. Slaves did not have to be paid for their labour although there were some forward thinking establishments who did pay small amounts they had to be purchased, fed, clothed and doctored. After all a slave was a valuable piece of property and had to be cared for in the same way as a prize stallion or hunting dog and in many cases in an increasingly sophisticated society they did not have the skills to 'earn their keep'. Slavery was also on the wane in the South where the lands that had produced tobacco (heavily dependent on   slaves)   were now nearly exhausted. In 1808 Congress had voted to abolish the international slave trade but the domestic slave trade was booming as never before, and all because of a Northerner called Eli Whitney.

Cotton grew well in the South but there was no fast way to separate the seed from the cotton other than by hand. In 1797 Whitney changed all that. He invented a cotton engine "gin" which used toothed-cylinders to snag the lint through a wire screen, leaving the seeds behind. It was simple but very effective. It had taken a slave ten hours to produce one pound of lint but one gin would eventually crank out up to one thousand pounds a day. The South exploded. "King Cotton" now supported the South in great style and the hungry cotton looms of England were being fed by ever increasing production. Slaves were needed now as never before and the flagging 'peculiar institution.' as Southerners so quaintly referred to slavery was not only revitalised but flourished as never before.

George Turner was one of the first to acquire a gin and Beaumont was immediately and dramatically transformed from a reasonably profitable plantation to one of heady success.

Thousands of acres were hacked from the wilderness and the number of slaves mushroomed. By the time George died in 1814 he handed his children the most successful plantation in South Carolina.

The twins usually stopped at a bend in the river to

look at their home. They had always thought it looked best from there. The house crested the hill overlooking the river. Today, it gleamed white and splendid in the sun. White porticos girdled the dwelling, creating a circular veranda.

In the early years of the century George's son William had caused something of a sensation when he decided to build a splendid new mansion. "We are going to have a house worthy of Beaumont. It's now the most important plantation in South Carolina and we can afford it. This house has just been added onto and added onto and it's just like a fat man's suit that just has to be let out every time he puts on a few pounds. It's a shapeless mess! We're going to have a white mansion of stone!"

Most plantation homes were still wooden or rather hotchpots versions of wood, brick and various other materials, giving a ramshackle appearance reminiscent of dwellings on a frontier which indeed the area had been until recently.

The building of Beaumont generated a huge amount local and, indeed national interest. Architects and stonemasons were brought in from England and the North. Furniture, paintings, porcelain and carpets were imported from England and France. When the work had been completed the mansion boasted some eighty rooms including a massive library which was now the envy of the neighbourhood and attracted many scholars; it stocked books in several languages, books relating to law, engineering and medicine as well as popular fiction by authors such as Dickens, Trollope and Thackeray.

As the twins gazed at their beloved home they both wondered how many more times they would sit together like this and how long their present lifestyle would last. As with many sets of twins a kind of telepathic communication existed between them. Each knew what the other was thinking but neither could bear to put thoughts into words.

Eventually Kate ventured. "There's one thing you don't have to worry about. I reckon I know almost as much about the plantation as Daddy. I'll be able to run it better than any manager."

"I know. Pa told me when I got back yesterday." Kate usually addressed her father and referred to him as 'Daddy' whereas Frank and her two older brothers preferred ' Pa' unless they were in any kind of trouble in which case 'Father' was usually used. "You've spent the last three months in the office. He says you know the account books better than he does .That doesn't surprise me. When we were tutored together at home you were much quicker with figures than me".

"Yes. And I've been riding around with him most days since I left the schoolroom and you went to Harvard. He knew that if war broke out all you men would go and somebody from the family has to run the place."

"He's just taken on that guy Harrison. What's he like?"

"Just the best of poor lot I guess. There were only three. One was a drunkard. You could smell the liquor on him and the other's references didn't sound too good. I saw Harrison with Father. I didn't like him much. He has spent too long time up North and has been a manager in engineering and is very full of himself but he grew up near Columbia and ,like many Southerners up North, the threat of war drove him home."

"I can vouch for the fact that it's uncomfortable for Southerners up North right now. And in the last two or three months the trains coming south have been packed. But how does engineering fit him for overseeing a plantation?"

"As I said he was the best of a poor lot. And he did grow up round a plantation. His Daddy was a sort of dirt farmer who used to help up at the plantation and he sometimes went with him. Despite that background he seemed arrogant and I can see him throwing his weight around. And he sure didn't seem impressed at being interviewed by a woman."

Frank grinned. "It sounds as though you'll get along just fine!"

Kate playfully flicked her whip at him. "Well with Daddy, four brothers and a house full of male visitors including boys of all ages I reckon I have had plenty of practice in figuring out the male species. You really are not that complicated you know."

Frank was not going to pursue that line of discussion. He knew it was pointless when Kate was discussing gender. "He sounds totally above himself but you'll handle him. I'm surprised though that Father thought he needed him when he's got you".

"Nice of you to say so but you know he's done it for appearance sake. You know he won't take advantage of the Twenty Slave Rule which they are talking about bringing in."

Frank nodded. "That's just not Father." Owners of plantations with more than twenty slaves would not be expected to serve in the Army if this would leave the plantation without a white man and thus vulnerable to slave -rebellion.

Hooves drummed as they crossed the bridge. They clicked to their tired horses and cantered up the sloping uncultivated parkland towards the house; they then instinctively turned right so that they could ride up to the house along the beautiful tree-lined drive which ran for about a mile from the road to the house, finishing by skirting well-tended lawns dotted with lovely shady oaks, palmettos and other trees.

The lawns and the veranda were alive with people standing, walking, sitting, eating and drinking. Despite regular, copious meals 'snacks' such as fried chicken could be ordered at any time of the day or night. Slaves would appear quietly and unobtrusively with food and drink and then, just as silently, remove the dirty plates and glasses. Children outnumbered the adults. Plantation families spawned prolifically with ten or more children not being uncommon. If a wife died a replacement was usually found quickly to begin a second brood. The Turner family of five was small by comparison with the majority.

Classes for the children had finished at lunchtime. Although Custis was the only Turner child being educated at home by a resident tutor, visiting children were also tutored as some guests often stayed for months, bringing tutors with them. The older children had finished riding or other sports, and were now playing with each other and the younger children.

Suddenly ,the busy but tranquil scene was interrupted by the dull sound of hooves and a yell. Kate turned round. "Oh, it's that mad head Tyler Lloyd."In the distance a young man, bestride a black horse which he was whipping mercilessly was galloping up the drive. This was a serious breach of the rules of the house which - for reasons of safety - forbade galloping or even cantering up the section of the drive which bordered the lawns. It was particularly dangerous now, due to the large number of people. Fortunately for the young man, Colonel Turner was in the house otherwise he would have received an immediate public dressing down. Just before Tyler reached the lawn he pulled up hard, causing his mount to rear spectacularly. Some of the younger element looked impressed, the older people looked annoyed. Nervous mothers and nursemaids watched their young children – some ran to them whisking them from harm's way. The twins' horses began to sidestep and frisk about. The riders managed to quieten them with a little difficulty. Frank's face was a mask of fury.

"What does that bloody fool think he's doing? I never could stand that guy. He's got a brain the size of a dime. Is he trying to impress the girls, or what?"

"Any girl who's impressed by him has the brain the size of a nickel. Daddy should send him home."

"Best kill him first. And then send him home in a box. Come on let's just get these horses back to the stables. We don't want them excited any more. We'll deal with that jerk later."

The twins steered the now docile horses right through the mass of vegetation which screened the house from the outbuildings - the dairy, smoke- house, stables, carriage-houses, grist-mill, cotton gin, smithy and workshops where the implements for the plantation were made and repaired. They clopped into the stable-yard where a number of grooms were involved in various tasks such as leading horses to and from the stables, cleaning hooves, mending tack, feeding or grooming horses. Others were watering horses in the huge horse pond, leading or quietly riding horses to or from the paddocks which lay further on towards the slave cabins which stood well away from the house.

The Turners usually entertained guests but the house was especially full now. April was a popular time to go visiting and this year was no exception despite the political unrest. The rules of Southern hospitality demanded that invitations were issued freely, and if requested, were not refused. Guests often stayed for months at a time and brought their own servants such as nursemaids, personal maids, tutors and grooms with them.

Cuffy,the fourteen- year old groom, held Jack's head talking to him quietly and stroking his nose whilst Kate dismounted at the mounting block. It was just in time as Tyler clopped into the yard – his horse sweating and blowing heavily. Some of the other horses began to move uneasily and required grooms' attention. "Ain't one of you niggers going to hold my horse or am I going to have to flog the lot of you?"

Frank walked up to him slowly so as not to frighten the horse and held the bridle. He was shaking with fury. "They can't, you idiot, because they are calming the horses which you have terrified with your ridiculous noise. They could hear your yelling and your horse snorting long before you appeared in the yard. Just what the hell do you think you are playing at ?. I can't stop you flogging your own groom but you are not flogging ours. Now be quiet! And get down. I have your horse."

Tyler dismounted wordlessly whilst Frank continued to vent his anger. " You've got that poor horse in a dreadful state. Look at the froth round his mouth. And he's soaked with sweat. He needs a rug immediately or he'll catch a chill. I shouldn't be surprised if Father doesn't send you home. You know the rules about riding near the house. You are lucky you didn't cause an accident .You frightened everybody to death. What's the matter with you?"

Kate looked on half-amused, half-disgusted. She was amused because Tyler was in a similar state to that of his horse. Sweat was running down his big meaty face. He was normally immaculately dressed but now his clothes were covered in dust, he was hatless and his coat and waistcoat were undone. 'He'll be frothing at the mouth himself soon.' She thought to herself.

Kate was disgusted because whereas Frank couldn't stand Tyler, she loathed him. He was conceited, haughty and overbearing, was convinced that most women were in love with him and when (as in most cases) his advances were rejected he just shrugged his shoulders and assumed there was something wrong with the woman concerned. Kate despised most of all his cruelty to those weaker than himself or who were in no position to fight back. Especially abhorrent to her was his cruelty to horses.

Cruelty was something that was never practised at Beaumont. Unlike some plantation owners Colonel Turner never ill-treated his wife, children, animals or slaves – some of whom he had freed. He whipped his slaves very seldom and he was always very critical of men who did. "That man is begging for a slave-rebellion." He often said when he heard of a particularly brutal incident. It was the same with horses. "A bad-tempered owner will never create a good-tempered horse" – was a principle that he instilled into his children.

Tyler for his part didn't just dislike Kate, he was terrified of her. When they were both about fifteen his family was paying another extended visit to the Turners. He had fumbled Kate on a couple of occasions only to receive some hard slaps across his face.

One morning Kate had decided to take an early ride before breakfast. She made her way towards the paddock to collect her horse and then take him to the stables where she would saddle him up. As she approached the paddock she heard the terrified snorting of a horse, shouting and the sound of hitting. She rushed round the screen of trees to see Tyler beating his horse round the head with a stick. "I'll teach you. You goddamn sonofabitch!" The animal was rearing up and thrashing in terror. At the moment when it looked as though he was going to smash Tyler's head with his hooves Kate ran up whip in hand.

"Stop that at once!" She screamed. She lashed out with her whip laying open Tyler's cheek. The boy screamed and fell to the ground. He started to cry.

"That's nothing to what that poor horse would have done to you had I not been here. He would have crushed your stupid head. Did you not realise that? Not that you don't deserve it! If I ever see you within one hundred yards of a horse holding a whip or stick again, I will kill you. And finish the job which this horse started! You can ill-treat slaves and animals who can't fight back but you can't take any punishment yourself. You're a booby and a coward. Look at you, great baby! Sobbing like you were two years old which is about the level of your intelligence. Get back to the house. I'll take care of the horse. Keep away from him. Can't you see he's terrified of you? His name is Bayard isn't it?"

Tyler nodded. The blubbering boy slunk off to the house staunching his cheek with his handkerchief. Bayard was now standing still but blowing hard, his eyes rolling with the reins dangling to the ground. Kate walked up to him quietly, talking to him constantly using his name. When she was near enough she blew into his nostrils. She patted and stroked him, chatting in a soothing way.

Kate heard a slight rustle and glanced round to see Matthew, the head groom standing by her holding a bowl of oats. As head groom he had status and respect from the family as well as the slave community. He was no longer a slave having been granted his freedom by the Colonel, and was now paid for his services.

"Respect from slaves and servants are not ours by right. It has to be earned. And in return they will hopefully reward you with loyalty. You can be sure that meanness guarantees resentment. Grudging obedience burns into a man's soul. And slaves do have souls despite what Judge Taney said. At some time in the future slavery will end (the Colonel always referred to slavery as just that and not 'our peculiar institution.' which was a term that many southerners euphemistically used). And if our way of life is to continue we will need staff that has been decently treated who, in turn, may treat us decently. Humanity is remembered just as much as harshness and both are repaid in kind. Not always but usually", the Colonel had told his family on more than one occasion.

Matthew had heard the commotion and knowing exactly what to do had arrived noiselessly with what was needed. He and Kate coaxed and wheedled the horse by slowly bringing the bowl to his mouth- to do it too quickly or jerkily would have startled him and he would have upset it. Bayard snuffled tentatively the inside of the bowl and gradually became more interested and finally he was munching away happily. When he had finished they walked him quietly to the stables ;one on either side, constantly talking and patting. They settled him in his stall and put a rug over him. Matthew said nothing about Tyler. Like most slaves he usually wore an inscrutable expression but his look of contempt was obvious.

Kate expected retribution when she returned to the house. Although her father was a fair man and would have applauded her actions inwardly, the fact remained that she had attacked a guest and to make matters worse she was a woman. Southern ladies were just not expected to behave in that way. However, to her surprise the event was never mentioned. Tyler knew he was in the wrong. His fear of Kate (to say nothing of his shame at having been beaten by a woman) was matched by his fear of his father who had beaten him on a number of occasions for his hasty temper and rough treatment of horses.The vigorous outdoor life, particularly when it involved horses and guns, caused many injuries and

Tyler was easily able to blame his relatively minor injury on collision with a tree whilst riding.

"I've always told that boy he rides horses too hard." His father said without even bothering to look up from the corn prices. "I hope he's learned his lesson. Tyler's mother was too occupied with her brood of seven children to pay him much attention. The constant arrival of babies ensured that the older children were left to their own devices.

Now, however, the effect of Frank's scolding had only momentary effect. He slapped his boot with his whip and emitted a shrill yell. Kate had heard it many times before from her brothers, and other young men when they were excited over something or riding hard. The yell was common over the South. It was generally thought to originate from a combination of cattle-calling and cries in the hunting field. It was to be known as the famous 'Rebel Yell.' Many Yankees who were to hear it in battle were to say how terrified they were by it. Kate had always been irritated by it, unlike some girls who were amused and swept into patriotic fervour. She thought it was ridiculous and immature. She now rounded on Tyler, her blue eyes ,blazing.

"Don't you ever learn anything you fool? Didn't you hear what Frank just told you? Stop acting like a boy of ten who has just shot his first rabbit. Now behave yourself. What on earth's the matter?"

For once Tyler was not to be daunted by Kate. "What's the matter? What's the matter? We've only just gone and fired on Fort Sumter. That's what the matter is; there's definitely going to be a war!"

In December of the previous year South Carolina had seceded from the Union and was quickly followed by Mississippi, Florida, Alabama, Georgia, Louisiana and Texas. Virginia had not yet seceded but seemed likely to follow. A Confederacy of the seceded states had been quickly formed and in February Jefferson Davis had been elected President of the Confederacy.

For three months a Union garrison had remained trapped in Fort Sumter in Charleston Harbour besieged by six thousand militia men and a semi-circle of artillery batteries. Lincoln ignored advice to abandon the fort; he would provision it but would not reinforce it or rearm it provided that neither it nor the fleet were attacked. He knew that war was now inevitable but he wasn't going to fire the first shot. The Confederacy had to be the aggressor. As expected they had now thrown fuel on the smouldering embers. War was now certain.

"Isn't it great?" Whooped Tyler again. "There's going to be war."

Frank looked grim. His face had gone white. His lips compressed together. He had difficulty in squeezing the words out. "No, it isn't great. The South will be ruined. Thousands of men will die. And if it can find it a Yankee bullet might even penetrate your miniscule brain. Now go back to the house, quietly mind! Get changed for dinner and don't say a word to anyone. I don't want you frightening the ladies with your bone-headed behaviour. Otherwise I will whip you myself. If there's any news to be broken, it will be done by my father in whose house you are a guest just in case you have forgotten."

Tyler looked surly. "Guess neither of you ever did like me did you."

"Not much. But there's no need to make it worse," replied Frank nastily. No point in pretending any more when bad behaviour rendered continuing politeness a mere sham. Furthermore the nation was now at war. Frank had read enough history to know that war strips away the social conventions which cloak human nature with a veneer of civilization to reveal the brutal and stark reality of the jungle beast that lies beneath us all.

Chapter Three

Hereford – England April 1861

"You mean to disobey me?" His father's voice was not angry any more but laden with helpless disbelief. For the first time in his life his nineteen-year old son had blatantly defied him. Richard had announced that he intended to spend the afternoon on the river instead of studying his law books as his father had ordered.

"Well, I have to go. I promised the others." Richard immediately knew that he had made a mistake by mentioning his friends.

"And who may 'the others' be?"

"You know very well Father."

"I do not know very well. That is why I'm asking you",replied George Clarke, painstakingly stressing each consonant as though he was talking to a little child.

"Bill Lloyd, George Wilson and Victor Lewis." Richard knew that the sons of two of the doctors in the city and the son of the Dean of Hereford, had to be acceptable to his sanctimonious father. George suspected there would be others. "And who else?."

"Arthur and Freddie Williams ", replied Richard staring at George levelly ,he did not want a row but he knew better than to lie to his father. He had been at school with Arthur and Freddie Williams. They were the sons of a wealthy client of George but as he was a brewer, George did not regard them suitable company for his son. Richard considered this attitude to be hypocritical.

"Christ kept the company of publicans and sinners Father. You know that. Anyway their father's money is not so tainted that you won't act for him".

George's heavy red face swelled with rage. He clutched the corner of the table to steady himself. He breathed hard, his eyes protruding like organ stops. For a moment Richard thought he was going to hit him. 'If he does I'll hit him back',.he thought to himself.

For the first time in their lives, the roles had been reversed. The son who had been brought up by his father to fear him now looked at that father with an amused contempt. The father gazed back at the son with incredulous impotent bewilderment.

George eventually recovered himself. "You have not heard the last of this. You will stay with your books until five o'clock." He muttered as he stumbled out of the room, slamming shut not only the door but more importantly any further argument.

When George had slammed the door, Richard sank back into the leather chair and contemplated the umbrella standing in the corner of the office. He had no intention of obeying his father's orders. George had started the contest by being so stuffy and unreasonable but Richard had won the first round. He intended to keep winning. He grabbed his stick, clapped on his hat at a rakish angle and sauntered into the street whistling.

The unexpected victory had given Richard a boost but had not altered the fact that he was highly dissatisfied with his life. For some time now he had been looking for a release but was at a loss as to how to put it into practice. He was bored. Bored with his father, bored with Hereford and bored with the office but he was not bored with life. He just wanted to change it.

Richard was an articled clerk in his father's firm of solicitors and as such was one of the privileged few destined to become a solicitor. Save for an allowance he was paid nothing and, had he not been articled to his father, a substantial premium would have had to be paid for his articles which lasted five years.

George had built up a successful practice in Hereford. The railway had opened some five years earlier which had brought much conveyancing in the sale of land to railway company. Further legal work had been created by the new commercial life that the railway had breathed into Hereford.

Much of Richard's work was repetitive and dull involving copying documents, drafting letters for somebody else's approval (who very often altered them which was frustrating), issuing and serving summonses and delivering items by hand. A large part of his spare time was occupied in studying to qualify as a solicitor,but he did have a taste for the law. He had passed the first part of the exams and was now working for the second. George was a hard taskmaster. Richard did not resent that in itself as he was not stupid or afraid of hard work but he did object to his every move being monitored at home, as well as in the office.

George was a keen participant in the Methodist movement which had swept the country. He diligently followed the principles of thrift, self-improvement, piety and hard work inflicting them on his children with such vigour and repetitiveness that the result was deep, silent and simmering resentment. Any disagreement was regarded as disobedience and immediately and sometimes brutally quashed. It is not surprising that Richard had never loved his father – in the worst moments of their relationship he had hated him and in his best had regarded him as a tyrant to be avoided.

Richard made his way from the office behind the cathedral into Hightown where the fair was in full swing. Hereford's many public houses were always busy but during the time of the fair they were overflowing.

40

He hadn't gone far when a leaflet was thrust in his hand by a member of the Temperance Movement, urging him to attend a meeting concerning the evils of drink. He politely declined; he had had enough preaching on the subject from his father. It was impossible to avoid such people nowadays as the Temperance Movement had swept the country but Richard did realise that they did have a point with such a high proportion of wages being spent in the pub and so many wives and children being beaten up, maimed and even killed. It was particularly evident this afternoon as he had to walk round drunks that were lying unconscious in the street.

Richard weaved through the throng of busy people bent on business, pleasure or both. He had to practise skilful footwork in avoiding the animal dung which the crossing sweepers had not had time to clear away. Although the auctions had finished, many animals still had not been driven home. He gave a wide berth to a young horse that was tethered to a post; the animal's left rear hoof was slightly raised from the ground and looked suspiciously poised for a kick.

Richard passed a roundabout powered by steam, a burly man wearing a sleeveless shirt thrusting blazing firebrands down his throat, an organ-grinder whose monkey darted about on a chain thrusting out a collecting bowl, a dancing-bear whose breast-bone had been broken in infancy to make it less powerful, jugglers, men on stilts and snake-charmers.

Richard ignored entreaties to have his fortune told, to be cured of all forms of diseases which happily he did not have and the promise of a good time by a gaudily dressed woman,who would have been attractive had she not opened her mouth and revealed several missing teeth.

Richard made his way up Broad Street past The

Green Dragon Hotel and turned right, then left into Bridge Street. As he was crossing the bridge he waved at his friends at Jordan's Boatyard. They cheered when they saw him. Richard was popular.

"Your pater let you off the leash then? You thought you might have trouble with him!" Victor lifted his fishing bag into the boat. Little Freddie Williams was struggling with a crate of beer which he and his brother had purloined from the cellar of their father's pub. He was a slight youth whose thin arms were not equal to the strain. He was trying to shore up the heavy crate with his knee. Richard ran to help him.

All the boys had attended the Hereford Cathedral School and had experienced many scrapes together. Most of these were quite harmless although some were dangerous and some others downright criminal such as poaching and 'borrowing boats'. Fortunately for Richard's relationship with his father, they had never been discovered.

It was a beautiful afternoon. The sunlight danced off the water. The boat skimmed over the river as the rowers sweated – heaving their oars out of the water, feathering, and then plunging them back in again until they reached their normal fishing spot which was a deep part of the river screened by a dark canopy of trees.

The river hummed with activity. Men rowed their families with anxious mothers taking care that children did not fall into the water. Younger men entertained their sweethearts – some of them looked entranced and never took their eyes off their loved ones. Other young women did not conceal their boredom and seemed more interested in worrying as to whether their light dresses became splashed, or hanging on to their gaily coloured hats with one hand whist angling their parasols with the other to prevent their skins becoming too sunburnt like those of the agricultural workers who had to slog away in all weathers.

The boys bantered with several boating parties that they knew. When they dropped anchor they cast their lines. Arthur opened the beer and passed it round. They took it in turns to fish. Victor lay on his back. The conversation had ceased while the fishermen concentrated. Eventually Victor broke the silence.

"Have you heard about Harry Harper?"

Richard was taking a rest from fishing. He was lying on his back with his hat over his face. " I haven't seen him for some time – not since his father's business went bust and he was wondering what to do.What about him ?." He hadn't moved his hat which moved up and down as he spoke.

"Well you won't be seeing him for some time either – if ever. As you say he did not know what to do and he didn't fancy staying round here and always being known as 'that bankrupt's son'. You know what people are like they never forget anything." Richard nodded in agreement. Hereford was a closed community .Victor shifted himself in his seat.

"He decided to make a completely fresh start. He's left for America to join the Army and fight that war that is just breaking out. Apparently you get bounty for joining – about three hundred dollars – sometimes more – and the wages are about thirteen dollars a month."

Arthur whistled. That was a great deal of money.

"Isn't it illegal though? Aren't we supposed to be neutral?" Asked George.

"Yes but they can't to anything to you when you are abroad. And I'm not sure if it is a criminal offence in this country for anybody to go and join the Army over there," informed Victor with an air of authority. Richard was very quiet for the rest of the trip.

When the trip ended Richard meandered slowly and thoughtfully along the towpath beside the river and up thorough the fields past the new waterworks to the new house which crowned Broomy Hill. Since the comments about Harry Harper he had been thinking about the possibility of going to America and joining the Union Army. The war wouldn't last long. Everybody said it would be over soon. He could save some money and then find work when the war was over. This was worth thinking about.

The young man wanted adventure and escape from the prison that he visualised that his life had become. The fact that he may be exchanging it for another prison of military discipline, bullying sergeants, disease injury or indeed of the Confederates was one that he had not considered.

Highlands had been built to George's specifications some three years previously. Whenever Richard could manage it, he had come up to watch the building. He had originally come to see the site when it was covered with scrub and trees. He had watched it being cleared and even helped hold the big patient horses whilst their carts were being loaded. He had stood sentinel over the laying of the trenches and gradually seen the building rise until it dominated the skyline with its' magnificent view over the open country across the Wye to the Black Mountains in the distance.

Richard looked at the house now. The solid handsome building represented the solid middle-class wealth which had created it. It was substantial and comfortable without being extravagant, comprising four storeys including the basement which was used for general storage purposes and for the preparation of food. There were some fifteen bedrooms including the attic where the servants slept. A large garden of some three acres encircled the house, with outhouses and stables set well to the rear.

As Richard turned into the drive he felt a pang at the thoughts which had occupied him that afternoon when he saw his Sister Laura walking towards him. Laura was two years older than Richard and they had always enjoyed a very close relationship. When Scarlet Fever carried off a younger brother and sister in earlier childhood, they were the only children of the family remaining. The bond between them had been strengthened, not only by the death of their mother in childbirth a few years earlier, but by the fact that they both regarded their father as a tyrant.

The brother and sister were alike in personality – both were outgoing, fun- loving and strong-willed but were also intelligent and capable of much reflection. They differed in looks with Laura being dark-haired with brown eyes and small delicate features whilst Richard was fair-haired with blue eyes and a strong determined chin.

George was conscious of his status as one of the leading professional men in the town and he never grudged his children money on dress. Richard was always smartly turned out and this evening Laura wore a fashionable informal walking dress of deep lilac with wide sleeves and gathered drapes. Her head was crowned with a pork-pie hat trimmed at the back with long ribbons known as 'follow-me-lads'. Fortunately, George was not sufficiently well-versed in the world of fashion to know that.

Laura had troubles of her own. She was in love with an impecunious doctor of whom George did not approve.

"It is such a lovely evening that I thought I would come and meet you. I expected you home at this time. Father has been called away suddenly so we needn't worry about him for a few days."

George often took unexplained absences from work, without any notice. He gave no reason and his children knew better than to ask him. It was assumed that his trips were connected with business.

Laura slipped her arm through Richard's as they strolled up the drive towards the house past the well-kept lawns and manicured flower-beds which the gardener's boy was still hoeing. He touched his hat respectfully to the son and daughter of the house as they walked past him. They passed the stables and into the garden at the rear of the house, along the neat gravel path known as ' the covered walk 'because of the metal arch which spanned it. Vegetation was being trained over it and when it had time to mature, it would have the effect of a tunnel.

The brother and sister wandered over the lawn and past the lily pond and cut through the vegetable garden down to the paddock. There was a joyful whinny and the two riding horses galloped up, leaving the carriage horses grazing sedately at the far end. Richard reached up and stroked the nose of Hotspur, the beautiful bay.

"Richard. Edwin and I are engaged."

"That is wonderful."

Richard hugged and kissed his sister, but then his face clouded.

"I know what you are going to say – 'What about Father?'. Well, I am of age and I don't need Father's consent. I love Edwin and he loves me and if I can't marry with Father's approval then I will marry without it."

"He'll cut you off without a shilling." They both laughed. George used that phrase at least three times a week- usually to Richard.

"If Father disinherits me, then he does. It won't be the end of the world. Edwin does not have any money but he is capable of earning it. He is well-educated and well-qualified and is a very good doctor. He will be able to keep both of us."

This statement of independence of course equated with Richard's views on his own life. However, he had decided to say nothing to his sister about his new idea.

He felt dreadful about it as they had always shared confidences but he knew that she would try to stop him, and even feel forced to tell George out of concern for his own safety. His conscience was, however, eased by Laura's announcement of her plans. Edwin was applying for posts outside Hereford and as soon as one had been secured, the couple would inform George. Laura was so full of her own happiness that she did not notice any remoteness in Richard's manner.

Over the next few days the idea gradually developed into a decision. Richard would go. He resisted the desire to record his thoughts in his diary. George had never been as devious as to rifle through his son's personal belongings but one couldn't be too careful.

Making a decision is one thing. Putting it into operation and planning the details to make it viable is another. He would have to leave the country without his father's knowledge, arrive in America and disembark, before the British Embassy could receive notification from his father and arrange for a representative to meet the ship and have him detained and returned to Britain. There was also the question of obtaining sufficient funds, choosing the port of departure and booking the passage which would have to be done under a false name.

Richard wondered when and how he would be able to achieve his wish. Fate would decide far sooner than he could have anticipated.

The Thursday afternoon following the fishing trip, Richard was sitting on his high stool copying out letters in the room which he shared with three other clerks. Stubbs, the managing clerk came into the room and shot a glance at Richard.

"Your father wants to see you." The other men looked at Richard sympathetically. They were all frightened of George who had been known to beat his younger clerks but they were particularly aware that he reserved the harshest treatment for his own son.

Richard had not seen his father since the confrontation of the previous Saturday. George had returned home late yesterday night and Richard had left for the office before his father had come downstairs. He expected retribution now. Well, he was ready for it. He straightened his full-skirted frock-coat, adjusted his waist-coat and watch- chain, climbed the stairs to his father's private office, knocked the door and turned the handle on receiving the summons to 'enter'.

George Clarke sat in his pleasant office overlooking the cathedral. He was a large portly man in his late fifties with the remnants of his grey hair matched by luxuriant whiskers. George's problem with his children was mainly one of communication. He was not a bad or unkind man and although his children were very wary of him his opinion of them (as they thought) was not low. Like many parents, he only wanted what was best for them but he could not put his views across to them in a way which did not cause them to feel resentful.

Richard would have been surprised to have known George's feeling about their row. George had been unnerved by it and did actually fear further revolt. He had decided that it was now time to give his son a little more responsibility. Richard stood in his usual position in front of his father's desk with his hands down by his side waiting for instructions or condemnation. If it was the latter he would retaliate.

"Sit down Richard." Surprised, Richard took his seat. This was a rare invitation indeed.

"Stubbs tells me that you are progressing well." Richard nearly fell off his chair but said nothing. "I have decided that I should give you a little more responsibility. I am trusting you with your first major task outside Hereford and you will not be supervised. I would have asked one of the others but as the firm is extremely busy at the moment, I will have to ask you to do it. I hope that you realise the trust that I am putting in you and that you won't disappoint me. You know that the Montague family is buying further property in London?"

Richard nodded. The Montague family were very important local landowners who had made vast sums of money out of the great boom in railways over the last twenty years which they had invested in industry and land in several parts of the country. George considered himself very fortunate to have retained such clients who had really outgrown the firm.

George was not looking directly at Richard but out of the window. This was a habit which, not only Richard, but a number of other people found disconcerting.

"I will want you to go to London for a few days and attend the office of the vendor's solicitors to make copies of the documents of title. As there are a number of properties you will have to spend some ten days to a fortnight in London. You will leave next week. You'll stay in a hotel in the Strand where I have stayed before. It is extremely, good value."

Richard managed to conceal a smirk. George would not stay anywhere that wasn't good value.

"They'll look after you very well. You will of course be given sufficient money for the hotel and other living expenses whilst in London." George warmed inwardly to Richard's enthusiastic expression. The boy would obviously respond to a greater trust and responsibility which he would give him provided he returned from London with his task suitably accomplished. He was proud of his son but he would never tell him so. "That will be all my boy."

"Thank you Father,I will do my best." Richard shut the door and leant against it for a moment. The opportunity of which he had dreamed over the last few days had come. Would he now have the guts to take advantage of it?

Richard held his sister tightly. "Careful. You are not going away for ever. I can't breathe." She wriggled away from him and laughed. Richard said nothing and forced a smile to his face, managing to blink back the tears. The brother and sister waved to each other until the carriage turned the corner of the drive of the house into Broomy Hill and down the muddy little lane which was seldom dry, as the trees on either side met in the middle forming a thick green canopy. It was a short distance to the station and Richard would have walked had he no luggage.

The last ten days had involved frenetic planning by Richard. He had taken Victor into his confidence, although Victor was concerned for his friend's safety, he had done all he could to help him. Richard had of course sworn him to secrecy and as usual he had proved to be a loyal and trusty friend.

The trip to London had enabled Richard to pack most of his clothes. He would sell some of these and the proceeds, together with the money that he had saved over the years combined with that given to him for his expenses would give him sufficient funds for his passage and normal spending until he joined the Army.

He would refund his father for his expenses once he was able to do so. He would not be accused of theft. Merely 'unauthorised borrowing' he told himself.

The young men had scrutinised the newspapers for details of sailings. There were plenty from London, Liverpool and Bristol. Richard could not make a booking from Hereford, although a shipping company had an agent there. He was too well-known. He would go to London as planned and make his booking there. Hopefully, by the time his disappearance had been made public, he would be on board ship.

At Paddington Station Richard found a hansom-cab to take him to his hotel in the Strand. He had never been to London before and he was amazed and horrified by the dirt,noise, crowds and the appalling poverty surrounding the wealth in the richest city in the world.The traffic roared with the sound of hooves and iron wheels on cobbles.

Richard was accustomed to the clear bright air of Hereford which was one of the healthiest cities in England. Now the acrid fug of London seeped into his lungs and mouth like heavy, smouldering treacle. By the time he left London his clothes would stink of the soot, smog and grime which stifled to death thousands of Londoners each year. White shirts and sheets quickly became a dowdy grey and black filth crept over stone buildings. The worst months were the winter months when deaths soared but even now although it was a spring day a light fog hung in the air making it thick and airless. The sun tried to struggle through resulting in a strange mixture of murky, grey hazy sunlight. To Richard it seemed as though somebody had hung up a lantern and then swathed it with filmy, misty gauze.

The cabman skilfully weaved through the tangle of carts,cabs, vans, pedestrians, push-carts, street-vendors, down past Hyde Park, past Buckingham Palace then clopping along St James' Park, and turning right into the Strand. Richard paid off the driver and booked into the hotel. A porter took his luggage up to his room. Richard tipped him. 'I must stop this'. He thought. 'I must save every penny I can. Who knows? I might soon be working as somebody else's porter.'

Richard called in at a shipping agent and found that the next available passage to New York would be from Liverpool in two days' time. He slid the fifteen pounds under the grill which covered food for the trip, but not alcohol.

Richard then returned to the hotel to finalise his plans. He would sell some surplus clothes and the next day he would dispatch a note to the solicitors stating that he was ill and unable to attend for a few days. He would then take the train to Liverpool the following day. He bundled up his spare clothes and visited three of the second- hand clothes shops in the area and concluded the best deal he could. It was still only early evening and Richard did not feel like spending the evening alone.

He wandered up to Covent Garden where the trading in fruit and vegetables for the day had ceased and eventually found his way through the maze of little streets to Fleet Street. He crossed the road by St Clement Danes Church and walked through the Temple which comprised the Middle and Inner Temples – two of the four Inns of Court.

Strolling though the gardens and the shady courts and alleyways Richard stood for a moment by the Temple Church. He went in and sat in a pew. He was alone save for the stone effigies of long- dead helmeted knights who lay with their eyes closed and their hands together in silent, eternal prayer. It was here that the Knights Templar had gathered to be blessed before departing for the Crusades to crush the wicked Infidel.

Richard pondered for a while about the tremendous sense of history that the towns and cities of England lived and breathed. It was possible to visualise the activities carried on in some streets of London by their names – Cornhill, Cheapside, Poultry, Old Jewry, Cripplegate, and Seething Lane – where Samuel Pepys worked for the Navy. Now he was leaving his country,he thought of its tremendous past. He was going to a country with very little history. He jolted himself back to the present and blinked as he left the gentle gloom of the old church for the brighter-albeit tarnished daylight of London..

Lawyers and clerks went about their business. Stately barristers crowned with dirty grey wigs, their black gowns contrasting with their whitish tabs and shirtfronts waddled like slow overfed magpies. Shabbily-dressed clerks scurried by carrying bundles of paper bound in pink ribbon – cases to counsel, writs and summonses to be issued and served – just to name a fraction of the many fragments of procedure which fuelled the complex, ancient and unwieldy legal system. Richard felt a slight tinge of regret because although he had found most of his duties as an articled clerk beneath his intelligence, he had begun to take an interest in the law and had done reasonably well in his intermediate examinations.

Richard arrived at the bank of the Thames and stared, fascinated by one of the busiest waterways in Europe which seethed with activity and every kind of vessel for conveying goods and people. Many Londoners travelled by river as journeying by horseback or vehicle of any kind was slow and chaotic with accidents being frequent. At the moment work was beginning on an underground railway between Paddington and Farringdon and was due to open in a couple of years. People were wondering as to whether it would make a difference to London's travel problems.

The smoke from boats contributed to the thick, heavy,oppressive atmosphere of London. Richard pushed his way through the throng of carts, cabs, stalls and people of every nationality and colour. He eventually found himself near Waterloo Bridge and walked up one of the small streets towards the Strand and stopped outside a music-hall.

Music- halls had always been denounced by his father as the focal point of every kind of vice and iniquity which would end in ruin in this life, and eternal damnation in the next. George's opposition had of course made these places all the more enticing to Richard although he had not had the opportunity to visit the one in Hereford as his father would be certain to hear of it. George had not been at home that morning having left for one of his trips three days earlier but, before he left, he had given Richard the expected homily as to his behaviour in London.

Richard now decided to judge for himself and paid his entry fee with an air of truculent defiance. Although the entertainment had not yet started the air was already redolent with smoke from pipes and cigars. Spittoons littered the floor. A piano was being played to jollify the audience in readiness for the programme.

Women walked about selling pies, oranges and various other goodies. People were sitting eating meals. Richard realised that he hadn't eaten properly since leaving Hereford. He sat at one of the wooden benches lining the long wooden tables and ordered a pint of porter, mutton chops and mashed potatoes. Three young men asked Richard if the spare seats were vacant. He invited them to sit down. One of them immediately took out a clay pipe and filled it from a pouch. From their dark, respectable but shabby dress and conversation Richard soon concluded correctly that they were legal clerks.

The entertainment began. The first artist was a cockney comedian who broke out into various songs one of which entreated the Queen to arrange for her unmarried daughters not to follow their sister Vicky's example and marry poverty-stricken German princes, but good solid Englishmen. He was followed by a conjurer, a saucy, female singer, tumblers and chorus – girls.

The interval came and Richard began indulging in mild banter with the three clerks who were convivial company. Suddenly, there was a disturbance as a large number of people trooped and jostled onto the balcony above. They were out of keeping with the rest of the audience, who, for the most part bore a threadbare, down-at- heel appearance. The men were middle-aged and well-dressed, whilst the women were all young and attractive. The party was in high spirits and appeared to have eaten or at least drunk well and there was a good deal of kissing and cuddling. One of the clerks turned to Richard.

"That's my Guv'ner up there. Lucky, he never recognises me. The likes of me are just part of the furniture to him. His sort just comes here to have a laugh at the rest of us and pretend they're slumming it. Every time I see him here he always has a different woman!"

The young man's levity tailed off as he gazed at Richard. "Whatever's the matter with you mate? Have you seen a ghost?"The question was not totally inappropriate.

For Richard was staring up at the balcony as though his face had been drained of all blood. It was motionless like the white plaster face of a statue. After what had seemed an eternity he grabbed his hat and stick and stumbled out of the building, followed by the puzzled looks of his companions.

He reached the street and stood with his back and head resting against a wall with his eyes closed.

One of the men in the balcony gazing into the eyes of a young blonde was his father.

CHAPTER FOUR

SOUTH CAROLINA – APRIL 1861

As Tyler slunk away, Kate put her arm through Frank's and they began to meander slowly back to the house. Frank stared ahead. His pale face drained of all emotion. Kate looked sadly up at him.

"You will be careful won't you Frank?"

"Sure I will. I'll be fine". Kate was not convinced. He certainly didn't look fine. What they both knew but could not say was that this was now an end to the life that they knew and loved. The future stretched out in front of them - bleak, uncertain and frightening.

Frank tried to inject some normality into his voice. "The trouble is there are lots of hotheads like him. The college at Charleston was full of them. In a way I'm surprised we weren't at war months ago".

They strolled across the lawn. Nursemaids were beginning to gather up the little children for bed to cries of protest as games with hoops and tops with the older children or playing with dogs was interrupted.

As well as horses, children's ponies were not allowed on the lawn. Some tots were now being carried back after riding lessons in the paddock – some older ones had ventured further afield. Most toddlers were placed on a quiet pony with a groom, leading them and either a servant or member of the family holding them on before they were two. By the time they were four they were riding unaided. Good horsemanship was an essential skill-and not just for sporting and social reasons- riding horses was the main means of transport in this rural world. In times of heavy rain the dirt roads became quagmires, making travel by wheeled vehicles impossible. Kate smiled as a protesting little boy with fair ringlets, dressed in a frock and petticoats was carried past on his way to the house, his chubby little fact puckered ready for a grizzle.

The lawns and veranda were littered with chairs and tables. Some people had already changed for dinner. The twins' two older brothers, Jeff and Harry, were lounging around on cane chairs talking to other young men. Many of these men were wearing uniforms of the various militias. These ranged in colour from a most impractical yellow to dark blue. Hats varied from small pillboxes to splendid brimmed affairs with feathers.

A few swords clanked ostentatiously at the sides of the wearers. They were not allowed inside the house. They could scratch floors and damage furniture and ornaments but, as soon as the martially minded owners stepped on the veranda, they were immediately and quite unnecessarily buckled on.

Butlers and footmen circled about unobtrusively with glasses, bottles and jugs. An order was given for a bottle of wine, soon it silently appeared swathed in white cloth, the label was shown and when the nod of approval was given, the slave slid away to open it returning to pour a little into the glass and on receiving a further cursory nod filled the glasses.

"Of course there's going to be a war." Jeff took a long swig of mint juleps. Unlike most of the other young men he was not in uniform. His white knee-length coat was open revealing a wine red waistcoat picked out in black, traversed by a gold watch-chain. His white panama hat was tilted back, his long legs stretched out.

"Hi, Professor." Greeted Jeff as the twins approached. Jeff had dubbed Frank that nickname when, unlike Jeff, Harry and many of the other local youths, he had declined to go to military academy, preferring to study at Harvard. After three years Jeff and Harry had not tired of the joke. Frank had resigned himself to the tedium and ignored it.

Like much of the planting South the general attitude of the area was highly militarised. Many of the men addressed each other as 'Captain' or 'Major' either from a former regular army commission or from a post held in the local militia. Young sons of owners of plantations attended military academy followed by a spell in the army.

Colonel Turner had the perception to accept Frank's decision to go to Harvard and not force him to follow a military career.

"Why, not Pa?" Complained Jeff. "Harry and I did. And you did. You went to West Point and held a regular commission and fought in the Mexican War! Why does Harry have to be different?"

"Well, he is different Jeff" explained the Colonel patiently. Harry has always liked books and music and had achieved success in his academic work. You and Harry are better suited to military college and Frank is better suited to Harvard."

"You mean that me and Harry are stoopid." Grumbled Jeff sulkily.

"No of course I don't mean that you two are stupid. And watch your grammar and your diction. If you are going to be an officer, you are going to have to learn to speak and behave like one." The Colonel was a thoughtful and sympathetic father and realised that the way to bring out the best in his children was to encourage them and not to berate them unnecessarily as was the wont of some fathers. He quietly agreed, partially anyway, with Jeff's statement : Frank was certainly more academically gifted than the other two who would have found the studies at Harvard very difficult. He had no doubt however that they would make successful careers in the Army.

"Not everybody is the same Jeff. Even brothers and

sisters, as you well know. I went to West Point because my father didn't give me any choice. Looking back now I wished I'd gone to Harvard. Frank is best suited to Harvard and you and Harry are best suited to military college and I am certain that you will both make fine officers." Mollified by this tactful and kindly response Jeff did not pursue the argument..

Now Jeff continued "You'd best be packing away those books of yours Professor and getting your kit together. Tyler says we're at war".

"You regard Tyler's wild announcements as official now do you Jeff? You know that every other day for the last three months there's been rumours that we have fired on Fort Sumter. If we'd taken every story as correct, we would never had stopped packing or unpacking. Anyway I told Tyler to leave making any announcements strictly to Pa".

Jeff nudged Harry and they grinned at each other. Although Frank and his two elder brothers got along well enough most of the time, his cultural interests set him apart from them and they regarded him as a suitable target for 'needling.' The fact that Frank and Kate were twins also created two natural rival ' camps' which had always been the source of friendly, and sometimes unfriendly, bickering.

These exchanges were interrupted by their mother, Solange, who came fluttering up. "Kate, where have you been? You should have been here to meet the Hansons. Charles has been longing to see you. And look at you! Those awful old clothes! And riding around the plantation like a field hand. And without a hat!" She wailed.

If guests had not been in earshot Kate would have retorted that although Charles Hanson was a nice enough boy and his family owned nearly as much land and slaves as her family and in Solange's opinion that made him a suitable match, he was after all only a boy. Kate was sick of him mooning around after her, blushing and making sheep's eyes every time he looked in her direction.

Kate had not thought much about marriage yet but she knew that when she did the candidate would be a man and not a boy: a man of her own choosing and not of her parents.

To Kate's relief this reproachful upbraiding (the type of which she had heard many times before) was broken by the Colonel looking grave. "Solange. Stop it. You know that I have been encouraging Kate to ride the plantation every day not just to exercise the horses, but for a reason. Now that reason is not just conjecture but reality. Hats and the state of one's clothes will not be an issue any more. We are talking about survival."

Solange looked at him aghast. "You mean we are at war ...." The last two words trailed faintly.

"I'm afraid so. I've just received an official dispatch. We're at war. I'm to join my regiment within the next three days". Solange said nothing but looked at her husband fearfully. He reassuringly put his hand round her. "You know we've been expecting this. It's no surprise".

"I know." She whispered. "But I hoped it would not happen."

"We all did. As you know Kate will be in charge of the plantation now that the boys and I will be gone. I've been preparing her for this for months. Not that she needed much grooming. She always knew much more than any of the boys. She knows every inch of the plantation and for the last six months she has been in the office every day. She knows as much about it as I do. She will look after you".

"I thought that was why you employed Harrison".

"You know why I employed Harrison. We have to

have at least one white man to stave of slave unrest. But overseers are just that – overseers – they are not members of the family. I can't depend on his loyalty or honesty. And he does not have a long knowledge of the history, and the depth of understanding of the plantation that Kate has. I know you don't approve of Kate doing this work, but women will be running most plantations now. After all many of them know as much about them as their husbands now. They just pretend they don't. I employed Harrison as a token for appearance sake. He was the best of a poor bunch".

As they had been talking, guests and slaves had been passing them and were now standing on the lawn. Colonel Turner had sent word round the house asking for everybody to assemble on the lawn. He now raised his voice asking for everybody on the veranda to move to the lawn. People moved wordlessly amidst the scraping of chairs and the sound of glasses being plonked on tables. Most of them had little doubt as to the reason for the address which they knew was coming. Colonel Turner stood on a small dais which he had arranged to be brought out. The sun was fading but it was not yet dusk.

Unlike many owners of plantations, Colonel Turner had been actively managing it rather than leaving everything to managers and overseers who could be slovenly and swindle. Kate had not just been learning from him in the last few months but by a sort of osmosis all her life. From the age of about six, she had spent as much time as possible with her father- riding with him and watching his conduct around the plantation. Frank accompanied them when his studies and other activities permitted. The Colonel was a good father to all his children but he had a special relationship with the twins with whom he was especially in tune both emotionally and intellectually. Jeff and Harry could be foolish and wayward (particularly Jeff) and young Custis was only just emerging from the 'puppy' stage and had not quite developed his own identifiable personality.

Kate looked at her father. She had always adored him and seeing him now with other men of similar age she felt especially proud of him. He was in his mid- fifties and still a handsome man with greying hair and moustache. His features were strong and arresting. Unlike some of the flabby men standing around him with soft bulging paunches, heavy jowls, red noses and broken veins, the Colonel's body was well- muscled with no surplus flesh. Here was a self-disciplined man born to train and command others.

The regular riding and other activities had prevented the Colonel's body from running to fat like many of his contemporaries. Unlike some of them he did not drink heavily nor, being faithful to his wife make visits to women in the town nor bother his female slaves. There were no mulatto slaves fathered by him. He detested the jokes of other slave-owners to the effect that 'their virility increased their wealth'.

Children born to slave- women became the property of their owners. In a market where the price of slaves continually increased,births on the plantation boosted stock at no cost. Slave–women had difficulty in resisting the advances of their owners or indeed of their young testosterone–filled teenage sons. Children born as a result of such couplings remained slaves unless freed by their fathers. The Colonel had forbidden his sons on the pain of strict punishments from having relations with the female slaves. "It is a severe abuse of our privilege". He had told them. This had not stopped Jeff on a few occasions but fortunately word of it had not come to the Colonel's ears and,even more fortunately, no pregnancies had occurred.

Now, children who were not young enough to have been sent to bed were standing solemnly beside their parents. They knew instinctively something was about to happen. Kate, Solange and Frank stood side-by – side. Custis stood in front of Frank who had his hands reassuringly on the boy's shoulders. The Colonel did not have to silence the subdued crowd. Those that were not party to Tyler's ill–judged revelations, had a good idea of what the Colonel was to announce.

"As you know there have been many rumours and counter–rumours in the last few days that Fort Sumter has been fired upon. I regret to have to inform you that I have received an official dispatch stating that this has happened. There has–thank God–been no bloodshed on either side. But we are at war with our fellow-Americans. I hoped I would never live to see this day".

Immediately there were Rebel yells from Jeff, Tyler and a number of other young men. This immediately resulted in a murmur of disapproval and stern orders of 'Sssshh' from the older members of the crowd. The Colonel's expression had been bleak and sad. Anger and irritation now riveted his handsome face. He looked pointedly at Jeff and then Tyler.

"I would like to remind my son Jefferson , Tyler Lloyd and those other young men who have been making those stupid yells and boasting that ' one Rebel can whip ten Yankees and that it will all be over in three weeks, six months or by Christmas', that I'm sick of hearing them". There were a few 'here heres'from the crowd.

"What I have to say to those young men is that you expect soon to be officers. How can you expect to control men if you can't control yourselves? Stop behaving like a bunch of twelve year old kids and grow up". The offenders looked down at their feet and said nothing. Jeff looked particularly uncomfortable. He always knew that he had seriously overstepped the mark when his father addressed him by his proper name of 'Jefferson'. Solange and some of the other women and girls were crying quietly. Kate was dry-eyed. She did not want this war but she certainly was not going to make an exhibition of herself in public. The slaves (as they often did) wore silent inscrutable expressions.

Although the Colonel was speaking to a large audience over an extended area. He did not bellow. His voice was level and firm and everybody could hear every word.

"Like many of you older men I have experience of war. It is no cause for celebration. It causes sickness, death and destruction and creates widows and orphans. Wars are far easier to start than to finish and I think that this war will last years rather than months". Some of the younger men appeared restive at this statement but did not dare risk another reprimand. The Colonel ignored the shuffling.

"As you know I served in the Mexican War and the American Army is the finest in the world. And although many officers and men are Southerners and will be coming back to fight for their homeland, it will be a very difficult army to defeat. I understand that General Robert.E. Lee is likely to be offered command. He is of course a Virginian and a Southerner but it is still possible that he won't accept. If he does not our task will be Herculean. If he does and takes command of our forces then it will be slightly easier". The silent crying among the women and girls had now become loud sobbing.

The Colonel raised his voice slightly. "This war is going to be hard and it is going to be bloody. The terrible thing is that Americans are going to be fighting

Americans. Families will be divided and it may be that some of you have relations who will be on the opposing side." He noticed one or two grimaces of disbelief. "Don't be offended, you will be in good company. You can start with the White House. President Lincoln has brothers - in- law who will join our Army ". There was a slight tremor of agreement in the crowd. Lincoln had only been President for three months or so but his wife Mary was quickly acquiring unpopularity in the Northern States. She had grown up in Kentucky and her family still owned slaves and a number of her brothers and half-brothers would fight for the South and she had not exactly helped herself by her haughty demeanour, her penchant for revealing dresses and her spendthrift ways.She was already lavishly redecorating and refurnishing the White House at public expense.

The Colonel shifted his stance a little. "You shouldn't be surprised. This is what happens in civil wars. They are the worst type of war. We have conquered this land. We have beaten the British, the French, the Spanish, the Indians and most of all we have tamed the wilderness and created a prosperous industrious nation at the cost of death, disease and hardship. But we have won through. And we will win through now and we will be one nation once again but it will be at a cost. It will be a clash of Titans. You will be fighting brave men who despite irreconcilable differences are your countrymen. Many people will die – probably some of you". This was a brutal statement but this was no time to spare anybody's feelings. The Colonel knew America was going to face its harshest ordeal since The War of Independence.

"Be brave, be steadfast but never forget the size and seriousness of the task and don't treat going to war as though it's some kind of fair". The Colonel looked meaningfully at Tyler who looked at the ground and shuffled his feet. His voice now softened.

"The barbecue and picnic tomorrow are cancelled. Dinner tonight is as normal. Tomorrow, gather your families and return to your homes so that those who have to can leave for their regiments as soon as possible. May God bless America. May God bless you all".

After a subdued dinner, most of the packing was done by the guests' slaves – sometimes supervised by their owners. Carriages were being prepared for early morning. Tyler and some of the other young men would not return to their own homes. Knowing that war was imminent, they had brought sufficient equipment so that they could report for duty straightway with their personal slaves. Further belongings would be sent on later.

Within a week Beaumont like many plantations was denuded of its white adult men. Only Harrison remained. Although she knew it would be useless, Solange made one final attempt to persuade her husband to stay behind and take advantage of the 'Twenty Slave Rule'.

"Anyway that rule does not technically apply to us now that we've got Harrison". The Colonel had told the protesting Solange". And we have to do our duty to our country".

"What about your duty to your family?"

"You know that our country comes first. Without a country there is no family. And you know there is the question of honour". Solange did know. Honour permeated the South down to the very pores. Honour to your country, honour to your regiment and at the last – honour to your family. This was the sort of conversation that was taking place in thousands of homes throughout the South. Solange ,like most of the other women, had been brought up with this code of honour. They did not want their husbands and sons to leave but expected them to do so and would have found it intolerable had they made a flimsy excuse to remain.

Jeff and Harry left two days after the news of declaration of war had reached the house.

"Just be careful". Kate had said to Jeff the day before his departure when he boasted about drinking champagne from 'Ole Abe Lincoln's boots' in Willard's Hotel, Washington. "Don't take stupid risks." She knew though that it was like telling an alcoholic not to drink too much. Jeff had been born reckless.

Jeff had nearly killed himself on a number of occasions- jumping horses over obstacles that were far too high, riding bulls, falling from a makeshift bridge formed by a tree trunk into the swollen river but the most ridiculous incident had been when he and another boy (who was a guest) had played ' William Tell' with guns. A shot had grazed through the other boy's shoulder. Kate had never seen her father so angry.

Contrary to his normal aberration to physical violence the Colonel had Jeff tied to a post in the stable yard and whipped him until the boy was screaming for him to stop. He was due to go to military academy in a year's time but he was sent within the week. The other boy was sent home in disgrace. Jeff had quietened down since then but was still capable of wild behaviour.

The Colonel left the day after Jeff and Harry. Father and daughter did not say much to each other. Not only were they too full of emotion to say much in front of the house- slaves but they had no need. They both knew that the parting was terrible for each of them. As for the practicalities of running the plantation, these had been discussed in every minute detail over the last few months. Kate had full confidence in herself, and her father had full confidence in her.

Frank left two days after his father. At about four o'clock in the afternoon, the day before his departure the twins went for a ride. They crossed the bridge and the horses toiled up the hillside towards a thick belt of woodland. Underneath the thick canopy of trees, the ground was thickly carpeted with pine needles and it felt as though the horses were plodding over a thick feather bed.

"What's going to happen to us Frank?" Kate asked worriedly looking up at Frank. "We are going to be alright aren't we?"

Frank sighed. "I just don't know. I wish I could say 'yes'. I wish I could be like Jeff and the others and say that we'll all be drinking champagne out of Abe's boots in Washington in three months. But I don't think so. We haven't got the industry to support a war. We haven't got the plant,or raw material to support ourselves in peacetime. We only have agriculture and slaves. Everything is imported either from Europe or the North. The Yankees will obviously stop supplying us and they will blockade our coast so that imports from Europe will be difficult. Where are we going to get our medical supplies, guns, ammunition, cannons, and uniforms? We don't make them ourselves. Are we suddenly going to build factories and obtain all the raw materials in the middle of war-time? Anything the Yankees need they can either make or obtain from Europe."

They had to part for a minute as an overhanging branch forced them to weave singly through trees at the side of the path. Frank continued when they were again side-by-side.

"And what about the men? The Yankees have five times as many as us, and again they have an endless supply of immigrants. Rumour has it that they are going to pay generous bounty to new recruits".

Kate sat sadly and silently in her saddle. She had heard these arguments many times before not just from Frank but from her father and some other older men, who had not been intoxicated by the war fervour which had engulfed the South since South Carolina's secession in December. For a minute the only sound was the muffled sound of hooves as the horses picked their way over the thick blanket of decaying vegetation. The sun poked through the trees leaving dappled patches of sunlight and shade.

The sense of pending doom was heavy and matched the dark enclosed atmosphere of the wood but Kate had to find a glimmer of hope. "But we have the better men and generals. Everybody says so."

"That's true of course. Most of our boys were reared in the country and can ride and shoot. We love our military schools in the South and we have some great generals – particularly now Virginia has seceded and Bobby Lee has accepted command of The Army of Northern Virginia. But as I said we're just outnumbered and the Yankees are not just city rats and immigrants. They have their fair share of farm boys too you know".

"Is there any hope at all?"

"The only way is for us to win some spectacular victories at the start before we run out of supplies, and get recognised by Britain and France as a country in our own right."

"How are we going to get through this?"

"The best way is not to think about the future. I'm told that a soldier should just live his life from day to day. Get through today and let tomorrow take care of itself. You should do that too." They were quiet and thoughtful for the rest of the ride – as so often silent telepathic communication was all that these twins needed.

The mode of Frank's departure was similar to those

of his father and brothers but for Kate it was far worse. She didn't like to think about it afterwards. Frank's horse was brought round to the front entrance. Solange and Custis were standing surrounded by house-slaves whose faces were expressionless. Custis was holding his puppy. Frank picked him up and gave him a long hug and then kissed his mother who could not resist a burst of tears. His last embrace was with Kate. Neither of them wanted to let each other go. They said nothing save a breathless 'bye' when they finally parted.

Frank rode down the drive accompanied by four slaves – two of whom were driving a wagon carrying his plate, crystal, wine, food, books, clothes and all manner of military equipment. He kept looking back and waving. Kate, Solange and Custis stayed until he was out of sight. Custis then turned and ran heavily in the direction of the stables clutching his puppy.

"Where are you going?" His mother managed to choke through her tears. "Come back into the house with us".

By some miracle of self-will Kate had managed to hold back her own tears. "Leave him. He needs to be alone. Can't you see he's crying?"

Following Frank's departure Kate concentrated on the daily affairs of the plantation. She rode part of it each day. And she did not do it by rotation. Sometimes she covered the same area two or three days in succession. The workforce could not be allowed to believe that just because there was a woman at the helm, they could be allowed to be sloppy or lazy. She never travelled without a rifle in her saddle or a Colt at her belt.

Six weeks after the Turner men had left, a young slave escaped. In order to safeguard themselves such persons as remained to run the plantations formed themselves into local co-operatives to deal with escape and rebellion. Kate, despite protests from her mother and the other men was the only woman to join the posse. The hounds quickly tracked down the man who was hiding up a tree. Kate found the triumphant cry of one of the posse – "We've treed the goddamn coon" followed by the Rebel yell – totally distasteful.

When the man was returned to Beaumont, Kate ordered him to be flogged whilst the other slaves were made to watch. Kate looked on with them, astride Jack. She loathed the experience. She shared her father's distaste of corporal punishment and knew it to be counter-productive. The local planting fraternity had received a salutary lesson a couple of years ago by the death of Major Williams who whipped his head groom mercilessly when he failed to rub down his favourite hunter to his satisfaction. The wounds became infected and the man died. Three weeks later the Major was riding home alone late at night. The next morning the alarm was raised when the riderless horse had made his own way home. A search party was sent out and the Major was found dead in the long grass by the side of the road, with his throat cut. The culprits were never identified. The questioning of the other slaves produced no information or any indicative expressions from the deadpan faces.

Despite this, Kate knew that she had to establish her authority. No slave had ever attempted to escape in her lifetime. By the general standards of plantations, the slaves at Beaumont were well-treated. She felt that this escape was a challenge to her authority as a woman. The community could not be allowed to regard her as a vulnerable young woman over whom it could take advantage. When the wretched man had been cut down, placed in a prone position on a stretcher and salt water had been thrown over the deep wounds,Kate addressed the gathering from her saddle.

"Colonel Turner is not here. But I am running this plantation on his authority. You will obey me in the same way as you would have obeyed him. When Jeremiah's wounds have healed, he will be sold. If anybody tries anything like that again, he or she knows what to expect."

During the beating and Kate's address, there had been no reactions from the impassive crowd save for the wails of Jeremiah's wife and mother which had now become loud screams. The sale of a slave- especially in a humanitarian plantation like Beaumont-was a momentous event and a disaster for the slave's family for which the parting would probably be permanent. The unfortunate Jeremiah's fate would be uncertain – especially if he was 'sold Down-River'. Normally the further South the plantation, the worse the treatment of slaves became.

As soon as she had finished speaking Kate yanked round Jack's head, dug her heels into his flanks and, with much kicking up of earth and skittering of stones, galloped off in a cloud of dust to the bend in the river – the twins' favourite spot. She dismounted, leant against a tree and sobbed her heart out. She hated what she had done but she would do whatever was necessary to save her home and her family.She had made the necessary example. She was worried over the next few weeks that there may be reprisals. There were none. The gamble had paid off. Her rule had been established and accepted.

The next important stand for her to make was with Harrison. She found his manner offhand and sometimes dismissive. It was obvious that he did not approve of women in authority.

Harrison, for his part, had been irritated when he found he was to be interviewed by Kate in the company of her father, but he did not suppose that she knew much about accounts, commissions, discounts, delayed payments and all that kind of thing even though she was technically in charge. He would be working unsupervised and the opportunities for a little peculation would be good.

When the Colonel had left, Harrison had not been surprised when Kate did not check the accounts at all (well, she wouldn't know what she was looking at if she did) neither did she supervise him very much. Then the day after Jeremiah was whipped, Kate strode into the office and asked to see the accounts. Harrison was taken aback-and the accounts were not really up to date anyway. Accounts were a chore-there was always something more important to do.

Harrison looked crafty. "It's not possible right now Miss Kate. I have to go down to Long Meadow."

"Now, please Harrison". Commanded Kate in a voice that would brook no argument. Harrison recognised that tone of voice which women use when any opposition to them is useless. He had first heard it at the age of five when his mother had told him to collect the eggs from the henhouse. He had refused. Within ten minutes a tearful boy with a very sore backside had brought the eggs into the kitchen.After much shifting of papers and books Harrison eventually unearthed the accounts book and shiftily slid it across the table to Kate.

"Actually, they are not quite up to date yet Miss Kate."

"I've never seen accounts which are. You can go down to Long Meadow now. I'll study the book while you are gone". Harrison gratefully made a speedy exit.

He delayed his return for as long as he reasonably could without arousing suspicion. Nearly three hours later he was surprised to find Kate still sitting at the table with the book still in front of her – and a few sheets of paper on which she had been making notes. She spoke without looking up at him.

"Harrison, how much did we get for that mare we sold to Mr Weston last month?"

"Sixty dollars Miss Kate".

"Are you sure you haven't made a mistake?"

"Quite sure, Miss. It's in the accounts".

"I know, that's why I'm asking". Kate frowned. "I saw Mr Weston recently and he told me that he gave you seventy."

Harrison looked fixedly at the door of the cupboard across the room. "Ah! Now I come to think of it it was seventy. I must have made a mistake".

"Sure you made a mistake. You did that deal when I was out riding the plantation and he brought the mare over unexpectedly – I thought he was coming the next day. You thought I wouldn't find out. What you did not know was that I have been checking the accounts since the Colonel left, when I knew that you would be well away in another part of the plantation or in town. I know every move you have made. I have found a number of discrepancies – here".

Kate shoved a piece of paper with notes and figures at Harrison's elbow. Now correct that book and I will check it tomorrow. And you will bring the account book right up to date tonight. And in future you will do the accounts on a daily basis each evening and I will check it the next morning. Try and cheat me again and I will have your butt out of here so fast that you won't have time to get your pants on. War or no war. You saw what happened to Jeremiah.Nobody is indispensable. And when they think they are, they very quickly find out that they aren't. And nobody ever EVER jerks me around. You got that Buster?"

Buster had. He was white and shaking. He held on to the table to steady himself. He never believed that this young Southern belle would have such a hard-nosed experience of business and dealing with staff so well beyond her years, and her language! It reminded him of a madam of a gambling saloon that he had ventured into once or twice up north. Kate left the office without a further word being spoken by either of them. There was no need. They had each other's measure.

Apart from the departure of the menfolk, the war had not as yet made much of an impact on their daily lives. Then in July came the news of Manassas Junction or Bull Run Creek as those Yankees called it. "They can't even agree on the names of the Battle!" Kate had observed to her mother. This double-naming would continue throughout the war with regard to many battles, with the South using the name of the nearest town or industrial feature such as a railroad junction, and the North adopting natural features.

Civilians had prepared to watch the battle and prepared for a gala day out to watch the 'fun'. Many, decked out in their best holiday finery, drove out in vehicles with picnics only to be greeted by the sight of fleeing blue-clad soldiers rushing towards them on the way back to Washington shouting to them that all was over and they had best turn back. Day-trippers joined the retreating soldiers in the 'great skedaddle' - the chaotic, panic- stricken rush to Washington. Carriages overturned, horses broke their legs and had to be shot and devastated civilians finally arrived back to the city having scrambled along roads strewn with detritus-dead horses, wrecked vehicles, children's toys,abandoned picnic hampers, dead and moaning soldiers and pleasure- seekers including children.

The Confederates under Generals Beauregard and Jackson (now nick-named 'Stonewall') had routed the Union Army under McDowell and were on the point of taking Washington save that they had not expected their success, had failed to prepare for it and consequently failed to consolidate their victory. This pattern of inability to 'go for the jugular and finish the job' would be repeated continually by both sides throughout the war.

Lincoln had been advised by some Northerners to surrender. The South went mad with jubilation. More cautious Southerners began to think that the wild boastings that one Rebel could whip ten Yankees might be true. Kate thought hopefully that Frank might be wrong and the likes of Jeff and the odious Tyler might be right and that everybody would be home by Christmas.

Then, in the first week of August, Kate had been out all day and returned to the house late in the afternoon. She opened the drawing –room door. Instinctively she knew something was wrong. Her mother was sitting facing the window with her back to the door. "Hallo"- ventured Kate cautiously. No answer; Kate passed round the motionless figure of her mother. Solange was gazing fixedly ahead, her face ashen. An open letter lay in her lap and slid to the floor. Kate, now very frightened, picked it up.

The letter was from Colonel Robertson to Mrs Turner. It was his sad duty to inform her of the death of her son Lieutenant Jefferson. J.Turner – 'a fine officer'. Jeff had not lived to drink champagne in Washington nor had he died bravely in action defending his homeland against the Yankees. He had died a mere one hundred and fifty miles away from home. Measles had swept through the camp and lying on the ground for three days had brought on pneumonia. Jeff was dead within the week.

An immediate surge of relief surged through Kate that it wasn't Frank or her father. She then felt a tremendous sense of guilt that the death of one brother was preferable to the death of another brother or her father. They were all members of her family.

She had never been particularly close to Jeff. When she and Frank were little, he had teased them mercilessly. As she grew up she realised that mentally she was about ten steps ahead of him- but he was her brother. He had been jovial, stupid and reckless .His rather robust jokes and pranks had been without malice and he had never meant anybody any serious harm. Fate had treated him cruelly. If he had to die why could it not have been gloriously in battle instead of in this sneaky underhand way?

The South was still celebrating. As yet no family in Kate's acquaintance had suffered bereavement. Tragedy had struck the Turner family first. Kate, Solange and Custis were wearing mourning. Paintings were draped in black and turned to face the wall. To Kate, her mother and brother the war was now real, deadly and grim.

Chapter Five

Richmond – April 1861

Two women watched a torchlight procession through the window, and the Confederate banner flying for the first time over Richmond.

The younger one fell to her knees with tears streaming down her cheeks. "Alas for those with loyalty in their hearts!" The older woman hugged her.

"We know what to do. We have set the scene already – we just carry on doing it but in secret". The younger woman nodded.

"But what about John? Won't the army take him?"

"We'll fight it. He's not strong. And he's got to run the store." The younger woman looked doubtful. 'Running the store' would hardly be a ground for exemption and she suspected that her mother knew that as well but if it gave her mother comfort to consider it possible, then so be it.

The women were Mrs Eliza Van Lew and her daughter Elizabeth. An observer would rightly conclude that the daughter was the more opinionated and voluble of the two – the mother being quiet and self-effacing and not a strong personality, which does not of itself constitute a weak character and it didn't in this case.

They were the widow and daughter of John Van Lew who had prospered as a hardware dealer. When he died ten years ago, he had left enough capital for his family to continue living in the large mansion with its six-columned portico on Church Hill where Patrick Henry had called for 'Liberty or Death'. His unspectacular but energetic son John took over the running of the business which continued to prosper.

Elizabeth's parents were both from the North and had made their home a centre of the arts and a focus for visiting celebrities such as Edgar Allen Poe and the singer Jenny Lind – known as 'the Swedish nightingale'. Elizabeth grew up in an atmosphere of grace and culture – of garden parties , balls and summer journeys to White Sulphur Springs in a carriage drawn by four white horses; however, she never took her life for granted and never forgot that it was provided by her father's hard work and industry – qualities which he had passed on to his daughter.

Elizabeth was sent north to her mother's city of Philadelphia to be educated and realised that she owed much of her comfortable existence to slavery, and in her own words, "imbibed abolitionism". Her family owned a number of slaves but, after her father's death, Elizabeth changed all that. She prevailed upon her mother to free all the slaves.She then spent the legacy bequeathed to her by her father buying their enslaved relatives and subsequently freeing them. She offered to pay for their travel north and to maintain them whilst they received education. Those, like her maid Jenny who chose to remain, received a proper wage as servants.

The Van Lew family were regarded by many of the upper echelons of Richmond Society as Yankees and with Yankee views, but they were tolerated with a certain amount of affection 'after all that is what one expects from Northerners' in the way one would regard a difficult child. However, when they started freeing their slaves feelings began to harden. The family were not as yet regarded with suspicion but in the same way as persons of a different class, country or religion.

" They are alright among their own kind but we just don't have anything in common with them". The invitations began to wane and had now ceased altogether.

Invitations had ceased but at least they had existed in the first place. The same could not be said for suitors for Elizabeth. As a young girl her petite blond looks had not been unpleasing – save for a huge chin which drew unkind comparisons to 'The Rock of Gibraltar' and wealth is never an obstacle to love. However Elizabeth had never been very interested in men, was not a flirt (no pouts, fluttering of eyelashes or the coy manipulation of a fan from her!) and those men who had not been sufficiently discouraged to pursue her, could not cope with her strong, opinionated views.

"Try to soften up a little". Her mother would advise. "Honey attracts. Vinegar doesn't". Although she could be charming when she chose Elizabeth took the view that people would have to take her as they found her and that included prospective husbands which explained why there weren't any. Now in her early forties her looks were fading, she took little trouble with her appearance and was regarded as an eccentric. Perpetual spinsterhood seemed certain - a prospect which did not worry her, or her mother who would have missed her daughter dreadfully. A strong bond had always existed between the two women and it had strengthened daily since the death of Elizabeth's father.

For some time now Elizabeth had been writing to Federal Officials keeping them abreast of current events. They had confidence in her. The ground had been prepared for the vital intelligence role that Elizabeth would play on behalf of the Union during the war which had now been declared.

Chapter Six

Liverpool England

June 1861

Liverpool. The second largest city in Europe and three quarters the size of New York. The Napoleonic wars had made the ports of the south coast of England too dangerous for commercial shipping and had breathed additional life into Liverpool.

The city's merchant princes were now the wealthiest in Britain having waxed fat – initially from the slave trade and privateering – but now from the vast volume of commercial traffic flowing through the port which had been boosted in the last decade by the huge growth in emigration.

No English city rivalled the centre of Liverpool and St George's Hall and the Law Courts were already being acclaimed as one of the greatest classical buildings of the nineteenth century. The docks, especially the Albert Docks, were unequalled both in size and grandeur boasting warehouses with cast – iron Doric pillars. The approach from the sea towards this fine stone façade was magnificent. Beside this great wealth existed great poverty.

The emigrant trade was now a substantial part of Liverpool's business. During the eighteen-fifties over two million people had emigrated from Britain and Ireland and of these over two-thirds had departed from Liverpool – mainly to America. Although the numbers had now dropped they were still substantial . Many emigrants were encouraged by the hope of a better life and in particular more food. Stories were told of

America being the land of three meals a day. Many British people were not used to more than two scanty meals a day.

Liverpool had dedicated entire streets and districts to the business of emigration and in particular to the divesting of the emigrants of whatever meagre savings they had managed to scrape together for the trip into 'the unknown' and for many of these desperately poor and ignorant people it was literally ' into the unknown'. Many could not place America on a map. Some had no idea of the length of the voyage and exclamations had been heard that America was in sight when approaching the coast of Ireland.

Richard elbowed his way through the crowds which thronged the new station at Lime Street. His luggage had now been reduced to two bags and although he looked presentable he was not wearing his best clothes. There was no point in making himself an obvious target for pickpockets or violent robbery. Most of his sovereigns were secured in a leather money-belt under his shirt.

Richard had read about the dangers of Liverpool in 'The Emigrant's Guide'. It was difficult enough just to escape from the station. He swore as he trod on dog's mess. Dogs abounded everywhere- some were on leads, some well-trained ones followed the heels of their masters and some were just running loose. A huge be-whiskered man, wearing a black broad-brimmed hat barred his way. He was holding onto a large, evil-looking, and slobbering mastiff. Richard reflected on the saying that dogs looked like their owners. Was it because some people unwittingly chose dogs that resembled themselves?

He spoke to Richard in an accent that he had never heard before and most of the endings of the words were not pronounced. Richard had to ask him to repeat himself twice. Eventually, he deciphered "Do you want lodgings? I know of some very good rates!" I'm sure you do thought Richard. The man's breath stank of booze. He was obviously one of the 'runners' he had heard so much about.

"No thank you." As laden as he was Richard deftly side-stepped both threatening man and his unattractive beast barging into a porter pushing a barrow laden with trunks. He bawled something in the same accent as the man with the dog. Richard couldn't understand it but it didn't sound complimentary.

Richard quietly threaded his way as best he could out of the station. People kept approaching him. He was now concentrating on understanding the accent with some success. Did he want lodgings? Did he want provisions for the voyage? Did he want tickets? They assumed he was planning to sail because most people arriving in Liverpool with luggage were planning to do just that.

Following the advice of the 'Emigrant's Guide' Richard had sent a telegraph from London booking a room in a recommended hotel in the city. It was false economy to stay in one of the cheaper lodging houses in the Emigrant's Quarter which charged exorbitant prices for poor accommodation and where there was danger of having luggage stolen or even its being cheekily held to ransom.

Eventually, Richard managed to find a hansom to take him to the hotel. He climbed into the raised seat beside the driver and wondered whether they would arrive that day as a solid mass of people, vehicles and animals stretched out into the distance. They inched alongside a huge brewers dray. Despite the fact that the barrels were lashed together, Richard felt nervous as they towered above him.

The swearing drayman showed his frustration as the

two heavy matching chestnuts were locked in the jam but Richard's skilful driver crawled past them, men on horseback, driven cows and sheep, ragged street urchins dodging their way through the crowds, people and carts laden with luggage and porters struggling with enormous baskets of produce. Richard's driver eventually stood up and peered into the distance. "The problem's a dead horse."

As they progressed painfully the driver never stopped talking. His accent was easier to understand than the others that Richard had heard and he could follow most of what the man had said.

"When are you sailing?"

"Tomorrow". Again, the assumption that everybody arriving with luggage was sailing.

"You are doing the right thing going to a hotel. The runners will fleece you of everything they can. Everyone takes his cut on food for the voyage, tickets, lodging and even medical attention. Everybody's in the pay of everybody else."

Richard could now see the cause of the delay a horse dragging a large vegetable cart had dropped dead between the shafts, breaking one of them as it fell. Richard watched with pity as the poor, worn-out old body was humped and dragged onto a cart by a number of sweating, swearing men and youths.

When they eventually arrived at the hotel Richard paid his garrulous companion who had given him plenty of information on where to go and what to do (and more importantly where not to go and what not to do) during his one night in Liverpool. As he was checking into the hotel Richard noticed that he was being observed by two similar-looking young men.

"Are you sailing on 'The White Queen'?", asked one of them in a strong accent which Richard knew to be Scottish. Two of the masters at school had been from Scotland. Richard nodded.

"Well, you'd better go down to the shipping office and make sure that you're booked on it." The men looked as though they were brothers. The speaker appeared the older of the two by a couple of years.

"But I've booked through an agent."

"That doesn't mean anything. We were booked last week but were told that there wasn't any room."

"Did you use an agent?"

"Yes, but we learnt to our cost that's no guarantee. Shipbrokers buy berths from the owners or charter whole ships and receive commissions on the sales which they either make themselves or through agents. Sometimes the shipbrokers repudiate the agents' bargain, sometimes the ship-owners repudiate the shipbroker's bargain and sometimes the dates and times are different."

Richard felt despondent. He had overcome so many obstacles just to get here. This was one he did not need. "Well, can't one do anything?"

"Not really. Nobody has the time to sue as they just want to board the ship as soon as possible and if they did have the time they probably wouldn't have the money. Anyway"---- the speaker stretched out his hand. "We should introduce ourselves. I'm Duncan MacLean and this is my brother Fergus. If you like we'll come down the shipping office with you. We haven't got anything else to do."

"Thanks. I'll be glad of the company – especially of somebody who knows the ropes !."

On the way to the office Richard discovered that the brothers were travelling to Pennsylvania to join their uncle who was a mining engineer. They passed through streets of grocery stores, spirit vaults, ticket agencies and many other enterprises all of which catered for the emigrant.

When the trio arrived at the shipping office they were assured that Richard's ticket was in order and that he would be sailing with the MacLeans the next day. Richard heaved a sigh of relief.

"Thank heaven for that. Come on. I'll buy you two a drink. Have you found a decent pub yet?" The brothers grinned.

Fergus spoke for the first time. "Finding a pub is no problem. The difficulty is finding one where you're not likely to be hit by flying glass or knocked over by a couple of brawling seamen. Still, we've found one that's not so bad."

As they talked, a particularly woe-be gone cargo of Irish passed who had just left the steamboat from Dublin. Although some ships sailed direct from Ireland to America far more had to travel from Cork or Dublin via Liverpool. Fergus took a tobacco pouch from his pocket and a shiny new pipe (' probably his first one thought' Richard , who after a few surreptitious puffs with his friends had decided that the habit wasn't for him) and began filling it.

"Look at those poor devils. We've spent last week watching the boats come in. The livestock travelling below has better conditions than the humans. They cram them together. There's nowhere for them to buy food or drink. They either fry or freeze to death." One or two strands of tobacco blew away. Richard wondered why he was bothering with his pipe at all. He would never be able to light it in this breeze but Fergus put the pipe in his mouth all the same. Showing off! thought Richard. After a few wet-sounding sucks Fergus removed it.

"We saw some come off the steamer last Friday when there'd been that terrible storm. They were soaked to the skin. They couldn't dry their clothes. They had had nowhere to lie down. The lurching of the ship meant that they'd all vomited over each other and when we saw them it had dried. It was disgusting!"

"Alright Fergus"reproved his brother. "Richard's got the message. There's no need to go into details." Richard smiled to himself at this sibling sparring. They eventually arrived at the pub. Richard tried to reach the bar avoiding the spittoons. Slops of beer glistened on the tables. The whole place stank of alcohol, stale tobacco and unwashed bodies. If this pub wasn't so bad Richard wondered what the others must have been like. He walked up to the bar to buy the beers whilst the brothers sat at the only remaining table.

Children ran around the floor playing 'catch' or played under the tables. One collided into an ill-kempt man causing him to spill his beer. "Watch where you're going. You smelly little bastard." He kicked the boy cruelly in the leg. The child fell to the floor and began to cry. "And if you don't shut up there's plenty more where that came from " snarled the brute.

Men sat around playing cribbage, dominoes, and all kinds of card games. Ships from all countries docked in Liverpool and there were a number of dark Mediterranean looking men speaking French or Italian as well as one or two black men. Women nursed infants whilst keeping a watchful eye on straying toddlers. Suddenly, there was the sound of barking, snapping and shouting. At the other end of the pub two dogs had started to fight. The swearing owners separated them and the one who was considered the aggressor was kicked whimpering into the street.

Richard assumed that most of the men were either seamen, emigrants or otherwise involved in the emigrant trade and gathered from snippets of chat that most of them were talking business. Eventually, he managed to struggle to the brothers with the beers. "I feel now that I have really achieved something."

"Oh! Hark at the young English gent"sneered a harsh voice in an accent that Richard knew to be Irish. Many Irish navvies had worked on the railway in Hereford. He now realised that his own accent- middle class softened by a mild Herefordshire burr was conspicuous among the medley of Scottish, Irish, Liverpool, foreign and a number of English regional accents with which he was unfamiliar. Richard turned round.

The speaker was respectably, if not smartly dressed in serviceable clothes of good quality – grubby white high-crowned hat, brown worsted coat and waistcoat with good boots.

"You English treat your dogs and horses better than you treat the Irish and Scots. You drive them from their homes like cattle; herd them onto ships to America and Canada. Most of them don't know where those places are. When they get there they can't support themselves. Many of them are penniless. You are just shoving problems overseas. It's just a step down from transportation to Australia." Richard winced. Transportation was a sensitive subject to him he agreed with the many people who had been agititating for it to stop. He was totally unprepared for this diatribe from a complete stranger. He would have liked to ignore him but it was impossible. The only response he could think of was foolish and one which he instantly regretted.

"Nobody makes them go."

"Of course they bloody do! What about the landlords in the Scottish Highlands who force their tenants to leave so that they can farm their land more profitably? What about those landlords in Ireland, who, because they don't receive any rent from their starving tenants get the army to force the poor bastards out of their hovels and burn them?".

The offensive man paused to take a long swig.

Richard wasn't surprised he was thirsty with all that pontificating. He hoped he would choke on it. No such luck. Another onslaught was coming.

"And none of the sodding landlords in Ireland are even Irish. They're all bloody English. And the Scottish landlords are so anglicised that they might as well be English. Where can the poor devils go? The landlords pay their passage to get them out of the way. They can't afford to move to another part of the country."

Richard found it difficult to reply to this vociferous, unpleasant speaker. Unfortunately the points that he made were all valid. There had been much publicity in the press about the Highland Clearances in Scotland and 'Shovelling Out' in Ireland where landlords induced tenants to leave by organising emigrant ships and paid their passages. Those who refused to leave were forced out of their homes which were immediately burned.

Having arrived on the other side of the Atlantic the American authorities were finding it difficult to deal with huge numbers of immigrants most of whom were uneducated and untrained for any specific skill. Resentment was also building up amongst the indigenous residents who regarded the new arrivals as parasites and as most of them were Catholic an ugly religious discriminatory flavour was added to the ill-feeling which had surged to the extent that an anti-immigration party had been founded – The American Party – known to its critics as the 'Know-Nothing Party' as it met in secret.

Duncan came to Richard's rescue. "What are you doing here? Are you emigrating?"

"No. I'm helping to run a Catholic Church mission for the Irish in Liverpool. There's a lot who come here to look for work apart from all those who arrive here intending to emigrate who either run out of money , or

90

have some problem finding a ship or just feel too exhausted to go any further and stay here . Anyway, I've got to go. I have a meeting." He downed his beer and much to Richard's relief left. "What an objectionable fellow!"

"Maybe. But you will be hearing a lot of views like that on the ship and certainly in America. So you'd better get used to it. There's an awful lot of anti-English feeling round here," assured Duncan.

The next morning the three presented themselves at the dockside to embark but before this was possible they had to undergo a medical examination. Richard groaned at the size of the queue. "There are only two doctors," advised Fergus as informative as ever.

"What! There must be over a thousand people here!"

Fergus put his bag down. "Oh. It doesn't take long. All they do is examine your tongue and stamp your ticket. It's scandalous when you think of some of the epidemics that break out during these voyages. There are enough problems on board without a plague."

Although the sailing time had been reduced by the steamship from thirty-five days to eleven the conditions were still terrible. Most passengers were subject to inadequate food, no hygiene, and no privacy, possible brutality from the crew or violence from the other passengers and injury from being tossed about in heavy seas. Water penetrated food, bedding, luggage and books;from dampness in mild weather to saturation in bad weather. The atmosphere was never free from vomit.

Richard and the MacLeans had booked cabins and their journey would be more comfortable than their less fortunate fellow-travellers. As they stowed their luggage Duncan picked up a menu. "Well,for breakfast there's beef steaks, mutton and pork chops ,veal cutlets, smoked salmon, broiled chicken, fried ham, cold meats, stews , boiled eggs, omelettes and hominy."

Richard was looking at the dinner menu. He saw there was soup, fish and every kind of meat and poultry. "And look at all those pies, puddings, tarts, pancakes and omelettes again! All included in the price of the ticket. We shan't starve."

"Assuming you don't spend half your time with your head down a bucket. The seas can be very heavy" warned Fergus the ever- present voice of doom.

"Oh. Shut up Fergus. Don't listen to him Richard. If the Angel Gabriel were to offer him nectar in a golden goblet he would ask him if it had gone off." Richard smiled at this brotherly badinage. Fergus gave his brother a playful punch on the arm.

"Not a bit of it. We're far better off than those poor wretches without cabins. I was talking to a member of the crew the other day. He said that the muck they serve he would not give to his pig! Most of them bring their own food as well but like as not it gets stale, becomes soaking wet or gets stolen."

Richard was now looking at a leaflet giving details of 'The White Queen'. "This ship's built of iron and the decks are wooden and corked with oakum and the wooden planking is bolted into iron beams below."

"We know" interrupted Duncan."And she weighs fifteen hundred and sixty tons and can reach eight or nine knots under steam. Her steam pressure is low."

" I'm sorry.I'm teaching my grandmother to suck eggs. I forgot I was talking to two engineers. I noticed that she has four masts with sails and one funnel. How many crew are there?"

Duncan wrinkled his forehead. "Oh. I should think about one hundred and fifty. Both steam and sail are very labour-intensive. Steam needs engineers to maintain the machinery and repair it because it's always breaking down and stokers always have to feed the furnaces with fuel."

Fergus took out his shiny new pipe again much to Richard's quiet amusement. "And what about the sails! I was talking to the boatswain of a similar vessel the other day. There's miles of them!" Fergus kept stabbing the air with the stem of his pipe as though to emphasize his points and now a particularly vicious stab. Richard thought he must be pronouncing a new addition to the Ten Commandments. "When they are being used there's all that hoisting, maintenance and adjustment and when they change over to steam they have to be hauled down and stowed and that takes ages. They use up a tremendous amount of room." Now an authoritarian tone and another stab. "Mind you, they try and use the sails as much as possible so they can save the money on fuel." Judgement having been pronounced Fergus put the pipe into his mouth, sucked on air and looked around him giving an air of satisfied self-importance.

Richard leant across the rail and watched the banks of the Mersey slip past as the tug pulled the ship out to sea. The river was crowded with big and small craft and whilst part of his mind was occupied with the manoeuvres of the vessels the major part was reflecting on the turbulent emotions that had swamped him two nights ago.

When he had collected himself somewhat after leaving the music-hall he had strode the streets. Passers-by thought that he was desperate to reach somewhere urgently. He stared blankly ahead and pushed several people who were in his way but was oblivious to their cries of protest. Luckily, he had blundered his way westward rather than into the stinking lanes and alleys of the East End where he would have been more likely to be attacked or robbed by the numerous evil-doers who swarmed London at night. Garrotting had become a pernicious evil. Sometimes a rag soaked with chloroform was forced over the victim's mouth rendering him unconscious which had resulted in a number of careful citizens wearing anti- garrotting collars made of steel with spikes sticking out. Whether the discomfort of wearing it was worth the assurance of safety was a moot point.

Fortunately no such fate was to add to Richard's troubles. Eventually, he calmed down a little and realised that his body was streaming with sweat and his clothes were splashed with mud from the filthy streets. After slaking his thirst at a public house he found his way to his hotel and threw himself on his bed. The sweat had now dried and he was shivering brought on by the shock and upset. It was a pale, drawn, tired and tense young man who boarded the train for Liverpool the next day.

George Clarke had built a life structure for Richard which he had destroyed in a moment. Until the day he had shown his defiance in the office he had been very cautious in his relationship with his father. He had often been afraid of him and on occasion hated him but he had always respected this man who had given him a privileged and careful upbringing but shown him little affection.

Now, Richard had seen that self-righteous slave-driver of his youth, the revered member of the Church, the exacting principal of a thriving solicitor's practice to whom many rich and powerful clients entrusted their private and commercial business-behaving like a besotted, depraved and pathetic old man pawing and slobbering over some cheap tart.

Paradoxically, what seemed to upset Richard more than anything else was that his father had let himself down and thus had sullied the canons of behaviour which he had taught Richard to follow. Although Richard had grumbled about them he had always accepted them as guidelines. He had not always followed them but he now realised that he had liked to know that they were there. Now, they had been kicked away. The young man felt terribly confused.

Richard, in his immaturity could not as yet look upon his father as a normal human being with normal human failings and desires who could kick over the traces occasionally.

"Mr Clarke?" Richard was shaken out of his reverie. He turned round to see a pleasant featured young man a few years older than himself.

"My name is Foster Matthews. We are sharing a cabin." Richard took the proffered hand. The man sounded American. Richard had never met an American before but he had heard the accent parodied.

"What takes you to my homeland Mr Clarke?" Richard was somewhat surprised by the frankness of the question from someone he had only just met. He had not told the MacLeans the true purpose of his journey thinking that until the ship had left harbour the fewer people that knew the better. However, he saw no reason to lie now.

"I'm going to join the Union Army."

"Well, so am I but then I will be fighting for my country. Why are you going? You look too well-to-do just to be going for the bounty. You are not a 'soldier of fortune' are you?"

Richard laughed. "Not exactly".

Young men from all countries in Europe were now beginning to cross the Atlantic. The poorer were attracted by the bounty and the prospect of a better life. Many wished to avoid conscription in their own countries.

Most countries in Europe – save Britain – conscripted young men for a spell of military service. Many men who were expecting to be called up had decided that if they were going to have to join an army they might as well be paid for it and took the advantage of the generous bounty and pay offered by the Federal Government. Leaving their own countries could be difficult as men who were of military age or nearing it could be detained at the borders or ports.

The prospect of adventure was also drawing men from the upper classes that identified with the South and the aristocratic way of life of the planters. Professional soldiers were travelling in an official capacity to observe a 'real war'. Other men who had a dubious past and an equally dubious future referred to themselves as 'soldiers of fortune'. Richard actually wouldn't have minded that description as it had a certain raffish cachet to it.

Over the next few days Richard told Foster the whole story and they quickly became good friends. It was good to have somebody to whom he could unburden his troubles. Foster whistled when he heard about the episode in the music-hall.

"Well, I must say! That for hypocrisy takes a good deal of beating. My father can be irritating at times but he seems a paragon compared to yours." Richard learnt that Foster's father was a distinguished doctor in New York, that his mother was Scottish and that they had met and married whilst Dr. Matthews had been gaining further medical experience in Edinburgh.

"Edinburgh has the best reputation in the world for medicine. My father insisted that I do all my training there so I haven't been home for nearly seven years."

"Did you enjoy it?"

"Yes. I had a great time. The training was excellent and the student life was a ball. It was just as well that I lodged at the university. My mom's relatives were keen that I live with them. I didn't fancy that! They are all Presbyterians. They really are a cheerless bunch. No liquor of course. And they frown if you go out too much. Enjoyment is a sin. And if I ever argued they kept on about 'showing respect for my elders'."

Richard smiled ruefully. "Sounds a bit like what my father used to preach. And then I found he wasn't practising it."

"Well, I found it all too difficult to swallow after my life at home. New York is very different to Edinburgh and both my parents are fairly relaxed. My dad has converted Mom to his ways. In the end I managed to see Mom's folks just once a week. That was enough!"

Richard, Foster and the MacLeans mingled with many other passengers who had accommodation in cabins. The more that Richard heard about the conditions of the passengers who travelled steerage the more he realised that the extra money that he had spent on a cabin had been a sound investment. Apart from the appalling food and sanitary conditions they had very little means of entertaining themselves. Their space was very limited and they could only sit on the stairs or lie on their bunks.

Those travelling by cabin had a much more relaxing time with constant entertainment and a church service on Sundays. The lounges were elegant and alcohol could be bought at most times during the day. Enforced idleness and drink are a bad mix and sometimes fights had to be broken up. Musicians performed regularly and card games, snooker, billiards, skittles and a number of other games were played.

A few evenings after they set sail Richard and Foster were sitting at a table when four men sat down at the next table and ordered two pints of Bourbon.

"Well, that is worth celebrating!" Pronounced one

of them. Richard glanced at the speaker whose exclamation was in an English upper-class accent. He was tall, and blonde with an air of arrogance about him. His clothes were perfectly cut and he gave the whole appearance of being an English aristocrat .Richard heard him being addressed as 'Bullingdon'.

As the conversation continued it was clear that they were talking about a somewhat complicated matter concerning business and money. One of them was tall and dark and spoke with a slight French accent. Richard had noticed him before.

The men talked quietly but the tenor of the conversation seemed increasingly urgent and the whispers became harsh. It was obvious to Richard that another man who spoke with an American accent was very frightened. The fourth man never spoke. After a while Foster rose. " Let's go play snooker."

"Why the blazes did you drag me away? that sounded very interesting" grumbled Richard, annoyed when they were out of earshot.

"Because if you had leant any closer your ear would have been in their water-jug. I'm surprised they didn't notice. I suppose they were too intent on their own conversations. I wouldn't like to cross those guys. You couldn't hear much of it anyway."

"I suppose you're right" admitted Richard grudgingly. "But they looked a nasty bunch. What did you make of all that?"

"I don't know. But it must have been something mighty tense. I've never seen anybody so frightened as that American. And I didn't like that Englishman!.There were a number of them like that at Edinburgh . They had all been to what you English call ' public schools'. They give the impression that they are born to rule the world and walk around as though they constantly have a nasty smell under their nose!."

They continued to discuss the matter but couldn't come to any conclusion.

For the next four days the ship was beset by storms. Richard and Foster like most of the passengers suffered from sea-sickness. On the fifth day they heeded the advice of the more seasoned passengers and walked on deck wrapped in scarves and greatcoats- it was too windy for hats which would have been blown into the sea.

Richard was grateful to be out in the fresh, salt-laden air and greedily gulped in large lungfuls. It was a welcome change from being below- deck where the atmosphere was fetid and laden with odours of food, vomit, urine, unwashed bodies and dampness which has its own particular smell.

Pale and weak after their confinement below deck the young men walked slowly clinging to the handrail. The crew were absorbed in their tasks as the sails needed constant attention due to the vagaries of the winds. Suddenly, Richard heard the creaking, splintering sound of wood combined with the soft flop of cloth followed by a scream of terror.

Richard and Foster ran in the direction of the sound and arrived to see a mass of tangled rope, splintered wood and folds of sail. Seamen were attempting to unravel the mess.

"Keep away!" ordered one of the crew. "There's somebody under there." Foster stepped nearer.

"In that case I'd better stay. I'm a doctor."

Both men helped the crew untangle the wreckage. Eventually, the face of the corpse was revealed. Richard gasped. It was the face of the frightened American man.

Chapter Seven
July 1861

The rest of the voyage passed uneventfully. The burial of the dead man took place the day after the death. Richard bowed his head in prayer as the coffin slid noiselessly into the sea to the sound of the practical, emotionless tones of the captain reading the service for the burial of the dead.

This was the only death on the voyage. As they neared America the captain informed Richard that this was good. Usually several people – mostly the elderly or young children died on a crossing. There had been a number of accidents amongst the steerage passengers during the violent storms – a few broken limbs and a fractured jaw but this had to be expected. The normal broken noses, black eyes and missing teeth had resulted from lost tempers due to alcohol, enforced inactivity and confined space.

The dead man's three companions remained separate from each other throughout the voyage and Richard and Foster took care to avoid them.

Foster had made Richard promise to spend a few days with his family in New York until they enlisted. They would not be able to disembark together as Richard would have to pass through Castle Garden with the other immigrants whilst Foster would set ashore .with the other American citizens. Richard had initially protested but Foster would not be dissuaded.

"You have to.Look! You are going to a rough violent city in a new country. New York is not like Hereford you know. You need to get used to the place and look around before you try to fend for yourself. You don't want to join the Army just yet. You want to see what the American people are like before fighting for them. You never know you might want to do another job. There are plenty."

"Well. I don't want to impose on your family. I might outstay my welcome."

"Oh! Richard don't be so English. In America we don't stand on ceremony like you do in England. We are a country of immigrants. They come in by every boat. We are used to them. Newcomers who have connections are welcome to stay with friends or relatives until they find their feet. In New York a newly-landed immigrant stands out a mile. It is full of crooks and conmen. Although it's better now we have Castle Garden." Foster took a long drink from his glass.

"It was terrible before. It was just like Liverpool in reverse. Runners used to wait at the docks and pounce on passengers and try to sell them tickets or lodgings or even steal their baggage and make them pay a ransom." Richard was persuaded. It all made sense and he mustn't let stubborn pride prevent him taking advantage of a generous offer which was kindly meant.

Richard felt a surge of excitement as land hove into sight and the small specks gradually magnified into large shadowy shapes which eventually assumed the lines of buildings. Before discharging any of its passengers 'The White Queen' had to anchor so that a doctor could board from a small lighter and make his inspection in the quarantine ground. This was a stretch of the bay marked by two buoys – one three quarters of a mile to the south of the marine hospital on Station Island and the other about half a mile. All passengers were examined and if any were suffering from any of a list of infections or contagious diseases such as typhus, smallpox or cholera then they were taken to hospital and the ship was quarantined for thirty days.

The MacLeans who between them seemed to be an

101

authority on all matters maritime explained that naturally ships captains did not want their ship quarantined as during that time it was not earning any money for the shipping company. Unscrupulous captains would do whatever they could to avoid this unwelcome delay- either by hiding sick passengers or by landing them illegally on the shores of New Jersey. If a ship was quarantined sometimes passengers who had not been taken to hospital would arrange (usually through a member of the crew who would do anything for money) to be taken off in boats and lighters.

Sick passengers were not the only source of imported infection into New York. Jettisoned rubbish, bunks and bedding would be quickly washed ashore where the inhabitants of New York would pick over it like scavengers and sell the more acceptable pieces.

Richard discovered that the medical examination for leaving the ship was as cursory as that for boarding it. A rope was drawn making a narrow passage just wide enough for one person to pass between the medical officer and his assistant who scrutinised passengers as they passed and if anybody had any disability such as blindness, lameness or he was obviously ill then that person would be questioned. Anybody who appeared to be fit was 'nodded through'. No sickness was diagnosed and much to everybody's relief permission was given to disembark.

As the ship approached the dock the passengers stood on deck watching with interest. For most of them it was the first sight of this great city of New York of which they had heard so much. Richard was unimpressed after the great new magnificent stone docks of Liverpool. The wharfs and docks were seedy and shabby and the wooden, run-down warehouses did nothing to enthuse the tired but hopeful immigrants who had incurred such trouble and expense to undergo a long and uncomfortable voyage to begin a new life in the 'Land of Opportunity'.

It had been agreed that Foster should go to his home immediately on leaving the ship and be reunited with his family whom he had not seen for some seven years. He would arrange for somebody to meet Richard when he had been released by the immigration officials.

Castle Garden was situated at the most southern tip of Manhattan. It had originally been built as a circular fort and then used as a place of entertainment but for the last few years it had been used as a reception centre for immigrants which Liverpool so lacked. Its purpose was to check the health and means of immigrants, to advise them on further arrangements for travel and to protect them against the evil-minded citizens of New York who could steal baggage and try to persuade them to stay at expensive lodgings or sell them tickets for further travel inland at inflated prices.

Richard walked in file past yet another medical officer who merely looked at him. His baggage was inspected and he had to state the amount of money he had in his possession. He was asked his destination but as it was New York no more action was taken but those who were travelling further were shown maps and sold tickets for railways, riverboats and canals at proper prices. Richard waited for the MacLeans whilst they bought railway tickets for Pennsylvania. As the brothers pocketed their change and tickets an official pointed to another queue.

"Over here now please. "

"What's that for?" asked Richard

"Your bath."

"What?"

"Everybody has to have a bath, Sir. It's regulations."

"But I'm perfectly clean!"

"Well, you'll be even cleaner now won't you Sir?"

Duncan dug Richard in the ribs. "It's no good arguing. You're in the Land of the Free now."

Disgruntled, Richard joined the two brothers in a long queue for the men's washroom where about twelve men and boys were standing in a bath and another fifty were scrubbing themselves in a large trough. Richard was astonished when the official in attendance told one youth to wash his crotch properly.

"What a diabolical liberty!" He muttered as he was handed soap and towels. Duncan started to unbutton his shirt.

"If you're going to join the Army you'll have plenty of people telling you what to do with your body – so if you find this humiliating you'd better give up the idea."

Richard said nothing as he sulkily undressed. Duncan was right of course. Not for the first time Richard regretted leaving England but these regrets were always temporary. Apart from the fact that to return home would result in a total loss of face his was not the sort of character to change his mind about a major decision. Although the initial resolution had been made on the afternoon of the boating trip this resulted from a situation that had been building up for some time. Thereafter he had planned his departure and considered it carefully. No momentary pang of regret or remorse would alter matters now.

The weather was stifling, but luckily the atmosphere was freshened by a running fountain cooled by a high jet. On leaving the washroom it was now time for Richard to leave the brothers which he did with regret. He had enjoyed the company of these sensible but humorous Scotsmen. The three of them and Foster had proved to be a convivial quartet on board ship.

Duncan gripped Richard's hand. "It's a pity we can't have a farewell dram. It had been publicised before disembarking that alcohol was forbidden in 'The Garden'. Even so, some tried to smuggle in liquor and looked on disconsolately when it had been found amongst their possessions and poured onto the floor.

The MacLeans had obtained food to cook in the kitchens and were sleeping overnight in the galleries along with about two thousand other people although the authorities tried to encourage people to leave the same day and begin their onward journeys immediately. The brothers would take the train for Pennsylvania the next day and not visit New York at all. Their uncle wanted them as soon as possible and as Duncan put it they had no spare 'siller' to splurge. Richard had taken their address in Pennsylvania and they finally parted company.

Having collected his luggage which had been successfully stowed through the various processes Richard passed through the exit. A tall well-built man approached him.

"Mr Clarke?"

"Yes."

"I am O'Sullivan – butler to Dr Matthews. Welcome to America." Foster had told Richard that he would probably be met by this man but he had never met him as he had been engaged during his absence. The years spent in America since adolescence had overlaid the native Irish accent with an American one. Richard found the combination unusual but he would soon become accustomed to it as well as the other fusions of American accents with British provincial and other European ones.

Sweat poured down from under Richard's hat as he struggled with his luggage. O'Sullivan helped him load the bags into a four-wheeled vehicle whilst keeping away potential thieves and eager bystanders who were willing to 'help' - for a fee of course. Richard noticed with interest the recruiting posts just outside Castle Garden and the large numbers of immigrants crowding around the enticing notices advertising bounty of three hundred dollars. He would continue to see such posts throughout the drive to the Matthews house.

As they started to trundle through the biggest port and most successful city in the United States O'Sullivan talked about his adopted home- most of what he was to say Richard knew already but there were also interesting new snippets of information.

New York was a lively mixture of ethnic origins, culture, sophistication, poverty, vice and filth. It boasted scores of eating houses with many serving fashionable Italian and French cuisine; the hotels were more lavish than any in Europe. Here lay the engine-room of the burgeoning economy of the United States and the poor immigrant who possessed intelligence, enterprise and thrift prospered.

Many such people had made fortunes. "I don't suppose you've heard of John Jacob Astor, Mr Clarke?" Richard shook his head. "Well, you soon will here. Astor was a poor lad born in Heidelberg. He scraped enough money together for a steerage passage to New York. One day he innocently strayed past the area reserved for steerage passengers and the captain rudely told him to return to his 'proper place' and not to leave it again. He was later to find that Astor's 'proper place' was that of the richest man in America with an income of over two million dollars a year."

"How did he manage that?" asked Richard amused at the captain's hubris. He always liked to hear of arrogant and self-important people getting their comeuppance.

"He started by beating skins in Gold Street. An appropriate name as it so happens. Many great businesses start from small beginnings like that. The trouble is that there are not enough immigrants like Astor. Too many of them think that the streets of New York are paved with gold but they soon learn firstly they are not paved with gold, secondly that many are not paved at all and thirdly the hardworking ones finish up paving them themselves and the lazy ones just finish up destitute. The trouble is Mr Clarke there are just too many of my own countrymen here at the moment that are really not good for anything – although that is not always their fault but it is stoking up one whole load of trouble."

The authorities in New York had become concerned with the swarms of immigrants who did not have the money or the initiative to leave New York and find work. They just drifted about the city until they were taken care of by the Almshouse Board or one of the many other societies that had been formed to take care of the poor. Unfortunately (particularly since the Potato Famine of the late 1840's) many of the newcomers were Irish Catholic and as a large proportion of the host population was Protestant and of Puritan leanings there was now a very unpleasant groundswell of anti -Irish and anti- Catholic prejudice. Many Irish felt that persecution had pursued them across the Atlantic.

"So you follow the example of Mr Astor and not the other type of immigrant and you won't go far wrong." O' Sullivan chuckled as the carriage floundered through Broadway which was ankle-deep in mud and refuse. Scavenging dogs and pigs roamed the streets. Richard's first unfavourable impression of the city as the ship drew into dock was not being dispelled as shabby buildings gave the impression of a shanty town.

"And there's another thing Mr Clarke. You ought not to go without firearms in this city. It's very violent and the police force is no good." Foster had also explained this to Richard on the ship. People did carry firearms in England but it was not a widespread habit.

Richard alighted from the vehicle and followed O'Sulllivan up some white steps leading to a handsome house of red-brick set in a terrace of similar houses. They passed through an imposing hall. O'Sullivan knocked on a door and Richard found himself in a spacious well furnished drawing-room.

Foster was talking to a handsome middle-aged couple. An elegant woman smiled at him and a distinguished-looking man with greying hair and a well trimmed beard rose and extended his hand. "Welcome to America, Richard and thank you for supporting our cause."

"It's a pleasure Sir."

"You are welcome to stay as long as you like and make this house your base whilst you are in New York – and indeed in America."

Mrs Matthews stood up and shook Richard by the hand. "You are a brave boy and some would say foolhardy to cross the Atlantic to fight the war of another country. There have not been that many battle losses yet but a number of boys have died of disease-particularly measles and bowel fever."

'Why don't you say what you really think'? thought Richard, somewhat overwhelmed by the bluntness of his hostess' overture. However, there was a twinkle in her eye and it appeared that she did not mean to give offence. Her face was strong with a nose that was large enough to give it character but not to render it ugly. Her chin was determined. The general effect was pleasing and radiated strength and a positive personality. This was the face of a woman who spoke her mind: this was clear from her opening sentence which stated her frank opinion and did not waste time on small talk such as ' how was your journey'.

Unlike the MacLeans she spoke only with the a trace of a Scottish accent which,Richard later discovered was middle-class Edinburgh – neither had she adopted an American accent producing strange hybrid tongues such as that of O' Sullivan. Her clothes were fashionable and of good quality without being fussy or flamboyant – as far as Richard could judge; like most young men he was not exactly an expert in feminine fashions.

"Madam, I made my decision before I left England. I knew the risks I was running and I also knew that when I had broken my ties with my father he would not wish to have anything further to do with me." Foster had explained the whole situation to his parents and as they were both broad-minded he had included the incident in the music-hall. Richard did not realise this and would have been horrified if he had known.

Dr Matthews took out his watch and glanced down at it. "It's time those girls were back. I told them to come straight home the first day their brother returns and no loitering with any young man that happens to be passing." This drew an amused reproof from his wife.

"John, I don't think they have the energy for that at the moment. Their nursing duties are really taking it out of them. And of course they wouldn't hang around when their dear brother comes home after seven years." She smiled at Foster who grinned. Richard was already appreciating the easy camaraderie of this family.

Dr Matthews turned to Richard. "I suspect you are wrong about your father young man. You know we parents care a lot more for our children than they think we do – even when they don't always do what we want. Have you written to your father yet? You are still his son whatever has gone on between the two of you."

"No, Sir. I decided that it was best to do nothing until I was outside British jurisdiction. If I had written before leaving Liverpool I could have been detained aboard ship on docking in New York as ' The White Queen' is a British registered ship my father could have held me on two counts- firstly that I am under age and secondly that I was intending to fight in a cause in which Britain is neutral". Dr Matthews laughed.

"Well, you seem to have the makings of a good lawyer, Richard. You have researched the situation properly."

Mrs Matthews was not going to be deterred from her opening comments to Richard. She didn't agree with his plans. Why should she care about a boy she had never met? Because she had a son of her own who was in a similar situation. Foster did not know it yet but his parents had plans to vary his own with regard to the Army.

"Richard, are you sure that you want to join the Army? There are plenty of jobs around in offices for intelligent, well educated young men. The war is giving a boost to our Northern economy."

Richard had not sat down since he entered the room but seemed to have walked into intense scrutiny. He suddenly felt exhausted. The voyage had been tiring, he had been through the various processes at Castle Garden and although none of them had been unpleasant or intimidating he had been apprehensive until they had finished with him because if anything had been found wrong he could have been refused entry. He had then made the journey through a strange city. The last thing he needed now was a grilling. The room started to spin round. He also felt as though he was still aboard ship. The room was moving up and down. He had felt this sensation as soon as he had set foot on dry land but it had suddenly become a lot worse. He was now quite giddy and put his hand out to grab the back of a chair.

Dr Matthews came to his rescue. He saw that

Richard was unwell. He took him by the arm and made him sit in the chair and put his head between his legs. He knew from professional experience when people had reached their limit.

"Mary. Enough! Can't you see this boy is exhausted? He's as white as a sheet. This is not the time to discuss this kind of thing. It can be done later. We'll get him up to his room; give him dinner there and something to help him sleep. He hasn't lost his 'sea-legs' yet. Neither for that matter has Foster but he seems to be in better shape but then he hasn't been through that performance in Castle Garden, neither has he arrived in a strange city. And he is a man of twenty-six. Richard is only a boy of nineteen. He hasn't grown into his full strength yet. There's a world of difference between nineteen and twenty-six."

During the next two or three days Richard slept a good deal and gradually recovered his strength. He completed the letters which he had begun on board ship to his father and Laura. His letter to George was respectful but factual giving his main reasons for leaving as being his wish for excitement and personal fulfilment together with his father's lack of understanding and sympathy. He could not bring himself to mention the music-hall and in any event that had nothing to do with his decision to leave.

The letter to Laura was much longer. He deeply regretted his sudden departure but he made it clear to her that he could not tell her the truth as she would feel compelled to tell George- not out of disloyalty to Richard but out of concern for his own safety.

During this short time Richard developed a rapport with this family .He was particularly impressed with the equal relationship that existed between husband and wife and also with the easy conversation between parents and children. This was a household of friendliness, mutual respect and support – quite unlike the authoritarian intimidation which had existed in his own home. Richard briefly met Foster's two sisters but as they had not seen their brother for seven years the three of them spent much of the time together and just allowed Richard to recover.

Susannah and Ann were training as nurses as the suggestion of their father. This had raised a certain amount of eyebrows amongst their acquaintances but the doctor and his wife had not brought up their children to be idle. The girls, as well as Foster had been well educated and all three had been taken round hospitals as children and had watched operations.

"Everybody says this war will be over by Christmas. It won't. The Confederates match us too evenly for that. We may have advantage of numbers and raw materials but they have many fine officers who have left the Union Army. And as for soldiers! All those country-bred rebel boys are crack shots and ride like Cossacks by the time they are ten." The doctor was talking just after Fort Sumter at the luncheon table. Coincidentally Foster was returning to America as his studies had finished.

"We have medical facilities for an army of sixteen thousand. The army will grow quickly and the medical side will have to grow with it. You girls had best get stuck in straightaway." Susannah aged twenty and Ann two years younger did not hesitate and quickly began their training. Everybody had respect for their father's medical opinion. He was working closely with Dr Jonathan Letterman in the setting up of the United States Sanitary Commission on aspects relating to surgery and was much involved in advising the Army Medical Department.

A few weeks later – just before Foster was due to sail from Liverpool – Susannah was reading a letter from him which she had received that morning. "Foster says that as soon as he gets home he is going to join the Army as a private." She glanced at her father tauntingly.

Dr Matthews looked up from his breakfast plate. "Well, that's what he thinks! I've never heard such a stupid idea in all my life. I've already made arrangements for him. He will help either in the Army Medical Department or in the Sanitary Commission – it hasn't been decided yet. We are desperately short of doctors. He may well join the Army later but it will be as a doctor. He can save lives doing something he knows rather than get killed doing something he doesn't."

"You can't stop him doing what he wants" replied Ann mischievously. Children have a habit of teasing their parents about the misdeeds or stupidities of their siblings. The last thing they intend is to put the parental minds at rest. Dr Matthews was used to controversial comments from his lively daughters and usually he encouraged it and enjoyed it but this morning he was not in the mood.

"The hell I can't!" He roared. His wife and daughters looked up in surprise. He hardly ever swore. " If he is so stupid as to join the Army as a private then he will just be ordered into whatever medical branch I and my colleagues decide to order him whether he likes it or not. So he might as well like it." The girls looked down at their plates.

"The Army needs doctors and those who join up will be used as such and not as cannon fodder. Foster will have no choice. In the Army you do as you are told. War is a serious business. It's not some football game which will be over in three hours. People get killed. It's not a joke. Do you understand?"

"Yes, Father the girls answered quietly almost in

unison".

"Now Ann, I will not hear any more of this foolishness either from Foster or from you. And that goes for both of you." Dr Matthews looked meaningfully at Susannah. Ann managed to slide a smirk at her sister who returned it but the girls were subdued. Baiting Father was regarded as something of a sport but they knew when they had reached the limit.

Dr Matthews's prophecy about the ability of the Confederates was proved sooner than he thought. Within a week of Richard's arrival they had won the resounding victory at Bull Run and at one time it was feared that Washington would fall. New York was devastated. Very few people had the foresight of Dr Matthews and considered that a Confederate victory might be possible. After all, Lincoln himself had made the same mistake. He had only called for initial enlistments for three months. Now, he rushed through a bill enabling enlistments for three years.

Kentucky, Missouri and Maryland were gripped by panic. They were all very seriously undecided as to whether to secede. Bull Run made this more likely and if it happened it would render disaster for the North all the more possible. Missouri remained divided throughout the war although Kentucky and Maryland remained loyal but only after causing a good deal of worry and uncertainty for Lincoln's government.

For Richard this uncertainty and tension only heightened his sense of awareness and excitement of his new environment. Within a few days after the defeat at Bull Run he had regained his strength. Foster and his sisters (when their nursing duties permitted) hosted him around New York introducing him to a large number of their friends.

New York provided a varied feast of culture, commercial activity, preoccupation with the war, sleaziness, ethnic mix and entertainment which this youth from a sheltered upbringing in a provincial English city found fascinating – if sometimes difficult to digest. He did ask questions and made one or two comments the ingenuousness of which, coupled with his accent his new friends (particularly the girls who considered him 'cute') found particularly engaging.

Richard went to restaurants, art galleries and theatres and explored the less desirable areas with Foster and his male friends roughly clad and carrying no valuables. They walked through the polyglot communities with their industrious energies concentrated into all forms of productive activity. There were French, Italians, and lots of Germans, Scandinavians, Greeks and immigrants from Eastern Europe. Jews from all over Europe seemed to dominate much of the tailoring and dealt in all kinds of commodity and everywhere there were Irish. By a kind of osmosis Richard absorbed this blend of culture.

When Richard had been in New York about ten days Dr and Mrs Matthews announced an evening at the theatre .They had to attend a reception for officials of the Government and other people of importance in the early evening; therefore it was arranged that Richard and Foster should meet the older couple in the foyer of the building where the reception was being held and they would then all go on to the theatre . The girls had planned to go but an unexpected trainload of wounded prevented them – much to Susannah's visible annoyance.

As the young men were waiting in the foyer a door opened and two men emerged. They walked quickly across the foyer and out into the street. As soon as the outer door had closed Foster nudged Richard who had also noticed that one of the men was the quiet man on the ship. Foster put his fingers to his lips as if to say 'keep quiet'. He had no need. Richard wasn't stupid.

Foster's parents then appeared and they all went straight to the theatre. There was no opportunity to discuss the matter until late at night when everybody else had gone to bed. Foster grabbed the whisky decanter and a couple of glasses.

"Let's go to the library. We won't be disturbed there." Foster splashed out two generous measures and walked over to the curtained window of the library with his glass held against his chest. He was silent for such a long time that Richard couldn't bear it.

"Who is he?"

"I've no idea. Don't forget I've been out of this country for seven years. But he's obviously important otherwise he wouldn't have been there. It wasn't a meeting for nobodies. What I don't understand is why somebody as important as that should be travelling on the ship in such a furtive manner."

Richard swallowed a large mouthful and had to wait a moment for the burning sensation in his mouth and throat to disperse. "It all seems very odd. Your father probably knows who he is. Why don't you ask him? "

"You're dead right it's odd. And no, I won't ask Father – at least for the time being. There are all kinds of things going on at the moment and I think we had best keep quiet about it for our own safety."

They discussed the matter until the small hours of the morning and agreed that they should not mention the matter to anybody else - including Foster's parents as even their safety could be compromised. They were both worried. Since their arrival in America they had heard that people had disappeared or otherwise met with a mishap. To stumble on knowledge which one was not supposed to have could be dangerous.

Fortunately they were not permitted to ponder on their danger for too long. The Matthews had thought the boys had rested enough. There was work to be done – idleness was not tolerated in this household where the work ethic was strong. As from the following Monday morning Foster was to take up an appointment at the hospital where his sisters were working. Two or three days after his return his father had put his proposals to him and would brook no argument; in any event Foster could not reasonably contest the logic of the reasoning. The skills of a doctor were invaluable. To throw them away on a vainglorious act – even if motivated by patriotism- was selfish as well as stupid and would deprive people of vital medical assistance who might otherwise die.

The Matthews family had made it clear to Richard that he could stay as long as he liked but Richard did not have the nature to abuse hospitality particularly in the current frenetic climate when just to do nothing seemed wrong.

After the defeat of Bull Run people were confused. Opinions were mixed, some thought that Lincoln should now come to an agreement with the Confederacy, the war fervour of others was heightened and they considered that the war should be prosecuted until the South was totally crushed and some people just did not care. As long as their income was not affected, food appeared on the table every day and their loved ones were not in danger they ignored the war and it was possible to do this. The North hardly suffered any shortages and the economy boomed.

Now Foster was starting work Richard had decided to enlist straightaway but Dr and Mrs Matthews had thought and planned in advance. Mrs Matthews had not changed her opinion which was so forcibly expressed on Richard's arrival that it was wrong for this nice English boy to come and fight another country's war. Dr Matthews agreed with her but he had his own reasons for dissuading Richard to enlist – anyway for the time being.

Two nights after the theatre Richard knocked on the door of Dr Matthews' study shortly before dinner. On being summoned to 'come in' he opened the door. Dr Matthews was sitting writing at his desk.

"I'm glad you came to see me Richard, because I was going to talk to you after dinner. A friend of mine who has a big lawyer's office would like to see you. He needs a junior clerk. The war has made things very busy for lawyers and there is a shortage of well-educated young men like you and you are partly legally trained."

"Yes, but in England."

"Well, as you know I am a doctor not a lawyer but even I know that our law is based on that in England. It should not be that strange for you."

"Actually, I came to tell you that I am going to enlist tomorrow." Dr Matthews reached for a cigar.

"And actually I also wanted to tell you I don't think that is a very good idea. You are not an American. You have no duty to fight. Indeed, if you want to serve America you could do a lot worse than take this job. I don't know how long this war will last but it will be a lot longer than people think. As I told Foster many men will die and when it ends what is America supposed to do with all her fine educated men buried underground and we are just left with cowards, drunks, shirkers, illiterates and penniless immigrants to rebuild the country?." Richard smiled at this.

"There's a great deal for trained men to do for America outside the Army you know." Richard said nothing. The idea sounded interesting.

"Look, all I say to you is just 'consider it'. If you meet Dick Jenkins and you decide that you still want to join the Army then fine. But just see him. That's all I ask. Will you do that? If you start the job and after a while decide that it is not for you then you can always join the Army later".

Richard was persuaded. "Thank you. I'd like to."

"Fine. He'll see you tomorrow at ten o'clock." Richard was quickly finding out that this was how Americans did things. None of this English. 'Well that is settled. I will tell him. And he will contact you and you can fix up a mutually convenient appointment.' No. In America it was 'Fine. He'll see you tomorrow at ten o'clock'.

"You see Richard. This war is creating masses of work for lawyers. I have never been so busy. There are real estate deals. The Government's buying up land and buildings all over the city. New businesses are starting up. Contracts have got to be drafted and approved for the supply of food, uniforms, arms – all kinds of things that we never did before the war. And with two of my best young lawyers having joined the Army I really need help."

Dick Jenkins looked at Richard intently. He seemed the sort of man who did everything intently. No half – hearted measures for this dynamic little man who had started up his own firm some fifteen years ago. Now it was one of the leading practices in New York. Papers and files were piled up high on his desk. Richard looked at him through two piles as through a little tunnel. 'Perhaps American law offices are not so very different from English ones'. He thought.

"Well. I've never worked in an American legal office before."

"Nor have any of the other immigrants that fill our legal and other office jobs. I think you can do it. If I didn't I wouldn't have asked to see you. If either of us think we have made a mistake you can always join the

Army later. I will start you on eleven dollars a month. Will that be alright?"

It would. That was only two dollars a week less than he would be paid if he joined the Army. Richard accepted, trying not to sound too eager. "When would you like me to start?"

"How about now?" Richard agreed. He was no longer surprised at the immediacy. This was how things were done in America.

"Thank you Matthews. That went just fine. You picked a good one there again. You seem to have an eye for it. His personality is right. He comes over pleasant and a bit naïve which is what we want. He seems to have a good brain but I will find out how good after he has been here a few months. Legal work always sorts people out."

Dr Matthews stretched out his legs in the serviceable but not too comfortable chair (Dick Jenkins never ordered chairs that were too comfortable. His staff was not there for a rest cure!). " That will also give him time to acclimatise to America for a bit. Let me know when you think he's ready for Washington."

Chapter Eight

South Carolina

May 1862

Kate walked Jack slowly back to the stables. She was lucky she still had him. She had heard how the Commissary swooped on farms and plantations without any notice and denuded them of supplies and animals so that it was extremely difficult to carry on production.

When faced with protests the standard answer of the official in charge was something like – "I'm only carrying out orders Ma'am. We've got to feed starving soldiers fighting for our freedom."

Kate wouldn't have minded so much had she been certain that everything would benefit the soldiers but she knew that was not the case. The efficiency of transporting supplies to the Army was deplorable. Much would be stolen or corruptly sold for personal profit; grain would lie abandoned in sheds or out in the open to rot. Horses and mules accompanying the Army shaved the ground of fodder. Many animals that were seized could not be properly fed and were either wastefully slaughtered or died of malnutrition.

Kate's father had warned her of the Commissary in the months before the war. When she had shown surprise he had shown uncustomary impatience. "Well, what to you expect? Armies have to be supplied and who other than plantations and farms is going to do that? We can't import anything."

However, the Colonel had taken precautions. Barns had been craftily built in separate isolated parts of the plantation – usually in the wooded areas. Beaumont was too vast to be thoroughly searched on one visit. Enough would be left in the main barns to avoid suspicion. Jack and the two other best horses were kept in a small field well away from the main paddocks. In the event of a visit, Cuffy was to spirit them away into the woods until the danger had passed. The Commissary had visited last week and the plan had worked.

Kate handed Jack over to Cuffy and wondered how long she would be able to do that. At the outbreak of war Beaumont's slave population numbered about five hundred. The family's capital assets were constantly maintained as babies born to slaves replaced those who died.

Now the collapse in the price of cotton and the lack of food had caused the departure of many of the skilled slaves – such as weavers, carpenters, millers, blacksmiths, teamsters or bricklayers – who had bought their freedom. All of these had now found lucrative work – some of it with the Army although not as soldiers. Negroes were not accepted into the Army. Barely three hundred slaves now remained of whom about twenty-five were children under the age of ten. The adults comprised mainly of the house slaves, the less intelligent ones who worked in the fields and those who could not be of any use either through old age or illness.

Kate, whip in hand, meandered towards the house. She had been in the saddle most of the day and was tired. She took off her hat and wiped her face. Beaumont was now beginning to show the effects of a year at war. The lawns were ragged and unkempt. Instead of being tightly clipped the bushes and shrubs were now sprouting ungainly, uneven strands. Weeds now dotted the previously immaculate drives and paths. Flower beds were weed- choked, and the sad ,and dying flowers had not been cleared out. An unknown grey horse was tethered to a hitching post which had recently been erected near the front door. A pile of dung swarmed with flies. Previously horses of visitors never remained at the front of the house. Immediately the visitor had dismounted, his horse was taken round to the stables by a slave-boy who remained there for the purpose and to keep the drive free of excrement.

Kate seldom entered the house without feeling depressed. As much as she tried to manage the house and the grounds she knew she was losing control. The house was beginning to look under- occupied, forlorn and shabby. No footman now received guests at the front entrance, many of the rooms had been shut up and the furniture covered with dust- sheets causing a smell of mustiness and dampness which pervaded the whole house; although the rooms that were still used were properly dusted and cleaned.

Nevertheless the rules of Southern hospitality had not changed in that any visitors who arrived unannounced should be welcomed and given hospitality. Guests were now rare. Few people had the time to entertain or be entertained. Most people who visited Beaumont were either for important personal or business reasons. Mere social visiting had totally ceased. Kate was apprehensive at meeting the owner of the grey horse. He was possibly some interfering government official or he may have brought bad news about her father or one of her brothers. Whatever the reason for his visit, it was not likely to make Kate happy.

The initial heady excitement of the first months of the war had now evaporated. Hardships and shortages were beginning to be felt. Reverses had suffered after Manassas. The Confederates had suffered a defeat a month ago at Shiloh although losses had been heavy on both sides. This battle had been a bloody action in which four thousand men had been killed and of the sixteen thousand wounded, some two thousand had died. Kate had heard that in some places the fallen bodies were so close together that it was possible to walk over them without touching the ground.

Kate's was not now the only bereaved family – mercifully as far as she knew her father and brothers were safe although she never stopped worrying about them hence her bad feelings about the owner of the grey.Tragedies were now engulfing her family and friends. Mary Gibson's husband had been blinded in a minor skirmish. She would now have to run the plantation as well as care for her three children under five, and nurse her husband. Kate's cousin Lisa had died two days after giving birth to a daughter, on learning of the death of her husband.

As Kate crossed the main hall still holding her hat and whip she heard raised voices from a room which had formerly been a small drawing room but which she now used as her office. She decided to listen rather than reveal herself. Solange's voice was angry.

"And I tell you for the last time Mr Schneider I will not part with my cotton to any agent or dealer I don't know. I don't want that cotton bought by the Yankees."

"Ma'am I've told you. I'm not going to sell it to the Yankees."

"Can you guarantee that it won't finish up with them? You are a dealer. You will sell it to the person who gives you the best price."

"Ma'am does it matter? I'm offering you good money for that cotton which I'm sure you can use, given the current state of things."

"Sir. How dare you speculate on the condition of my finances! Do you not realise that this country is at war for our freedom? I have lost one son and my husband

and other two sons are risking their lives along with all the other real men of the South. Why are you not in uniform serving your country instead of pursuing doubtful deals with defenceless women?"

"A full belly makes for fine words Ma'am. Just let me know if you change your mind."

"That will never happen!"

Mr Schneider realising that there was no point in furthering the argument,shuffled into the hall. He grinned slyly at Kate who put her finger to her lips to signify that he should say nothing and followed him out of the front door. They stood outside the front door. Kate did not like what she saw. Before the war such a man would not have been given access to the front door. He was short, with long black greasy hair. His dark eyes shiftily slid about. His grubby white suit strained across his bulging belly. Kate didn't stand on ceremony.

"I gather you want to buy our cotton." An oily ingratiating smile spread across the fat features.

"That depends on whether we can agree the price Ma'am."

"Of course. Well you don't deal with my mother . You deal with me. Why did you come to the house rather than to the manager's office? That is the normal procedure."

"I did, but I was told he was the other side of the river."

"Well, go there now. You know where it is and wait for me there. I will be with you shortly. Lead your grey. There's no need to ride him. The drive is in enough mess as it is."

Schneider, realising that smarmy words would not have any effect on this woman with the ice-blue eyes, untethered the horse and led him over the uneven drive.

Kate stormed into the small drawing room where

Solange was sitting - her black clothes matching her mournful and helpless expression.

"Why did you send that man away?"

"I am not going to sell my cotton to people like him. You don't know where it will end up?"

"Our cotton. You mean! You know we have difficulty in paying our bills. I was up until midnight last night sorting out which we can pay now, and which we can't. You realise don't you that if we can't sell it we may have to burn it? You should have asked him to wait for Harrison or me. Harrison is paid for that sort of thing and I run the place. Father gave me the job because he knew that I could do it, and he knew that you would be hopeless at making deals."

Kate immediately felt guilty but only momentarily. Her struggle to keep Beaumont viable was for survival. Guilt was a luxury she could no longer afford.

"Kate we can't allow cotton to fall into the hands of the enemy by whatever means. I'd rather starve," wailed Solange. Kate's eyes were hard and flinty. Solange felt weak. She knew the power of that stare. Over the last few months she had sometimes been afraid of her daughter.

"Oh. That's just fine isn't it? That's a great help to the South! And will Father thank you for your high principles when he comes home and finds Beaumont ruined and you starving to death? And when I say 'you' I mean 'you'. I don't intend to starve to death and I won't let Custis do so either. Not while he is a child anyway. When he's a man he can do what he likes."

Solange sank down on the sofa and started to weep. Kate sat down beside her mother put her arms round her and brought her head down onto her chest where Solange sobbed quietly. Kate cradled her mother's head in her arms and kissed her neck.

"I'm sorry darling. I didn't mean it. It's just that you

make me so angry sometimes. It's a hard job keeping this plantation going and we have to use every advantage that comes our way even it means doing business with people like Schneider. Father left me with the job of managing Beaumont to the best of my ability, together with looking after you and Custis, and I mean to do it."

"You're right of course" sighed Solange. "Oh I do hate the way we have to live now."

As Kate held her mother she considered (not for the first time) that the minute her father left, the traditional roles of mother and daughter were reversed. Solange was not fitted by character or upbringing for the world into which she had been catapulted by war. To exacerbate the changes were her grief for Jeff and her worries about Frank, Harry and the Colonel. Although all three wrote regularly and were not currently in action   (as far as Kate and Solange were aware) things could change very quickly and as Jeff's fate had proved, sickness was scything through the Confederate ranks far more effectively than Yankee bullets.

If the war had shattered Solange's world it had widely expanded Kate's. Women could now indulge in business openly. The careful teaching of her father had fed her natural aptitude. Kate was now respected (and in some cases feared) by the people with whom she did business.

Kate kissed her mother and withdrew her arms. "I must go now and talk to Harrison. Let's not have these rows again. It's a question of survival. You do understand don't you?", Solange nodded sadly.

As Kate reached the horse pond she saw Rachel, the beautiful seamstress.

"Rachel. Is Harrison in his office?"

"I believe so Miss Kate." Rachel chose not to speak in the vernacular adopted by most slaves. Kate thought to herself that Rachel almost certainly knew where Harrison would be. The plantation was a close community. Everybody knew why Rachel kept visiting the office of the plantation manager so frequently. As Kate had expected, Schneider's grey was tied to the hitching post outside the office. The two men rose as she entered.

"Carry on, gentlemen." Harrison was now accustom-med to Kate taking part in negotiations. Since the affair of Mr Weston's mare, he had accepted that Kate was in command. He had learned his lesson. Kate sat near the window behind Schneider and said nothing. When Schneider mentioned a certain figure, Kate gave Harrison a nod of approval. Harrison agreed it with Schneider who took out a wad of notes and counted them out on the table. Kate now walked in front of Schneider.

"Mr Schneider, I must apologise for the behaviour of my mother in the house. She can't really cope in these troubled times. If you wish to do business with this plantation, please come to this office. Don't use the front drive. Turn down the teamsters' trail about half a mile further down the road. A path branches from it and leads here. Cuffy will show you the way when you leave. All your dealings will be with Harrison or me."

"Sure Ma'am. Any time." Schneider grinned as he sidled out of the office.

"We did a good deal there, Harrison. We want to shift as much cotton as possible. We don't want to have to burn it." Harrison nodded in agreement.

Kate knew that the war had created a glut of cotton, partly because export was made impossible by the Federal Navy's blockade of the Confederate coast and partly because the North was not buying the South's cotton – officially anyway. Unofficially, parties from both sides illicitly traded with each other which was the reason for Solange's concern with dealing with Schneider.

The Confederate Government wanted to encourage the planting of more crops and limit the production of cotton, and there were instances where cotton was ordered to be destroyed. Kate was desperate to avoid this happening at Beaumont. The hope of the Government was that if the European markets were starved of cotton, this would be an important inducement of their governments to recognise the Confederacy in its' own right.

Unfortunately this plan had misfired. Although Britain was suffering from its' silent cotton mills in Lancashire, the European markets were quick to find another source of cotton in India. The South's cotton and its' shortage of manufactured goods had created fertile ground for a healthy black-market between people whose countries were at war. As Kate intended to hand back a flourishing plantation to her father rather than a bankrupt one, she had reluctantly decided that she would participate in this banned trade if necessary.

When Kate had passed Rachel on her way to see Harrison, she had given her little thought. Kate was concentrating on her dealings with Schneider. Rachel, however, was glowing with feelings of happiness with her relationship with Harrison although this did not prevent her from inwardly seething every time she was in the presence of Kate.

Rachel was one of the most beautiful women in the county and knew it. She always refused the advances of men from the Turners' class who found the copper coloured skin, lithe body and perfect features of this quadroon irresistible. Rachel did not intend to be the mistress of any man whom she knew would never marry her for the reasons of her colour and status.

The Turner family protected her from these men if

they became difficult when she rejected their advances. Unlike some Southern men, Colonel Turner did not hold the view that hospitality extended to his male guests having access to his female slaves. Rachel was not grateful to the Turners for their protection. Why not? Because she was one of them.

A young uncle of the Colonel's had fathered Rachel's mother when he was fifteen. His father had been disgusted and had packed the boy off to military college- that convenient destination for the wayward sons of the gentry.

Disgust for his son however did not move the Colonel's grandfather to sufficient compassion to free his little granddaughter. The boy died in his early twenties and the relationship was never mentioned in the Turner family. Gossip among slaves however had ensured that Rachel had been made aware of her ancestry at an early age. She was intelligent and had been taught to read and write by her Uncle Nathaniel, who had learnt these crafts in the household despite the laws forbidding it.

The general view held by the authorities was that if slaves were educated they 'might get ideas above their station'; it was safer to keep them ignorant. The Turners, like a number of owners, did not take that view. Literate slaves could be useful for clerical work and could read to children and sick members of the family and even act as tutors to the children. Young slaves who worked in the house who had quick and enquiring minds would see books and papers lying about the place, and, in many cases, taught themselves without much assistance

When she was about eight, Rachel protested to her mother that as she was related to Kate and her brothers she should be free like them. Her mother struck her across the face knocking her from her stool.

"You say dings like dat an' you get us sold to a cruel Massa who whips us. Dese Turner folk's deys treat us good."

Rachel was sobbing and holding her face but she was crying more from surprised injustice than from pain. She was only expressing an opinion. "But if my grandmother was good enough for a member of the family to lie down with, then we are equal." Rachel had an understanding far beyond her years and she did not speak in the vernacular adopted by most slaves- even now despite her anger and hurt feelings.

"But dem white folks dey is different. We be slaves an' we must do as we be told or we be beat and sold."

Rachel was well aware that the white folks were different but unlike her mother did not accept the fact. However, she knew that it was no use arguing with her mother again, but, in due course, she was to have a conversation that would set the course of the life.

When slave children were about eleven, the Turners assessed them for their future role on the plantation. Those who were considered to have sufficient aptitude were taught a skill or taken to work in the house. The rest were destined to spend their lives working in the fields and were sometimes contemptuously referred to as 'field niggers' by whites and those blacks who had been selected for a more superior role.

Rachel's mother was delighted, but Rachel was furious. As she knew that her mother would take no notice of her point of view, she expressed her disgust to Nathaniel at 'pricking her fingers for her white family' when she should be wearing the same clothes as them. She might as well work in the fields. Nathaniel drew her to follow him a few hundred yards, where they sat down under a tree.

"Rachel. You know that in my youth I worked in the

house and had all the food and clothes and read all the books I wanted but like you I resented my slavery and twice I ran away."

"You were very brave."

"I was very stupid." Rachel looked puzzled.

"Twice I was caught, brought back and whipped. After the first time I was sent to work in the fields. After the second time I was told that if I did it again I would be sold and I knew that they meant it. I never saw the inside of the house and library again."

"What! Never? Why not?"

"Because they had identified me as a troublemaker, you silly girl! And, worse than that, if there was any unrest they always suspected me first. And the threat of being sold was always there. They probably wouldn't do it now at my age, but I can't be that certain."

Rachel looked solemn. Slaves lived in fear of being sold which was an uncertain fate that could befall any of them at any time.Slaves would be sold for any reason – a perceived misdemeanour on their part, a change in the fortunes or on whim of their owner. Sometimes they were given away as gifts. The death of an owner could be a worrying time, particularly if his wealth was broken up and distributed amongst other members of the family. A sale probably meant that the slave would never see his blood relatives again and if he was unlucky, he would finish up with a cruel or neglectful owner.

"We must never lose hope. The world does not end at the boundaries of Beaumont or even at the boundaries of South Carolina. Nor is it restricted to the Southern United States. There are lots of organisations to free us in the North and in England. Particularly now everybody's read 'Uncle Tom's Cabin' which came out a few years ago. It was written by a Northerner – Mrs Beecher Stowe."

Rachel now looked interested. "What's it about?"

Nathaniel gave a brief summary of the harrowing tale. Rachel sat spellbound at the way that the death of Tom's master (who was about to free Tom) resulted in his sale to a brutal owner who had an even more brutal overseer – Simon Le Gree. "It's very difficult to get a copy in the South. I managed it through my connections and passed it on. It should be read by as many slaves as possible. Any slave found with a copy will probably be whipped – or worse. They say Queen Victoria cried when she read it and the British are really on our side. They abolished it in their colonies some years ago."

"How do you know all this?"

"What you don't know you can't tell, and, more importantly, can't be forced out of you. When you are older I might tell you some things but if, and only if, I think you will be useful to us and we can count on your discretion. And I will never be able to do that if you are just going to be angry and resentful. You will have to learn to control yourself. Now are you are going to listen to what I have to say or are you going to just sit and simmer like a pot on the stove?."

Rachel smiled slightly and nodded. She was quiet and had that thoughtful look on her face that children have when they are being given advice that they have never thought of before but which they instinctively know is right.

"Never forget, Rachel what I am about to tell you. The classics taught me a lot of things. You remember the story I told you a few weeks ago about the Trojan horse?"

"You mean the one where the soldiers were hid in a huge wooden horse which was dragged into the town and when it was night they jumped out and murdered all the townsfolk?"

"Yes. That's the one. The Greeks had gained the city's trust by intelligence and stealth and struck at the right moment – when the city was unsuspecting and weak. Much cleverer to do that than to attack when they are ready for you and to storm the walls from without than when they are bristling with defenders and the drawbridge has been taken up. Do you see what I mean?"

"Yes." Rachel looked at Nathaniel intently. Her hands were now planted on her knees with her elbows akimbo.

"Now listen very carefully. Take Mrs Turner's offer. Go and learn in the house of the white folks. The closer you get to them the more you can learn from them. Read their books, listen to their talk and get to know their ways. And mind your mouth."

Rachel smiled. She knew that Nathaniel was telling the truth. "The more education and skills you acquire, the more use to them you will be and the more they will respect and trust you. That way you will be the more use to us when the time comes to win our freedom. Over the subsequent years Nathaniel knew of the abolition movements in the North which also drew sympathy from some Southerners, and he did keep Rachel informed of these. She continually pestered him for the source of his information but he refused to tell her. "People who have unnecessary information can be a danger to us." He would say.

Nathaniel reprimanded Rachel for impatience. "We must bide our time. The South will secede. There will be war. The South will lose and then our moment will arrive. To become involved in any premature, hot-headed plantation revolt which will be brutally crushed will put our cause back years."

When Rachel passed Kate that afternoon she thought (not for the first time) that her freedom was in

134

sight and the words 'Master' and 'Miss' need never pass her lips again. She couldn't stand Kate. Her brothers were fine – she was adept at dealing with the male sex- but two intelligent self-willed women – one a slave and one a mistress were not destined to be a happy combination, and they were not; particularly when they were related.

The two young women had seldom openly clashed but Kate felt that Rachel's cool politeness just managed to conceal an insolence and sense of superiority which she found intensely irritating. The underlying tension was tightened by the fact that Rachel was never openly defiant and therefore could not be criticised.

When Kate strode into the drawing room her mother looked up from the settee where she lay with her head buried in her arms. She had been too preoccupied with her own thoughts to worry about the cotton and Mr Schneider. She stretched over to the side-table which was crowded with sepia photographs of her men folk and picked up one of her husband and gazed at it. She did this several times a day.

When war was imminent, photographers in both north and south had done a roaring trade. The new science was now very popular. Couples had flocked to have their pictures taken with the woman's arm tucked into that of a uniformed one. The pairs stood proudly possessive of each other. Those men who had not had the time to be photographed before they left had used the services of professionals who thronged the camps keen to scoop the plentiful business.

Like many of the younger soldiers Jeff and Harry struck martial attitudes. As befitted his nature, Frank cut no extravagant poses and looked thoughtful. Not many photographs were taken in the South now as like many other items chemicals were in short supply due to the blockade. However, Solange's contemplation of the photographs was interrupted by Sam the butler who slid noiselessly into the room. Sam had not joined the exodus of slaves. He was in his late fifties, considered that he was in a comfortable position and had decided to stay in it.

Kate moved in between her mother and Sam in order to conceal Solange's emotion from the slave. "What is it Sam?"

"It's Mr Miller, Miss."

In his quarters Harrison lay on his bed. The furnishings for the manager were functional but basic. The thin, faded curtains fluttered gently in the light breeze, the cracked paint peeled from the dry woodwork. A shabby metal washstand, jug and bowl provided the washing facilities. The life of a manager on plantations(which were always a few miles from the nearest town) was often lonely. He was apart from the planter's family and slaves alike – below the one and above the other. Many found solace in drink and slave women. Harrison was happy. He had found solace in Rachel. A slave woman with a difference.

Rachel would be visiting him again tonight. It was not just their sexual relationship that was successful. Their personalities, sense of humour and views meshed.

They were both intelligent and self-educated. Rachel was desperate to see the end of slavery of which Harrison had always disapproved and he was anxious that the stranglehold that the leading white families had on Southern life be cut. For Harrison, the dirt- grubbing life led by many poor whites formed a different kind of servitude and he hated the expression 'white trash': it had been applied to himself and his family.

Noah Harrison had come from a poor white family which was hardworking and managed to eke out a meagre subsistence on its sparse holding.. The family owned no slaves. Noah was a clever boy who had learnt to read and write and made the most of the rudimentary education which was handed out by the minister and his wife in the wooden school at the side of the house. Much of the reading was from the Bible. The church lay a few hundred yards away surrounded by trees. The Petersons had the use of a large garden and small farm which they managed with the help of three slaves. Noah went to school whenever he could.

When Noah was eleven, he was the oldest pupil in the school. Attendance at the best of times was spasmodic as children were often kept home to help about the home and farm. There was no school in times of planting and harvesting. Many areas had no schools at all.

One day Noah, as senior pupil was sitting in a corner of the room instructing some of the younger pupils in reading. Despite the open door the stuffy room was airless and somnolent. Apart from the whispers of Noah and his young charges the only sounds were the persistent buzzing of flies and the scratching of chalk on slates made by the rest of the pupils who sat on benches pulled up to rough tables serving as desks. The children's clothes were shabby, worn and in many cases carefully patched. Much of the clothing was cut down from larger garments worn by older brothers and sisters or parents. All the children were barefoot.

Reverend Petersen sat on his raised desk. He was reading. His cane was propped up against the blackboard. Occasionally he would slide a suspicious glance under his glasses at the class.

Suddenly, the silence was broken by grunting, squealing and a man shouting. The minister stood up. "I'm going outside for a moment. Noah. You're in charge." He walked quickly and fussily. Noah had never seen him run.

A moment later he returned. "The pigs are out again. Noah! Get the six biggest children and come with me. Stay here the rest of you. One sound and I will just pick out any three of you and cane them." This ensured silence. The Minster's canings on the hand were often savage.

Noah and the six helpers ran out and were told to get into the upper orchard. A sow and her litter of piglets had broken out of her sty and were running over the orchard and farmyard. The minister, his wife, the children and the slaves eventually managed to shoo the sow and her piglets back into the sty. The minister, unused to this exertion took out a handkerchief and wiped his hot, shining face.

He turned in fury to his oldest slave. "Joseph! How many times have I told you to keep that pigpen fixed? This has happened too many times."

"Massa I did. I looked at it last week."

"Well. You didn't do it this week. Go to the stable and get my whip'".

Joseph fell to his knees. "Massa, please. I did try."

"Not enough. I said 'Go get my whip.' Joseph walked slowly and came back with a cruel looking whip. The minister tied Joseph to the well head and administered at least twenty five strokes to the screaming sobbing man.

Noah, the other children and slaves looked on in silence. The slaves wore an inscrutable, disgusted air. To Noah it seemed that the minister was enjoying himself. Eventually the whipping stopped. Joseph's back was a mass of blood. "See to him." The minister barked to the other slaves. They loosened his bonds from the well head and then laid him on the ground and fetched salt water to throw over his wounds. They then placed him on a stretcher and carried him to the slave cabins.

Joseph's wounds turned sceptic and festered. Ten days later he was dead

The minister then turned to the children. "Get back to class." Noah stood still gazing in front of him at nothing in particular. The other children trailed off to the classroom. The minister shouted again. "Noah! Did you hear what I said? Get back to class!" Noah remained fixed to the ground still staring ahead. "Noah!" The minister came right up to Noah and bent down. "Noah! Did you hear me?"

Noah looked up at him. "We read in the bible that all men are equal and that God loves us all. How come you own slaves? How come you whip a man like that and you a man of God?"

The minister was dumbfounded. His church served a poor area. His parishioners had very little education and regarded him with reverence. He was only used to being addressed as an equal by those of his own social standing which-in truth - was not that much higher than this parishioners. To those of a higher social standing such as planters' families he was obsequious and ingratiating. Children had never spoken to him like that. He grabbed Noah by the arm and started to drag him towards the schoolroom. The boy struggled and punched but the man was too strong for him. The minister eventually pulled the Noah to the front of the frightened class.

"This boy has had the impudence to question the right to own slaves. Not only is it part of the constitution of our great country and our state but it is in the Bible. I quote you Genesis Chapter 9 Verse 25. 'Cursed be Canaan; a servant of servants shall he be unto his brethren'. And who was the father of Canaan?"

"Ham". Chorused the apprehensive children save for Noah who was now still.

"Right. And you know the saying that'the children of Ham shall be the hewers of wood and the drawers of water'. Don't ever one of you question slavery again. I'm going to teach this boy a lesson." The minister reached for his cane. This caused him to loosen his grip slightly and Noah shook himself free. He ran to the door. "You ain't right. It ain't right for one man to own another and to beat him like that. I ain't never coming back."

Noah ran home. He told his parents. They were not too bothered. They had not thought much about the rights or wrongs of slavery. They couldn't afford any anyway. Slaves were for 'rich folks' who as far as they were concerned lived in another world. As for Noah's schoolin, they could hardly afford the meagre fee. They were glad to have another pair of hands about the place whilst Noah was still living with them.

Both Noah and his parents knew that he would leave as soon as he was old enough. There were too many younger children and Noah had already set his horizons wider than that of his parents. Their hand to mouth subsistence living was not for him. Noah continued to read whatever sparse, grubby books he could lay his hands on and he continued to practise his arithmetic. When he was fourteen he left home to work his way up North. He obtained jobs helping teamsters, he helped drive herds and he worked on boats. Eventually he arrived in Philadelphia and obtained employment in an engineering business at the lowest level. He was intelligent and hardworking and his qualities were recognised. He obtained qualifications, was promoted and eventually became the manager.

In his spare time Noah continued to educate himself. The schooling provided by the Petersens may have been rudimentary but it proved to be a sound base for further learning. He attended evening classes and learnt maths, politics, literature and philosophy including the works of political theorists such as Adam Smith, Rousseau and Jeremy Bentham but he was most influenced by Karl Marx – Das Kapital which had been recently published. Harrison became even more aware of the injustices of the world – not just slavery in the south but the inequalities that he was seeing around him every day.

Pennsylvania taught Harrison that slavery exists in many forms. In some cases workers were worse off than the slaves in the south. Although they had freedom of movement they were subject to a different kind of bondage.

Many of these unfortunate people were immigrants who had come to America to escape political persecution or economic hardship or both. America promised a better life. Now in that 'better life' they were exploited by the industrialists and had to struggle for the most miserable pittance, with children starting work at the age of eight. When they were exhausted through ill-health or fatigue, they were dismissed.

About a year before the war Noah received a letter from his sister stating that their mother was becoming increasingly infirm and that she (sister), having six children and another on the way, to say nothing of a shiftless ne'er-do-well husband (who did nothing but drink liquor, chew tobacco and whittle all day), could not be expected to take on this additional burden. As Noah was unmarried and had no responsibilities save to his mother, it was high time that he should shoulder these and come home where he should be able to find suitable employment.

Noah did not want to go 'home'. Philadelphia, Pennsylvania was now his home.He loved his mother and had regularly sent money back to her after the death of his father (whom he had always respected but considered that he had worked too hard, in the wrong place and to no avail),but he would not have considered going back to her under normal circumstances. In his opinion he had done his duty and would continue to do so until his mother drew her last breath.

However, these were not normal circumstances. War looked certain and southerners were being regarded with hostility and were returning home in increasing numbers. His elevated position at the factory gave him a certain protection from jibes at work for the moment. In the event of war he could well expect dismissal despite his value to the firm- there were plenty of able northerners keen to take over his coveted position. Society was becoming increasingly polarised with many southerners and northerners not mixing with each other unless it was absolutely necessary. Increasingly he heard sneers of 'copperhead' or similar unflattering names for southerners.

Harrison decided to comply with his sister's request. He gave in his notice at which his employers expressed genuine regret, cashed in his considerable savings and took one of the increasingly laden trains southwards. The train journey itself made Harrison speculate as to the likelihood of the South being successful in a war. With the highly lucrative ' King Cotton' and slave labour the South had no incentive to emulate the North and invest in new modes of agriculture , plant, machinery, roads and railways. Much of the South was not even mapped.

As an engineer Harrison was astounded by the railways. He had never travelled in the South by rail before. He discovered that there was not a uniform gauge and several times transfers were made from one gauge to another. This was expensive and time - consuming. He wondered (not for the first time) whether he had made the right decision to return to the South and not just 'taken his chances' by remaining in the North. But he came to the conclusion that 'what is done is done', and it was too late to change anything. He arrived home, stayed with his mother for a few days, made arrangements for somebody to care for her, and applied for the advertised post of manager at the neighbouring plantation of Beaumont.

The Colonel and Harrison did not care for each other on sight, but in spite of the latter's lack of recent experience on a plantation, lack of deference and self-opinionated manner, he had grown up on a farm and as a child had occasionally helped out on a plantation . He also had plenty of managerial experience and excellent references from his previous employers. Time was limited, secession was imminent and the Colonel would have to leave soon. Harrison was the only suitable candidate and was engaged.

Harrison did not like the Colonel whom he considered to be typical of the old patrician ruling class which he had always regarded as odious but now from his readings of Marx was unacceptable. This type of family was soon to be extinct and Harrison would rejoice in their downfall. However, a job was a job which he wanted for the time being although, financially he could have existed without one for some considerable period.Nevertheless, the habit of thrift, which had brought him so far in life would not desert him. The chances of lining his pockets were also excellent. He had no qualms in taking advantage of the Turner family whom he considered to be part of a corrupt system and had benefited from it for years. He had reckoned without Kate.

As Preston Miller entered into the room, Solange fluttered up to him and threw herself into his arms. He was fond of his sister – as far as he was fond of anybody. The only person whom he had truly loved had been his first wife. He held Solange tightly – smoothing and patting her hair.

"I just don't know how I'm going to cope anymore." She began to sob uncontrollably. Miller held her until the weeping began to subside.

They then made their way to the settee where Miller kept his arm around his sister. With the other hand he reached for the brandy which Sam had noiselessly brought in on a silver tray and placed on the sideboard. Sam never asked Miller what he wanted on his arrival. He just brought the brandy.

It was automatically accepted that Miller would stay at least one night. Although the practice of Southern hospitality had changed with the war, the principle had not.

Despite the lack of luxuries space was still in abundance. Food was not as plentiful as previously but most of it was produced on the plantation and there was enough if properly managed. Nobody went hungry. The number of house-slaves had been reduced but that did not greatly inconvenience the family – those that remained just had to work harder.

When Solange had retired upstairs for a rest ,Miller and Kate indulged in conversation about the family. Eventually Miller decided to broach more practical matters.

"I understand that your ingenuity in beating the blockade has been tremendous. You have my congratulations."

"Thank you, Uncle, but I am only doing what is necessary."

"Considerably more than is necessary I would say. It would not occur to many people to make their own shoe blacking out of soot and oil or to save the bristles from slaughtered hogs and use them for brushes. Or to preserve all the brine left in the barrels when the pork has been salted down and to boil it and convert it back into salt again."

Kate looked at him surprised. "How do you know all this Uncle?"

Preston smiled. "Oh. I have my sources." He stretched and stood up. "Come and show me how you are spinning your own cotton. I've heard about that too."

As they wandered down to the sheds, they chatted and Kate informed Miller how like so many others she was making her own dyes from shrubs such as myrtle which produced the colour grey or from mixtures or roots, berries and walnuts and a variety of other concoctions which produced a dark-brown colour.

"The uniforms will all be brown soon. There is not any more grey dye due to the blockade and there will not be enough myrtles to make what we need." Observed Miller as they entered the spinning sheds.

The South had never boasted many cotton mills and now Beaumont like many other establishments had to spin its' own cotton. They walked into a miniature cotton factory with nine or ten slaves working with cards, spinning wheels, warping frames and looms. Miller and Kate stood and watched for about ten minutes and then strolled back to the house.

Coffee had soared in price and Kate explained how she had tried to find a substitute from okra, yams, potatoes, browned wheat and burnt corn but none of these had been successful. She told Miller how she used the leaves of the raspberry,blackberry and huckleberry plants for tea, how she made starch from the bran of wheat, flour , green corn and sweet potatoes and how she concocted putty from Spanish potatoes roasted in hot ashes which were then peeled and mashed in flour.

Miller said very little. He knew all of this and much more because Miller made it his business to know anything which might concern him. Beaumont did concern him. Despite Kate's superb management her continued presence at the plantation did not suit his plans.

Whatever was not convenient for Miller had to be changed. Kate's running of the plantation was not convenient for Miller; she would have to be removed. Harrison's management was convenient for Miller. Harrison would remain.

Chapter Nine

Washington

May 1862

Richard struggled through Washington. His carpet bag was heavy and bumped against his calves. He kept stopping and changing hands to spread the burden. Sweat ran down his face from under his hat. He had to make his way from the station to Willard's hotel for further information, and, possibly, instructions. He had no idea as to what the meeting would propose but that only contributed towards his anticipation. Normally he would have asked a porter to carry his bag but he had been told to trust nobody for risk of theft.

Richard did not really know what he expected from the capital city of this big, young country in which he had been living for just under a year. He had spent all his previous time in New York. In Washington he had expected to see great and beautiful buildings and there were some. He could see the Capitol which would be impressive once the roof had been completed. He also knew there would be poverty. After all poverty existed next to wealth in British cities such as London and Bristol, but the different neighbourhoods were usually well-defined.

What he had not expected was the curious undeveloped aspect of Washington. Shanty areas lapped against well-built brick buildings. Pigs wandered loose in the muddy, filthy roads rooting for food. Every kind of military traffic splashed, bounced and clanked about everywhere. The time that he had spent in New York had accustomed him to the sight of

Negroes. Many were ragged but some looked relatively prosperous.

The city grilled under the sun. Richard had not yet become accustomed to the sudden stark changes in climate that he had discovered in the East Coast of America. He was used to being gently nursed by the English spring from winter in to summer, and from autumn back into winter.

Richard found an excuse to rest for a minute. A party of sweating, swearing soldiers was working to shift a huge gun carriage which had sunk in the mud. Some tried to shore up the wheels with planks whilst others pushed and pulled along the back and sides. At the front a further group tried to coax and lead the horses. Suddenly the vehicle lunged forward with squeals and splashes as the wheels were forced up out of the rut. The working party wiped their hands and dusted down their uniforms.

The small crowd which had gathered round cheered. A large fat man wearing a straining brown and yellow checked suit and brown bowler hat gesticulated as he spoke raking the air with a cigar wedged between the second and third finger of his right hand.

Occasionally the cigar would travel a circular gesture to the speaker's mouth when he would take a long, wet soggy puff and blow out smoke mingled with saliva. He was one of those 'know-alls' who as long as he has an audience takes it upon himself to expound in an authoritative manner.

Many listeners either say nothing or give the appearance of agreement - it is easier to do that than argue. Others just disengage their minds and gaze listlessly into space or just wander off without the speaker noticing ,because he is too full of his own self-importance.

"Of course those men were professional teamsters

before the war. Anybody who had a proper trade is still doing it in the Army". As nobody replied and he now decided he wanted a reaction he gesticulated towards Richard.

"You look lost, boy. Where are you headed?"

"Willard's Hotel."

"Willard's! You look too young for a general or a politician. Perhaps you're somebody's son ?.One or two of the bystanders started to titter.

" Yes, I am somebody's son". Further tittering from the onlookers .

Richard was too hot, apprehensive and too keen to reach his destination to indulge in tedious jokes.

"You're English?"

"Yes. I'm English. Now can you please tell me the way to Willard's?"

"Come with me. I'm going that way." A friendly looking young man about Richard's age motioned with his head. Richard picked up his bag and followed him gratefully taking care to avoid treading on the various different kinds of dung that lay in the road. They stepped aside as a detail of soldiers approached. Richard thanked him. The young man waved his hand. "You gave me an excuse to get away from that old bore. I know him well. You're not in the Army are you? Plenty of immigrants are joining up as soon as they get off the ship. The bounty's so good!"

"Not at the moment. How about you?

"Not yet. My pa wants me to join up straight away now the Army's short of men and many of the original enlistment periods have expired. He says it's my job to save the Union. My Ma says there are enough drunks lying about the streets and those immigrant Irish sitting about, doing nothing and getting into fights, that can go and get their heads blown off first."

Richard waved away an eager street vendor who

was holding out a loaded tray of buns. "The Confederates have just brought in the draft. All enlistments have been extended for three years and all white men between eighteen and thirty five will be drafted for three years. They may bring in something like that here? What do you think?" His companion looked impressed.

"Say, you know a lot! You haven't been here long judging by your accent!"

Richard smiled. His accent had caused a good deal of favourable comment. He spoke with a Herefordshire burr which was strong enough to be noticed but not so pronounced that people could not understand what he was saying. "Just under a year. What do you think about them bringing in the draft?"

"They may but not yet. We've got much more men than the Secesh and all these immigrants coming in, and Congress are even making it law so that Negroes can enlist. They'll hold off the draft as long as they can. It's not American. Most Americans or their ancestors came to America to get away from things like that. Anyway we're here. Nice to meet you. Good luck. My name's Sam Parker."

Richard introduced himself and shook his informative companion by the hand and parted from him with regret. He liked the welcoming and friendly approach of the Americans, which was very different from the reserved, distant attitude of the British. He had now become accustomed to it. He put down his bag for a few minutes. He wanted to cool down and tidy his clothes. He did not want to greet the official he was due to meet, with his face red and shining with sweat, untidy neck-wear and dusty clothes.

Richard had never stopped wondering about the strange trail of events since that afternoon almost exactly a year ago when he had confronted his father.

If George had not irritated him so much on that particular day would he still be a bored solicitor's articled clerk in the Cathedral City of Hereford? Or would he be where he was now? Meeting American Government officials who were going to make him some mysterious proposal. He always reached the same answer. He would have come to America anyway although it may have been slightly later. He knew that his life was unsatisfactory. The row had just given him the jolt to move at that particular moment.

After Richard had spent a few minutes preparing himself, he picked up his bag. He was approached by a doorman. "I've come to see Mr Snow." The man allowed him to pass through to where a number of page boys were standing around waiting to be of assistance to those who asked for it, or to those who just stood around looking bewildered. Richard obviously fell into the latter category as one lad came up and asked if he could be of help.

Richard stated his business. "Come with me, sir." People filled the foyer. Richard felt that it would be difficult to move an inch without being accused of assault. He had not been jammed in such a crowed since disembarking at New York. Eventually, Richard found himself in a large chamber on the first floor and he now had freedom to move about him.

Willard's was where everything happened, and where everybody met in Washington. If you wanted anything done or wanted to meet anybody important then you went to Willard's. Richard had heard that even Julia Ward Howe had written 'The Battle Hymn of the American Republic' at Willard's.

Groups of men sat or stood around the room and some sat at tables writing and were presumably in some sort of official capacity. Many were in uniform. The page indicated a table where a large man with a long white beard resting on his chest sat writing with one hand and holding a large cigar with the other.

Queues of people stood by each table. Next to Mr Snow stood a young man whom Richard judged to be some sort of aide. Richard handed him the short note that he had been instructed to give Mr Snow. The aide smiled pleasantly and asked him to wait at the end of the line.

The people in the other queues were talking garrulously to each other whilst the people in Richard's queue were silent. Richard suspected the reason. However a couple of men in the next queue smiled at him and exchanged pleasantries which developed into conversation especially when they realised he was English.

"I'm not going to ask you what you are here for just in case you can't tell me." Said one of them. People are here today for two reasons. Either they've been sent for in which case they can't say why, or they want something in which case they don't stop talking about it. I can tell you why I'm here."

"Why". Asked Richard interested although he suspected that the speaker would need no encouragement. These men looked as though they might provide some entertainment during what could be a long and boring wait.

"I'm after a contract with the Army for the supply of shoes. There's a whole bunch of us after Army contracts. My buddy here wants to supply the Army with beef and the guy over there wants the contract for blankets. And you see the table in the corner?" He paused waiting for Richard to say 'yes'.

'Yes'.

"Well that's the inventions table. The fat guy has just patented shoes in the shape of canoes so that men can walk on water and wants to supply the Government, and the tall guy has just invented two cannon balls joined together by a chain so that ten men can have their heads cut off at once." Richard laughed but his amusing informer was interrupted.

Suddenly, the door opened and in flooded a small crowd of people surrounding a tall spindly man who was chatting informally and laughing. He had thin long features complemented by a beard which suits that type of face very well. The face seemed familiar. Then Richard realised that it seemed just like President Lincoln – he had seen the face on posters but he could not believe that the President would just arrive when nobody seemed to be expecting him. He leaned across to his informer and asked quietly. "That isn't President Lincoln is it?"

"Sure, that's Abe."

"But nobody said he was coming!"

"Oh Abe doesn't stand on ceremony. He drops in sometimes and chats to people." Richard had heard that the President's approach was informal and casual. He preferred dealing with individuals and small groups rather than large formal gatherings and received so many visitors that the White House had taken on the character of a transit camp. He also wrote letters to all kinds of people indiscriminately throughout the country.

Richard watched the President of the United States of America tell what appeared to be a dubious story as those in his immediate vicinity rocked with ribald masculine laughter, and then, slapping one of his aides on the back, shambled from the room.

"He seems very jovial. Hasn't he recently lost his son?"

"Yes. Willie was eleven and got typhoid and his younger brother Tad nearly died of it as well. Abe was heartbroken but ole Abe just gets on with things. They say his wife Mary is out of her mind with grief. And they lost another son Teddy some years ago."

Richard eventually found himself at the front of the queue. Mr Snow motioned to him to sit down and read a paper that had been placed in front of him without looking up at Richard. He then motioned to his aide to come forward and whispered something to him. He then turned to Richard. "Please go with Mr Croft." Richard, pleased to leave the Mr Snow of Few Words and Less Charm,picked up his bag and followed Mr Croft out of the room, up two flights of stairs and along a series of corridors where he was shown into a room where two men were sitting. One was in the uniform of a Colonel and the other wore civilian dress.

The Colonel looked up. "Sit down Mr Clarke. Before we go any further I just want to check some details. Please give me your name, date and place of birth, how you travelled to this country and where you have been living since your arrival."

"My name is Richard Clarke. I was born on 14th October 1841 in Hereford, England. I travelled from Liverpool to New York aboard 'The White Queen' and I have been staying with Dr Matthews in New York."

"Good. This fits with the details that I have been given and your personal description also matches. "Six feet tall, fair hair, blue eyes and broad athletic build'. If, one day, everybody uses these daguerreotypes which soldiers are so fond of having taken and sending to their loved ones, then that will make our lives so much easier. We have to deal with impostors all the time. Bounty jumping is nightmare."

The Colonel stood up. "Now I know you are who they say you are, we can proceed. I am Colonel Wilmer and this is Major Allen. He is a detective". The detective stood up and shook Richard by the hand. Like most men he was bearded. He wore a crumpled knee-length coat. His bowler hat lay on the table.

"Pleased to meet you Mr Clarke." The accent was strongly Scottish. "I know quite a lot about you. In addition to what Colonel Wilmer has said, I know that your father is George Clarke, a solicitor from Hereford. You attended Hereford Cathedral School. You have one sister living and that you lost your mother in childbirth three years ago." The Colonel could see that Richard winced at the mention of his mother. Her death had affected him very deeply.

"Alright Major. I think you have made your point. We did not want to upset you Mr Clarke but you must realise that we know a lot about a lot of people. You are here because Dr Matthews gave us your name as somebody who might be able to help us. We then investigated you and when we found that you were suitable we decided to ask you to help us."

Richard was quiet. He thought that was somewhat devious of Dr Matthews whom he had regarded as a generous host, but he supposed that was how people behaved when their countries were at war. They put the interests of the nation first. He was also intrigued. "How on earth did you find out about my family land my school in England?"

The detective smiled. "You will be surprised at the sophistication of our intelligence. We have a number of agents in Britain together with a wealth of information from all kinds of other sources such as trade connections. The Confederates also have a very good network over there-our agents and their agents are constantly falling over each other – there are so many. They are especially strong in Liverpool which has always had strong connections with the South."

"I suppose that's because the cotton has always been shipped there."

The Colonel leaned forward. "That's right Mr Clarke. It's always been very convenient for those Lancashire cotton mills and our blockade is now hitting the mills hard. Liverpool is now making up for it with all those Southern ships that are being built in their shipyards especially those damned commerce raiders which are wreaking such havoc with our fleet." The Colonel spoke with such vehemence that Richard felt quite guilty but now his voice softened. "Now Richard just tell us what you know about why you are here."

"Well, Sir. I met Dr Matthews' son Foster on the ship coming over."

"Yes. We know that." 'Of course you do' thought Richard grimly 'you know everything about me.'

"I had decided to join the Army straightaway as I only had a limited amount of money but Foster pressed me to stay with his family. After I had been there a short time Dr Matthews suggested that I might like to get to know the country a bit better before fighting for it, and found me work in a legal office.After a while it was suggested to me that the Government might have other work for me to do and it will involve travelling but I don't know where"

"Yes. Richard that's all you know and all you were meant to know up to this moment. I can tell you now that it will involve you travelling to Richmond into enemy territory,and you will be involved in intelligence work for the American Government."

Richard was surprised but not totally dumbfounded. He realised that if the Government had sent for him it must have had a good reason but he never thought that it would be work of that nature.

"You mean spying?"

"If you like to put it like that. I would prefer to describe it as 'intelligence gathering'."

"But why me? I'm English. I don't know the

country. And I'm only twenty. What possible use can I be?"

Major Allen intervened. Richard wondered why he wasn't in uniform. "It is precisely because you are English that you don't know the country and that you are only twenty that you can be of considerable use to us and that is why you are here. There are Northerners visiting or living in the South who are suspect and the same applies to Southerners in the North. Similarly there are Southerners and Northerners living in their respective territories who support the other side." Richard nodded. He had heard all this before. Major Allen continued.

"This is a civil war Mr Clarke where brother fights brother. There are natives of every Rebel state serving in Federal regiments. Our Senator John Crittenden has a son in each army. And you know that the President's wife has a brother and three half-brothers in the Confederate Army?" Richard had heard a great deal about this. Mary Lincoln was not a likeable person at the best of times and her Confederate connections didn't help her. Colonel Wilmer leaned forward.

"So is her brother-in-law. And that is even after the President offered him a commission in our Army. The trouble with this damned war is that you don't know who your enemies are. As far as I'm concerned if you're American, you're suspect." Major Allen began to fill his pipe.

"So you see Mr Clarke you are ideal for our purpose. Few people are going to suspect a twenty - year old Englishman. We don't even have to change your name or your reason for being in this country. You came here for adventure and now you're getting it. You will be provided with a number of contacts. Some of these will be 'friends' of your family in England. They or members of their family will have visited England

and there is no reason why they should not know you or your relatives."

"What I am to do?" Asked Richard.

"You will soon realise that the safest thing is for people in your position to know as little as possible. You will be contacted by our agents where you are required to be of service. During that time you will be a guest in and around Richmond. So enjoy yourself. But you should know that you will be required to watch this woman." The Major pushed a photograph across the table. Richard saw a handsome woman with her arm around a little girl.

"This is Rose Greenhow. She has been a prisoner for the best part of a year. She is a Confederate spy and is more deadly than four Rebel regiments. She was responsible for our defeat at Bull Run. She supplied the enemy with details for all our troop movements –even with the number of blankets we had. She will soon be released."

"I didn't realise women were spies!"

The Colonel laughed. "They most certainly are and very effective ones and the Major here uses them. Don't you Major?"

"Yes Colonel. You see Mr Clarke they can conceal things very easily with all their elaborate hairstyles and clothes and those huge crinolines can hide all sorts of things, even arms. They are also less likely to be suspected than men – even now. If they are with a male spy posing as say his wife or sweetheart they can give him useful cover whereas a man on his own or two men together arouse suspicion more readily. They are also better at extracting information out of both women and men – women talk very easily to other women and men tend to brag about their exploits to women. Where necessary, women have affairs to extract information."

Richard was intrigued. "Why are you letting her go

if she is such a dangerous spy?" The Major looked at the Colonel who answered.

"Because she seemed to be almost as effective a spy in prison as when she was free. The trouble is that she knows everybody both nationally and internationally and has many friends on our side. She was a leading hostess in Washington before the war. She speaks several languages. Her husband Robert was a diplomat and they were both very highly regarded in Government circles. They met the likes of Washington Irvine and your Charles Dickens when they came to Washington. She and Robert were involved in land deals in San Francisco where he was killed in a fall caused by road works and she finished up suing the City of San Francisco, and received ten thousand dollars. She had only just given birth to little Rose – the girl you see in the photograph. She is as beautiful as she is clever and has been having affairs more or less since Robert died. Men are infatuated with her. That's how she obtains much of her information. She seems to be able to operate from gaol because half her gaolers are in love with her. She could manipulate a tree. The sooner she is packed off back to her own country the better."

"But if she is so dangerous and she has so much information about our side ...." Richard had just realised that he had said 'our side'. He was beginning to think of himself as a Northerner. The other men had noticed it as well. "Why do you let her go? Why don't you just shoot her?"

The Colonel laughed. "You have a lot to learn about politics son. For one thing she has many friends in our Government and in our Army. Friendships are not just extinguished by war. For another, neither side likes to shoot a woman – it's just not done – that's another reason for using women. They are not so harshly treated as men. And for another, the South might just retaliate by shooting some of our people that they have in captivity. And we are not just 'letting her go'. She is being released in exchange for some of our people."

"How long will you want me to be there?"

"We can't say for certain.We will pull you out when we think you can't be any more use to us, or we think you are getting stale (everybody gets stale after a while) or we think that the other side are starting to suspect you. Or it may be that we lick the other side very soon and then of course everything will change but that is unlikely to happen.

Now that is all we can tell you at the moment. We are not going to ask you if you can handle it. We know you can otherwise we would not have come this far. But are you interested? If not, then just say so and the matter stops here. We will just pay your expenses for coming here and you can go away and join the Army. You will be able to join anyway of course when you have finished working for us."

Without hesitation Richard announced:"I'm interested".

The Colonel settled back in his chair and folded his arms across his chest. "Good, we knew you would". 'Of course you did', Richard thought. "Now I expect you have been wondering about money"? Richard had. "We will pay you five hundred dollars as a down payment in gold, and twenty five dollars a month plus expenses. Do you find that satisfactory?" Richard did.

"O.K. Let's get to work. Hopefully we shall take Richmond soon. It may even be before you get there. In which case our plans for you will change. In war time everything changes from day to day."

When the door closed on Richard the Colonel stood up. "That went well Allan. I will inform Elizabeth Van Lew in Richmond. I received a message from her this morning. She liked the details we had sent her about Clarke."

When the Colonel described 'Major Allen' to Richard as a 'detective' it was similar to describing the Chief Justice of the United States as a 'lawyer'. Major Allen ran the Federal Secret Service and his real name was Allan Pinkerton who had set up the Pinkerton Detective Agency before the war. He had initiated the employment of female operatives and was therefore the best person to have extolled their attributes to Richard. Pinkerton however looked grim.

"I am arranging for Timothy's widow to be told the dreadful news. What can we do about Hattie? Can't we try and exchange her for Greenhow."

"Difficult. We have already negotiated Greenhow's terms. I'm sure it's too soon. Hattie's only just started her sentence."

The two men had both agreed that Richard 'did not need to know' the fate of Timothy Webster and Hattie Lawton. These were two of Pinkerton's operatives who went to Richmond to gather intelligence posing as husband and wife. They had been discovered, arrested and found guilty. Webster had been hanged on 21st April – the first spy of the war to be executed. Pinkerton was right when he said that women were less harshly treated, as Hattie Lawton was sentenced to one year's imprisonment in Castle Thunder–although nobody who had spent time there would have described any sentence in that dreadful place as 'lenient'. Richard's remit as to Rose Greenhow was just a test of his effectiveness.

There would be many other people watching her. Nobody thought that Richard would provide information that the Federal agents did not already have.

Two weeks later Richard was on his way to Richmond. He had undergone an extensive briefing as to the politics of both North and South, slavery and the structure of both Armies.There had been a certain amount of role- playing in preparation for some of the situations which he might face. He had also been given instruction on ciphers and codes. His instructors were impressed with him. Shortly before he had finished his course one of them sat down with him.

"You have a keen intelligence. That is why we picked you, but try and play that down a bit when you're down South. Don't act stupid exactly. That could cause comment and draw unnecessary attention. Just give the impression of a bland, pleasant English youth who is just interested in visiting another country. That in itself will not cause suspicion. There are a lot of English in the South at the moment." This was true. Much of the English upper classes sympathised with the Confederacy as they saw similarities between the Southern ruling class and the English aristocracy. A good number of English (as well as Europeans) were visiting the South out of interest. There were also a large number of military and other representatives who were observing the war in an official capacity.

"And don't be drawn into serious conversations about the war or politics with anybody. You never know when you are being tested. And on no account express any opposition to slavery or 'their peculiar institution' as they so quaintly call it. But don't appear to be too enthusiastically in favour of it either. That could raise suspicion. Just be neutral. Plenty of foreigners visiting the South voice no opinion at all. Be one of those."

Richard had been told when to recognise an agent who was making contact with him. The person would mention his mother's maiden name in the first few sentences. "Nobody forgets their mother's maiden name and it's something very few other people know." Richard's mother had been Mary Felmingham. Naturally Pinkerton's people had discovered that.

Richard had been given a good deal of further information about Rose Greenhow. Colonel Wilmer met him the day before he left. "Be careful Richard. Men seem to tumble before her like leaves in the fall although she doesn't usually go for men of your age. She prefers mature types. Perhaps even I might stand a chance! Still. Young men have been known to become infatuated with her so be warned."

Richard's journey to Richmond had begun with the Army, riding on a horse or in a wagon when he became tired. The style of saddle and method of riding were different to what he had been used to in England but he soon became accustomed to it. In order to avoid suspicion the later stage could not be with the Army, and had been a complicated one of clattering rail journeys with many changes caused by the battles raging round Richmond and had finished by boat.

Richard had been given clear instructions as to the address so there was no need to ask the way. His first impression of Richmond was of beautiful tranquillity mingled with dreadful calamity and foreboding. It seemed eerie and unreal. Richmond was a lovely city and reminded him of some of the more attractive English towns. The city was surrounded by green hills but they echoed with the noise of cannons and white smoke drifted above them. The placid James River flowing through Richmond was not decorated with pleasure craft but bristled with boats loaded with ammunition and other supplies.

Trees drooping with foliage and blossom lined the gracious wide streets along which trundled ambulances taking the wounded to the makeshift dressing stations and hospitals that had sprung up in and around the city. The cries of these stricken men in the beautiful sunshine under the brilliant blue sky seemed even more pitiful and out of place. Richard now realised that he had always associated wounds, pain, sickness and death with storm and darkness.

The houses looked spacious and elegant. The gardens were large, drives were long and wide and radiant flower beds bordered green lawns. Richard had been told that he would be staying with the Smythe family. He had been given a substantial briefing about them. They had friends in England and letters purporting to be from them had been written asking if Richard could visit. In accordance with the rules of Southern hospitality Mrs Smythe had replied freely giving the invitation which was nestling in Richard's pocket next to his chest.

Apart from the military traffic, wagons and ambulances carrying their wailing cargoes Richard could sense panic. Carts loaded with household goods jostled with the other vehicles; men and women on horseback tried to overtake; people scurried along on foot, holding whatever they could carry. Richard found the address and turned into the gate just avoiding collision with a large bustling black woman who was firmly holding onto the wrists of two bewildered white children. She glared at Richard in annoyance.

Richard turned into the drive of the beautiful porticoed mansion. Immediately he was hit by a sense of foreboding. An ambulance was just driving away. The driver and the two orderlies didn't even look at him. Their mouths were drawn in a tight line. Intimidated, Richard walked up to the front door and knocked on the door. He had to wait a few minutes before it opened and was greeted by a black manservant. Richard stated his name. "Come in sir, but this really is a terrible time."

Richard had seen some dreadful sights in the streets but this was nothing to what confronted him in the hall. About thirty wounded men lay so closely packed that those attending to them could hardly walk without standing on somebody. The manservant made his way over to a woman who was lifting the grizzled head of a soldier with one hand and holding a cup of water to his mouth with the other. The manservant said something to her which Richard couldn't hear.

She didn't look up. "Not now Gabriel. Can't you see I'm busy." Richard felt unwanted by a frantic hostess in this house of mutilated men in a city of terrified people where invasion was imminent.

Chapter Ten

South Carolina

May 1862

Preston Miller sat in the magnificent library sipping brandy and contemplating his plans. He was a tall, imposing man in his late fifties. His intelligent face and high forehead were framed by a fine mane of grey hair which nursed his collar. His prominent chin was not concealed by the customary beard so popular among other men. He sat upright in the high backed chair. His was the body of a man who had always maintained his fitness and pursued vigorous sports. Here was a man born into an influential family which considered that it had a natural right to control whatever it touched. Anybody who crossed this man would regret it and many people had.

Miller was clever both academically and commercially-not always a common marriage of talent. Both Miller and Solange had been brought up bilingually by their French mother. To add to these attributes, Miller was an expert horseman, a deadly swordsman (which skill he perfected during his year at Heidelberg University at the age of eighteen where he became fluent in German) and a killing shot. When he left Germany he spent three years in business houses in London and Liverpool.

Liverpool was the most important British port and city as far as the United States were concerned. It welcomed cargoes of tobacco, grain and cotton. Vessels returned loaded with emigrants and luxuries that were not manufactured in the Southern States.

When Miller returned home, he immediately threw himself into his father's commercial interests. The older man was happy to relinquish activity in favour of his intelligent and energetic son. When he was twenty eight Miller soldered his interests to one of the other main commercial families of South Carolina by marrying their only daughter, who quickly bore him six children. The prominent families of South Carolina cliquishly referred to themselves as 'F.F.S.C.' Miller's place among them was now safely assured.

Despite being a marriage of convenience the union was a happy one and Miller was devastated when his wife died of Milk Fever on the birth of the last child. Death associated with childbirth was a common occurrence and widowers were expected to remarry ; the household needed to be run, slaves managed, children brought up and beds warmed. Miller remarried and although the couple lived under the same roof, the marriage was not a particularly happy one although the framework of respectability was maintained.

Miller ingeniously developed the business interests acquired from his father and his wife into a huge network of agents and offices covering the United States, Great Britain and Western Europe. His operations included commercial properties, banking, shipping, plantations, timber and agriculture. He was also involved in trading in a wide variety of commodities including slaves, cotton, metals, liquor and various foodstuffs.

Due to the war, the South was now suffering from a severe shortage of commodities and a desperate, unprecedented need for goods and raw materials. These demands had created spiralling prices and a haven for agents and middlemen. Shortages had bred corruption, and corruption had engendered new fortunes and swollen existing ones such as that of Preston Miller.

Intelligent Americans had known for years that war was inevitable. The only question was 'when'? Miller was an intelligent American. Intelligent Americans had also known that a Southern victory was unlikely. The North had a Navy – albeit inadequate – but the South had no navy at all. The North had great industrial production and the South had to import most manufactured goods. The fact that the South now had a Navy and an effective industry was one of the great marvels of the war ,but Miller knew that it was not enough.

'The Anaconda Plan' of the North to deprive the South of much-needed imports was working. The blockade of the Confederate coast and the control of the huge slow rivers that penetrated deep into the Confederacy were having a devastating effect.

Manpower was also a serious problem for the South. The North's population of twenty five million was supplemented by a steady stream of immigrants and there was even talk of allowing Negroes to enlist. The white population of the South was a mere six million and it was totally out of the question for Negroes to bear arms, although they were used by the Army as labourers. The South had good generals, a strong military tradition, many graduates of military academies, and a majority of men from all classes who had been brought up to ride and shoot. It was not enough.

Miller knew that the only lifeline for the Confederacy was to achieve sufficient military success for it to be recognised as a country in its' own right by Europe. Britain and France were still dealing and trading with both sides and were watching the conflict with interest. The Union was becoming increasingly irritated by their attitude. Miller suspected that the inevitable major Southern defeat would ruin all chances of the Confederacy being recognised by Europe.

Miller had never intended to be ruined along with the rest of the South, and as much of his wealth as possible was held outside the Southern States. In 1859 he had realised that war was imminent and, foreseeing a shortage of cotton and tobacco in Europe, had increased production on his own plantations and shipped these commodities to Europe along with other cotton and tobacco he had bought. Two months ago he had sold it all for a huge sum.

Miller was also involved in blockade-running, importing arms and luxuries such as whisky, perfume and frames for bonnets into the South and selling them at enormous profits ,howcver these operations were dwarfed by the extent of his other schemes and enterprises.

Despite Miller's plans for his own future, he had the full confidence of the Government and had been consulted by Jefferson Davis from the start of the war and had spent much time in Richmond. He had now been at Beaumont for twenty-four hours and was pleased. His plans were carefully laid and everything and everybody was working well, and being carefully watched. Kate and Beaumont were part of those plans and yesterday had brought wonderful news. Rose Greenhow was to be released and would soon be on her way home. This would be the proof of his commitment to the Southern cause. He and others in the Government had been working for her release for months.

Miller nursed his brandy-glass in both hands and took a gulp of the strong liquid, rolling it about in his mouth then swallowing with relish. Within two days Kate would be removed from Beaumont and Miller would be well on the way to becoming the richest man on the whole continent of North America.

As Kate dressed for dinner, she was unaware of the

fact that her uncle was thinking of her. She however was thinking of him and wondering how long he would be staying. He had ridden round the plantation with her today and his constant questions and comments (although many of them were favourable) made her irritable. She felt that her authority and competence was being questioned.

"My father has enough faith in me to leave me in charge so why haven't you? Anyway it's nothing to do with you. Beaumont belongs to my father. And you can only be here because you are shirking your military duties and-furthermore-you have taken care to see that your sons never see cannon!"

Kate felt like saying these things but she didn't. Her uncle was one of the senior male figures in her family and was to be obeyed- ostensibly at any rate. She had never had any affection for him or his sons' although she had always enjoyed the company of his three daughters who were jolly, uncomplicated companions. She had regarded Miller as remote and authoritarian and his sons as colourless and very much under their father's control.

Kate fumbled with her clothes. Despite the war Solange still insisted on dressing for dinner. "There's no need to change our civilised customs just because we are fighting the Yankees", she was fond of saying when there was any suggestion of relaxing the old customs. "If we do that, then they have won."

Dressing had become a great deal easier since the introduction of the cage crinoline a few years ago. This was a light metal framework that was now cheaply mass-produced. Formerly, some Southern belles had worn as many as sixteen petticoats in the evening. Even so, dressing for dinner was still a performance.

Kate fulminated as her maid Susie handed her garments. Miller was younger than her father and could have entered active service. So he thought he was too important to fight!. Many more important men than he had donned uniform.For example ,Nathan Bedford Forrest was the son of a blacksmith who had made himself a millionaire from dealing in cotton, property and slaves. At the start of the war he had enlisted as a private and was now forming his own company.

Kate now pulled on her drawers and her low-cut chemise. Miller's abstention from duty rankled but what she found intolerable – especially since the loss of Jeff and the news of other casualties among her wider family and friends – was that Miller had kept his sons out of the Army. Conscription was riddled with exemptions which favoured the rich, although there were strong social and moral pressures to enlist but social and moral pressures didn't worry Miller.

Now, Kate had to wrestle with the hip-length corset which prevented her legs being shown by the swaying of the cage. Then she slipped over a long white petticoat. She could now step into the cage crinoline and struggle into yet another white petticoat. Susie helped her into the plain black evening dress and stood behind her to fasten the back.

"Oh damn!" Kate yelled "I'm still in mourning for Jeff. He wouldn't have wanted it. Jeff loved fun and playing jokes." She knew Jeff would have been very happy for her to wear her favourite silk evening dress of the Parisian fashion from the year before the war. This was light green in colour with a tight bodice and full skirt gathered into a medium-low waist.

"Calm yourself Mees Kate. Meester Miller is downstairs."

"I know Mister Miller is downstairs and calm! I'm not going to be bloody calm. I'm bloody furious. Especially because Mister Miller is downstairs. I've lost one brother. I may lose my other brothers and my father, while he and those mealy–mouthed slugs of cousins of mine sit out the war in comfort!"

Kate had received one of Frank's many letters that morning, which always gave her a boost but as always it was only temporary. He and Harry were safe from the enemy at the moment but for how long? And poor Jeff's death was a constant reminder that disease was a greater killer than enemy bullets and shells. Chimbarazo Hospital in Richmond was one of the Confederacy's largest military hospitals which held more sufferers from diarrhoea and dysentery than from wounds, and it was said that one in ten of these patients died.

Even Solange had raised her eyebrows over Miller's actions over his sons. His eldest son was in Europe and had been told to stay there until the war was over, despite the fact that many Southerners who were abroad had rushed back to enlist. This however paled into insignificance when he manipulated the 'twenty slave rule' to excuse the other two boys. This was reviled by most Southerners and by the poor who could not afford to avoid conscription. Miller had hived off part of one of his plantations, creating two small units and then placed twenty slaves in each.

"Now, be careful Miss Kate. You're crosser than an ole bullfrog. Don't go like a whirlwind." Kate could rarely resist Susie's humour and despite her annoyance she smiled and began to cruise slowly to her mother's room taking care not to knock over furniture and ornaments. Women in crinolines could devastate a room and last year a neighbour had suffered serious burns where her dress had been set alight, when standing by the fire. The heavy cladding had prevented her from feeling the heat.

Kate tapped at the door. Her mother's maid opened it. Solange was sitting at the dressing table. Her deep mourning did not suit her. Bright or pastel shades complemented her dark complexion much better. Kate stood behind her mother and put her arms around her, leaning down to hug and kiss her face and neck. Solange leant back relishing the affection and comfort. They remained like that for a few minutes in silence full of understanding, mutual grief and compassion. Eventually Kate stood upright but with her arm draped over her mother's shoulder holding her hand.

"Are you sure you want to go down tonight?" Solange nodded.

"I can't be rude to Preston. I didn't go down last night."

"He'll understand."

"No, Kate. I may lose everything else but I will keep my code of behaviour." Kate sighed. Arms entwined, they walked downstairs. Miller heard them in the library and came out to meet them. The susurration of silks, the crackling of starched petticoats and the creak of shoes ensured that a woman dressed for the evening could be heard some distance away.

Young Custis was sitting disconsolately in the hall fiddling with a toy cannon. Kate held out her hand. Sadly, the little boy stood up and placed his hand in his sister's. He missed his father and brothers - especially Frank. Like many younger brothers he had found his older brothers stimulating. They had the time and interest to teach him things which his father hadn't. They had taught him so much. Apart from riding, shooting, swimming and fencing, his knowledge of the plantation and field-lore was impressive. Kate had ensured that the boy's education had not been neglected. The departure of so many slaves had forced Kate to be more flexible. Much to the old man's delight she had brought Nathaniel back into the house as a tutor for Custis - at his age Nathaniel was unlikely to be a danger. When Custis wasn't at his lessons, his time was spent either on his own or in the company of slave-boys. He was also becoming increasingly useful about the plantation.

They sat down to dinner and talked whilst the soup was being served. Before the war, small talk would have been made at this stage of the meal but now the number, importance and momentum of events had obliterated the relevance of petty chat.

Conversations would now begin immediately with the price of commodities, shortages, the armies and the progress of the war. The other main topic was the fate of relatives or friends who were serving in the Army or Navy – especially those who had been reported killed, wounded, missing or taken prisoner.

"You seem to be doing well with the lighting."Complimented Miller. This was now becoming a problem due to the shortage of kerosene.

"Yes, sir. We use cotton seed oil and ground peas. We even make our own candles. We mix beeswax and tallow. I do most of it myself." Custis announced proudly.

Kate put down her soup spoon. "Custis is the man of the house now, I don't know what I'd without him." Miller asked further searching questions about the plantation which were answered curtly by Kate who had difficulty in masking her increasing irritation, or enthusiastically by Custis pleased at being elevated to 'man of the house'. Solange was relatively silent throughout the meal. After the main course Miller excused himself and returned after a few minutes.

When the dessert had been served Miller decided to broach one of the two objects of his visit.

"Kate you now have an opportunity to serve your country."

"I thought I was serving it now."

"Kate, don't answer your uncle back like that. I'm sorry, Preston. It's this war. She would never have spoken to you like that before."

Miller raised his hand. "Don't mention it Solange. Women of the South like Kate are making a great contribution to this war. They are now showing qualities which they have always had, but they have never needed to use before and if it means they speak or behave in a more assertive manner then we just have to accept it." He drew out an envelope from his pocket and handed it to Kate. "A letter for you."

Kate frowned. "For me? Who is it from?" She carefully opened the letter. "It's from the President of the Confederacy. He wants me to go to Richmond in two day's time. She handed the letter to her mother who read it several times with incredulity. "It's signed personally by Jefferson Davis. You must go."

"I can't. I've got to stay here and run Beaumont. I promised Father."

"Which brings me to my second letter." Miller drew out another envelope from his pocket. "It's from your father."

Kate almost snatched it from him and read it eagerly and handed to to her mother who was watching expectantly. The Colonel was now in Richmond advising the Government. As so many men were in uniform the Government was short of able people. The President wanted Kate to work for the Confederacy.She must obey his wish forthwith. The Colonel and Miller could supervise Beaumont. Regular visits could be made either by them or their agents, and Harrison was competent.

"Thank God your father's safe." Solange turned to Miller sharply. "I wish I'd known. Why didn't you tell us earlier?"

"I have only just received these letters. They had

arrived by special messenger and I was handed them when I left the room for a few minutes after the main course. I knew it would probably happen but I didn't want to give you welcome news about William, only for it to be wrong and for you to be disappointed."

Solange had seldom smiled since the loss of Jeff. With her mournful expression, sallow complexion and black clothes she resembled a woebegone blackbird. Kate loved her mother's beautiful smile. She smiled now, radiating warmth and charm as when light suddenly illuminates a darkened room.

The next day Miller enacted the second part of his plan. Kate and her mother were involved in frantic preparations for Kate's departure and had no time to pay attention to Miller's activities.

Harrison was supervising in the northerly end of the plantation when Miller cantered up to him, astride a powerful black stallion. Both horse and rider made a handsome and impressive team. The stallion's gleaming black coat and powerful sinews bore a rider who looked very capable of handling him. Miller's thighs, bulging with saddle-muscles, were encased in tightly fitting white breeches topped by a well-tailored blue coat and white Panama hat. A silver- topped whip was curled in the elegantly gloved hand but was seldom used and then only lightly. There was no need. Horse and rider understood each other perfectly.

Although they had never met both knew the identity of the other, Harrison had known of Miller's arrival from gossip among the slaves. Miller had found out all about Harrison. The private detective who had been employed to investigate the manager had been ordered to probe thoroughly and explore and report any weaknesses.

The detective had earned his money and reported that Harrison had a healthy but not abnormal interest in women. The fact that he was sleeping with a slave-woman belonging to his employer was regarded as just routine, in fact it was not discouraged – a sexually active manager boosted the plantation's stock. A reasonable but not destructive partiality to alcohol and embezzlement from his former employers was also revealed.

What Miller's investigators had discovered, and Harrison's employers had not, was that their hardworking reliable manager had made several thousand dollars out of bribes for placing orders with certain suppliers and from the sales of pilfered goods. A former colleague who was jealous of Harrison's preferment over him proved very talkative when a few gold coins loosened his tongue.

"Morning, Harrison. As you know Miss Kate and I will be leaving for Richmond in the morning. I will call at your quarters at nine this evening to discuss the running of the plantation whilst she is away." It was not a request. It was a statement. Harrison touched his hat but he managed to do it with a superior sort of acquiescence rather than obedience which Miller found irritating. Miller gently clicked to his mount which needed no encouragement. The animal bounded forward, kicking up the earth behind him.

At nine o'clock Harrison was sitting outside his quarters. Miller strode ,up carrying something wrapped up in a cloth. Harrison opened the door and Miller stepped in and motioned to Harrison to shut the door. Much to Harrison's surprise, Miller produced a bottle of whisky from under the cloth and plonked it on the table.

"All we need now is glasses." Harrison silently produced these. Miller uncorked the bottle and splashed the generous measures into each glass.

"We have some talking to do. We can be of use to

each other." Harrison was nonplussed. He certainly did not expect Miller to be talking to him in this conspiratorial manner. He had been expecting terse orders for the management of the plantation in Kate's absence with a certain amount of trepidation, thinking that Miller had learnt of his dishonesty from Kate.

"I'll come straight to the point Harrison. Both you and I know that this war is a waste of time, money and men and that the South will lose." Harrison said nothing and looked and felt very uncomfortable.

"I expect you are wondering how I know your views. That is because I take the trouble to find out about things and people that concern me. And you concern me. I found out about your views like I found out about your little plans for pilfering here. Don't worry. Kate didn't tell me. And the fact that you are sleeping with one of the slaves and also your little sidelines whilst you were working for Robertsons in Philadelphia."

Harrison was white and shaking now. He didn't even try to deny anything. He knew he was cornered. His mouth was dry. He managed to quaver.

"How did you find out about Robertsons?"

"Because, Harrison, I have eyes and ears everywhere. I am one of the richest men in America and I plan to be the richest. Help me and I will make you rich. Obstruct me and you will be found in a ditch somewhere shot, stabbed or garrotted depending on which of my agents I choose. Are we in business?"

"It looks as though I have no choice."

"You're right. You haven't but there is no need to look at it like that. Think positively. What is there here for you anyway? Or anywhere in the South for that matter? The South is all washed up. Defeat is certain and the best thing that could happen now would be a negotiated peace but those honourable patriotic fools won't be satisfied until their beloved South becomes a wasteland, their homes blackened ruins, their economy devastated and all their men under ground,dead and buried." Miller took a long swig from his tumbler.

"The likes of the Turners won't be able to feed you turnips let along pay you wages. You may as well be rich supporting me ,as destitute supporting them."

The way that Harrison was nodding his head in positive agreement rather than in a subservient way to a more powerful man, indicated to Miller that he had been right in his assessment. Harrison had no faith in the South, was interested in providing for himself and, in short, would be a great asset. Miller had judged his target perfectly. Had Miller discovered that he had been wrong, Harrison would not have survived the week.

"I will not go into details now Harrison. I just wanted to establish the principles tonight. Beaumont will be vital to my operation and you will receive constant instructions from me or my agents. You've met one of them already." Harrison looked startled.

"I'm not telling you his or her identity. I never divulge the names of any of my agents." Miller gave a sigh of satisfaction. Schneider had done his work well.

"You mean you employ women?"

"Why restrict myself to using just half the population? Some of the best spies both North and South are women." Miller opened his coat and revealed a leather belt round his waist that had a pouch as an integral part of it. He removed it and slid it across the table. "This is for you. Open it."

Harrison felt the pouch which was heavy. He unfastened the straps and put his hand inside. He felt coins. He spilt them out. Gold coins slithered across the table, glinting in the lamplight. Without even counting it he could see that there was enough to pay his wages for at least six months and it was in gold. Confederate money devalued daily.

Miller picked up his hat. "This is the first of many payments. You will be contacted by me or my agents. Stay a friend and you will prosper. You know what happens to my enemies." Harrison nodded. There was no choice. Miller left the room without a further word.

Rose Greenhow sat in Old Capitol Prison, Washington where in happier days she had been a popular guest – dining, dancing and being pursued by admirers. She hugged her eight year old daughter Rose. The mother and child had been imprisoned for about eight months and the strain was beginning to tell on both of them. They had both been ill, the food was sparse and the facilities for washing and general hygiene were very basic. The general conditions were Spartan and many of the other inmates were the sort of people with whom Rose would not have passed the time of day under normal circumstances. Most people would have expected life in prison to be uncomfortable, but Rose was not like 'most people'. She always considered that she should be a special case.

Technically Little Rose (as she was always known) was not a prisoner but as her mother had chosen to keep the child with her,she was subject to prison regulations.

However, today was a happy day. Rose had just been told of her release. She and her child would be leaving for Richmond. She had many friends in both the North and South who had worked for her freedom, and a number of the men were in love with her. Their efforts had been rewarded. The most important Confederate prisoner was going home.

Chapter Eleven

Columbia South Carolina

June 1862

Columbia, the capital of South Carolina, was now a very important city, as not only did it house the Mint but also the Government had established many factories there. It was socially as well as economically vibrant. Now it played host to the Confederate Congress which had fled from Richmond together with Varina Davis, the wife of the Confederate President and her children.

Preston Miller had taken Kate directly to Richmond as the President wanted her 'urgently'. As her father was there, Miller did not consider that he had any responsibility for her once they had arrived. Miller had joined in the rush from Richmond to Columbia, but he was quite happy to leave his wife and daughters behind to face a possible invasion. "My business interests will best be served by me being in Columbia ,but you and the girls have your civic duties to carry out. You'd best stay here." He had told Henrietta.

Many wives would have been distressed by this callous lack of concern but not Henrietta. The arranged marriage between the widower with six children and the girl more than twenty years his junior had been loveless from the beginning. She never missed him and indeed had her own reasons for welcoming his absences.

Miller now sat in his imposing wood-panelled office. The room suited its' occupant who would tolerate nothing less than the best. The scale model of one of his ships stood near the door. The shelves contained books on law, leather-bound copies of Lloyds Register showing the movements of ships and folders containing information concerning the various stock-exchanges throughout the world.

Miller had a good idea of the whereabouts of any of his ships. It could not be more than a good idea given the vagaries of the winds and tides – especially now the country was at war, but many owners with half as many ships again were not nearly so well- informed as Miller as to their location.

Miller stood up and stretched out his hand as his visitor entered the room. The man was tall, well-built with black hair and a swarthy complexion indicating that he was of Creole stock. He was immaculately dressed in a brown frock-coat, fawn trousers and a yellow brocaded waistcoat. He handed his ebony silver-topped cane and white top hat with a curly brim to the footman, who slipped away noiselessly.

Without wasting time on opening civilities, the two men began to discuss their complicated business arrangements which included the blockade- running of a consignment of cotton which would be shipped to Nassau in the Bahamas and then transferred to a Northern ship. As trading with the other side was so necessary, both Governments winked at it whilst officially banning it.

It was clear from the conversation that Miller was the controlling influence as indeed Miller controlled everything which concerned him; DuFresne only permitted this because he knew that Miller was far more commercially powerful than he. DuFresne was not the sort of man that anybody could dominate. An observer of the two men together would conclude that a clash between them would be a clash of Titans.

Now the important business had been discussed

Miller glanced at his visitor approvingly. "Bullingdon is now back in England but he will be returning later in the year. I was happy with the disposal of Forbes on 'The White Queen'. You and he did well there. I had my doubts about him for sometime but when they were confirmed he had to be silenced." DuFresne nodded . The death of an associate who had proved to be unstable was a small matter in comparison with the far weightier business matters under discussion. It warranted no further attention.

DuFresne now broached the subject which he had regarded as one of the main purposes of his visit.. "You haven't mentioned your niece." DuFresne's English was good, with a French accent which many women found attractive – as indeed they did the rest of him.

"As you know I should have been in Richmond but as it looked precarious I left Kate there and came onto Columbia." 'Thus making sure that your own skin was safe'. DuFresne felt like saying but one didn't say things like that to Miller who continued; "Richmond will not fall now – at least not yet; McClellan could and should have finished the job but of course he didn't. They say he is either a coward or traitor – or both. Lincoln is certain to replace him. Richmond is safe for the time being. We will go there in a few days time. You will meet her then." DuFresne noted that Miller said 'we will go there in a few days time.' Not 'I am going to Richmond in a few days time. Will it suit you to come at the same time?'

"Do you think she will be difficult?"

"In a word – yes. I would never have got her away from that plantation unless I'd be able to work on Jeff Davis and her father. She is far too clever for a woman. She was running that plantation perfectly and she is a shrewd judge of character."

"It's a pity we had to choose her."

"We didn't choose her. 'I' chose her – or rather I chose Beaumont which is ideal for our purposes with the men out of the way, the manager in our pocket and my knowledge of the place and my family connections. My poor dear sister is fine running the house, supervising the family and slaves and ministering to their ailments but she is about as much use in running the plantation as a lily in a quick- set hedge. Kate had to be removed."

"You certainly have picked me a tough one."

"Well, DuFresne that just gives you all the more opportunity to exercise your famous charm doesn't it? You've never had any difficulty in that department. You may just have to work a little harder on my niece that's all."

"Can't wait to meet the little hoyden."

Miller looked at him sharply. " You forget yourself DuFresne. Remember just to whom you are speaking and that you are speaking about my niece. I am running this operation and you are only in it because you are of use to me but I know enough about you to finish you. Make one mistake and I will break you like a twig. Understood?"

DuFresne nodded. He understood.

Chapter Twelve

Richmond Virginia

June / July 1862

Richard did not know what to do and just stood helplessly for a moment. "Can I do anything to help?" He asked Gabriel as the man came back somewhat perplexed. Gabriel's expression did not change. "You'd best come with me."

They started climbing the stairs. For the first time Richard was able to look round him since he had entered the house. He now realised that the hall in which he had seen those dreadful scenes was spacious and lined with paintings, portraits and miniatures. An impressive chandelier hung from the ceiling. The occasional piece of furniture punctuated the lower part of the walls. Fine oak doors with heavy brass handles led off the large airy landings. Various alcoves created spacious recesses containing the odd chair or table. In one alcove lay an army of toy soldiers but they were in disarray, some having been knocked over by the toy cannons. Presumably a battle had been in progress when the young participants had been called away to help when the real soldiers had been carried into the house.

When they reached the landing on the third floor they picked their way through people cutting up sheets, shirts, nightdresses and all kinds of linen. Black and white women and children worked together without laughter or chatter. Communication was grim, reduced to necessity such as "pass me that sheet" or "take the scissors over to Mary". Two boys worked together.

They appeared to be about a year apart in age – around eleven and twelve and similar in appearance. Presumably these were the generals of the toy army. They looked up as Gabriel and Richard reached them.

"Walter, Martin-this is Mr. Clarke. He is a guest. Show him what to do."

"Yes. Uncle Gabriel." They replied respectfully, almost in unison. For a moment Richard thought this was strange. These boys were presumably the sons of the house and were being given orders by a slave whom they not only addressed as a superior but as 'Uncle'. Then he remembered 'Uncle Tom's Cabin' where the slave had been addressed as 'Uncle Tom' by the children of his owner, and had been regarded as a valued member of the household.

This point had also been emphasized during his briefings in Washington. "This is what makes the problem so complex and so much part of the fabric of southern slave-owing society," he had been told. "Many Europeans think it is all whips, collars and working in the boiling sun for sixteen hours a day in high season. It's not, although regrettably that happens; many of them are treated almost as though they are part of the family and in some cases of course they are part of the family."

The boys were courteous and competent and guided Richard expertly in this emergency in a strange house in enemy territory. He was grateful to them, but was beginning to feel uncomfortable about being there under false pretences. He had been warned about this also. "You may have feelings of guilt about abusing hospitality – especially if you start to become fond of the family. It is only human nature. Overcome them. You can bet your bottom dollar that the South is being just as devious in all sorts of situations and our people are being captured and killed as a result."

For the next few hours Richard worked – tearing up bandages, helping to make splints from canes or pieces of furniture, taking food and drink to the wounded, placing pillows under hot, feverish, sweating heads and acting as stretcher- bearer, taking the suffering out to the street where they could be loaded onto wagons and transported to the tobacco warehouses which had hastily been converted into makeshift hospitals. Carts and wagons trundled past heaped with dead and wounded. Richard looked at one cart piled with dead bodies. In one of them a stiff arm was raised and shook as the vehicle jolted down the street, as though the dead man was protesting.

Some of the dead faces carried life-like expressions – grins, shock, terror or just total surprise. Richard realised later that during this time he had not felt much emotion, compassion or anger at the destruction that humans could cause to each other(these would come later) but, at present, he was just too occupied in dealing mechanically with every crisis that arose.

The situation continued over the next three days although it gradually became calmer. Each night Richard collapsed onto the bed in the small bedroom into which he had been shown by Gabriel on the first night, and sank into a heavy sleep but punctuated by nightmares depicting scenes of even more exaggerated horror than he had seen. A mutual respect had grown up between the slave and the Englishman. Gabriel was impressed by Richard's willingness to cope with a totally strange and unexpected situation. Richard, for his part liked this intelligent and dignified Negro. He had a noble, almost regal face and had the air of a man who was used to exercising authority with a quiet assurance rather than submitting to it, as though he was descended from a long line of kings or chieftains.

Meals were snatched and eaten in relays, so that

there was always somebody on duty. Although there had been no time for Richard to have long conversations with the family, working together forged the bond which is created by striving towards a common goal.

Then the last of the broken, wretched men left the house. The frenetic panic which had gripped the city subsided into a worried preoccupation tinged with excitement. The week had been a terrible one for the Confederacy which had lost twenty thousand men and it had only won one of these battles which came to be known as 'The Battles of Seven Days',yet the ever cautious General McClellan failed to consolidate the Federal victories and retreated. By July 3rd Richmond realised that it was safe for the time being, and drew breath.

For the first time the Smythe household could relax a little. Walter and Martin had taken Richard into the garden to show him the mysteries of baseball, when Gabriel strode majestically over the lawn. The man moved with a lithe, easy grace of a panther.Richard thought he would make a superb athlete. "Mr Clarke, Mrs Smythe would like you to join her in the drawing room."

Richard had never met any Southern ladies before and only had a very sketchy idea of what they must be like coming mainly from the planter's wife in 'Uncle Tom's Cabin' which he had read a few years before. That lady was always feeling ill, tired or faint. She seemed to spend most of her time lying on the settee, fanning herself and moaning. She was never able to fetch anything for herself. Most of her needs were anticipated but if one wasn't, all she had to do was to languidly lift a limp hand for somebody to rush to her side. The briefing in Washington had tried to disabuse him of that notion "running a household cannot just be left to the slaves. Many of the wives do involve themselves,even though in many cases it is managing others rather than doing the jobs herself". Richard thought of the role Mrs Smythe had played during the last few days. She had not just been managing, she had been working harder than anybody without worrying about her appearance which had been unkempt. Her clothes had been old and drab, but she had still conducted herself with unruffled efficiency as though she had been running a hospital all her life.

When Richard entered the drawing room he found it difficult to repress a chuckle. Mrs Smythe was reclining on the settee with a glass in her hand, exactly like the planter's wife. She was now dressed for the evening in the fashion of the year before the war – a beautiful deep pink silk gown off the shoulder and low cut which complemented her dark hair and eyes.A diamond necklace sparkled at her throat. Her hair had been properly dressed.

A radiant smile illuminated the exhausted face and Richard realised for the first time that he was looking at a beautiful woman. Maturity, together with the confidence and love that had grown from a lifetime of prosperity and comfortable surroundings, a happy marriage and healthy well-adjusted children had developed a face that had been lovely in youth to one of serenity and confidence in middle-age.

"I'm afraid I've been a very poor hostess, Richard. What can you think of Southern hospitality? You arrived as a guest in a new country and were put to work immediately – just like a servant." Indeed he had realised he had made a good effort which had assuaged – a little – the guilt that had accumulated.

"I was only too happy to help Ma'am. I didn't do anything that the family did not do, and your boys are

189

great teachers."

"Yes. They are good boys, although I say it myself. Of course they miss their father terribly."

More drinks were brought and Richard chose mint-julep which he had never had before. It was refreshing. He relaxed. "Richard you have been a tremendous help to us over the last few days. Consider this house your home for as long as you like." The guilt welled up in him again.

The next day was July 4th – Independence day. Mrs Smythe and her boys had been invited to a barbecue and they insisted that Richard join them. The event had been planned some time previously. Independence Day was Independence Day and a small matter like a series of defeats was not going to stop the celebrations – to say nothing of the fact that the city had been threatened with invasion, which had only been thwarted by the indecision of the enemy's general. Richard just had to admire these people.

After breakfast, a note that had just been delivered to the house was handed to Richard. A friend of his father wished to meet him at the junction of two streets. The name of the signatory, T. Jenkinson, was one that Richard did not recognise.

Richard arrived a minute early. He did not want to be late, but to arrive too soon and wait around would make him conspicuous. People passed him. One or two men on their own seemed likely customers but they took no notice of him. Richard was beginning to wonder if there had been a change of plan. Two pretty, young women in their early twenties were approaching. Richard could not help his admiring glances. A mixture of interest and exhilaration flooded through him when they stopped. One asked him for directions.

"I'm sorry I'm new in this city." The second woman addressed her companion without acknowledging

Richard.

"Are you sure that Mary Felmingham gave us the right address?" Richard looked startled. "Come with us. We are just going for a walk. I am Clara and this is Amelia." They were similarly dressed in white, long-sleeved blouses, with stand- up collars, multi-coloured skirts and French bonnets. They each carried parasols. "You look surprised Mr Clarke." Clara adjusted her parasol.

"It was just that I was not ...."

"Expecting women. Few of the new agents do, although they are told to expect us. Women still have the advantage in that although there are more of us most people tend not to suspect us and we are less severely treated if we are caught." They then walked along the road, with the two women engaging in inconsequential chatter. Presumably, Richard thought to put him at his ease.

Richard was finding the company of these two attractive women enjoyable. Clara was the more vivacious of the two with mischievous dark eyes. Dark curls bobbed from under her bonnet. Amelia was quieter, with blonde hair and large, thoughtful blue eyes. Neither of them spoke with the slow Southern drawl of Mrs Smythe or her sons.

"Why are you doing this? What would happen to you if you were caught?"

Clara stepped aside to allow a couple to pass. "It's more likely now than at the start of the war when it was regarded as a bit of a game. The authorities have started to clamp down hard on suspected Union sympathisers and women are not immune. Martial Law has been in force for a couple of months covering a ten– mile radius of Richmond and there is now at least one woman imprisoned there for crossing Confederate lines. What's worse, they have power to confiscate your property and deport you up North."

"And they can just lock you up for being a Union sympathiser, you don't even have to have done anything." Amelia added.

"That's terrible!" Richard had grown up with and studied the ingrained British principle of Habeas Corpus.

Clara linked arms with Richard. "Come on; loosen up a little. We have to behave as though we have known each other a long time. If they did imprison us they would let us out after a short time. They have let a lot of people out already – there has been such an outcry. And the good thing about it is that when people are released the other Union sympathisers know who they are. Before, everybody kept quiet about it so it was difficult to know whose side people were on. As we are both married women, all the property we have belongs to our husbands and, as they are both fighting for the Confederacy, they are not going to take that. We wouldn't mind being deported back North as we have never felt at home here." Amelia was looking at Richard in quiet appraisal with a faint smile playing on her lips.

"We grew up together in Boston. We are cousins twice over. Our mothers are sisters from here in Richmond and our fathers are brothers from Boston. Our marriages were more or less arranged when we were children, and we were married at seventeen with brothers that were second cousins of our mothers. Although we had been here on visits before, that is very different from living here."

"What went wrong?" Amelia waved at somebody passing in one of the rare private carriages to be seen which was weaving around the mass of military traffic.. Horses and vehicles had been requisitioned in large numbers by the Army and were in short supply. The occupant of the carriage must have been somebody of importance.

"Well we had known our husbands from childhood. They were alright but we never fell in love with them. We had been used to a great deal of freedom up North but here women have to be chaperoned all the time,before the war anyway. That's one good thing about the war. We have far more independence now. We had lots of rows with our husbands' families about that." Once Amelia decided to speak, she was quite eloquent.

"We could never really accept slavery either. We had grown up in Boston which, as you know, is the centre of the abolitionist movement and we had read the abolitionist press. We'd experienced slavery when we came down here on visits which we did almost every year as children, but we had never lived with it before. Visiting a place and living there are two very different things. The trouble is we married at seventeen, which is much too young. We did not know our own minds and were caught up with all the excitement of the preparations for the wedding. Now I'm twenty- two and Clara is twenty- three it seems a lifetime away." Amelia stopped for a moment and looked at Richard intently. "What do you think about slavery Mr Clarke?"

Richard was aware that this was a trap. He had been prepared for this kind of probing in his role-playing sessions.

"Well, obviously I grew up in a country where it does not exist. But it's not my place to come into somebody else's country and tell them what to do." He decided to deflect the question. "Where are your husbands? You said they were both in the Army."

"That's right," replied Clara. My husband is riding with Beauty Stuart and Amelia's is with Lee."

"Are they alright ?"

"So far." Clara did not show much feeling. Richard had the impression that they did not seem to care very much whether the men were safe or not. "Anyway, you have to go now. You have a barbecue to attend".

"How do you know that?" Richard was astonished.

"Honey, our organisation knows everything. You sneeze and we know about it."

"Goodbye, now. Somebody will be in touch with you." They minced away, their parasols touched. 'What brilliant cover!', thought Richard – 'they appear like two silly giggling girls but that frivolity conceals shrewd brains' ,Allen knows his job.' It would be some considerable time before he would know the true identity of 'Major Allen'.

Richard realised that the meeting had just been a 'testing out' on the enemy territory. They had told him nothing about anything important. He did not even know as to whether they had told him the truth about their backgrounds. If they had, they hadn't seemed particularly concerned about their husbands. Richard reflected that should he ever marry he would not care for his wife to be so relaxed if he was ever to be in danger.

He also realised with satisfaction that if the women had told him little, he had not told them much either.

Richard returned to the Smythe household just in time to leave for the barbecue. If Mrs Smythe had wondered where he had been or was irritated at the fact that he had only returned just before they were due to leave, she didn't show it. Due to the shortage of horses and vehicles Mrs Smythe had decided to walk. Anyway, walking was easier as the streets were still jammed with military traffic. Mrs Smythe took his arm and he walked on the outside nearest the street. Richard felt proud to be escorting this charming lovely woman. Walter and Martin trotted ahead. Like many little boys they wore regimental ribbons in in their lapels and military style caps.

"The barbecue won't be anything like those before the war but they will do their best." They turned from the tree-lined avenue into the large brick gate posts of the mansion. The gates and railings had been removed as indeed they had from all the other houses. Richard was to learn that they had been taken to make cannons.

Large trees provided welcome shade on the drive and the lawns which were somewhat brown, but dotted with bushes, shrubs and flowerbeds blazing with colour. The ambience of summer permeated the atmosphere. Richard felt that he was floating in a warm bath of heavy fragrance. Scents of flowers mingling with pollen and balm from trees were tinged with the slightly acrid smell of smoke from the barbecues. Bees droned as they lazily and heavily blundered from flower to flower.

Richard was not a nervous or uncertain young man but he now felt rather bewildered and out of his own sphere. He had been taken as a guest to a large social occasion by Mrs Smythe with whom he was staying under false pretences, in an enemy country which he had entered as a spy. Despite his briefings in Washington, these waves of guilt would never leave him.

Richard's discomfiture was increased by the number of women in heavy mourning and older men with black coats and neckwear. The fact that all the young men were in uniform, and some were recovering from serious wounds did not make him feel any better. Four soldiers with three legs between them sat on flimsy wicker chairs with wheels the like of which Richard had never seen before. Later he was to learn that fortunes were being made from the manufacture of these chairs, as well as from artificial limbs.

Two or three men had their faces heavily bandaged; three had only one arm and a number had an arm in a sling. A young dark- haired woman was spooning food into the mouth of a uniformed youth who had been blinded. Richard could not help contrasting the loving, caring look on her face with the attitude of Clara and Amelia.

The young women outnumbered the men. Despite the blockade they looked attractive in expensive summer dresses. Richard correctly assumed that they came from wealthy families and had a large stock of clothes from previous years. Some of them looked provocative with low necklines revealing cleavages, bare arms and shoulders. Other women were very plainly dressed and wore no jewellery. He noticed one young woman with red hair, whose looks were arresting despite her dowdy clothes. Mrs Smythe introduced him to a couple of very pretty girls who started chatting to him easily and with interest. His confidence was quickly restored.

Kate had spent the morning at the hospital and was particularly glad to leave the stench and suffering. She had not started working for the Government yet. The battles had disrupted everything. Miller departed promptly for Columbia leaving Kate with his wife Henrietta and his three daughters. Kate had been disappointed that she could not see her father who had had to leave due to the emergency. Kate had previously found the company of her cousins pleasant enough but now they appeared to her to be shallow and immature. The year spent running the plantation had given her maturity and made her very intolerant of superficial chatter.

Not that there was much time for superficial chatter. Women who were otherwise unoccupied (which was most of those who had other people to run the house and care for children as well as single and childless women) were swept immediately into hospitals. Henrietta made sure that her stepdaughters and Kate reported for duty immediately. When the girls arrived at the hospital, the matron sent them home to change. "Has not anybody told you the rules? No bare arms, the neck must be properly covered up, no jewellery, no hooped skirts and no make-up."

"Right battle-axe", grumbled Millie on the way home. "Just because no man would ever look at her even if she was decked out in the latest Paris fashions." Her sisters Sarah and Helen giggled. Kate had very quickly become bored with these girls. It seemed almost impossible to have any sort of conversation with them. Any kind of serious statement was met with giggles or some stupid comment. The problem was that Kate had changed. Her cousins had not.

"Don't you think it might be for our own protection?" Kate snapped. "On the way over from Beaumont I heard of some woman who was attacked in a hospital by a man she was nursing. Don't forget that most of these poor wretches probably haven't seen a woman for over a year. And the men in these hospitals are all sorts. Very few of them are well-groomed college boys, you know". Millie pouted and exchanged conspiratorial side-long glances with her sisters. Since Kate had arrived, her cousins had not enjoyed her company much.

"She used to be such fun!, complained Sarah later. "Now anybody would think she's a maiden aunt of about seventy." It was true that Kate was no fun. The last year had not provided any fun but she would never be a maiden aunt of seventy or any other age. Womanhood surged too strongly in her.

To be fair to Kate's cousins, although they had not been subjected to the same responsibilities as Kate, they had not been idle despite their seeming frivolity. Like most women they had been supporting bazaars, picnics and balls in favour of hospitals, wounded soldiers and their families. They collected blankets and linen for bandages and attended the endless knitting and sewing sessions to make garments for troops. It was also considered essential for young unmarried women to carry out minor duties at hospitals.

These girls who had never lifted a duster now had to carry out non-medical tasks such as cleaning, preparing bandages, feeding and reading to the men. However, they had not been told to regulate their appearance before and these sudden new rules imposed by a new matron had come as a shock.

The population of men folk had become so depleted that the hospitals had brought a new source of interest. Some of the men were not as badly wounded as all that, and a number of girls had become engaged. Hospitals seemed one of the few places that a girl could meet a man these days.

Kate had heard about the terrible physical cost of the war but she had only seen it for the first time since coming to Richmond. The sight of disfigured men walking about the streets was bad enough, but the horror of these paled into insignificance compared with the sights she had seen in the hospital. She decided immediately that she was not an angel of mercy. She would rather run a hundred plantations any day. She was glad that the casualties were no longer pouring in and she would soon be able to do the work for which she had been sent.

When Kate knew that she would be able to leave the hospital early enough to go to the barbecue, she couldn't remove her apron quickly enough. Her only regret was that she didn't have time to go home to change. She almost bounded up the drive and onto the lawn where slaves were carrying round the food. Despite the shortages, the hostess had managed to provide a reasonable spread.

Kate took a glass from the tray that was held out to her by the footman. She wondered how long this would last. Many slaves had run away behind Northern lines and others had been requisitioned by the Commissary for labouring work for the Army. She looked round at the young men in uniform.

Kate was not immune from the common female attraction to men in uniform. The most insignificant man in civilian dress awakens female interest once he dons military attire, although by now some of the uniforms were looking decidedly shabby. The war began with a confusing array of uniforms in both North and South as many regiments had their own. Some Southern uniforms were blue and some Northern ones were grey leading to tragic confusion in some early battles.

After Bull Run, the North adopted the standard blue and the South the Confederate grey. The grey dyes were soon exhausted due to the blockade ,and now an increasing number of men paraded in uniforms coloured by home-made substitutes from walnut shells, giving them a shade of butternut.

Only one young man did not wear uniform. He was good-looking certainly – tall, fair-haired, with broad shoulders. He was wearing a white hat, blue knee-length coat and white trousers. For once a man in civilian dress looked more desirable than the poor broken soldiers in their dowdy makeshift uniforms. Even the men who had not been wounded looked tired and haggard and as though they hadn't eaten properly for a month – which was indeed the case.

This young man looked like the indulged heir to a plantation who had never lacked for anything in his life, and was used to having every whim obeyed by slaves, his doting mother and a bevy of adoring sisters. He was talking to a cluster of admiring girls with an easy assurance.

Much to her annoyance, a servant from the hospital came up to Kate and informed her that she was needed back at the hospital immediately as an unexpected consignment of wounded had arrived. Kate bade a hasty farewell to her host and hurried after the servant feeling cross. She had wanted to meet this young man. His good looks and confidence both attracted and irritated her. Neither had Kate been impressed by the coterie of young women who were paying him such rapt attention. Some of them were in mourning for a brother, husband, sweetheart or father and should have been asking him why he was not fighting for his country, instead of simpering and fluttering their eyelashes at him as though he were a returning victorious general.

"Who was he? Why was he not in the Army or Navy? Did he work for the Government in some capacity? Or was he one of those men who, like Miller's sons, were taking advantage of the Twenty Slave Rule and whom Kate held in deep contempt. She intended to find out.

Chapter Thirteen

Richmond Virginia

July 1862

Richard was accompanying Mrs Smythe home from the barbecue whilst the boys ran on ahead firing imaginary pistols and dodging imaginary bullets. The evening was sinking beautifully and gracefully, the sun was setting bloody red in the west, suffusing the sky with pink. The buildings and trees cast dark and lengthy shadows, midges danced and began to bite.

"You were a great success today, Richard, particularly with the girls. I think everybody was just pleased to see somebody who had not been bashed and battered by war. It's so refreshing".

"I feel rather guilty actually."

"No need to feel guilty at all. It's not your country, not even your continent. What have you got to feel guilty about?" Mrs Smythe had misinterpreted Richard's meaning. This made him feel worse.

"There was something I wanted to ask you actually, Richard." The conversation paused as they approached an ugly brindled mongrel sniffing around a tree. It cocked its leg and urinated, a strong, yellow ugly stream ran down the bark and onto the ground sinking into the dirt. The dog then caught up with them and started to snuffle in a desultory fashion around Mrs Smythe's skirt. Richard quickly steered her a few steps away. The pressure on his arm tightened. The military traffic had quietened down and was now reduced to the odd horseman riding singly – probably on an errand or for a business reason. Not many social visits were made these days.

"What is it? I will do anything to help."

"I need to visit our plantation within the next few days. It's dangerous to go without a man. I would prefer Gabriel to stay in Richmond to look after the house. Will you come with me?"

"Of course I will …….. Incidentally, who was that girl with red hair? Mrs Smythe concealed a smile. The casualness of the question was just a little bit too contrived for there to be anything 'incidental' about it.

"That will be Kate Turner. I don't know her very well but I do know her family. They are one of the most important families in South Carolina."

Mrs Smythe had been fortunate in that she had been able to keep her blood horses from the Commissary due to her husband's influence and, as she was very near to the seat of Government, she could quickly call on friendly contacts should any officials arrive and prove difficult.

The plantation lay only a few miles outside Richmond and the Federals had retreated so it was now relatively safe. Richard and Mrs Smythe rode horses, whilst two slaves followed driving the carry-all. Mrs Smythe and Richard were armed. It was against the law for slaves to carry arms.

Their departure from Richmond was slowed by three funeral processions. They were all Confederate officers. Their caps and swords had been placed on top of the coffins draped with the Confederate flag. In one procession the dead man's horse was led with his boots in the stirrups turned back to front.

"It won't be long before somebody else is wearing those boots. They are in such short supply. If they are not careful, somebody will steal them before there's time to give them away. That's Hal Bennett. He got it at Malvern Hill. They had to take both legs off. Nobody expected him to survive." Mrs Smythe tried to calm her fidgeting horse and raised her hand in a subdued salute to a woman in deep mourning. Richard thought the woman could not have seen the gesture because she was so heavily veiled – anyway she didn't acknowledge it. Behind the widow two little girls in black dresses and hats were each being held by the hand by a slave- woman. They looked the same size, possibly they were twins. A strong feeling of compassion welled up in him.

"Did you know the family well?"

"Reasonably well. In normal circumstances I would have gone to the funeral but there are too many now. If I went to every funeral there wouldn't be time to do anything else, anyway it's too depressing. His wife, I mean widow, is-was his cousin. You see she has twin girls of two years old. I know their plantation is heavily mortgaged and she knows little about business. Some of their slaves have run off or been requisitioned and she'll probably lose more. I don't know how she'll manage."

They continued when the cortege had passed. Mrs Smythe cut an elegant figure in a well-tailored riding-habit. "Of course it's absolutely scandalous in Richmond at the moment. The speculators have got the city by the throat. The price of fish is exorbitant and plug-uglies have been hired by the fishmongers to make sure that it is not undersold. And all the flour has been hoarded so that it can be sold at the highest possible price."

Richard held in his horse as a military cart, stacked full of harnesses and saddles, approached. When it had passed and they were again side by side he could reply. "They were complaining at the barbecue that when the

203

Federals were advancing towards Richmond, and it looked as though there was going to be serious fighting, speculators even bought up all the coffins and mourning crepe and have been selling them at a vast profit. I think that's disgraceful."

"Of course it is. I'm disgusted that my countrymen should behave in this way. But it's not just them. A lot of people have come down from the North and from Europe".

They made relatively slow time. The roads were busy. Richard was glad they were armed. A number of ragged –looking men walking or sitting by the roadside made requests for money or food. "Most of these men are probably deserters. A lot of our men are just giving up and going home. But there are a number of Northerners as well. We are only two miles away from Mulberry." As Mrs Smythe spoke they were approaching a bend. Richard noticed a movement in the foliage at the side of the road. But Mrs Smythe had noticed it first.

"Watch out! There's somebody hiding. We can't go back there's too much traffic. Make sure that you have your revolver at the ready." Richard felt for reassurance from the smooth solid metal of his Colt .36 calibre, six shot, single action percussion weapon nestling in its' holster under his coat. The weapon had come onto the market at the outbreak of war and the sales had been phenomenal. Mrs Smythe was wearing a short jacket over her riding-habit which concealed a holster. She grasped both reins in her left hand and drew out her Colt with her right. "Get yours out." She barked at Richard in the voice she had used to Gabriel when he had first entered the house. "It's no good just fingering it. You may have to use It.!"

When they turned the corner, three filthy, ragged, barefoot, hungry – looking men were standing in the middle of the road. One of them stepped forward. Dirty, ginger hair straggled out from under a forage cap whose peak was skewed sideways.

"Give us some food Ma'am," he whined. "We ain't eaten for two days."

"Then get back to your unit. They'll have food there."

"But we've got to get home. My wife has written saying she's desperate. She can't run our few acres by herself. And we've got five children." He stepped in front of her.

"You are deserters! Take one step nearer me and I'll shoot." Whilst the man was talking the other two were sidling nearer. One of them made to grab her bridle. Instantly a shot rang out. The man fell to the ground with blood pouring from his throat. Mrs Smythe's horse reared up. A second shot, and the spokesman fell to the ground clutching his leg.

The swiftness of the woman's reactions amazed Richard who had just sat holding his revolver controlling his uneasy horse. The third man ran off. Mrs Smythe was now calming her own horse by cantering up the road for a few hundred yards. She then managed to slow him down by talking to him gently, and returned to Richard who had not moved. Meanwhile the carry-all with the slaves caught up with them and skirted round the two bodies lying in the road. The spokesman was screaming and moaning. Richard felt useless but he had to say something.

"What are we going to do about him?"

"Leave him," snapped Mrs Smythe. "Somebody will pick him up or better still shoot him. It's his own fault for deserting. We have to get on. And Young Man! You need to be able to react more quickly if you want to live much longer. It's no good just sitting there. If it had not been for me, you'd have been off your horse and on the ground with them at your throat in two ticks. I brought you to protect me – not the other way around. This is a dangerous country now. As you can see there are a lot of destitute, desperate men about. Everybody's been brutalised by war."

'Including you,' thought Richard. He was both shocked and impressed by the quick, ruthless way in which this elegant, sophisticated woman had reacted . She could ride like a cavalryman and shoot like a marksman.

Richard was quiet for a while. The whole incident had been deeply disturbing and he felt shamefaced that he had sat, inert like a pudding, and left this woman to save the situation.

Eventually, Mrs Smythe broke the brooding uncomfortable silence. "Look, I'm sorry that I spoke to you like that. I know you are English and that you have not been brought up to ride and shoot from the cradle like a Southern boy but you are now in a country at war. And you do need to practise just to protect yourself. Your riding is not bad but it can be improved. However, your shooting is just not quick enough." Richard had done a certain amount of game-shooting in England and during his training in Washington he had practised with the revolver, but it obviously wasn't sufficient.

"Where did you learn to ride and shoot like that?" Richard asked. The tension was easing.

Mrs Smythe laughed. "As I said, Southern boys are taught to ride from when they are toddlers and to shoot certainly before they are nine or ten and that goes for girls as well – especially if they grew up on a plantation like me. If you can't ride a horse, you just never go anywhere. You are isolated and where there are roads they are either baked hard or rutted in the dry weather or like a swamp in the wet weather. Anyway, we

Southern ladies are always encouraged to ride for our health. And, as for shooting, I used to practise with my brothers and cousins."

They spent four days at the plantation. Despite the fact that Mrs Smythe said that it was nothing like it was before the war, things could have been a lot worse. The Commissary had not visited yet, not many of the slaves had run away and the overseer was doing his job reasonably well. Richard learnt that it was not uncommon for overseers to be almost perpetually drunk whilst the owners were away. The house was a disappointment. He had expected a grand, stone affair with columns in the Palladian style but it was an unimpressive wooden building and looked decidedly shabby. Shortly after they arrived Mrs Smythe began to tell Richard about the property and her family.

"I married my cousin. This was his home and my father owned a lot of adjoining land so it formed part of my dowry." Marrying cousins appeared to be common in the South. Clara and Amelia were married to cousins and he had heard more talk of such marriages since he had been in Richmond. Hal Bennett, of the riderless horse with the boots reversed, had also been married to his cousin.

"Cousins seem to marry each other quite a lot round here."

"Oh yes. It's a way of keeping land and money within the family. And you also know who you're marrying, and husbands are more likely to behave themselves when they marry family. Some friends of mine who married men from families they didn't know well have had some nasty shocks. One poor girl married somebody who got drunk on their wedding night and beat her up. She finished up by going back to her parents when she was in a condition (this was the phrase that southern ladies used for an expectant mother) . When her father went to remonstrate with her husband he was beaten up as well. She tried to get a divorce but couldn't. She had to return to her husband because he could insist on the children being returned." Richard was surprised he didn't think that so-called southern gentlemen behaved like that.

"Another thing is that a number of men marry their dead wives' sisters and vice versa. Planters need a wife to look after the domestic side and care for the slaves. And widows find it difficult to run plantations themselves, and deal with the business side. And it's better for the children if the new marriage is within their own family rather than to somebody they don't know.

Richard spent the time riding round the plantation. Not much cotton was being planted now. The emphasis was on growing food. The South now had to feed itself. As far as he could tell the place was well –run. The slaves looked well-fed and cared for. He could see no evidence of whips and collars about which he had heard so much in England, and in the North. Again he remembered his briefings.

"A slave is a valuable asset." He had been told. "A great deal of wealth is tied up in slaves. If a slave is badly treated not only will he not work as well but he is more likely fall ill and depreciate in value or worse die, when he will be worthless."

"It sounds as though you are talking about a valuable horse or cow" commented Richard caustically.

"Exactly so." You are now beginning to understand the economics and mind of a Southern planter."

Richard spent some time following Mrs Smythe about her household duties and decided that the role of the planter's wife was even more different than that of the woman in 'Uncle Tom's Cabin'. He expressed surprise when she showed him the smokehouse and the store house which seemed to him to be well-stocked in these lean times.

"It's nothing to what it used to be.There used to be rows of hams and sides of meat hanging from those beams. You had to bend over to move and you couldn't see the floor for tubs of pickled pork and corned beef. We used to have rows of nine pound loaves of white sugar, barrels of flour, cases of olive oil, wine, brandy and all kinds of things. Nothing is the same since this war started.

Richard saw the clothing store for the slaves and was told that each slave was issued with a set of clothing for winter and summer. He was shown the account books for the purchase of the cloth. "Now of course we are making our own cloth. And the slave-women have always made the clothes themselves." He was shown the hospital where the sick slaves were tended. "Fortunately, we just have this boy with a broken leg. It's his own fault. He fell out of a tree. You're quite a nuisance aren't you Tom?" Tom didn't answer – one had not been expected. It was not a question. It was a statement.

"I'm glad we haven't any infectious diseases at the moment. If there were, we wouldn't have left Richmond. Five years ago we suffered a terrible cholera epidemic. We lost sixteen slaves – and my little girl who was five." Mrs Smythe said this in a matter of fact way. Richard could not even detect a tremor in her voice.

"I'm sorry," murmured Richard. He felt clumsy. He knew he had to say something but didn't know what.

"No good being sorry. Children die all the time. Most of my friends have lost at least one. Its part of life and life can be tough for the mistress of a plantation. It's not all balls, picnics, drawing-rooms and summer breaks to Sulphur Springs." Richard was realising that.

Chastened by Mrs Smythe's criticism of his shooting, Richard had practised hard whilst at Mulberry. However, the journey back to Richmond was safe enough. A detachment of troops called for water and fodder just as they were leaving. As they were going towards Richmond, they invited Mrs Smythe and Richard to accompany them.

A Major Connor rode with them for a while and talked pleasantly. "This is a complicated war. I'd rather fight the Indians or the Mexicans any day. You might be fighting your college friend, your cousin or even your brother. And I think the men feel the same way. On Independence Day our boys and the Federals were even picking blackberries together and trading tobacco and sugar in the fields around Richmond."

The day after they arrived home Richard received a note to meet the next day. It was signed again 'T Jenkinson'.

"English!" Kate exclaimed. "I thought he must be some shirker. Mind you I never heard him speak."

"He's got a lovely voice," enthused Millie. It's upper –class English like that Englishman we all met at Beaumont some years ago. You remember the one?" Kate nodded.

"Oh, but it's much nicer than that. It has softness about it. It has as sort of a burr and he rolls his rs. It's lovely" sighed Sarah. "Maria Lewington is quite in love with him already." 'She's not the only one', thought Kate.

Kate plonked her cup down on the table. "I will obviously have to take a closer look at this paragon if I see him again."

Chapter Fourteen

Washington

July 1862

Rose Greenhow sat at the rough wooden table which at the moment served, amongst other things, as her dressing table. She gently placed the silver-backed hairbrush with the others on the silver tray. She had managed to keep these items from the Federals when they had ransacked her home in Washington. They had kept her there for several months under house arrest before transferring her to Old Capitol Prison.

Her face gazed back at her from the looking glass which measured a mere six by eight inches. She was now forty-six and looked it. A year ago her appearance had not changed much since her early twenties.

Her finely chiselled features gave her an air of authority and her slim, athletic body moved with ease and grace at the social gatherings which had been her natural environment. Her dark hair, black eyes and olive skin indicated that she may have been of Spanish or Italian descent; this was possible, but her forbears who had settled in America were Irish.

The year's imprisonment had left its mark. Poor food, lack of exercise, uncertainty and tension had rendered her face gaunt and lined it with deep furrows. Her hair now bore strong streaks of grey and her agile well- proportioned figure was beginning to thicken.

Hair and body may change in adversity but eyes and temperament do not. Rose's eyes were now sunken but they still flashed and showed her moody, tempestuous nature. They had always been very mobile and displayed wit, brilliance and anger. Now they showed steady, strong determination. They were never dull or expressionless. Similarly, her temperament had been her constant support. Not only had she resolutely refused to disclose anything to the Federals but she had managed to continue her espionage in prison.

Rose was of revolutionary stock and proud of it. One of her ancestors was among the Roman Catholic colonists who landed in America in the sixteen – thirties. Now 'Rebel Rose', as she was known by some, was working tirelessly for the Confederates and had been prepared to put herself and her child in danger.

Hopefully today was a good day. Rose was to be released, provided that the Federal authorities were to be trusted. She would not feel totally safe until she was behind Confederate lines. She had defiantly wound the Confederate flag around her, beneath a light summer shawl. As she stepped outside the doors into the warm sunlight a feeling of dread assailed her – a military escort was waiting.

A young lieutenant was sitting astride a fine chestnut gelding. He touched his cap. So this was the famous Mrs Greenhow he had heard so much about. The most dangerous woman in the Confederacy – clever, devious and a temptress who oozed sexuality – against whose wiles Senator Wilson and a number of other top Federal politicians and soldiers had proved powerless. A large crowd of people had assembled as though to watch a show.

Little Rose walked imperiously before her mother and gathered up her skirt to step into the carriage with not so much a glance at the sergeant holding open the door – as though she was the Queen and he the lowliest servant. The child was now almost as famous as her mother for throwing tantrums, and being difficult.

Rose had been as troublesome as possible and had

plagued her jailers with a mixture of flattery, coquetry and abuse worthy of a fishwife. She also frightened those in authority by writing continuous letters of complaint to her extensive and powerful contacts in Washington. The Governor of the prison had made it no secret that he was heartily relieved to see 'the back of the pair of them'.

Rose acknowledged the Lieutenant's salute. The young man didn't realise it,but she was extremely nervous. The possibility was never far from her mind that she had been considered so much trouble that she was being moved to a remote Northern prison where she would be held quietly until the end of the war. After all, Habeas Corpus had been suspended and both the Union and the Confederacy had no compunction about the thousands of prisoners who were now languishing without trial. Rose walked up to him.

"Sir. I am asking you, not as Lincoln's officer, but as a man of honour and a gentleman. Are you taking me to a northern prison or the Confederacy?" The officer was uneasy. He was in charge and she was his prisoner but with her influence she could cause him a great deal of damage if he showed her what could be construed as the slightest disrespect. She appeared to him to be haughty, arrogant and terrifying. Everything he had heard about her was true. He took an instant dislike to her.

"Madam. On my honour, my orders are to take you to Fortress Monroe and then to the Confederacy. Here is the order of transportation." Rose took it and looked at it in the manner of a schoolmistress checking a schoolboy's homework, handed it back without further comment, nodded briefly to the audience as though they were her assembled courtiers, and stepped into the carriage.

Two other prisoners were being repatriated at the

same time as Rose and her daughter. Rose ignored them as best she could. She found them bad-mannered and ill-bred. Her active mind never stopped working during the journey south. She made a mental note of anything she noticed which might be of interest to her country – particularly fortifications, which fascinated her.

The distance from Washington to Richmond is just over one hundred miles but because of security precautions and the military activity around Richmond, the journey lasted some four days. The last leg took them by boat up the James River towards Richmond. The sun had beaten down relentlessly since they had left Washington. The last night was airless and Rose sat with Little Rose on deck. They had stifled downstairs and the child had felt that somebody was smothering her with a pillow to stop her breathing. Incarceration had done the child no good whatsoever. It was not just her physical health that had suffered in the same way as her mother but, unlike her mother, this developing child had suffered psychologically being very distrustful and nervous of strangers. The disruption to her life manifested itself in bad behaviour, precocity and rudeness-never attractive qualities in a child, and this child was regarded as odious by anybody who was unfortunate enough to come into contact with her.

Not that mother and daughter would have spent much time sleeping anyway owing to shouting of commands by the crew and manoeuvring of the ship. The river was difficult to navigate. The Confederates had removed the buoys. Hulks of sunken vessels littered the river.

"Look." Rose said to the child. "There's the Congress." That was sunk by the 'Virginia'. She was built by us from the Yankee ship 'Merrimac' which they scuttled when we forced them out of Norfolk."

Rose knew that there would be no public reception for her on the quay. Her work was secret. A mule cart stood waiting for them. The animals were tied to a hitching-post whilst the driver loaded their trunks which served as seats. Rose clutched her daughter as they jolted and lurched through the city.

Rose did not know were she was being taken but assumed that lodgings had been found for her. She was right. The Government was grateful to her and there was work still for her to do. She was in the Service. The cart pulled up at Ballard House. The driver helped Rose down and held the child by the waist (despite her squawks-Little Rose didn't like being touched by anybody other than her mother) and swung her firmly to the ground. Rose left her two travelling companions without regret. The feeling was mutual.

The next few days were rest and readjustment for Rose. General Winder, the Provost Marshall of Richmond did her the honour of calling on her the first evening. Despite official secrecy the papers did not take long to trumpet the news of her return. The greatest acknowledgement however took place the second evening after arrival in Richmond. Rose was relaxing by reading French (Rose never relaxed by doing nothing or something inconsequential) her mind always had to be employed. The maid entered. "It's President Davis for you Ma'am."

Jefferson Davis bowed and took her hand. "Ma'am thank you for all you have done for us. You realise, don't you that, but for you, there would have been no victory at the Battle of Bull Run". Rose did know. She never under -estimated her achievements but she was extremely touched by the President's gesture and she was also a skilful diplomat.

"It is an honour to do anything for my country and I would happily die serving it." Neither of them realised that her words were prophetic.

They looked at each other. Both were shocked by the change in the other's appearance. She saw a tall, gaunt man. He was of a nervous disposition. His cheek twitched constantly. The people who worked under him found him difficult and aloof. He didn't address anybody by their first names – even his slaves. Since the advance of the Federals, he had grown even more worried and fidgety. He had sent his wife and children to Columbia and safety. His neuralgia and dyspepsia were attacking him as they always did when he was under pressure. He was also shocked by what he saw. This beautiful, commanding woman now looked haggard, uncertain and older. Her eyes were sunken and the dark, olive-skinned face heavily lined. The war had taken its toll on both of them.

By the time the President had left, Rose had been promised the sum of two and a half thousand dollars out of the small fund that was at his disposal for the Secret Service, and her future role had been discussed. Her important service for the Confederacy would continue until the end of the war.

"Well, how did you enjoy your visit to a plantation?" Clara, Amelia and Richard were sitting on one of a cluster of benches in a copse at the edge of one of Richmond's major parks. The heavy, shady ceiling of trees protected them from the shimmering heat. The park was now empty. Children had been gathered up by their nursemaids and had been taken home for their lunch and rest. They would not return with their hoops and pet dogs until early evening.

"Interesting!" Said Richard. "Had they not prepared me for it in Washington, I would have expected a fainting owner's wife and slaves whipped regularly by the likes of Simon Legree. Mrs Smythe works really hard." The girls laughed.

"Yes. It's not all like 'Uncle Tom's Cabin'. Plantations are businesses and go bankrupt if they are not run properly. That was the case before the war of course but even more so now." Amelia waved away an insect that was buzzing round her. "Now you were told in Washington that one of your tasks could concern Mrs Greenhow." Richard nodded. "She has just arrived here in Richmond . At the moment all you have to do is to study her and find out where she goes and who she sees. You've been told how to do these things." Richard had.

When observing people the approach was one of 'eyes open and mouth shut'. The person had to be watched surreptitiously. The appropriate social gatherings had to be attended. He had to listen to conversations without taking part in them too much and, especially, he should not ask any questions beyond those of inconsequential social proprieties. The young women spent the next half an hour telling Richard about Mrs Greenhow. He had known much already but he was furnished with the odd scrap of additional information. She and her husband had been a formidable team.

Robert Greenhow's life had been brilliant, and tinged with tragedy. When he was twelve he had attended Richmond theatre with his parents. The theatre had caught fire. His mother had burned to death and his father had just managed to drag the boy to safety.

Robert had subsequently obtained medical degrees from the Universities of Columbia and Edinburgh and had walked the hospital wards of London and Paris, where he had occupied his spare time in taking a law course at the Sorbonne. He spoke French, German, Italian and Spanish. On his return to America ,he had involved himself in diplomacy and had become a noted explorer on the American continent. When he was thirty-five he had married the eighteen- year old Rose O'Neal. He had also found time to become an expert in land boundaries. Rose accompanied him when the American Government sent him to Mexico City to advise on the confusion of titles to land in California, resulting from the Mexican War.

The vibrant new city of San Francisco had grown up round the Gold Rush. The Greenhows moved there so that Robert could set up a legal office to settle land and mining claims which had often been decided by fistfights and brawls. Rose was heartbroken when Robert was killed in 1854. The marriage of this passionate pair had pulsed with excitement and mutual stimulation.

Rose disposed of Robert's land and business interests, pocketed the ten thousand dollars damages paid to her by the City of San Francisco, and also managed to become embroiled in a massive fraud over land and became the major witness in the subsequent trial. She then returned to Washington where she became heavily involved with pre-war politics and was seen in diplomatic circles. She met the Prince of Wales. Her grief for Robert did not prevent passionate affairs with Colonel Keys, Senator Henry Wilson and a number of others.

Richard slowly made his way back to the Smythe's across the park and adjusted his white Panama hat so that the back of the brim protected his neck against the blazing sun. His mind had been buzzing for the last few weeks with his briefing in Washington, the terrible scenes on his arrival in Richmond and the visit to the plantation. The striking red-headed girl that he had met at the barbecue was seldom out of his thoughts. He regretted that he could not keep up his journal. He had been forbidden to continue with it in his briefings in

Washington. This was, of course, commonsense but he was irritated that they knew he kept one – he suspected that his belongings were searched when he was staying at the home of Dr Matthews.

Now the girls had given Richard orders for a couple of assignments. He did not realise that these were 'dummy runs' of no consequence and were just to test him. He had been given no specific instructions as to Mrs Greenhow as yet-just to find out as much about her as possible and to try and attend functions where she was present ,but at the same time to keep a low profile.

It would not be easy for a young unimportant English youth to shadow one of the most important people in the Confederacy but, as he was reminded, it was because he was young, unimportant and English that he had been picked for the task. "We know it's difficult." Colonel Wilmer had said. "But that is why we are paying you so well. We don't pay people for doing things that are easy. We know you have the brains and ability otherwise we wouldn't have chosen you. For one thing you've proved you have initiative with your journey over from England."

"It seems to me." Richard had told the young women. "That this Rose Greenhow is trouble; wherever she is excitement or intrigues are never far away."

"You're dead right." Said Amelia. "And watch out for little Rose as well. That child is a demon. She had only been in Richmond a week when she spotted one of McClellan's officers disguised in a Confederate Uniform at the America Hotel. The poor man was quietly having dinner when he saw the little witch looking at him. He said that he felt as though her eyes were boring into him like gimlets. He just cut and ran before he could be captured."

Chapter Fifteen

Richmond

August 1862

DuFresne was ushered into a large drawing-room by the butler. He was confronted by an enticing blend of light, scent, and sound. A hum of steady conversation from cultured, well modulated voices, mingled with the music of Mozart played in an alcove at the end of the room. Gaslight and candlelight reflected from necklaces, earrings, silver, exquisite crystal chandeliers and silk dresses.

The gathering radiated sophistication, education, confidence and power. A casual, disinterested observer would have wondered if this really was a country at war that was facing severe shortages and was recently so close to being invaded that it's leading citizens and government evacuated and had only just recently returned. DuFresne took a glass of ice-cold champagne by the stem from a silver salver proffered to him by a white-wigged slave, wearing livery of the eighteenth century.

Miller saw DuFresne enter the room. He did not approach him at first as that would have been too obvious. Eventually he drifted up. "Good to see you DuFresne. Come and meet my daughters." DuFresne felt slightly irritated. He had come to meet the niece whom he was supposed to be marrying. Miller introduced him to Millie and Sarah. The girls blushed, glanced at each other and giggled.

'I hope the niece is more mature than these'. DuFresne thought to himself. 'They seem as though they should still be in the schoolroom.' Miller whispered a few words to Millie "Come and meet our cousin", she said. DuFresne followed her and Sarah, manoeuvring his way through the crowd to where Kate was talking vivaciously to a clutch of admiring young men in uniform.

Kate had cast off her mourning. Jeff had been dead for a year now. She couldn't be in mourning for ever – anyway her mother wasn't around. There were far too many black dresses about. It was so depressing. She had brought most of her wardrobe from Beaumont and had decided to wear one her dresses which had arrived from Paris shortly before the war.

To her delight she had discovered two days ago that Frank was being posted to Richmond. She had met him that morning. Much to his disgust he learnt that he would be in Richmond for the foreseeable future. Kate was just relieved that he would be out of harm's way. She was in an exuberant mood she felt vivacious and flirtatious.

DuFresne saw a beautiful young woman whose face was full of liveliness and intelligence, wearing a low-cut, pale-green dress complementing her red hair. Both blended well with the emerald earrings and diamond necklace. Millie made the introductions. Kate saw a darkly handsome man, mature, tall and well-built with an amused mocking glint in his eyes. DuFresne bent down and kissed her hand with head bent but eyes raised. "Your servant Ma'am". The French accent only added to the attraction.

"I'm delighted to meet you Mr DuFresne." The two of them looked at each other surrounded by the circle of disgruntled young men. Millie, somewhat put out by the fact that the impact that she had made on DuFresne was obviously nothing compared with Kate's, interrupted the locked gaze of the two people and introduced the rest of the circle. Kate however was determined to proceed with the conversation.

"What line of business are you in Mr DuFresne? DuFresne was taken aback. This was a very direct question for a southern woman to ask.

"I work for the Government, Miss Turner, but I also work for myself."

"Don't you find that your loyalties conflict?" DuFresne reflected that Miller was right. This young woman would need a good deal of careful handling.

"When I am working for myself, Ma'am, I am loyal to myself and when I am working for the Government I am loyal to the Government."

"Would not your time and loyalties to your Government be best spent serving in the Army?" queried one young soldier truculently. The youth had an immature and unsophisticated air about him. He was sticking his chin out defiantly. DuFresne was used to such criticism whether veiled or as obvious as this

"You, Sir, serve your country in the best way that your talents allow and I do likewise. The South will not win by military means alone. Commerce and agriculture play a vital part in keeping the people and the Army fed and supplied with food, weapons and equipment. As you know, Napoleon said 'An army marches on its stomach'." DuFresne doubted whether the young man knew that at all. He didn't give the appearance of being particularly well-read or informed and he now seemed bewildered and fell silent. DuFresne continued.

"It's not just the Army and Navy that play an important role in war, but civilians have a vital part. If every male of military age joined the Army then the country would be left with just the women, slaves, children and old men. The northern generals would be drinking champagne here in Richmond in no time. Our country is best served by us using all our talents in the manner which is most beneficial to her. I use mine to the best of my abilities as I'm sure you use yours. Now, Miss Turner, would you like to accompany me to the other end of the room and watch and listen to the musicians they are so good? Thus, skilfully, preventing any further discussion.

Kate accepted gracefully. She was impressed by this attractive man. He had given a mature and courteous answer to an immature and antagonistic question. The boy had been thwarted, but not humiliated, which would have spoilt the tone of a pleasant, social gathering. When they arrived in front of the musicians, she looked up at his dark mocking eyes.

"You certainly put Michael Lafayette in his place but you were very civilised about it."

"Well, he's entitled to his opinion. I know that since the war started, people have been locked up for expressing their opinions but I still like to think we still have freedom of speech in this country despite the war. He is also very young and has probably lost some friends and will probably lose a lot more. People of his age are too young to be facing the dangers and responsibilities that have been thrust on them."

"How do you know my uncle, Mr DuFresne?"

"Through business."

"And what sort of business might that be?"

"Nothing that you need worry your pretty little head about. Kate flushed angrily.

"Don't patronise me, Sir. I have been running my father's plantation since he and my brothers left for the war. And now I am working for the Government. As most of you men have gone off to war (she nearly said 'real men'; men not in uniform still irked her) leaving the women to run their businesses, farms and plantations we have to worry our pretty little heads otherwise on your return you will find no food to fill your stomachs, your children dead from starvation and your bank accounts empty. What would be the result now if we women were to follow the excellent advice of that clever Mr Charles Kinglsey? –'For men must work and women must weep.' If there are no men to do any work nothing is going to be achieved by women weeping.

DuFresne smiled at this tart response. "You are certainly a match for most lawyers I have met Miss Turner. And you are very well-read."

"Well-read is well-prepared Mr DuFresne."

"Would you like to come riding with me?" Kate laughed in spite of herself. The man's nerve was unbelievable but she was becoming very interested.

"You are bold, Sir. We have only just met."

"I will ask permission of your uncle." Kate was annoyed. Her father was still in Richmond and he was the one to give consent but her interest in DuFresne was overriding her irritation.

"And what about your wife Mr DuFresne?"

"I'm not married Ma'am." Kate was surprised. He looked as though he was in his late thirties. He appeared to be a vigorous, healthy man, it was obvious that he liked women and from the surreptitious glances being slid in his direction it was clear that she was not the only woman who liked him.

"I look after people."

"I didn't think of you being in the medical profession." Observed Kate dryly.

"I'm not; although I can provide medicines when required."

"Are you a blockade-runner?"

"That is one of my little pastimes. Yes. People want things. I supply them. They pay me. They're happy. I'm happy."

"I'm not surprised at the profits you make."

"You have absolutely no idea as to the profits I make."

"I have. I work in the Government offices. I know what some of you people make."

"And lose."

"Yes. And lose." But you don't look as though you are losing very much at the moment. For one thing you are the best-dressed man in the room." Kate eyed DuFresne from head to foot. His immaculately cut wine-red frock-coat, yellow waistcoat, white trousers and English- made shoes were conspicuous against the shabby uniforms of the soldiers. Most of the male civilians were reasonably well- dressed but that would change as the war progressed.

DuFresne was right. The South was completely lacking in heavy industry and had to create it from almost nothing, and the fact that she was managing to do so was one of the greatest surprises of the war. Many plants making agricultural implements had been quickly converted into armament factories. Metal objects from pots, pans, and railings to church bells were collected and melted down. Nothing was overlooked or wasted. Contents of chamber pots were collected to be rendered into nitre for gunpowder. Liquor stills were converted to produce percussion caps for rifles.

Whatever valiant efforts the South made to build its industry, they would never be sufficient and imports were still necessary. The North was quick to capitalise on this weakness with the blockade of the Confederate coast, and the advance down the Mississippi.

Tactics is like a game of Chess. Moves produce counter-moves and the North's pincer activities quickly engendered blockade –running and privateering by the South. The risks were huge as the rebel ships played 'tag' using smokeless fuel from Welsh anthracite pits, and were in danger of being blasted by the mines littering the entrance to the harbours which were laid by both sides. However, if the hazards were large then so were the profits. Blockading the Confederate coast, which stretched for some four thousand miles, was a formidable task and many ships remained unscathed.

The South issued privateering licenses to any shipowner who applied, whatever the nationality. The holders of such licences were allowed to sell as contraband any cargoes captured from northern merchant vessels, and up to a fifth of the value of a Federal ship was offered to the privateer responsible.

Much to the fury of the Federal Government, many Britons indulged in blockade- running and had licences to act as privateer. Tensions between Britain and the North were aggravated by the fact that the South chartered British ships with British captains and crews. Commerce-raiders were built in British ship-yards- the most famous of which was 'The Alabama'. These ships wreaked devastation on the northern merchant fleet.

The blockade was usually penetrated at night and the Confederate Government expected the ships, which left loaded with cotton, to return with essential items such as ammunition, weapons, food and clothing.

Regrettably, men like Miller and DuFresne who were prepared to run considerable risks, were not disposed to follow the dictates of the Government if there was more money to be made from pandering to the whims of the public who demanded luxuries. The most glittering of these profits were to be made by the importation of non-essential goods such as frames for crinolines and bonnets, perfume, brandy, cigars and a large array of foodstuffs such as Stilton cheese, coffee and tea. If, however, these highly-priced cargoes finished up at the bottom of the sea, the losses could be devastating. Men who indulged in this kind of activity were admired for their daring and were also useful to know.

DuFresne combined the ingredients of recklessness, sophistication, maturity, good looks, desirability and mocking courtesy. These qualities, combined with his subtle seduction which did not extend to blatant,tasteless flirtation and the suspicion that he was arrogant and not quite respectable aroused Kate's sexuality. The good-looking, fair, English boy, whom she had now seen on two or three occasions but to whom she had not yet spoken, paled into insignificance when compared to this dark, dangerous man.

"With all your booty Mr DuFresne you must be sought after by the ladies!"

Again, the sardonic smile and mocking eyes but before the sparring with words and eyes could continue, Miller's wife swirled up. Kate had spent far too much time with that handsome business friend of Preston's – all that pouting and telling glances between a young unmarried girl and a much older man was not respectable.

"Kate, you must meet Mr Wilson.He's off to camp for the first time tomorrow." Henrietta indicated the youth at her elbow. Kate looked grudgingly at the young man in his private's uniform. Most young men from 'good' families did not automatically obtain a commission as was common in the North. Wilson was not quite eighteen. Like the young Englishman, this boy could not compete with the sophisticated, rich, dark, daring blockade-runner with a French accent. After the taste of brandy, milk had no appeal.

Meanwhile, Henrietta had steered DuFresne away and Kate looked on in irritation whilst her aunt chatted animatedly to him. The hapless Mr Wilson received the barest civility from her. Kate was unable to be alone with DuFresne for the rest of the evening and hoped that he would not forget the invitation to ride. If DuFresne forgot ,then Kate certainly wouldn't and if no invitation came then Kate would engineer a meeting-somehow. Kate had decided they would meet again and when Kate decided something, then it usually happened.

However, it would not be necessary for Kate to use her ingenuity as Miller raised the matter at dinner the next evening.

"Kate you must have made an impression on Mr DuFresne as he has asked my permission to take you riding." Henrietta looked up from her fish and put down her knife.

"Of course, you refused him. Preston you can't possibly agree to it. Kate has only met him once and we know nothing about him."

"Well, my dear you certainly seemed to be putting that right last night. You were talking to him for a good half an hour."

"No. It can't have been more than fifteen minutes", retorted Henrietta.

"Oh. You were obviously counting them then!" From his wife's expression Miller could see that it would not be wise to continue this kind of verbal sparring. Probably, because it was too close to the truth. He was aware of his wife's penchant for handsome men. Still, the business concerning Kate had to be finished.

"If, as you say, you know nothing about him it doesn't matter because I do know something about him as I do business with him. He is a perfectly respectable man with whom I can trust my niece and you know that the rules of chaperones and courtship are not the same now since the start of the war. Anyway, why shouldn't people have a little fun in wartime? After all, Kate like many other women, is now working with men.

Henrietta knew she was defeated on that line of argument. As men were now available for only short snatches of time, the old elaborate rules had been swept away. Courtships accelerated and in some cases marriages were taking place only a few days after the couple had met, so that the man could die in battle leaving a bereaved widow rather than a bereaved fiancée. Henrietta now tried another tack.

"You may know something about his business but you know nothing about his family. And another thing. He must be at least fifteen years older than Kate if not twenty."

"A slightly, smaller age difference than exists between you and I my dear. And for knowing nothing about his family. Judging by the qualities of people whose families we do know that fact should not condemn a man out of hand." Kate suppressed a smile. The stormy chemistry between husband and wife was entertaining and had dispelled the annoyance of her being discussed as though she was not present, as well as the fact that Miller had taken it upon himself to give consent when her father was in Richmond.

"But what about Kate's reputation? Don't you care about that? Your own niece!" Henrietta wailed.

"Of course I care about it as I'm sure she does but according to the current wartime standards, it is quite in order for a girl to ride out with a man alone. Kate comes from one of South Carolina's leading families and is working for the Government. If people haven't anything better to do than gossip about an innocent girl's reputation, then they can't be contributing much to the war effort. Case closed now, Henrietta. I have nothing further to say on the matter."

Miller knew the reason for Henrietta's thunderous expression. She had taken a fancy to DuFresne herself.

229

Miller knew of his wife's susceptibility to men although he knew she had done nothing improper. If she had, he would have known about it. Self-interested people would have told him. Southern conventions could not override basic human instincts and passions. Married people did have affairs which were usually kept discreet, although they did sometimes boil over into open associations when 'Society' would close many of its doors to them. It was of course accepted that some men needed to visit whores and keep mistresses but these women were not part of 'Society' so they didn't count. Slave-owners relations with their slave-women caused no comment.

Miller's first marriage had not only been advantageous for business reasons but had been very happy. He had genuinely mourned his wife's death but a man like Miller needed a wife. He had to have somebody to superintend his household and act as hostess at his many functions.

Miller had married Henrietta some eighteen months after the death of his first wife. In the opinion of Henrietta's family, Miller's age and his six children were more than compensated by the fact that he was one of the wealthiest and most powerful men in the State. Henrietta,for her part, had been spurned by a man with whom she was deeply in love, and was in a frame of mind in which she would marry anybody eligible and approved by her family.

Henrietta was beautiful and accomplished and knew how to run a home ,she was a competent stepmother but emotionally the marriage was not a success. The rapport which is necessary for a happy union was missing. Since the still-birth of their only baby, little intimacy had existed between the couple. As long as his wife was discreet and performed all the functions of a wife expected by Southern Society, Miller was not concerned as to how she conducted her life. He had far more pressing matters on his mind.

Kate tried to keep her excitement from being too apparent and looking levelly at her uncle, coolly asked him when he had met DuFresne that day.

"He came to my office and mentioned it to me then." Indeed, Kate was an item which took up a very small proportion of the intensely, long and involved conversation which had taken place between the two men.

Kate was blissfully unaware of anything other than DuFresne. The ruthless business woman and current employee of the Government was, for the moment, a young dizzy girl happily visualising scenes between her and this man of magnetic attraction – he pressing her with invitations and she showing reluctance and only after much pouting, eye-work and teasing with her fan, would she accept.

Chapter Sixteen

September 1862

South Carolina

DuFresne, Miller and Harrison drained their glasses in Harrison's quarters. Beaumont had buzzed with activity over the last few weeks. Solange was aware of it but assumed that it was all connected with the work of the plantation and, anyway,'Dear Preston' was 'handling everything' and she was therefore happy to resume her old role of managing the house and caring for the slaves when they were sick. Not that there were so many of them now. More had bought their freedom, some had been taken by the Commissary for labouring work in the Army, and others had run off – probably behind the Union lines.

Solange was grateful that her husband was now safe. He had been involved in those terrible battles around Richmond but, praise God, he had not been injured. Jeff Davis had now sent William to England as some kind of envoy to persuade the British Government to recognise the Confederacy in its own right.

Solange had been worried about William crossing the Atlantic, with all those mines and those dreadful, vicious Northern ships. Thankfully, she had heard a couple of days ago that he had arrived. She prayed fervently that he would now be out of harm's way for the rest of the war.

William had been able to visit Beaumont for just two days before he sailed. Kate had returned with her father from Richmond. Solange wanted her to stay longer but she insisted on returning with William, although he had offered to try to obtain further leave for her, by intervening on her behalf. She seemed rather strange and distant. It was probably all that work she was doing for the Government.

Solange was now starved of adult company except for slaves. There were just Mammy, Rachel and Nathaniel to whom she could talk on some companionable type of basis. The old man was now living in the house. He spent most of his spare time in his beloved library. He had been a good and calming influence on Custis. At the start of the war the little boy had been very unsettled by the departure of his father and brothers. He had even, outrageously, mentioned joining the Amy as a bugler.

"All the real men are in the Army or Navy" he grumbled. He was sitting on the veranda with Nathaniel. It was early evening and Nathaniel had suggested that as there was an hour between now and dinner, it would be a good idea to work on Latin verbs. That was not disposed to improve the boy's immediate humour but Nathaniel knew that he was seriously discontented. The problem had to be addressed. Boys of ten and eleven were running off to join the Army and in some cases they were not sent home. Initially, they had a value as musicians but were bearing arms all too soon.

"We won't do any Latin now. We'll go for a walk." During that time Nathaniel explained that 'real men' did not leave their womenfolk unprotected to the mercies of invaders and insurrections by slaves. His father would not have gone leaving Custis in charge if he did not think he was a 'real man'.

"He didn't leave me in charge – it was Kate," muttered the boy.

"We know that they all said that. And she was

running the place. But it is very important that you are here – especially now that Kate is in Richmond. We need one male member of the family here. The best way you can help your country is to work at your education. The Confederacy doesn't need to be governed by fools in the future". He nudged the boy, and he began to smile. The old man was psychologist enough to know that the best way to get through to children and get them on your side is to make them laugh. "Practice your shooting, your riding and continue to learn as much as you can about farming and the running of the plantation. You know quite a lot already." Custis' confidence and self-esteem were now boosted, and Nathaniel ensured that it was kept that way. There was now no further talk of leaving.

Nathaniel was torn between his longing for a Union victory and his affection for the Turner family – especially Solange and Custis. Whilst living in the house he had developed a strong emotional bond with these two – the one because of her nature, and the other because of his youth. Nathaniel wished no harm to come to them, or to any of the family.

However, he was a slave and what he had longed for and worked for all his life now seemed attainable. Had he been a younger man he would have run away north and possibly joined the Federal Army or at least tried to buy his freedom, but he was too old now and would soon be meeting his Maker. He had to leave that kind of thing to the younger generation for whom he had constantly sown seeds. His work was done. He was disappointed with the progress of the war. He had hoped for an early Confederate defeat early in the war, and had been devastated by Bull Run. The South was proving far more resilient than it was thought possible and even now many Northerners thought she might win, despite the recent setbacks.

Solange was grateful for the support of the slaves in the house ,but they were not on an equal footing. She was lonely, depressed and desperately worried about Frank and Harry. William was safe for the time being but she missed him terribly and was still grief-stricken for Jeff. Kate's leaving made matters much worse.

For Solange – as for many mistresses of plantations – separation from her husband had always been a fact of life. Planters often had to spend long periods of time away on business, sometimes mixed with pleasure.The wife usually had to remain at home to care for the house and slaves, and to generally maintain a 'presence' as far as the running of the plantation was concerned, although the daily responsibilities lay with the manager.

Plantations were very isolated and unless sisters, female cousins or women friends could be persuaded to pay an extended visit, these periods were extremely desolate. It had always been difficult to organise long journeys for women before the war as it was unthinkable that they should travel without a male escort, although the war had relaxed this convention, as it had many others.

Solange therefore was no stranger to loneliness but this time was worse. Now, there was no definite end in sight and previously more of her children had been with her. Now she just had Custis. She had turned to her previous support in times of desolation – laudanum. Like many Southerners, Solange used this tincture of opium when she had been ill or suffering from 'female complaints'. She also gave it to her children when they were ill and used it to help her depression and insomnia. She was taking it now in increasing quantities.

Colonel Turner had been pleased with the progress of Beaumont. Kate had done well and Harrison was continuing the good work. A year before the outbreak of war the Colonel had foreseen the difficulties that would ensue if war had become a reality and had increased the farming area of Beaumont's activities such as the growing of Indian corn, sweet potatoes, peas, beans, and rice, the raising of cattle , sheep, hens and pigs. Kate and Harrison had developed these products much further and now had a considerable number of customers in the neighbourhood.

Beaumont was an ideal location for the storage of arms, other equipment and cotton. At the far south of the plantation lay swampland which was not fit for agricultural use. It was here that Miller had arranged for some makeshift sheds to be erected. They were well-camouflaged, being screened with trees and foliage. Miller's own slaves had been brought in to do the building so that the slaves of Beaumont were not involved and they had no interest in it as the building area was unhealthy, unattractive and insect-ridden.

Miller had made certain that Colonel Turner would not interfere with his plans. He had used his influence with Jeff Davis so that the Colonel would be sent to England in the same way that he had influenced Kate's being sent to Richmond. He was lucky in that the President had been considering the Colonel as an ideal candidate for the post but then Miller was often lucky- that was what made him so successful.

Kate had often wondered why the President had seen fit to summon her to Richmond. As the battles had been raging when she arrived, she had been told not to report for duty but to concentrate on the immediate emergencies such as working in the hospitals and the rolling and preparation of bandages.

When the crisis had passed she arrived at the Government buildings and was put to work filing and taking messages. She found the work repetitive, dull and well beneath her capabilities. "This is what I left running my plantation for" she complained to her father who was about to leave for England.

The Colonel laughed."Your plantation now is it? Be patient. You have been brought here for a good reason. They are just giving you those mundane tasks to acclimatise you to life in a government department. I have a good idea as to why Davis sent for you. You were chosen because you have proved your ability in running Beaumont and also because you are from one of the South's leading families and can be trusted." This loyal and honourable southern gentleman had no idea that any member of his family (or from any family such as his) could be anything but steadfast to the Confederacy. When he was eventually to learn of Miller's treachery, the poor man broke down and never fully recovered. The dishonour of this brother-in-law was the most terrible of the host of troubles which were to rain down on the old man.

After two or three weeks, an official summoned Kate to his office and invited her to sit down. It was only when she had sat that Kate noticed a dark, sallow woman sitting in the corner of the room. "This is Mrs Rose Greenhow. You will be working for her from now onwards." Kate was not often lost for words but she was now. She looked at the woman in awe and felt nervous. So this was the famous Rose Greenhow – the heroine of Bull Run." She would be working for the most venerated woman of the Confederacy.

"I will now leave you to get to know each other." The official rose. In normal circumstances, two visitors to his office would have to 'get to know each other' elsewhere. It was a sign of the reverence in which Rose was held that she was taking over this man's office. When the door shut Rose stood up and made her way to the official's desk with her back to the window.

Kate saw a tall, graceful woman who sailed to the desk with an arrogance and confidence with which she had been born. Kate had learnt that she had managed to intimidate her jailers, and make them feel inferior. Rose, however, did not intend to intimidate Kate. She would be working closely with Kate and to intimidate her would be counter-productive. Rose knew how to obtain the best from people. She knew how to wheedle and coax when necessary, and her ability to manipulate men in particular was legendary.

Not that Kate looked as though she would be easily scared. Rose saw a beautiful young woman who exuded the intelligence and self-assurance which comes from a well-educated person, who is a member of a wealthy and secure family. "I'm delighted to meet you, my dear." Rose held out her hand to Kate and smiled. "I'm sure we will get on famously together."

Over the next few weeks, Kate agreed with Rose's prophesy. The two women had a marvellous rapport. They shared the same level of intelligence although Rose was more of an intellectual and had the greater culture, learning and knowledge which nearly thirty years seniority must give. Kate quickly realised that the work for which she was being recruited was 'special'. During the next few months she was to learn the complex world of espionage and 'double-dealing' at its highest level.

In the meantime she followed Rose's advice to indulge in the frenetic social life of Richmond as much as possible. She should be observant, remember names and report anything suspicious. Richmond was crawling with Federal spies – not only Yankees but southerners with northern abolitionist sympathies. It had also been reported that the Federals were using foreigners,a good move as initially non-Americans raised little suspicion. A Norwegian woman had been arrested at the border. A routine search had revealed a large packet of papers under her crinoline.

A significant proportion of Kate's duties comprised accompanying Rose to social functions. This was easy. She enjoyed her company. They regularly called on President Davis and his wife Varina. Kate liked Davis. He was a gentle, thoughtful man. As a planter he had decreed that punishments must only be given to his slaves by a black judge, and had only retained the right to reduce sentences that he thought were too harsh.

Kate had heard that Davis was sensitive to criticism and if attacked too vehemently, would suffer from acute dyspepsia. Like Rose his intellectual powers were impressive. He could speak an Indian language fluently and was well-acquainted with Indian traditions from his days in the West. He also knew Spanish, Greek and Latin.

When Varina Davis returned to Richmond from Columbia after the battles the family moved into a handsome old mansion which had been purchased by the City of Richmond from Dr John Brockenborough, for renting to the Confederate Government as a home for the President and his family. The house consisted of four stories, and was situated on the brow of a hill surrounded by attractive terraced gardens containing cherry, apple and pear trees. The Carrarra marble mantelpieces provided an impressive background for Varina's entertainments.

Initially, Kate was very wary of Varina. She had sympathy with those who referred to her as 'Empress Eugenie' because of her haughty manner and with the 'Richmond Examiner' which accused her of aping Royalty by putting her servants in livery and not returning visits. It was inevitable that she evoked comparisons to her northern counterpart, Mary Lincoln – both these women owed their positions to their husbands but whereas both the men were relatively modest and unassuming in their behaviour towards others, the wives were arrogant,self-important, condescending and unpopular with many people of lower rank who came into contact with them.

Varina was well-read and cultured, but her tongue could be so vicious it had been described as 'forked'. Kate quickly heard of a famous exchange at the start of the war which was now legendary.

At a gathering, a woman who was the same age as Varina had indelicately and stupidly hinted that if her husband was killed she would have fun finding a replacement. Varina retorted. "What! When we see all that you could do in your youth and beauty! If George is the best you could do when you were fresh and young, what better chance could you hope for now you're old?" The silly woman left the room in tears. When Kate heard the tale she sincerely hoped that the most injured person of all, the hapless George who had done nothing to harm anybody, would never learn of the incident.

The anecdotes about Varina were legion. Just after meeting Varina for the first time, Kate was hurrying to work when she heard a shout of recognition. It was an old family friend, Captain Blackford who was now serving under General Stuart. When Kate mentioned Varina, he whistled and raised his eyes to Heaven. "I'd rather come across a dozen Yankees any day than her in full flow. I passed her the other day. She had caught a groom handling a horse roughly. You should have heard her cursing. Worse than any drover! I didn't know who to feel sorrier for, the groom or the horse."

Davis loved his home and would clatter up the hill for a respite from the worries of war, whenever possible. Kate's first visit was enlivened when the President entered the room unexpectedly with General

Lee and their staff officers. As soon as Lee entered the room, he apologised to Varina for splashing mud from his ride over her light carpet.

"Don't worry about it. Have a café au lait." Varina had been making it in a little silver saucepan on the hearth. The brew was precious as coffee was difficult to obtain. The delicate little cup looked scanty in Lee's great paw of a hand.

Kate was introduced. Despite the fact that she had grown up in a home where generals, statesmen and people of substance were frequent visitors, she felt awe at meeting this great man on whose shoulders were heaped the responsibility for saving the South.. However, she took his hand with poise and assurance.

"I know your family well and I know you are helping us. Thank you." Lee said, smiling.

Kate knew the man was an aristocrat and he looked it. His father had been the well known 'Light Horse Harry' Lee who had fought in the Revolution, but had subsequently gone bankrupt. Lee had grown up in genteel poverty and had been an honour cadet at West Point. He had married his childhood sweetheart – Mary Custis who was one of Virginia's great heiresses and a step- granddaughter of George Washington despite her father's disapproval of her marrying a penniless young officer,albeit an aristocrat. Mary was also of noble descent. Her ancestor, Colonel Parke had taken Marlborough's message of victory from the battlefield at Blenheim to Queen Anne.

Kate had been told that a year of war had now taken its toll on the General but, to her, he appeared to be an imposing figure. His hair and beard had turned totally grey within the year but the fifty-five year old man had not lost his military bearing and looked taller than his five feet eleven inches.

Lee weighed one hundred and seventy pounds but

looked heavier. Kate noticed that his physique was slightly distorted. His huge head rising from a short , thick neck was in the right proportion to his massive chest and shoulders but then his body tapered from the narrow hips and slight legs down to small feet, rather like an inverted isosceles triangle, one Northern newspaper had unkindly observed. ; but it was his face that overwhelmed Kate.

Kate would hesitate to describe a male face as beautiful – particularly in a man of Lee's age but she could not find another adjective to describe it. The face was handsome but what gave it rare quality was the expression of serenity and calm self-assurance; it was this which had inspired confidence in soldiers, children, Secretaries of War and two Presidents who had offered him Supreme Command. Women admired him and many were in love with him.

Lee's stature had increased since the Battles of the Seven Days of last June. McClellan, despite his victories, was incapable of advancing and the Confederate Joe Johnston was incapable of anything other than retreating and had he continued to do so this would have ended in a Union siege of Richmond and, perhaps, the end of the war. Luckily, Johnston had been wounded and Lee had not only diverted defeat but since the recent Second Battle of Bull Run his army was now standing on the banks of the Potomac. The North was under threat again and Southerners were appreciating Lee's ability.

"How is Mrs Lee?" Asked Rose. "I know she arrived in Richmond slightly before me and that she's had a very upsetting time."

"Improving slowly thank you Ma'am. Her arthritis is still very bad. The Federals were good enough to give her protection and made sure she arrived here safely but she's still very upset about White House

Landing. It belonged to her father who willed it to our son Rooney."

It was well known that Mary Lee had fled Arlington House, which had belonged to her family and where she and Lee had set up home. It was a fine mansion with parkland descending down to the Potomac. From the house could be seen the half-finished dome of Washington's Capitol. She had managed to elude the Federals for most of the journey but finally had to obtain permission to pass through their lines. Mary stopped at her son Rooney's house and pinned a defiant note on the door requesting the Northern soldiers to respect the property of the descendants of the wife of George Washington.

The enemy arrived just after Mary had left. General McClellan allowed her to proceed under a white flag and posted a guard to protect the house. Unfortunately after McClellan had moved on, a Federal straggler in a mindless act of vandalism set the beautiful old house on fire. Mary was distraught.When she finally arrived in Richmond, Lee was shocked at her appearance for, apart from the toll which the flight and the burning of the house had taken, her arthritis was so bad she could hardly walk.

These were just a few and the most famous of the many people that Kate was to meet and work with over the next few months. Now, she felt stimulated and buoyant. She was operating in the centre of the universe. What these people did (and what she was now doing) was to affect the lives of many people – sometimes resulting in the saving of lives of their countrymen and women although sometimes, sadly resulting in the losing of such lives. This realisation often gave her frissons of excitement. The atmosphere was electric and, indeed, sexually charged.

Men and women were engaged together in vital

work. They possessed the vitality and formidable intellect necessary for that kind of activity. Such people tend to have magnetism. Affairs which before the war would have been unthinkable were now inevitable. Kate had heard of Rose's reputation as a femme fatale and was amused to see that it had not taken long for her to be pursued by a general and a leading statesman who seemed to be vying for her favours. Kate had seen a number of men who interested her,but that was before she met DuFresne

Richard was still staying with Mrs Smythe. He had been worried that he may outstay his welcome but Clara and Amelia assured him that it was not uncommon for guests to stay indefinitely. He saw the girls often but never in the same place twice. Sometimes the meeting fixed the next one. Sometimes a note was sent by a servant. The note always mentioned Mary Felmingham.

It was not until the fourth or fifth occasion that he met the girls that they told him that Mrs Smythe was a cousin of Rose Greenhow. He was astonished and annoyed.

"Why on earth didn't you tell me earlier? I suppose I shouldn't have been that surprised. Everybody seems to be a cousin of everybody else round here. But surely that is a vital fact that I should know."

"It was decided that you didn't need to know earlier. The powers that be wanted to see how you settled in". Amelia brought down her parasol to shoo away a yapping little terrier that had scampered over to worry them.

"What you really mean is that you wanted to see whether I messed up or not. Anyway what if Mrs Smythe had mentioned her cousin to me?"

"Well you haven't messed up and as for Mrs

Smythe mentioning it, that was something that we were sure you could take in your stride. If you couldn't, you wouldn't have been selected. And don't scowl. You don't look nearly as handsome when your brow is all wrinkled and furrowed. You look a cross, grumpy old bear." Clara playfully tapped him on the cheek with her fan. Richard smiled in spite of himself.

"That's better! You have done really well in your assignments." Richard had been busy. He had followed people, observed them and given written accounts of the individuals and their actions in code to Clara and Amelia. He had been given messages by the girls to decode. The girls had reported to their 'superiors' whom Richard had not met and never would.

Richard had also taken packages from places and taken them to other places where he had hidden them for collection. What he had not realised was the people he had followed were not regarded as being of any significance whatsoever; they included a cotton broker's manager, a housewife , a schoolmaster and a clerk in a warehouse. None of the people realised he was watching them. What was unknown to Richard was that he was, in turn, being watched by somebody he would never know and that the 'important packages' were just parcels of paper . His 'employers' were now satisfied with his performance and he was approved for further duties.

It had not been difficult to absent himself from Mrs Smythe' house. She was too busy with her own activities such as organising hospitals, medical supplies, raising money for charities for dead and wounded soldiers' families and running a household in a climate of diminishing products and soaring prices, to concern herself with the movements of a visiting youth. When she asked him questions they were out of polite interest rather than real curiosity.

Richard had more trouble with the boys Walter and Martin who had taken a real liking to him, and seemed to regard him as some kind of surrogate elder brother. The South was teeming with all too many boys like them now. They really missed adult male company in the absence of their fathers and elder brothers. The boys tended to ask Richard where he was going and could they come? Richard hated to see the disappointment in their young faces when he had to refuse. He made it up to them as best he could by practising shooting with them, and playing football and baseball to which they had introduced him – he had proved to be an apt pupil. Still, the problem would soon be solved with school starting.

For a young single man with money in his pocket Richmond was now the place to be. Every fortnight an 'undress military review' was staged. Thousands of people attended these, the military bands played non-stop. Richard had heard 'Dixieland' so many times that he could now sing it by heart. It was a great tune and was as popular in the North as in the South. Richard was surprised to learn that it was written by a northerner. Members of the Cabinet, heads of bureau and Generals from the front mingled with the crowds. People pointed out to Richard men such as Generals Johnston, Longstreet, the blonde giant John Bell Hood and the bearded J.E.B. (Beauty) Stuart, amongst others.

Clara and Amelia were hard taskmistresses. Richard now had to give a summary of his activities – almost hour by hour. As he was forbidden to keep a diary remembering every detail was difficult. Every morning, afternoon and evening had to be accounted for. He complained to the girls. "We know it's difficult. You were chosen because you were considered capable of doing this difficult job. And that is why you are well paid," responded Amelia. This is what Colonel Wilmer had said to him. He had no answer to it.

Evenings spent at home were frowned on unless a good reason was given – such as Mrs Smythe was entertaining and therefore he may be seeing people that could be of some interest. When Richard was not following specific assignments, he was expected to be going out, meeting and observing people and reporting back to Clara and Amelia.

It had been made clear to Richard in Washington by Colonel Wilmer in no uncertain terms that the Federal Government paid by results. He could be called back to Washington and dismissed at any time with no reason being given. The possible circumstances outlined were that his cover had been 'blown', or he had just been in Richmond for too long and had become too familiar with everybody. Before the war young men without any obvious form of occupation would not have aroused suspicion but now they were conspicuous. He would obviously be recalled once they had been satisfied that his work had been done, or if he was just idle or ineffectual.

Not that going out in Richmond was any hardship. The city seethed with every kind of interest, vice and activity. Soldiers on leave had money to spend and little time in which to spend it. They had either been in action, were about to go into action or both. Everywhere amongst civilians and soldiers the attitude pervaded - 'Live and enjoy today because tomorrow you might be dead.'

One of the evenings planned by Clara and Amelia was a visit to a casino. The girls kept reminding Richard of Colonel Wilmer's instructions not to go anywhere without his Colt.36 calibre-less cumbersome than the massive.44."This is not provincial England, Richard. Richmond is now a violent city and you might as well be without your gun as without your pants."

The fact that his shooting had left Mrs Smythe less than impressed had made a deeper impression on Richard than he cared to admit. His male pride at being out shot by a woman had been seriously hurt. The incident had also emphasized the fact that danger was now a daily visitor. He had continued his practice regularly- with either hand - and had become a reasonable shot.

When Richard first arrived in Richmond the violence to which the Colonel referred was not noticeable. The battles were still raging, and citizens were too busy dealing with the dead and wounded or with the threat of invasion to bother with crime. Soldiers were engaged in battle or other official activity. Those people who entered Richmond did so for a purpose.

Now, not only had the criminals, gamblers and prostitutes re-emerged to ply their various professions but there was the added evil of the drunken soldier on leave. The offenders were not those who came home to visit their families but those who were stationed in camps near Richmond who arrived in large groups for short spells. Many of them were simple farm boys who had never before been more than ten miles from home. Temptation loomed large for these lads who arrived in sizeable groups in a city like Richmond ,with money in their pockets. Often, they became the victims of crime themselves, being beaten up and robbed.

Richard made his way along the shady avenues. The warm dusk was gathering fast. Lights were now blazing. Loud, jarring piano music jangled out from open doors of saloons. He could see crowds of soldiers – mostly in shabby uniforms – downing large glasses of beer or measures of whisky. He quickly stepped aside as one inebriate was quickly pulled out on the street by two companions. The man crouched down on the ground and immediately vomited.

As Richard rounded a corner he collided with a soldier that was leading a rabble of about ten others. "Cocksucker!" exclaimed the man.

"Sorry" said Richard and stepped aside

"Say sorry" snarled the ruffian who was unsteady on his feet. Even by the current standards his uniform(such as it was) looked scruffy. Most men at least tried to keep their clothes clean. His was stained and dirty as though he couldn't be bothered. Richard knew enough about the Confederate Army by now to judge that the officers in charge of this man must be sloppy.

"I've said sorry. I didn't see you coming!"

"Well say it again cocksucking sonafabitch." He turned to his companions. "Say, he talks kind of funny. Where's you from? You a furriner? Richard was now becoming reasonably familiar with the different shades of the southern accent. He judged that this man was probably from Alabama. Probably illiterate, and from the sort of background contemptuously referred to by Negroes as well as superior whites as 'white trash'.

Richard was now seriously worried. The other men began to crowd round him. He could see they were all very much the worse for drink. That would give him a distinct advantage. The best thing would be not to instigate any action because that would bring certain retaliation but he had to be ready. His fingers curled round the handle of his Colt which was inside his jacket. He would try and talk to them as long as necessary.

"I'm from England."

"Why you dressed so fine? And why aren't you in the Army? You some kind of yeller belly?"

For some time now Richard had realised that he was becoming increasingly noticeable because of his lack of uniform. Nearly all men of his age were in the Army or Navy. People openly asked him why he was in civilian dress. Most of them were satisfied that he was English but there were still those who thought that foreigners should not be exempt from conscription. He had mentioned this fact to Clara and Amelia. He had left England to join the Union Army. He was determined not to finish up being drafted into an Army that supported slavery.

"Don't worry. They have enough to do at the moment without that." Clara assured him. "Besides, foreigners are needed here for all sorts of reasons." Despite this encouragement Richard was increasingly noticing resentment – either implied or openly voiced.

Now Richard tried to pass. The spokesman stepped nearer. Richard could not move without touching him. "Give me your money." Richard now had a reason to act. There was no way he could extricate himself from this situation peacefully. He had been taught self-defence in Washington where he had usefully built on the rudiments he had learnt from the militia in Hereford, which had held its summer camps on Broomy Hill. He and his friends had spent many hours watching activities and had been invited to participate in certain things-including self-defence. He felt confident. The man was taller than he but looked thin and poorly fed. He was also very drunk.

Richard's left hand was now firmly gripped round the butt of his Colt. He smashed his knee in the spokesman's groin. The man screamed and fell forward clutching his testicles. Richard now brought his right hand up flattened like a plate and smacked the edge across the man's throat. The man crumpled to the ground. Richard being right-handed now quickly changed the Colt from his left to his right hand and immediately jumped into the roadway, just avoiding an oncoming carriage.

"Watch where the hell you're going you crazy

sonofabitch!" yelled the driver.

The carriage had given Richard valuable time and enabled him to put distance between himself and the other men whose movements were dulled by drink – also their main concern was for their friend who was inert on the ground. They stood round him looking stupid and ineffectual. Richard fired a shot over their heads and ran. People saw what was going on but such sights were familiar now in Richmond,particularly where soldiers were concerned.

Nobody in the vicinity wanted to become involved. It could result in becoming injured or entangled with the authorities who might just ask awkward questions about one's own activities.

Richard ducked into an alleyway and snaked through various streets – he now knew the geography of Richmond well. He stopped in a doorway to recover his breath – and he did not want to arrive at the casino in a lather of sweat. That would cause suspicion. He did not know as to whether or not he had killed the man. The swipe across the throat could have broken his neck – not that anybody would bother too much. Drunken soldiers were often being killed in accidents or brawls.

Richard would be safe at the casino. The security on the door was good. Drunken, tattered soldiers – whether they had a genuine grievance or not – would never get near the place. After a few minutes he walked quickly, looking straight ahead of him until he reached the casino. Two armed doormen searched him and took his Colt from him. "You'll have to check your gun in. Tempers tend to become frayed in casinos." Amelia had advised.

Richard looked round him. A number of people , including Mrs Smythe, Clara and Amelia had told him that Richmond had totally changed in character from a busy provincial capital, to resemble the wild frontier towns such as San Francisco that were springing up in the West. Richmond, being the capital of the whole Confederacy now drew everybody like a magnet. Traders and businessmen wanted contracts from the government to supply items such as clothing, footwear or beef. Builders, bricklayers, carpenters, engineers and other artisans were in great demand - particularly those involved in the railroads.

Buildings and railroads were always being erected, extended or renewed and the constant destruction by the enemy had to be made good, and the Government had lucrative contracts to hand out. Lobbying and bribery were rife.

Soldiers who had been in battle, or had been riding raids with J.E.B. Stuart, or had spent months holed up in water batteries off the Mississippi, had accumulated earnings which they had not had the opportunity to spend. They would rectify that in Richmond where there was a lot of money to be spent in such a short time. Cries of recognition rang out as old comrades were recognised.

Men sat with large cigars jammed in their mouths or chewed tobacco, occasionally leaning over to gob in the spittoons which liberally adorned the floor. Tables of various kinds made it difficult to move. Waitresses in low-cut and low-backed evening dresses or with legs just encased in tights brought round drinks and gambling chips. They made an impression on these men, many of whom hadn't seen a reasonable looking woman for months.

Cards slapped down on tables, ivory chips and dice rattled. Conversation round the tables was limited to cryptic and spare phrases such as "see you", "raise you a hundred" or "that's me cleaned out."

Inflation was worsening daily. Richard was glad he had been paid in gold which was secured in a belt strapped round his waist. Clara and Amelia paid him regularly. People with gold could live like kings and he was told not to be extravagant. Each day the Confederate Treasury desperately ground out its bank notes as the paper money daily sank in value. A hotel room in Richmond now cost one dollar in gold and twenty dollars in Confederate bills, whilst a suit of clothes paid for in Confederate bills cost ten times one paid for in gold.

A beautiful young quadroon in a red low-cut shimmering dress with a pink flower in her dark hair suddenly appeared at Richard's side, carrying a glass of whisky on a tray and offered it to him.

"I didn't order this."

"It's been ordered for you. Take it." Bewildered, Richard took it and thanked the girl who swished off on another errand.

"I don't believe it!" Richard swivelled round to see the speaker of those angry words. He was a large man with straggly side-whiskers. A grubby, yellow waistcoat strained across his bulging belly. At the other side of the table a small quiet man with a green shade over his forehead leaned forward and raked in a heap of chips.

"One last chance", pleaded Yellow Waistcoat.

"Nope. You've got nothin' left." The laconic Green Shade didn't even look at him but just chewed on tobacco.

"Oh please!" The plea had now lifted into the higher pitch of a whine. "I'll stake my horse, this watch, this ring and my gold claim in California." Yellow Waistcoat slowly and painfully wiggled off a large gold signet ring from his podgy finger and banged it on the table. He then fumbled with his waistcoat until he finally placed his watch and chain on the table with the grudging determination and concentration of one who is worse for drink.

Yellow Waistcoat then drew out a tattered envelope from the inside pocket of his coat and slapped it down on the table. "There's the deed to my gold claim." Other games had stopped. There was now a large gathering round the table which was littered with chips, cards, glasses, tobacco and slops of spilt drink glistening in the subdued light.

The expressionless Green Shade turned his head aside and spat,still chewing,"Where's the deeds to the horse?", The audience sniggered.

Yellow Waistcoat barked "Pen and Paper". These were provided. With his tongue slightly protruding from his mouth he slowly and laboriously wrote in large, round childish handwriting, and then banged the pen down on the table and slid the paper across to Green Shade who picked it up and read.

"I, Herbert Waller hereby authorise Franklins Stables to hand over the bay gelding known as 'Worthy' to the bearer of this paper."

The game started. Green Shade's white parchment of a face was still devoid of any kind of movement whilst in contrast Yellow Waistcoat was sweating and breathing hard. Eventually, Green Shade fanned out a spread of cards on the table showing three aces and two kings.

Yellow Waistcoat was now shaking. "It's rigged!" he shouted and slumped on his chair. Meanwhile Green Shade noiselessly gathered up the paper, deeds, watch and ring. Yellow Waistcoat put his head in his hands on the table and started to sob. Richard felt quite sorry for him. Somebody tapped on his shoulder and he turned to see a short, insignificant man holding two glasses of whisky. He handed one to Richard who had just put down his empty glass.

"Now you see the results of gambling. Mary

Felmingham doesn't want you to do it but she doesn't mind the odd glass of whisky. "Surprised, Richard took the glass.

"Tomorrow, you will be accompanying Mrs Smythe to a dance in support of 'clothing for soldiers'. You will meet Rose Greenhow and her new assistant,Kate Turner." The man spoke in a low mutter.

Richard felt a frisson of excitement. He would meet Kate Turner at last. The girls had not told him that she was working for Rose. Perhaps that was something else 'he did not need to know'. It was true that he had not mentioned to them that he had met Kate but they probably knew anyway. They seemed to know everything.

The man took a long swig from his glass and continued his low mutter.

"You won't be able to miss Kate Turner. She has bright red hair. Engage them in a little conversation. Remember, be pleasant, listen don't tell them much and don't express opinions. Just come over as a young English boy who is nice but a bit naive. You will receive instructions at a later date. I'm going now. Leave in ten minutes time. Don't take part in any games. You are safe from your attackers. You did good work there. The man isn't dead but if he was, it wouldn't have mattered too much. His friends have taken him back to camp."

Richard knew better than to ask the man how he knew all that. Anyway, he had no chance. The man disappeared into the heavy, smoky air.

Chapter Seventeen

Richmond

September 1862

Elizabeth Van Lew sat writing at her desk. Her maid quietly brought in breakfast and laid it down on the small table at the side. Mary knew better than to disturb her mistress when she was working. They understood each other. Mary had been taught to read and write. This was not unknown although the law expressly forbade it. Owners were restricted by the law as to how their slaves were occupied. Before the war Elizabeth had been fined when one of her slaves had been found travelling without a pass. The constraint on education was an area which did intrude on the household of a forward – thinking owner.

The official view was that if slaves were educated this would give them ideas above their station and could lead to rebellions more sustained and controlled than the isolated revolts on individual plantations. These amounted to little more than unplanned surges of resentment and were easily crushed. Illiterate slaves from different plantations could not communicate and organise effective, cohesive action.

However, the more progressive families did not believe in promoting ignorance and realised that emancipation must come at some time in the future and ignored the law, and the practice of employing educated slaves as tutors to owners' children was becoming more common.

The world would not allow their'peculiar institution' to last for ever and what would happen when millions of illiterate, untrained slaves were suddenly freed and for the first time became responsible for themselves and their own upkeep? Lessons had to be learned from the freeing of the slaves in the British colonies. Slavery had shackled their minds as well as their bodies. The basics of life had been provided and when suddenly they had to take care of themselves and their families many found the transition very difficult.

Mary had been born as a slave on John Van Lew's plantation. When she was very young members of her family were sold to other owners and she never saw them again. When John died Mary was freed by Elizabeth, and then worked for her as a paid servant. Elizabeth, realising Mary's intelligence sent her to be educated at the Quaker School for Negroes in Philadelphia. When Mary returned to Richmond she was arrested for breaking the law which forbade blacks to return to Virginia after having left to be educated. Mary protested that she had not been given her freedom but had only been allowed to go away on a visit and was returned to the keeping of Elizabeth. Mary Bowser was to become a vital part of Elizabeth's spy ring.

Elizabeth and her mother refused a request from a delegation of women to sew clothes and banners for the Confederacy in the early days of the war. The delegation knew that help would be unlikely to be forthcoming but this was a test to force the Van Lews to show their true loyalties.

Elizabeth put down her pen as her mother entered the room. Eliza Van Lew was a handsome, well-preserved woman in her mid-sixties. She carried herself with dignity and was always well-dressed. Indeed, her daughter's lack of care in her appearance constantly irritated her. "It makes them think I'm madder than I already am. They're less likely to take me seriously"-

was the tenor of her normal reply when chided by her mother.

Eliza realised that her daughter was deep in thought. " You look very pensive- is something troubling you ?."

"You know, Mother, I wish we had been more subtle and not made our opinions so well-known before the war. We would have been more acceptable to society and more useful in obtaining inside information."

"Subtle! You are as subtle as a charging herd of buffaloes. You can never keep your views to yourself. You are much too open for that. I am more discreet." They both laughed. They knew what Eliza said was true.

"Anyway, we are not just Yankee sympathisers. We are Yankees. Everybody knows that. They know I am from Philadelphia and that you went to school there and that we freed our slaves. In fact, you could say that we would be more suspected if, as Yankees we had vociferously supported the South and joined the sock-sewing circles. And John's exemption on medical grounds has made us even greater pariahs. Some families are encouraging their sons to enlist no matter how unfit they are. Look at poor Richard Bury! He can't see without his glasses, he looks as though a puff of wind would blow him away, yet his father made him join up." Eliza helped herself to a cup of the poor substitute coffee and sat down on the settee.

"He's not much of a specimen I agree. What was his mother thinking about? She should have stopped it."

"She was as much for it as the father. You know what these Confederate women are like they are crazier than the men! What these people don't know of course is that we're actively working for the Yankees. Nobody can prove anything."

258

Elizabeth frowned. "They don't have to. They could just slap us in Castle Thunder."

"Well, they haven't yet and they have to be very careful about doing things like that to people like us." Come on Elizabeth start your breakfast. Don't let it get cold. You won't be helping the cause by starving to death."

"Like those boys in Libby Prison."

"Both you and I are doing a great job in helping them. And to keep on helping them you have to keep your strength up. We've got a great team together. Have you had the latest report on that young Englishman?"

"Richard Clarke. Yes. I read it before breakfast. Clara and Amelia are doing an excellent job with him. Contact was made with him last night in the casino. I arranged that." As luck would have it he was accosted by drunken soldiers on his way to the casino and acquitted himself really well."

"Did you 'arrange' that as well Elizabeth?" Elizabeth smiled.

"No. Not this time. I had heard he had not been that impressive when he and Susan Smythe were attacked but she is a crack shot and her standards are high. But he has been practising since and he really is quite good now. He's meeting Rose Greenhow and Kate Turner at the dance tonight. Mary Chesnut will be there as well. She is bound to spill some background information which will be useful to Clarke. You know she always talks to everybody about everything."

"Of course I do. You know I can't stand her. She is so opinionated and pretentious. She is always making classical allusions to the Greeks, Romans and Spartans. The other day she referred to Helen of Troy and poor old Abe Leaford said he did not think he had met her and asked where she lived." Elizabeth had difficulty in swallowing her coffee. She plonked the cup down and shook with laughter. Eventually, she managed to put her cup down.

"Well, putting Abe and Mary together is going from the sublime to the ridiculous. Poor old Abe can barely write his name. The only thing he can do is make money."

"Well if you can only do one thing making money is not a bad choice." Commented Eliza. "Anyway, pretentious or not you and Mary will never get on. She is a committed Southerner. What I can never understand though is that she hates slavery. It doesn't make sense!"

"Mother! Let's not go through all that again. You know we never agree. Many Southerners hate slavery but would never take up arms against their homeland. And when you say it doesn't make sense. Nothing in this war makes sense."

Elizabeth had built up a very efficient network of espionage which started before the war. Early in the war she had arranged visits to prisons which had begun as mere acts of kindness to the Yankees who had been taken prisoner at Bull Run. At that stage of the war very little thought had been given to the housing and care of prisoners. Then suddenly the Confederate Government was faced with the problem of dealing with thousands of men who had to be incarcerated, guarded and fed.

Large warehouses and other suitable buildings were commandeered and had to be quickly converted into prisons. The warehouse belonging to the Libby Brothers who carried on a ships chandlery and grocery business was situated in Tobacco Row and now housed some seven hundred prisoners who were crammed into six large dark rooms.

Elizabeth, together with a small number of Christian citizens of Richmond expressed sympathy for these fellow Americans who, after all, were only serving their country and who were sons, husbands, fathers and brothers in the same way as the Confederates. She requested permission from the commandant of Libby Prison to be able to visit the inmates and bring them small comforts. Her compassion concealed other motives.

To add to the many conundrums of this war the commandant was Lieutenant David Todd who not only had strong anti-Northern views but just happened to be the half- brother of Mary Lincoln. Elizabeth asked Todd for access on the grounds of Christian charity and humanity. Todd refused. She then adopted the more pragmatic approach which was that if Federal prisoners were treated worse than cattle what sort of treatment could the Southerners expect?

When it appeared that Todd's lack of concern for his fellow countrymen equalled his callous indifference towards the Yankee prisoners Elizabeth knew she had to try elsewhere. Elizabeth was always one to start at the top and thought about the Confederate Secretary to the Treasury-Christopher Memminger whom she had met on a number of occasions. He was a devout Lutheran who had arrived from Germany with his widowed mother at the age of twelve. He found himself orphaned shortly afterwards when his mother died of Yellow Fever but had been adopted by a family who had sent the bright boy to law school.

She didn't even try to make an appointment and walked into his office where he was sitting alone. As always he was dapper and clean-shaven which revealed his strong jaw. Being a civil man he stood up, smiled and shook Elizabeth by the hand.

Straight to the point as always Elizabeth explained

the reason for her visit. Memminger looked stern. "I hardly think that men such as that are worthy of the attention of a lady such as yourself." He still spoke with the traces of a German accent. She was expecting this sort of response and was ready for it.

"You remember the time shortly before the war that you gave a discourse at that religious convention. It was such a beautiful talk." Memminger beamed seraphically.

"Oh yes. I remember every word of it, I'm so glad you liked it."

"Do you remember what you said about charity?"

Memminger put his hands together. "I said that love was the fulfilling of the law, and if we wished 'our cause' to succeed, we must begin with charity to the thankless, the unworthy ......" His words trailed off and his smiled faded as he realised that Elizabeth's gimlet eyes were boring into him, her chin protruding.

"Precisely."

Memminger shuffled in his seat and put his hands up as though in submission. "Alright Elizabeth, I concede your point. What do you wish me to do specifically?"

"Arrange for me to meet General Winder." Two minutes later Elizabeth left the room holding a note of introduction to General Winder.

Eliza looked meaningfully at her daughter when she recounted her visit to Memminger. "You remembered what I said about honey and vinegar then- honey attracts , vinegar repels. You used flattery. Flattery always works on men. Their egos are so big they never see any motive behind it. Use it on Winder. Be a sunflower Elizabeth. Not a snapdragon!" They both smiled. Behind Eliza's quietness lay a shrewd and nimble mind which enabled her to make her point very

262

effectively and without causing offence.

General Winder had been an instructor at West Point and had taught President Davis who had remembered his old tutor and on the outbreak of war had appointed him Brigadier General and Provost Marshal, which ranks did not reflect Winder's ability. In an army which had to be created from nothing, anybody with any previous military experience rose very rapidly. During the relatively short time that he had held the post Winder had succeeded in making himself more hated than most Yankees.

"Of course he is second-rate." Elizabeth had heard a loyal southerner say at one of the few social functions she attended. If he was any good he'd be out there fighting the Yankees. They only ever put the dregs in charge of prisons." From what Elizabeth had heard of Winder she had to agree with that statement.

Winder had come from a background of privileged mediocrity. His father had been a general in the war of 1812 and had managed to transform the battle of Bladensburg from certain victory for the Americans into a crushing defeat by the British who had begun from an inferior position with a smaller force. They then marched into Washington and burned it – including the Capitol the rebuilding of which had been interrupted by the present war.

Incompetence in some people leads to their being promoted to a position which is superior but where they can do less harm. So it was with Winder Senior. He was appointed to a leading post at West Point (to which his son owed his teaching appointment) and when Washington was rebuilt there was even a building named after him.

When Davis gave Winder Junior his appointments it was clear that he had inherited the inadequacies of his father. He was the prototype of a man who had been promoted beyond his abilities. He had recruited a number of men who were mainly Yankees and that fact alone made them unpopular. If civilians were required to do tasks such as repair roads or build bridges Winder's 'plug –uglies'- as they were called - abducted them at gunpoint. Many of his arrests were overturned and a number of prosecutions failed. Rumour had it that he would soon be replaced.

In addition to prisons, Winder had the responsibility for fixing prices. These were often too low and many farmers who were already in dire financial straits faced ruin. One farmer who ran a large family farm had the temerity to criticise Winder in a letter to the local newspaper. One night, whilst drinking in the Exchange Bar he was arrested at gunpoint and carted off to a disgusting old factory in Cary Street where Winder imprisoned those whom he considered to be 'undesirable'.

The introductory note given by Memminger was no guarantee that Elizabeth would have any success in her mission. She wasn't looking forward to meeting Winder. In addition to his other attributes he had a filthy temper and regarded women with contempt. The only facet about his personality which gave her any hope at all was that he was corrupt.

When she entered the building Elizabeth immediately began to have doubts. A number of dishevelled men whom she took to be Winder's 'detectives' sat slumped on benches behind a counter. They looked at Elizabeth. One unshaven lout dug another in the ribs, whispered something and they both sniggered. Two slovenly clerks appeared not to be very busy. They were arguing in a particularly unpleasant and aggressive manner; one was drinking beer; the other was chewing tobacco. After five minutes of being totally ignored Elizabeth rapped the desk with her umbrella. Chewer spat into a spittoon. "Yeah?"

Elizabeth announced that she had an appointment with the Provost Marshall. "Take a seat," decreed Chewer and immediately resumed arguing with Drinker. As she waited she witnessed a trail of people with pleas- some of them tearfully asking about the fate of their relatives. A man who had an appointment before her complained when it was more than an hour overdue. Chewer looked up.

"Your appointment's cancelled. Come back next week." The man began to protest. "Get him out of here" ,ordered Chewer laconically to the thugs who hustled him down the stairs. Elizabeth knew better than to say anything. In the last few months she had seen the effects of a small amount of authority on men of limited intelligence and poor character who now considered themselves masters of the very little they surveyed. However, Elizabeth had been born into a family that was not used to being treated with contempt neither did she have the personality to tolerate it. Her appointment was some forty–five minutes overdue when Chewer stood up and announced to the world. "I'm going to go take a shit!" and slouched out of the room

That was enough! Elizabeth strode to the counter. Drinker was sitting with his head on his chest, the beer bottle dangling by his side, saliva dribbled from his mouth down his unwashed, unshaven chin..She rapped the counter again with her umbrella, flinching at the fetid breath. Drinker opened one eye. "My appointment was forty-five minutes ago. I have a letter of introduction from the Confederate Secretary Memminger to the Provost Marshall. If you don't go into his office within two minutes to tell him I'm here I will have no alternative to report the matter to the Confederate Secretary and tell him that the Provost

Marshall's underlings have been discourteous, and drunk. If the Provost Marshall decides he is too busy to see me then that is his decision. Not yours."

This seemed to have an effect on Drinker who stumbled to his feet and shuffled away. He returned immediately. "The Provost Marshall will see you now Ma'am."

Elizabeth had heard that Winder was sixty. He looked seventy. He slumped in his chair. His uniform coat was open and large folds of belly flopped over the top of his trousers. He stank of booze, tobacco and lack of washing. Uncombed, unkempt white hair contrasted with his florid, red face. Dandruff liberally dappled his shoulders. His bulbous filmy eyes glared at Elizabeth suspiciously as she sat down without being invited. His mouth appeared to be fixed in a permanent sulk.

"What do you want?" Elizabeth put her case. "Why do you want to waste your time with Yankee scum? They are the enemy. Let them rot in jail. The more that die there the better. It'll solve the overcrowding problems."

Elizabeth had heard from a number of sources that Winder had two major weaknesses amongst a myriad of others. One was vanity (extraordinary from this slob of a man) the other was greed. She also knew better than to plead humanity and Christian duty but put the argument that bad treatment by Southerners could result in reciprocal behaviour by the Federals. Winder was taken off guard. He had not heard this argument before. He did not look convinced but seemed to be thinking of an answer and sat silent and glowering. Now was the time for Elizabeth to play her trump card.

She sat back and smiled. "Your hair would adorn the Temple of Janus. It looks out of place here." Irony and sarcasm were lost on Winder. The slit of a mouth grudgingly struggled into a grimace which she supposed was a smile. She then slid a small cloth bag across the table to Winder. He held it upside down. Gold coins tumbled onto the table. He counted them. The grimace momentarily widened into a sort of a leer and then vanished. Without a further word he grabbed a piece of paper, scratched a few lines and shoved it towards Elizabeth. It was an order to Todd to give her and her mother unlimited visiting rights to Libby Prison. "Thank you." She said. Winder grunted. She managed to keep her face expressionless until she reached the street when she heaved a sigh of relief. Now the most vital stage of her work could begin.

Chapter Eighteen

Richmond

September 1862

The morning following the night in the casino Richard tried to show no surprise when, at breakfast, Mrs Smythe announced that they had been invited to a dance that evening in support of the hospitals for wounded soldiers in Richmond. Like many of these fund-raising events it had been arranged very quickly. After the fear and panic of The Battles of the Seven Days in June a sense of relief had settled on Richmond. For the time being the enemy had been driven back. Lee's victory at Second Manassas (or Bull Run) had increased his standing in the South to one of near deity. Nobody called him 'Granny Lee' any longer.

The tempo of life in Richmond had now become very hectic. Tension still pervaded the air but it now appeared in the form of frenetic gaiety rather than worried strain. Lee had announced "My boys must be entertained" and there were plenty of young women ready to entertain them. They rushed from their sewing circles, bandage-rolling, lint-scraping and hospital duties to 'danceable teas', dinners, balls and dances.

Richard sat in the hall waiting for Mrs Smythe to come down. Eventually she rustled down the stairs in a rose-pink evening gown which harmonized well with her dark complexion. Her emerald and diamond necklace sparkled. She gave Richard her arm as they walked down the front steps to the carriage. Richard enjoyed having the pressure of the arm of this beautiful sophisticated woman on his own. She now did not seem like the same woman who had ridden like a cavalryman, shot like a crack marksman and berated him for his poor shooting when she had made him feel like an inadequate schoolboy being scolded by his mother.

Now she was charming and witty which made him feel charming and witty-a sort of sophisticated protector. He handed her into the carriage and waited whilst she arranged her large dress. He rapped on the roof and the two Kentucky blood horses stepped out. Lee had bought time. The frantic evacuations and requisitioning of June were over. Carriages and horses were now being used again for social outings.

The early evening was warm and beautiful with the sky just beginning to pink with the setting of the sun. The air was heavy with the scent of magnolia. Fuchsia bushes showered their magenta and scarlet bells over white walls. Jessamine dangled from trellises. The feeling of calmness and plenty seemed unreal to Richard after the terrible scenes he had witnessed a few weeks earlier. He had an eerie sense of foreboding, of the lull before the gathering storm. Mrs Smythe did not give him much time for these reflections.

"My cousin, Rose Greenhow will be there. She had just been released by the Yankees who treated her abominably by all accounts. I should have seen her before now but there just hasn't been the opportunity. We have just both been so busy but we have sent each other notes." Richard said nothing. Wilmer had said to him. "If anybody mentions a 'sensitive subject' say nothing they will usually not think about it and just talk blithely on."

So it was now with Mrs Smythe. "You remember Kate Turner – that red-haired girl that you saw at the barbecue?" She looked at Richard meaningfully.

This required an answer, "I----'m not certain that I

do." Richard replied after having given the matter some thought. Mrs Smythe was not going to let him get away with that.

"You know. You asked me about her."

Richard looked thoughtful. "Oh. I do think I remember her now."

Mrs Smythe found it impossible to conceal a smile and turned her face towards the carriage window. She knew the interest that the boy had shown in Kate was not just idle curiosity. Why did he not just admit it? Well, he was English. That must explain it. She had always heard that the English were reserved and the few English people that she had met had given her no reason to disagree with that view. If a Southern boy liked a girl he made no secret of the fact.

"Well, anyway she will be there. Oh. You will also meet Mary Chesnut. She is part of the fabric of Richmond society. I like her but not everybody does. She is a great talker. Some people find her overbearing and pushy. She also tends to air her knowledge. She is a great friend of Varina Davis. The general opinion is that she is disappointed in her husband's achievements. She would have liked him to have risen high in the Army. He had the ability. He did very well at Sumter and First Bull Run and there was also talk of him being appointed to the London or Paris mission. Mary would have loved that." Her flow was interrupted for a moment when the carriage swerved to avoid an ambulance. There was certain amount of jostling and the coachman had to say a few words of calm to the horses. Mrs Smythe continued.

"The trouble is that Mary has always complained that James is too much an old-fashioned South Carolinian gentleman to push on his own behalf. She had tried to do his pushing for him but he won't hear of it. At the moment he has some post involving the military affairs of South Carolina. It seems a messy and thankless task. There is however talk of him being appointed as an aide to Jeff Davis."

The carriage turned into a huge military encampment which had previously been a field. Richard could see rows and rows of tents and huts in the distance. A guard stopped them and talked to the coachman. They jolted over the clumpy ground and halted. The coachman put the drag on the coach and came round to pull down the steps on Mrs Smythe's side and opened the door. Meanwhile, Richard had walked round to help her down, making sure that her wide dress did not become caught or torn. Fortunately, the ground was hard after the dry weather so there was no danger of it becoming stained with mud.

They made their way to the sound of the military band playing the ubiquitous 'Dixie'. Richard knew the words of this by heart together with those of 'Lorena' and 'Bonnie Blue Flag'. He was to hear these pieces of music together with many other patriotic favourites over and over again this evening.

No detail had been spared in preparing the event. After all, when an Army is putting on a show free labour is never in short supply. An open-air dancing area had been prepared with a wooden floor. Chinese lanterns had been placed in the surrounding trees and on the outside of the huge marquee where dancing would also be held.

As they entered the marquee Richard marvelled at the energy and planning which had been expended on this event during a time of emergency and potential siege – even if there had been a temporary respite. Evergreens festooned the interior together with garlands of flowers which had been expertly arranged. Although the price of food was still high, the city was free of famine. Many women had returned to their plantations or farms during the summer months. Although there had been insufficient labour to support much of a harvest there had been a good deal of production of beef, pork, mutton, poultry, eggs and dairy produce.

Even so, Richard was amazed at the delicacies attractively laid out on the crowded tables. A poultry table was laden with goose, wild turkey, partridge and quails as well as the usual chicken and duck. The next table groaned under vegetables, salads and all meats including venison. Fish, sweets and cheese abounded. Queues were forming early so that the dancing and socialising could make an early start.

Soldiers in immaculate grey uniforms stood behind the tables helping the guests to food whilst others circled with all kinds of drinks and buckets of ice.

Mrs Smythe voiced Richard's thoughts. "This is all lovely Richard but it doesn't seem right that my poor husband and all those other poor boys in the field are hungry whilst we have all this plenty." Richard had yet to meet Mrs Smythe's husband and doubted he ever would. He was out in Mississippi. She looked at Richard. He wasn't paying attention to her. His mind and certainly his eyes were elsewhere. She smiled to herself. It was not difficult to see why.

Richard had never seen so many beautiful girls in one place in all his life. Crinolines spread like mushrooms from wasp-like waists. Flowers nestled in perfectly coiffured hair, low necklines and bare arms and shoulders abounded. Jewels sparked against slender white throats and from shapely fingers which it was difficult to imagine had during the last year been employed in unaccustomed work such as endless sewing, hospital duties and labours on farms and plantations.

Many of these girls were now leaning on the arms of

gold-braided, brass-buttoned, epauletted sword-belted manhood. Eyes were locked in rapturous gazes and and there was already surreptitious kissing. A few decorously wounded men with arms in slings were assiduously waited on by adoring wives, girl-friends or sisters. Horribly disfigured men were nowhere to be seen. Tonight's event was to boost morale as well as funds. No tattered or scruffy uniforms were in sight. If a man could not find a reasonable uniform then his attendance was not required.

Richard heard a voice behind him. "You know what Mrs Roger Prior said the other day- 'The soldier dances with the lady of his love at night and on the morrow dances in the deadly trenches of the line.'"

They swivelled round. Richard saw a smallish, plumpish woman, probably in her early forties. "Mary!" Exclaimed Mrs Smythe. "That's an outrageous thing to say! Even for you! Particularly at an event such as this." Richard had to agree. The remark was in extremely poor taste.

"I didn't initiate it. Mrs Roger Pryor did." The woman smiled mischievously. She had a lively intelligent face and eyes that sparked with interest and humour.

"Well, you don't have to repeat it." Mrs Smythe was mollified but still slightly irritated. "I accept, Mary, that your brain acts fast but unfortunately your mouth acts even faster. The first needs to control the second."

"Come now Susan. I'm sorry .She looked anything but sorry." Introduce me to this handsome young man He doesn't look as though he's from here. His clothes are not shabby enough." Smiling, despite herself Mrs Smythe introduced Richard.

"Oh. You're English!"

"I'm afraid so!" Richard could not help laughing. This busy little woman appeared to be as amusing as she was outrageous. Her personality radiated a magnetism which was irresistible.

"I hope you read Mr Clarke."

"Sometimes".

"England is producing some marvellous writers at the moment. Thackeray's 'Henry Esmond' is his best in my view although most people prefer Vanity Fair. The portrayal of unrequited love is brilliant although Esmond's attraction for his beloved's mother and subsequent marriage to her I find particularly revolting. I think that Trollope in 'Castle Richmond' treats his elderly lady in love much better. Have you read either of those?"

"I've read 'Esmond'. I think his treatment of the period and his description of Esmond's life in Marlborough's army is particularly fine."

"Oh you men! You're all so fascinated by war and armies. Anyway you've got plenty of that here at the moment. Do you read Dickens? I met Dickens you know when he gave one of his readings in New York. His reading of poor Nancy's death was electric. But I didn't like his views of America expressed in 'Martin Chuzzlewit.' Do you read Lamb, George Elliott or Charles Kingsley? And you don't happen to have any of the English reviews do you? I used to have them all – Blackwoods, Atlantic, Harper's, Cornhill. I wasted my last subscription money. Everything stopped with Fort Sumter."

"Mary! Let the poor boy answer one question at a time."

Richard stepped aside to allow a large, beribboned, purple-faced brigadier – general pass through. The man appeared arrogant, aggressive and capable of pushing anybody who didn't move away quickly enough. Richard took an instant dislike to him. "Yes, I have read all the authors you mentioned but not all their works. I am afraid that I do not have any of the reviews."

"I didn't think you would but it was worth a try. We must talk books sometime. We obviously have a love of reading in common. I see, Susan that neither Winder's manners nor his appearance have improved since his appointment. If he doesn't explode through temper his gut will do it for him. They say he eats non-stop and he's a real sponge for wine and port! And he never pays for anything now. 'Windbag' would be a better name for him. He's full of his self-importance."

Mrs Smythe had to put her glass down on a nearby table to stop spilling it through laughing. "Really, Mary you do me good. I haven't seen you for a while. I've been feeling rather down the last few days. You're a great cure for depression!" She turned to Richard who was looking on in quiet amusement. "That is our revered Provost- Marshall. He's probably more disliked in Richmond than Lincoln. Mary, I'm longing to see Rose Greenhow. She'll be here tonight. I haven't seen her since the Yankees released her. I've heard she doesn't look at all well."

"Well, I'm not surprised. The poor woman has been kept imprisoned for months. For over a week she had to keep her doors open whilst sentinels guarded her day and night. She couldn't even undress or go to sleep in privacy whilst soldiers tramped about and sniggered. I know she's beautiful but no woman wants to be gaped at whilst she's at her toilette. She says she was worse used than Marie Antoinette who had a letter snatched from her bosom."

Richard agreed with Mrs Smythe's view expressed in the coach that Mary Chesnut displayed her knowledge unnecessarily. Anybody who did not know anything about history or literature would not have a clue as to what she was talking about.

It also seemed to Richard that Rose had fared much better than Marie Antoinette who had lost her head. Considering that Rose was responsible for the defeat of the Federals at Bull Run (or First Manassas) as these Confederates insisted on calling it she had been treated very leniently. However, he needn't speculate on the lady any further as Kate Turner accompanied by a dark, handsome young man in uniform(who immediately aroused in Richard a totally unreasonable surge of jealousy) and a dark, gaunt good- looking woman whom he took to be Rose Greenhow came up to them.

Kate had found working with Rose demanding but exhilarating. The best doors were opened to them. Although those in office had 'unofficially' stated on several occasions that she was no longer in the Service nobody believed them. Her fame after First Bull Run was legendary and her imprisonment had given her an aura of martyrdom. Some people were afraid of her – especially if they knew that some aspects of their own conduct would not bear too much scrutiny from her penetrating intelligence network.

An important task for Kate was to assist Rose in writing ' debriefs' of the amazing amount of information that she had gathered whilst imprisoned. Material ranged from troop strengths, munitions and supplies of food and medicine to subjects such as clothing, footwear, animal feed, breeds of horses and mules, the number of cattle accompanying each march, veterinary officers, butchers and dentists. She had a brilliant grasp of detail when looking at a map or document and could memorise with almost photographic accuracy. She obtained the dimensions and other characterisations of the new Navy gunboats whilst they were still in the early blueprint stage.

Rose had not even wasted her journey South after her release. Details of all fortifications (a great interest of her's), military traffic and anything else that she had considered relevant had been memorised and noted down as soon as the Yankees had ceased to escort her.

Now the important information had been passed to the authorities Kate was helping Rose on the preparation of her diaries for publication. She had recovered her basic notes and was reconstructing the whole whilst her memories were still fresh. There was a considerable amount of information which could not be included in the first edition as it was still too sensitive – this was reserved for a further edition to be published after the war.

It was not just the details that Rose had obtained that fascinated Kate but her observance of characters and personalities. Rose had moved in the highest social, political and diplomatic circles; this fact together with her prodigious self-education had made her a merciless critic. President Lincoln was a backwoodsman catapulted to prominence and although his wife's origins were far less humble neither of them bore the sophistication of Rose's normal social milieu.

Rose was kinder to Lincoln than to his wife. She never referred to him as that 'gorilla' or 'that ignorant baboon' which was common practice among some southerners. Indeed, some of his gaucheness was becoming. At an official dinner when a servant asked him which wine he would take he replied with touching simplicity "I don't know: which would you have?" On another occasion he spilled tea on a guest's gown and was covered with confusion. This bumbling awkwardness gave him an air of vulnerability which endeared him to his staff who sought to protect him. As one diplomat observed to Rose "he appears constantly surprised to be in his position and always seems to apologise for being here but nobody likes his wife. Anybody would think that she is President herself".

Kate chuckled as she read what Rose had written about Mary Lincoln . "She is a short, broad, flat figure, with sallow mottled complexion, light grey eyes, with scant light eyelashes and exceedingly thin pinched lips; self-complacency, and a slight scornful expression characterise her bearing as if to rebuke one for invading her noble presence."

"You really don't like her at all do you Rose?" Kate put the paper down on the table and sat back in her chair. Rose looked up from her work and smiled.

"Well, Kate if people get themselves into positions of power then they should learn how to behave and that goes for wives as well- actually even more so, after all, they are only there because of the success of their husbands." Kate realised that she was working for a woman of the utmost skill and intelligence when she discovered the details as to how Rose engineered the victory of First Bull Run. This was the greatest espionage coup that either side achieved during the war.

On July 16th 1861 General McDowell's men marched away from Washington with supplies for three days in their knapsacks. The plan was to take Richmond right away. What they did not realise was that the Confederate generals Johnston and Beauregard were waiting for them. Rose had seen their marching orders and had sent word to Richmond some days before.

Rose had ensnared John Callan, a young clerk of the Senate Military Committee. The hapless man stood no chance against the advances of this mature, beautiful, sexy woman. Soon Rose was in possession of detailed plans.

Shortly afterwards , a farm girl- Betty Duval – was

bouncing out of Washington via the Chain Bridge in a cart full of butter and eggs. She wore a bonnet and plain calico dress. No Federal checkpoints took any notice of this simple country girl driving her farm cart , save for mild attempts at flirtatious badinage by teenage farm boys – turned soldiers which were met with coy smiles , lowered eyes and blushes.

Once in Virginia, the cart drew up in front of a fine house. The farm girl knocked on the door and was admitted. She removed her bonnet which revealed that her hair had been elaborately dressed with a tucking comb. Less than half an hour later a sophisticated, beautiful young woman dressed in a fashionable riding habit and hat sauntered down the front steps holding a whip. A fine bay gelding stood with a slave at his head. The man helped Betty into the saddle. She kicked the animal into action and cantered off.

The bored sentries at the picket outpost heard the sound of galloping hooves and raised their muskets. They relaxed when they realised that it was a lone woman. Before they could ask her business they were addressed imperiously from her saddle.

"Take me to General Bonham at once."

"Who are you Ma'am?"

"Never mind that. Just take me."

Had the stranger been a man the soldiers would have been a little more persistent but this woman was obviously well-connected and nobody bent on unlawful business would have demanded to be taken straight to a general. Strict adherence to procedures would obviously irritate this important woman and mean trouble for them. They looked at each other and nodded simultaneously. One took Betty's rein and led her through the camp.

Men who had not seen a decently dressed woman for months looked up from their games of dice, flea races or cards and the more literate ones from their letter writing or reading of newspapers, books, bibles or the many religious tracts that were circulated about the army and read by many men with zeal. The tired horse was now blowing with his flanks heaving and his head lowered as he was led over the flattened grass.

Betty sat impassively in her saddle. Her eyes were fixed straight ahead – impervious to the admiring glances in her direction. There were no comments or wolf-whistles. The men had realised that this was the sort of woman to whom one did not do things like that. Those were reserved for the wives of the lower ranks, washer –women or women who came to perform a more personal service.

General Bonham sat outside his tent. It was a lovely evening. The smoke from the fires drifted towards him giving off a pleasant woody smell. He had just finished writing to his wife. Although he had served in the Mexican War this lawyer and Congressman from South Carolina needed a gentle introduction to military duties; the object was to try to keep the inexperienced generals away from areas of expected conflict. Not a great deal had been happening so far. Bonham looked up to see a private approaching leading a fine bay horse. The woman seated on the horse side- saddle dressed in a very stylish riding-habit was more handsome still; the combination of woman and horse evoked power and class. Things could be getting more interesting. The general was soon to find out how interesting.

"General Bonham?"Inquired the lady authoritatively from her saddle. Bonham was taken aback. It was usually he who asked people their names- not the other way around. He felt like a private being addressed by a senior officer.

He quickly recovered himself. "That's me Ma'am. May I ask your name?"

"I need to see you in private urgently. I'll tell you everything then." Even more bemused the general put down his pen.

"Alright. Private -take the lady's horse. Come with me Ma'am."

Betty followed him into his tent. He turned round and saw she was looking at him intently. Her black eyes mirrored commanding power. "I have a message for General Beauregard. Please will you give me your word to take it to him immediately?" This was a blatant command- not even a command couched in the form of a request.

Although Bonham had not been a general for very long he had been used to being in authority all his life. He was not accustomed to being addressed in such a manner – particularly by a woman. However this woman spoke with such a passionate intensity mingled with authority that he felt she must be genuine and nodded in assent.

To Bonham's astonishment Betty removed her hat and took out her tucking comb. A luxuriant curtain of dark brown hair cascaded down below her shoulders. She leant her head forward and put her hands behind her head. She seemed to be untying something. She handed him a small package sewn in silk.

"Here is the message for General Beauregard. Please take it to him immediately." Again, Bonham felt like a subordinate being addressed by a superior but he knew he had to ask.

"Please tell me your name Ma'am and who sent you."

"No. I cannot do that. The less anybody knows the better. All I can say is that the consequences if Beauregard does not get the message will be terrible." The woman's eyes burned with conviction to the point of fanaticism. There was no doubt that she was genuine. The deep feelings which she displayed could not be faked.

Bonham sent the message to Beauregard immediately who rushed it to Richmond with a request for reinforcements. The information gave Beauregard a chance to place his forces to the best advantage behind the banks of Bull Run Creek and to place his batteries in the best defensive position. It ruined the Federals' plan to surprise the Confederates with greater numbers, to break through their lines and to March on Richmond and enabled the South to win the first major battle of the war.

Betty Duval had been selected by Rose. The message had been ciphered by Rose on information prepared by Rose and sewn in silk by Rose.

Chapter Nineteen

Richmond

September 1862

Richard of course knew all about Rose's part in Bull Run. When Wilmer and Pinkerton (Richard had now learnt the true identity of ' Major Allen' from Clara and Amelia) had briefed him in Washington they had described it with such professional admiration as a perfectly executed act of espionage that there was no suggestion of any grudging tone in their voices.

The sun was now beginning to sink below the hills surrounding Richmond. The green of the hills subsided into red gently merging into a mauve pink which was now beginning to slide fingers into the pale blue sky-firstly breaking it into pieces then gradually suffusing it.

Although he had been impatient to see Kate again Richard just had to observe the 'Notorious Rose' or the 'Heroic Rose' depending on which side you were on. Some famous people like Lincoln did not mirror their fame. You could just pass them by in the street as a person of no consequence.

Such was not the case with Rose. Her beauty itself commanded attention but hers was not the kind of beauty that fades with age or hardship as happens with some pretty girls of indefinite character. Certainly her year in prison had aged her and rendered her gaunt but this if anything had increased her charisma. The strength of her character and activity of her mind burned from those intense dark eyes and radiated her face with intelligence and awareness. Richard had of course seen a photograph of Rose. He was fascinated to meet in person somebody about whom he had heard so much intriguing detail. On seeing her he immediately realised why men found her irresistible. He wanted to keep looking at her but politeness prevented it.

To Kate's relief the obnoxious Little Rose had not been brought to the dance, much to the child's disgust which she displayed by throwing a china ornament across the living room of her mother's lodging and smashing it. In Kate's opinion this should have warranted a sound spanking and sending to bed for the rest of the day without any meals. Rose however treated it as a normal occurrence. The only one facet about Rose which Kate did not admire was her lax treatment of this wayward and unattractive child.

Although Richard had thought of Kate a great deal since the barbecue she paled beside the vibrancy of the mature, sexy Rose. His irritation at the young man on Kate's arm subsided and was extinguished when Kate introduced him as her twin brother Captain Frank Turner.

A private brought round a tray of drinks. Richard exchanged his empty glass for a full one without noticing the man; then Kate said a few inconsequential words to the private which prompted a reply. On hearing the voice Richard felt a shiver of familiarity. He was careful not to look at the man immediately but then observed him as he walked away and then managed a surreptitious side-long glance at him a few minutes later.

When Kate arrived home late that afternoon she was delighted to find Frank waiting for her. She rushed into his arms. After the usual initial delight that the twins always experienced after a separation Kate's mood lifted into euphoria when she discovered that Frank had been promoted to Captain and would now be working for the War Department in Richmond where – for the time being – he would be out of harm's way. The posting had been confirmed today. Rose would have known of course but Kate realised that the rules and her own professionalism would have prevented Rose from telling her. Tomorrow, Frank had to report to Colonel Bledsoe who was in charge of operations. "Thank God you'll be safe for a while."

That was of course the worst thing she could have said. Frank then bemoaned the fact that he had seen very little action so far and that the best contribution he could make was in the field. "Oh. So now we are a captain of a days' promotion we think we know more than a general now do we? General Lee obviously thinks that the best contribution you can make is in the war office so we'll let him be the best judge of that shall we?" Frank grinned. Kate always knew how to put him in a good humour.

Frank had arrived just in time to go to the dance. His three cousins were thrilled to see him. They adored Frank. Kate was disappointed that as they would all make their way to the dance together she did not have the time to tell Frank about DuFresne. Still, she could do it later tonight or tomorrow. She must be grateful that she could tell him at all. His unexpected arrival made up for everything – even for DuFresne not being there. She was disappointed when she learnt that he had to leave for a short visit to Columbia.

Kate was in love with DuFresne. She knew it was irrational. He was much older and obviously followed a very risky occupation and like most of his ilk was disapproved of by many of the 'right thinking' people of Richmond – the men anyway. The women tended to make excuses for him. Love, of course is irrational and his blockade – running, his dubious past and the fact that people disapproved made him all the more attractive.

The trouble was that DuFresne made most other men appear inadequate or insipid in Kate's eyes. She had been quite attracted to the young Englishman when she first saw him but now, although he seemed pleasant enough he paled beside DuFresne - a colt compared to a stallion.

Richard found Kate polite, but distant. He did try to make conversation but she did not seem particularly interested so he gave up. Perhaps she was in a bad mood. Maybe he'd try again if they met another time. Indeed, her brother was better company. It appeared that he was with the cavalry. Richard asked him how he was faring.

"All I'm riding is a desk at the moment. I have been shifted to the War Office."

"Presumably that's because you have a college education. You're of more use there than in the field."

"That's certainly not my view. For me there is one place for me and that is the field. But it was General Lee's decision and as my dear sister said earlier this evening who am I – a lowly captain of just one day to argue with a general? And the relevance of a college education depends on your regiment. Some regiments are all college boys. In those types of regiments – like mine – where everybody's educated a lot of people are still privates who would now be officers in other regiments. Education is no big deal. You get elected officer by the men." Frank was too modest to add that he was elected officer shortly after the start of the war."

Frank stopped for a moment whilst another tray of food was brought round. It was not the same private that had given Richard that eerie feeling which was still troubling him. Richard reflected again on this practice of electing officers. Knowing the practice of the British Army he found it strange. He had often wondered as to whether it could result in ineffectual officers whom the men thought would give them an easy time. Still, that would not apply to Frank. He appeared to be a strong but likeable character who would command the respect of his men.

Frank took a long swig from the glass that he had just been given. "That was welcome. Sorry. Where was I? Oh yes. Well, General Lee got to know me and posted me here. He also knows my family. But I hope the reason for the posting was that he thought I was good. You don't say 'no' to General Lee and I daresay the experience will be useful but I hope to get back into the field before too long." He was then interrupted by Mary Chesnut who had been listening with all the others. She had been quiet for at least two and a half minutes which was a long time for her.

Richard, with the others fell about laughing when she told a story about one of her visits to Chimbarozo Hospital when a wounded soldier decided to entertain his comrades by imitating the facial expressions of the dead on the battlefield.

"Mary!" Expostulated Mrs Smythe once she had managed to collect some words. That is terrible."

"Yes. But it's funny isn't it?"responded Mary. The others, by their mirth had already admitted that it was.

"Sometimes funereal humour is funny. And we have so much misery round here. It's now normal to see people walking about with tears streaming down their faces . You see at least one funeral most days with black-plumed horses, women in black and heavily – veiled with shocked, bewildered children in tow. We hear 'The Dead March from Saul' more often now than 'Dixie'. If we don't laugh sometimes we will all finish

up by slitting our own throats if not each others'".
Nobody disagreed.

There was no doubt that Kate was beautiful but
beside Mrs Smythe, Mary Chesnut and Rose Greenhow
she appeared young and lacking in conversation.
Richard couldn't remember having spent such an
enjoyable evening. He had never come across such a
clutch of amusing, cultured, educated and attractive
women. There had been no women approaching
anything like that in Hereford. His mother and her
friends had been pleasant enough but Hereford was a
provincial backwater. The only woman he had met who
could match the present company in any way was Mrs
Matthews in New York.

Richmond had always been a centre of culture,
commerce and politics but now it was the capital of the
Confederacy and the pivotal point of all decisions
which, together with the constant threat of invasion
gave it a thrilling sense of excitement and its population
a greater piquancy to every sensation and emotion.
People's wit was sharper, their love stronger, their
hatred more violent and their grief (and there was
plenty of it) more searing.

At about one o'clock Mrs Smythe suggested they go
home. To Richard it seemed still about ten. He was
kissed farewell by Rose Greenhow (he relished the
thought of telling that to Clara and Amelia; he had
followed their instructions to 'get close' to her to the
letter) and Mary Chesnut who gave Mrs Smythe
instructions to produce her handsome young
Englishman again soon – she had kept him to herself
for far too long. Kate's farewell was polite but distant ,
Frank's took the part of a firm honest handshake –
which mirrored Richard's assessment of his character –
and a smile with a ' hope to see you again soon'.

Mrs Smythe clung to Richard's arm as they picked

their way over the clumpy ground for which her heels were not suitable. The band was still playing slow numbers, couples clung to each other on the dance floor, and others sat together in dark unobtrusive places or by the glowing wood fires. It was now becoming chilly and some girls were sitting wrapped in blankets inside army wagons which had been provided to take them home. That night saw a number of engagements – some by couples who had known each other less than a week.

Candles glowed through the darkness and lanterns flickered. Richard helped Mrs Smythe arrange her dress in the coach"I've had a wonderful evening" and he meant it.

"Thank you for your company. You've come a long way in the last few months." Richard knew she did not just mean in distance. As he sat back in the coach he reflected the tremendous strides that his life had taken in the last sixteen or so months. The callow law student from England had now matured into a fully fledged spy in a hostile country consorting with mature sophisticated women.

The private serving the drinks was still troubling him and would continue to do so until he had resolved the situation in his own mind. He had been alerted to the voice – the soft Herefordshire burr- not unlike his own. The build, face and gait all pointed to the same person -Harry Harper- with whom he had attended the Hereford Cathedral School. It was he of course whose father had gone bankrupt and the news that he had gone to America to join the Union Army was responsible for Richard sitting in this coach spying for a country which was not his own.

It couldn't possibly be Harry. Could it ?.

Chapter Twenty

Richmond

November 1862

The harsh, bitter cold of the weather matched the mood of Richmond. The feverish expectancy of September was now giving way to gloom and depression. The price of food was escalating. The poor were suffering hardships in ways which were not as yet affecting the better-off.

Other tragedies of war however, are no respecters of rank or social condition. Every day brought its new clutch of widows and orphans. Women with ashen tear-stained faces accompanied by frightened, sad bewildered children were now a normal sight whether they were well-fed and clad in expensive black crepe or rags flapping round their scrawny bodies.

Poor women flocked into Richmond with their children to seek assistance at the centres which had been established to help families of absent or dead soldiers. These were women who had never owned slaves but they and their men folk were paying the price for their rulers ' peculiar institution' . Only a minority of soldiers in the Confederate Army owned slaves; the majority were poor whites who were either conscripts, shiftless drifters for whom armies have always provided shelter and regular meals of sorts or those swept along in the initial euphoric wave of enlistment.

The late summer and early autumn had been a false

dawn in the Confederate fortunes. News of the war was now not good. Lee's losses at Sharpsburg (or Antietam Creek as the Federals called it) were terrible. He was lucky that his army had not been destroyed. Then there had been Lincoln's Emancipation Proclamation freeing those slaves living in the states that had seceded from the Union and joined the Confederacy

. For all practical purposes this did not immediately change the situation of slaves at all as slaves in the loyal border states of Maryland,Missouri,West Virginia, Kentucky and Maryland remained in bondage. Lincoln had to make a very difficult decision with regard to these border states which remained loyal to the union although by virtue of their proximity to the south many inhabitants felt a strong sympathy with the secessionists. Slavery was still very much ingrained in the structure of these states and any attempt at emancipation could 'tip the balance' resulting in their changing loyalties to the Confederacy.

It was a modest first step to total emancipation but it was a start. Even so the Confederate President Davis called it 'the most execrable measure recorded in the history of guilty man' and it did worry many slave-holding southerners. Only the most stubborn and unrealistic refused to believe that slavery was not doomed.

Now that the end was in sight, people such as Mary Chesnut who had argued that slavery could not be maintained were in a quandary. It was likely that their wishes would be achieved but as 'the peculiar institution' had underpinned the southern economy their way of life would be changed for ever. Mary and her husband James had owned about five hundred slaves at the start of the war and the value of the slaves formed a significant proportion of their capital.

Like many other owners the Chesnuts, the Turners and Mrs Smythe and her husband were watching their wealth being quickly eroded. From the start of the war they had been constantly losing slaves who had been running off or had been requisitioned by the Confederate Government.

Since the Emancipation Proclamation the trickle of runaways was now becoming a flood. The Union Army had recently allowed Negroes to enlist and many were now doing so or working for it as labourers. With total freedom many slave-owning families faced total ruin, particularly those whose plantations were heavily mortgaged and whose slaves formed part of their collateral.

Richard had very little sleep the night of the dance in September. He was unable to dismiss from his mind the Confederate private who had been serving drinks. He could not believe that he was Harry Harper but everything about this man – especially the voice indicated otherwise. Accents from Herefordshire, England did not abound in Richmond, Virginia. He was due to meet Clara and Amelia the next morning and would tell them immediately. Would he be discharged and sent back to Washington? That would be a bitter blow! He was enjoying himself and was under the impression that he was doing well.

Richard met the girls the next morning in the Park. They were sitting on a seat when he arrived and sat down between them. After the initial greeting he was about to reveal his thoughts about Harry but didn't have the chance. Clara swivelled round so that she was facing him, their knees touching, her eyes were dancing mischievously.

"Harry Harper reported that you performed very well last night." Richard should have realised by now that nothing should surprise him but it was clear that he obviously hadn't. He sat open mouthed.

"What the blazes! What on earth ...."

"Is he doing in Richmond in Confederate uniform when he left Hereford to join the Union Army shortly before you did?"voiced Clara smiling – her dimples were very pronounced today. 'She looks very attractive and she's got such a great personality' thought Richard not for the first time. Under different circumstances – well- best not to think about that.

Amelia as usual entered into conversation later than Clara. She now turned to Richard so that he was sandwiched between the two of them who were facing him intently.

"Well at first all went according to plan. He sailed from Liverpool. On arriving at New York he walked down the gang-plank straight to one of the recruiting posts at the dockside, joined the Army and was paid his bounty. He adapted well to the Army and was made corporal but was captured at Malvern Hills and thrown into Libby Prison. He was given the option to join the Confederacy as the price for his liberty. Many foreigners do that and you can't blame them. They have more chance of eventually gaining their freedom. If they are holed up in prison for a while the chances are they will die. If they change sides they at least have the possibility of escaping and going back to Federal territory and even rejoining the Army. Captured Confederates do the same.

"What about the oaths they have sworn?"

"Well. I don't suppose that means a great deal to immigrants, it's not as though they are betraying their own country." Clara nodded in agreement with Amelia. "I know if it was a question of changing sides or staying in prison I know what choice I would make." The pragmatic views of these two never ceased to amaze Richard. They would do anything to save their own skins.

"Anyway how do you two know so much about him and that he knows me? And why did you not tell me about him earlier. ? Oh. I know-- I didn't need to know. But what if I had let slip last night that I know him?"

Clara shook out her fan and started to fan herself extravagantly. "Well we didn't think you would and you didn't. And even if you did it wouldn't have been the end of the world. You would just have been two Englishmen who were at school together and happened to meet up."

"So this doesn't change anything. I' m not going to be sent back?"

"Certainly not. There's no reason for that – anyway too much time and money has been invested in you and you have too much to do."

"From what you say he is working for you as well and he knows why I am here?" Amelia straightened her skirt.

"That's it. He obviously has limited time due to his military duties. Anyway, enough about him." Richard was not going to allow the subject to be dismissed like that.

"I know the reason for all this secrecy. But one final thing-will I ever meet him? What if I run into him in the street?"

"We cannot rule out the possibility you may work together but nothing is planned at the moment. If you meet by chance then you should acknowledge each other - and now after last night Harry has also been told that- after all coincidences do happen. If ever you are both arrested and it is discovered that you both come from the same town in England and pretend not to know each other then that will arouse suspicion in itself."

Richard had been working hard. He had managed to become reasonably close to Rose Greenhow. He was bringing useful pieces of information to Clara and Amelia some of which they knew already – but by no means all. Beauchamp's Oyster House on Main Street was being used as a mailbox for sending post to the North. Rose was communicating with contacts in Washington – not only with regard to obtaining information but was also involved in dealings with securities, bank currencies, stocks and bonds both on her own behalf and on behalf of the Confederate Government. Richard had been intercepting some of these letters and had made copies which he passed on to Clara and Amelia.

Elizabeth Van Lew knew all about Richard's progress. He knew nothing about her – save from gossip about that 'batty rich woman who was sympathetic to the Yankees but was harmless enough.' He did not know that she was 'running him'. He was not alone. Nobody knew very much about any of Elizabeth's activities save her mother and – to a lesser extent her brother John. Nobody knew that she had managed to arrange for her maid Mary Bowser – the very one that brought her the coffee- to be employed as a servant in President Davis' household thus obtaining valuable information.

As every body expected Negroes – especially the women-to be illiterate, papers were left around carelessly which Mary read and memorised. Mary was also present when important discussions took place and nearly as much information could be gleaned from informal conversations in her presence - servants were regarded as part of the furniture.

When Elizabeth had managed to wheedle access to Libby Prison she bribed the jailers to allow sick prisoners to be transferred to hospitals in the city. It was not only no secret – it was expected. Bribery was commonplace in Richmond – it was often the only way to persuade officials to do anything. The demands of these unsophisticated, poor, corruptible guards were not that great – a few chews of tobacco would do.

If people had thought about it (they probably didn't) they would have assumed that Elizabeth would have chatted to these mostly semi-literate former farm boys when she bribed them. These simple men were doing a boring job and starved of female company – any woman (whether attractive or not) who bothered to talk to them was welcome. What people did not know was that she was extracting as much information from them as possible. Although guarding prisoners was regarded as a lowly occupation reserved for the less talented soldiery there was constant traffic to prisons and guards learnt much from gossip of escorts of new prisoners and from the captives themselves.

People knew that Elizabeth was talking to the prisoners both in prison and in hospital. What people did not know was that she spent most of her visiting time talking to the most recently captured men who unwittingly gave her much information. Elizabeth was adept at obtaining knowledge from people without them realising it. She would begin by asking questions about their health and their families back home. These dispirited, hungry exhausted men would then just ramble on about all kinds of military matters – particularly of the events which led to their capture. Elizabeth was adept at drawing them out –mainly by lending a sympathetic ear and offering the occasional platitude. She reserved her questions strictly to family and personal matters – if she probed on military subjects they may become suspicious and clam up. She stored a wealth of intelligence- including troop movements, supplies, medical arrangements, shortages, diseases, mules and cavalry mounts. This was sent north as soon as possible.

It was on one of these prison visits that Elizabeth met Harry Harper. Young soldiers brought out the motherly instinct in mature women. Elizabeth had no children but if she had they would be in their late teens/ early twenties – the ages of these young soldiers (some of whom were even younger) – when she saw this young boy sitting disconsolately in a corner she went up to him and gave him some bread and cheese. He thanked her politely. She immediately established that he was English and they fell easily into interesting conversation – from this, his looks and his manner it was clear to her that he was educated. Now the practical side of her overtook the maternal. He would be useful to her. She would now have no further direct contact with him – this would be done by her underlings. He must not associate her with anything other than charity work.

Over the next few weeks Harry was visited by members of Elizabeth's team. It was suggested that he take the Confederacy offer of freedom provided that he join their Army. When he protested that he would never fight for slavery it was suggested that rather than live out the war (or more probably not living it out) incarcerated in this hell- hole the chances of changing sides would give him a better chance of freedom and it was 'hinted' that there may be other work for him to do for the North. Harry's eyes lit up. He had shown interest. He would be contacted some time after he had joined the Confederacy.

In the same way that trading between both sides was officially forbidden but was carried on anyway because it was necessary – so it was with communication between the two capitals just one hundred miles apart.

Private mail services operated between Richmond and Washington. Elizabeth used them when necessary but it was far too risky. She had to find an alternative. The phrase 'Fate takes a hand' is often used but a person needs to be intelligent and perspicacious enough to realise when Fate is at hand and to use her to the best advantage – Elizabeth was both intelligent and perspicacious. Fate now appeared in the person of Dr Hauptman.

Since she had been a child Elizabeth had been tended by their family doctor. Some years previously Dr Freeman had taken on an assistant. Dr Hauptman was a young German immigrant. He was quiet and studious. He began to visit the household when Eliza suffered the odd minor ailment.

Elizabeth first met the German shortly after his arrival in America. He seemed shy and hesitant – save when he was talking about medical matters. She warmed to this young doctor who blinked at her nervously from behind his gold-rimmed spectacles. She felt protective towards him. Like her he was an outsider – she because of her abolitionist views and he because of his lowly immigrant standing, which, due to his intelligence and sensitivity he felt keenly. They became close friends.

Hauptman's professional status gained him access to the best houses but in his medical capacity only. It was constantly made clear to him by implication that he was regarded as an inadequate substitute for Dr Freeman. "'Oh. Can't Dr Freeman come? What a pity!' They say. They don't quite go on to say. 'Well, I suppose we'll have to make do with you.' But I can tell that is what they mean." His voice was bitter.

Germany had been in tumult after the revolutions of 1848 which had engulfed Europe. Many Germans had been obliged to flee the country for political reasons.

Economic forces had compelled many others to emigrate. Hauptman had recently graduated from medical school but not many people could afford doctors. When Elizabeth discovered that he hated slavery as much as she did she asked him why he had chosen to come to the slave-owning South rather than the North.

"As the English say 'beggars can't be choosers'. I didn't even have the money for my ticket. Then Dr Freeman offered me the post in his practice and sent me my fare and enough money to live on until I arrived. Dr Freeman is a cousin of my mother."

"I didn't realise that Dr Freeman is German!"

"He doesn't advertise it and he doesn't like it to be generally known. His parents brought him to America as a small child and they wanted to integrate into American society. Wilhelm Frieman became William Freeman. He also asked me to keep quiet about the fact that we are related. To have a cousin who is a poor German immigrant would not be an advantage as far as his rich friends and patients are concerned."

"That is a shame. Not to acknowledge your own relatives." Hauptmann shrugged.

"I'm not sure I fit in here. They are as you say 'cliquey'. I miss my own country. They mimic my accent and I don't like it. I will probably go back some day."

Elizabeth tried to restrain a smile. This very worthy, pleasant young man was so serious and mirthless; he did not have much of a sense of humour.

"And why do Americans always call Germans 'Dutchmen'? It doesn't make sense. After all they call real Dutchmen 'Dutchmen' as well." Now Elizabeth really did laugh.

"They say it's a corruption of 'Deutsch' but nobody really seems to know."

Well, I think it's silly." Elizabeth thought that it would probably be just as well that this straight-laced German returns to his own country. Nevertheless, he had a living to earn and over the years had settled in after a fashion.

However, since the outbreak of war he had felt increasingly uncomfortable in Richmond. He was a foreigner in a country whose structure he had never accepted and which he felt had never accepted him. Now that country was at war to preserve that structure. He also found the fervent patriotism offensive but apart from that there was the risk that he may be conscripted. Foreigners were not being drafted yet but there was talk of it happening soon and as doctors were always in demand he would be called up early. The decision had now been made.

Hauptman was returning to Germany. The situation was better there now. He had been offered a teaching post in his old university. He had discussed this with Elizabeth who had tried to persuade him to remain in America but travel north. A doctor would always find employment. No, he missed his own country. He had never felt at home in America. When it was clear that he was determined to leave Elizabeth considered that perhaps she could put his return to good use. She began to devise a plan.

Three weeks later Hauptman had obtained a passport to leave Richmond and departed via Fort Monroe in Tidewater, Virginia where he delivered a message to General Benjamin Butler. The reply was sent in invisible ink. This was the beginning of an effective conduit of communication which was to last throughout the war and became even more effective when Elizabeth developed her own cipher.

Elizabeth had now succeeded in the very dangerous activity of recruiting her own spies from a variety of backgrounds – including housewives, merchants , government employees and domestic servants. No opportunity was lost – Northern prisoners such as Harry Harper who had joined the Confederate Army were very useful. Nobody mistrusted a man in the right uniform. Clara and Amelia were 'running him' well and they met when his military duties permitted. There was little danger in this. What was wrong with two attractive young women meeting and flirting with a good-looking young Confederate soldier? Sometimes, to allay any possible suspicion he was told to bring a friend when no sensitive subjects were discussed and no notes passed.

Elizabeth was an astute judge of character and never recruited a double agent. Her spies were effective – and where possible kept ignorant of each others identity. Richard Clarke was doing well. Elizabeth had plans for him. When these had been achieved he would be sent north. His work would be done.

Chapter Twenty one

Richmond

November 1862

There were many reasons why Kate should have been happy. The social life was good, her work for Rose was fascinating and the two women got on well. Her father was in England. Frank was safely in Richmond and she saw him regularly, although he was still grousing that he wasn't fighting the 'real war'- particularly since he had learnt that his old friend and adversary Robert Gould Shaw was now Colonel of a new black regiment. This news had caused considerable controversy in the North but in the South it had been received with disbelief and terror.

Kate was in love with DuFresne but that was her problem. Her love was not that gentle, quiet love that lifts one on to a higher plain of happiness, the fulfilment of giving love and the security of knowing that love is returned.

Kate's love was that violent, destructive kind of love that regularly has the heart pounding, the stomach churning and interferes with sleep and appetite. It is an insecure, turbulent love wrapped in jealously and uncertainty.

Kate was obsessed with knowing where DuFresne was all the time, what he was doing and with whom he was doing it. He went away regularly – usually to Columbia or Charleston. He gave her little reassurance as to his constancy although he was charming and loving whenever they met. He would then disappear with little notice for weeks leaving Kate in ignorance and torment and then reappear suddenly.

In many relationships the strength of love between the parties is unequal. There is the 'lover' and the 'lovee'. Kate had never been the lover before. She knew that young men had liked her such as Charles Hanson whose father owned adjoining land to Beaumont and had been regarded as a 'suitable match' by her mother. Her father had more sense than to become involved in planning his children's relationships. Sadly, Charles was now dead from a bullet through the head at Shiloh. Kate had received the news with the same regret that she received the news of the death of the now all too many friends and acquaintances but nothing stronger.

Kate had regarded these young men with a mild indifference tinged with amusement. If their attentions became too assiduous she gently pushed them away. She was never unkind. They were sufficiently well-bred to take the hint. Kate had always been in control of her admirers just as she had always been in control of everything else in her life. She had always assumed that she would marry someday and that despite Southern conventions she would be in control of her husband.

Kate was not in control of DuFresne. His winning ways and consideration could quickly give way to irritation and anger. Nobody had ever spoken to her in that way before – not even her parents who whenever she had misbehaved as a child had dealt with her fairly. They may have punished her but neither of them had lost their temper. Kate was now faced with a situation with which she did not know how to deal. When DuFresne went away he never told her his destination. She only learnt on his return. She did ask Miller who had introduced them but his answers were always vague. What Miller suspected and what Kate did not know was that by this behaviour DuFresne, the experienced manipulator of women, was purposely stoking up Kate's violent feelings by his apparent casual attitude. There was nothing casual about the planning of it.

Kate had many 'woman to woman' conversations with Rose. To her surprise Rose had neither met DuFresne nor had she even heard of him. Rose seemed to have met half the people in the world and have heard of the other half. Rose asked her about his background. She was surprised when Kate didn't know. "Well ask him. You come from a good family and must marry into a good family. You don't know if he's ever been married or has had children. Men of that age usually have married at some point in their lives. If he is a gentleman he will understand."

However, it was when Kate told Rose about DuFresne's short temper she became concerned. "If there are things about you that irritate him now what's going to happen if you marry? He seems too dubious to me. And I worry that I haven't heard of him. I should be very careful about taking it further until you are absolutely sure and you have found out more about his background."

"Well, my Uncle Preston Miller knows him. He does business with him. He wouldn't have introduced us if he hadn't thought him suitable for me." Rose did not respond to this point. She knew a lot about Preston Miller and had done so for years. His affairs were very complex and his associates were to be handled with caution. However she knew nothing certain to his discredit and even Rose would think very carefully about airing doubts about one of the most influential businessmen in the Confederacy to his niece. She chose a different tack.

"Well do you have to go for somebody so much

older than you? After all there are hundreds of eligible young men coming in to Richmond all the time and I dare say many of those would marry you like a shot. You are always getting admiring glances. Makes me quite jealous at times."

Such is the perversity of human nature that it was just that kind of advice that made it all the more necessary for Kate to marry DuFresne.

"You know, Kate", Rose said one day, "I like that nice young Richard Clarke. He is charming and good-looking. If we knew more about his family in England you could consider him"

"Well, he's nice enough. But I do not think of him in that way." She didn't say that Richard seemed to like Rose more than herself. Kate's primary relationship with Rose was that of underling and although they were friends that would be presuming the friendship too far.

Kate was also not quite sure what Richard was doing in Richmond anyway. He had been here five months now. Unlike most able-bodied young men he was not in the army and was not working. He always seemed to be at social events. She commented on the fact to Rose.

"Well he's English," replied Rose as though that explained everything.

"What's that got to do with it? I've met a number of Englishmen and other nationalities as well in Richmond. They are either serving or observing in our army, connected to our government in some way or here on business. They are all here for a purpose. He just seems to be having a good time.

Rose put her face-mirror back in her reticule and snapped it shut. "Now you come to mention it he does seem rather a dilettante. His family must be very wealthy. I've said before you ought to find out more about them." Kate was not going to do that. She was not interested in Richard. She was only interested in DuFresne. She had not heard from him for three weeks now. She was desperate. People commented that she was looking pale and thin.

If Richard had heard Rose describe him as a 'dilettante' he would have been delighted. That is exactly what he wanted people to think. He would not have been so delighted had he known that Rose had not voiced her real thoughts to Kate. Rose was becoming suspicious of Richard. The North was beginning to use foreigners for espionage work. A Norwegian woman was arrested only last week. However, she was not going to mention her doubts to anybody at the moment. She would first do some quiet 'digging' on her own.

Whilst Kate was wondering about DuFresne's whereabouts her suspicions would not have been quietened had she known that he, Miller and Harrison were at her own plantation sitting in Harrison's quarters swigging whisky. Beaumont had buzzed with activity over the last few weeks. Solange was happy that the plantation was so busy. 'Dear Preston' always handled everything so well. She had written to William in England and told him that he need not have to worry about anything.

Solange had slid happily back into her old role managing the house and caring for the slaves when they were sick or in childbirth- at least she thought she had . Rachel and Harrison knew the true situation.

Solange had now accepted Harrison. He seemed to be extremely competent and she now considered that she was very lucky to have him. She still didn't like him but that didn't matter. It was not necessary to like one's manager as long as he did his job. One certainly did not socialise with him.

DuFresne drained his glass. Nobody said anything. Harrison sat uncomfortably. Both these men made him nervous. Miller's warning that Harrison had better remain a friend because he knew what happened to his enemies had not gone unheeded. Keeping silent is a tactic. It can unnerve one's opponent or frighten him into making a false move or volunteering information. All DuFresne and Miller wanted to do was to keep Harrison unnerved. They knew they had him exactly where they wanted him. Harrison could stand it no longer.

"What is the next step?" He asked hesitantly. DuFresne leant over to the table and splashed a generous measure of whisky into his glass, leant back in his chair, crossed one elegant buckskin thigh over the other and took a mouthful rolling it round his mouth luxuriating in the hot, strong taste of the spirit.

"We will give you the information when we consider you need it my friend. " Replied DuFresne silkily, but menacingly. Harrison looked mystified and frightened. Miller said nothing. The network was efficient and effective. A considerable number of people were involved but hardly any of them had any knowledge of the true nature of the activity.

Back in the impressive library of Beaumont Miller reached for a cigar, cut the end fastidiously with his cutter and strolled over to the fire where he lit the cigar with a spool. "I don't think we'll have any trouble with Harrison. Sewing a mixture of fear and greed always works."

DuFresne stood with his back to the fire holding up the tails of his coat warming his legs. A bitter wind laden with flurries of snow had seared through the two men on their walk over from Harrison's quarters. They had been here now for nearly a week. DuFresne was anxious to leave Beaumont. As things were going well here there was no need to stay.

Beaumont was now a bleak place. Large houses are like most men and women. They need constant care lavished upon them; without it they quickly look unloved, neglected and tatty. Few people flourish in isolation. Even sheer lack of occupation has an effect on a house. People keep the air circulated and warm. Empty, unused rooms soon assume an air of mustiness, dampness and decay which is accelerated by winter. The attitude of the slaves was also contributing to the general deterioration of Beaumont. DuFresne was determined not to accompany Miller on his next visit.

The trickle of slaves departing from Beaumont as a result of buying their freedom, running off to join the Union Army or being requisitioned by the Confederate Government had now become a flood and had created a serious shortage of labour. Cuffey the young groom had been the last to go. He had told Nathaniel that he was going to join the Union Army. "You go with my blessing but try and become an army groom. Use your skill. There is no sense in becoming cannon fodder in a white man's war. Let them decimate each other and we reap the benefits." This advice was probably too philosophical for the young man although he listened very politely. Afterwards he told Rachel that he was going to try and join the fighting. He wanted to kill as many planters as possible.

Both Miller and DuFresne had noticed a change in the attitude of the slaves that remained. This was common now throughout the South. Mary Chesnut had commented on the inscrutability of the slaves. Now nobody knew what they were thinking. There was little downright rudeness; just a quiet almost superior confidence that the whole social fabric was about to come crashing down.

DuFresne had always been extremely fastidious about his dress at the best of times but as the South was increasingly suffering from shortages his clothes were especially conspicuous even in former centres of fashion such as Columbia. The Confederate grey was an increasingly rare sight. Indeed, uniforms of any kind were not that common- either of the butternut shade or dark brown resulting from captured Yankee uniforms dyed from walnut shells. Dead or captured Yankees were stripped of anything that could be of use. The first things to be taken were money or items of value and then footwear followed by clothing.

The dress of civilians was also showing signs of the difficulties with many respectable and former wealthy citizens wearing frayed and skilfully patched clothes..

DuFresne bore witness to no such shortages as he lowered his immaculately clad frame into his chair and stretched out in a leonine fashion. Most of his wardrobe had been obtained from England. His beautiful boots had been made by Lobb of St James's in London's West End. The skin-tight buckskin breeches had been tailored in Saville Row as had his wine-coloured frock-coat and white silk waistcoat picked out with yellow flowers. Naturally, neither Miller nor any of his family showed any evidence of the hardships.

"DuFresne we are finally settling the details and we will soon be able to start moving but not yet. It will be some time before my British agents can notify me that the money is sitting in the specified accounts in Lombard's Bank. Bullingdon has arranged that. He is on his way back from England". DuFresne looked uncomfortable.

Miller felt reassurance was needed." If you are worried about that business aboard 'The White Queen' don't be. Nobody saw the actual accident only the mess

309

afterwards." " Are you certain?."

Miller pulled on his cigar and let out a long column of smoke. " Bullingdon is certain and that is enough for me. And that should be for you."

Dufresne nodded. Bullingdon would have satisfied himself that there were no witnesses to the 'accident' – living ones anyway.

"You seem to be doing pretty well with Kate. She is always asking me about you, where you are? And when you will be coming back? Your famous way with women always works."

A self-satisfied beam lightened up the dark saturnine features. Like many conceited men DuFresne was fully aware of his successes with the opposite sex. Men of his ilk tend to polarise women. Some are quickly smitten; others take an instant dislike to self-assured, over-bearing confidence in seduction. Few women are totally unmoved by such men. When DuFresne was rebuffed he was unaffected , assumed there was something wrong with the woman or decided that he didn't like her anyway and moved on to the next conquest.

"When do you think we ought to get married?" DuFresne ignored the fact that he had not asked Kate to marry him yet and it did not occur to him that she might turn him down.

"Not yet. Not only do we not need it at the moment but she is usefully employed by Rose Greenhow. That in itself could provide useful information. I know you haven't got anything from her yet."

"No. She never talks about the details – only where she is going and whom she is seeing socially. If ever I try and ask her more she always falls silent or changes the subject."

"She is obviously doing her job well and taking her responsibility seriously. I would expect no less from a member of my family. My niece is a sophisticated and intelligent young woman. My influence may have got her the post with Greenhow but if she had been no good they would have got rid of her by now. When our plan is more underway I will tell you when to move. And until then there is always the chance that she will let something drop about her work with Greenhow.

Miller knew there was a fine line to draw about the timing of the marriage. DuFresne was not well-regarded by the authorities. He was not fighting for his country (if indeed this was his country – nobody seemed to know what his country was); he was a blockade- runner, a chancer and to make matters a lot worse nobody knew anything about his background. Few regarded him as a gentleman and he was not readily acceptable in Government or military circles.

Once they were married Kate would probably not be able to continue to work for Rose – but nobody knew in this war. Situations and opinions changed daily and the old conventions of behaviour seemed to have crumbled. The advantage of marriage would be that should Miller's scheme be derailed then Kate would be forced by Southern conventions not to disclose anything. Her duty would be to DuFresne which would override any feelings of patriotism.

DuFresne once asked Miller. "What if she puts her duty to her country before that to her husband?" Miller lifted the paper weight on his desk and brought it down with a resounding thud.

"Well that is your responsibility to ensure that she doesn't. Silence her or you will be silenced. Understand?" DuFresne said nothing. He understood.

DuFresne was a ruthless man who was used to dealing with ruthless men but he had never yet come across anybody who would sacrifice a member of their own family who might stand in their way. Now he had.

He had no doubt that Miller meant what he said; but that was alright, DuFresne could deal with that. Nobody would 'silence' him. If there was any silencing to be done he would do it.

Harrison stood and watched Miller canter down the drive safely out of sight. DuFresne had left the day before. Harrison was in sole charge again and that was the way he liked it. He was always nervous when those two were around. He and Rachel were now happily in control – he of the plantation and she of the house although Solange did not appear to have realised it – or if she did she did not care. If other people wanted to manage things it meant less work and worry for her. Mammy the old housekeeper was slowing up and her health was deteriorating. In normal circumstances a successor would have been groomed for the role by degrees but now there was no time for such formalities and anyway suitable candidates were lacking.

Rachel saw this as her opportunity and started to inch herself informally into the role. Slowly she had assumed responsibility for various duties such as dealing with the slave's clothing allocations, assigning duties to children that were now old enough to work, keeping the store houses stocked and arranging essential repairs to the house. The more she assumed responsibility the less Solange wanted to do and by degrees she slid into lethargic oblivion assisted by laudanum and alcohol.

Solange would never have realised that items were missing from Kate's cupboards and drawers. She never looked in them anyway- that was the maids' job. When she saw Rachel wearing a dress or an item of jewellery belonging to Kate she assumed that Kate had either given them to Rachel or granted her permission to use them before her departure. Rachel had the sense not to touch any of Solange's own clothes or jewellery – that would be foolhardy.

As Solange never visited the wine cellar she did not know that Harrison and Rachel were helping themselves to wine or brandy.Most nights she wafted up to bed in a haze of alcohol and drugs and did not notice that Harrison and Rachel were spending most nights in Kate's bed. The only person likely to tell her was the maid Susie but she lived in fear of Rachel. Shortly before the war Rachel had caught her and Jeff behaving like a couple of dogs in one of the store-rooms. If Solange had found out about that Susie would have been returned to the fields and slave-cabins immediately. This gave Rachel total power over the girl.

Custis, like most boys, never noticed what piece of jewellery or article of clothing women wore and as he always went to bed before the servants and got up after them he was not likely to notice the sleeping arrangements. Rachel had insidiously and very firmly assumed control over the house. Miller had grasped the situation on his visits but an enfeebled Solange suited his purposes.

Chapter Twenty Two

Richmond

February 1863

Savage cold, accompanied by desperate hunger howled through Richmond. The news of the war was slightly better if far from brilliant. The South had inflicted a defeat over the North at Fredericksburg just before Christmas but desertions from the Army were now heavy. The price of food had spiralled; the average family food bill had risen eleven-fold since the start of the war. Speculation and hoarding of food to obtain the highest possible price were rife. Wealthy people were trading unashamedly with the North. Dealers and speculators on both sides were bribed whilst cotton moved north and gold and Federal currency moved south.

It was difficult for the South to remain truly independent as Federal currency was worth four times that of the Confederacy and Northern gold pieces were particularly coveted. The poor hungry Confederate soldier was paid about a quarter less than his Federal counterpart in a depreciating currency which was often paid late.

No wonder troops were embittered at civilians enriching themselves through breaking the law whilst they starved. No wonder soldiers from poor backgrounds who owned no slaves were deserting in droves. They had always regarded the war as a 'rich man's war and a poor man's fight', a quarrel between Governments and this feeling had now strengthened. Many men received pleas to return home from their desperate wives who were now at their wits' end in trying to feed hungry and often sick children. Other soldiers changed over to the North. 'Johnny Reb' had no problem with 'Billy Yank' and at least the food and pay were better.

Richard was aware that he was now very conspicuous due to his lack of apparent inactivity. Grief, worry and deprivation were now hardening attitudes towards everything. Women whose men folk had been killed or maimed were now not so enthused with the 'young good-looking English boy whose accent was so cute'. He was now openly asked at social functions (which were becoming more sparse and basic in terms of food and drink) what he intended to do and when he intended doing it. He didn't think he could depend on evasive platitudes for much longer.

Richard was also feeling increasingly under pressure in the Smythe household and that he was outstaying his welcome. He was assured by everybody that under the code of southern hospitality he could stay as long as he liked. However that code had developed over a long period when numerous servants, unlimited food and plenty of space abounded. Although space was no problem for Mrs Smythe food and servants were.

The lordly Gabriel still reined supreme but other slaves had been requisitioned or had run off. Mrs Smythe received produce from her plantation and although much of this was pilfered en route she was not in such a desperate state as some former well-to-do people. Nevertheless she was still suffering from the high prices. Despite her protests Richard had managed to persuade her to accept a weekly contribution towards his keep. Before the war it would have been considered bad manners for such an offer to be made and absolutely unthinkable for it to be accepted.

Richard was also finding the personal side difficult.

He had now been living with Mrs Smythe for more than nine months. He was now almost regarded as a part of the family and the boys – Walter and Martin – were beginning to cause him concern. They missed their father and although Gabriel could dispense adult male company – and discipline where necessary – they were now treating Richard as a kind of elder brother involving him as a kind of arbiter in arguments with their mother who herself was beginning to give Richard some concern.

She was an attractive woman who was under a great deal of pressure not previously experienced who missed her husband and often felt lonely. As social functions had decreased Richard could not reasonably maintain his former commitment to socialising most evenings. On many evenings Mrs Smythe and Richard were the only adults in the house who were not servants. The relationship between them was becoming close. She had begun to confide in him about her money troubles, problems with the slaves or the plantation and gradually some of the difficulties in her marriage.

Mrs Smythe was a loyal wife and in the first few months of Richard's stay he had only heard Colonel Smythe spoken of in the most glowing terms but recently, bit by bit, various cracks in the marriage began to emerge. There are three major factors which test a relationship or marriage – prolonged separation, financial hardship and serious illness to each other or in the family. The first factor was present and the second factor was becoming increasingly more pertinent.

Richard began to learn of the Colonel's surreptitious womanising, his occasional heavy drinking and his sudden bouts of uncontrolled temper- sometimes he beat his boys quite severely. This last itself was not that unusual – boys were quite often beaten by their fathers as Richard had been by George but this had always

316

been in a controlled way. The Colonel had hit his sons in uncontrolled frenzy. Mrs Smythe never launched into a diatribe about the Colonel's failings; she was too loyal and well-bred for that – but sometimes she let slip some small detail and by degrees Richard had built up a picture of a still sound but far from ideal marriage.

Although Richard was in most ways mature for his age his experience with girls was limited and any amatory relationship with older women was non-existent. Mrs Smythe was a tactile woman who was missing relations with her husband and was starved of any affection. Increasingly she would sit next to Richard on the settee and when talking to him sometimes touch him. She probably didn't mean much by these movements. The problem was that Richard had not been brought up in a tactile household. His father had never showed him any affection and his mother, though loving, had never hugged or kissed him a great deal.

The poor lad was in a situation with which he did not know how to deal. He was confused. He did not know whether Mrs Smythe was making advances to him or not. He found her attractive but would never have considered taking the matter further any more than he would have with an aunt.

Everybody has their limits and in early February Mrs Smythe had reached hers. She had had a particularly difficult day buying fish. Martin the younger boy had a fever and she decided that he needed fish. Not only had merchants filled their warehouses with flour and hoarded it until they could obtain the highest possible price but the fishmongers had hiked their prices and hired thugs to make sure they were not undersold. Before the war it would have been unthinkable for ladies such as Mrs Smythe to perform such mundane tasks as to queue for fish. It was just one of the unwelcome changes that the war had brought. She queued for two hours in the biting wind and finally bought fish at an exorbitant price. When the fish had been cooked Martin was worse and did not want it.

Mrs Smythe sent one of the servants for the doctor but all the doctors were at the hospital dealing with troops following a fresh detachment of wounded. A dull but persistent toothache had lasted for three days and laudanum had not improved it. She was worried that it might blow up into something more serious – again the Army had taken a number of dentists leaving a shortage. Now the realisation that she had not received a letter from her husband for two months had seared her to the core.

The final straw came in the evening when one of the slave girls had been found pilfering food. Although always a misdemeanour which warranted punishment this would not have been much of a problem in normal times when food was plentiful. Now it was a much more serious matter. Richard had happened to walk down to the kitchen and saw an altercation was beginning. The girl started to deny the theft.

"Don't you lie to me you little slut"- screamed her mistress penetrating every corner of the large house. Richard was astounded to hear such a tone from this ladylike woman – even the shooting incident on the way to the plantation had not prepared him for it. He had heard nothing like it since he had visited a farm near Hereford when a farm boy had brought eggs across the yard to the farmer's wife and dropped them. Anybody would have thought that he had dropped the family's entire savings down the well.

A large stick constantly stood in the corner of the kitchen as a stern sentinel over the servants although it was hardly ever used.. Mrs Smythe grabbed the stick and started hitting the girl indiscriminately over the body. The girl raised her arms to protect her face and head. Richard looked on helplessly. His instinct was to grab the stick and break it but he knew he could not do that. He had been briefed against interference in such situations in Washington. "You will see sights that you have never seen before and which will disgust you. Ignore them and whatever you do don't intervene – this will make you conspicuous. We appreciate that you will find it difficult but everybody who lives in Richmond accepts them as part of normal life even if they do not agree with them." Richard had seen a boy being savagely beaten in the street shortly after he arrived in Richmond and since then had seen similar demonstrations of cruelty. He had never got used to them.

What particularly appalled him were the identity of the assailant and the victim's complete lack of ability to defend herself. Such an assault by an illiterate foreman down a salt mine would have been more forgivable but this was by a supposedly cultured and civilised woman. This just emphasised as to how engrained in the whole fabric of southern society was this total domination of one race by another. Richard could stand the girl's screams no longer and climbed the stairs to the drawing-room.

After a few minutes he heard a loud sobbing coming up the stairs and assumed it was the girl. He stood up when the door burst open. It was not the slave-girl but Mrs Smythe; she rushed up to him, put her arms round him and sobbed hysterically into his shoulder. Through her sobs she tried to talk but even the few words that Richard managed to understand did not seem to make any sense; but then distraught people do not make sense. He could make out phrases such as 'the war is lost', 'the Yankees might as well come and burn down this house and kill me and the children because they have destroyed my soul.'

Raw, naked human emotion can be shocking and difficult to cope with especially if one is not used to it and Richard was not used to it. He did not know what to do so he just stood with his arms around the distraught woman giving her the occasional ineffectual pat. Gradually the sobs began to subside into whimpers. She started to nuzzle up to him. The desire for mere affection and comfort, rather than sex was now overpowering her.

Richard held her. With the closeness of this woman his normal male reactions were beginning to overcome the obvious social taboo of close contact with a married woman who was old enough to be his mother and more importantly was his hostess. He felt his penis hardening. He started to kiss her hair. Her lips began to nibble his neck. Then her mouth clamped down on his; it opened and they were now kissing voraciously with tongues snaking around each other. Richard had never done this before. He hadn't realised that womens,' tongues were so big. For him it was a totally electrifying experience. Suddenly she wrenched away and held him at arms length and looked at him intently. "I'm so sorry." She croaked in a tearful whisper and rushed out of the room.

Late that night Elizabeth Van Lew was writing at her desk. There was a tap on the door and as usual Jenny (the replacement maid for Mary Bowser who was proving invaluable in the house of President Davis) entered without waiting for an answer. "You have a visitor. He's right here." She held the door back. Gabriel entered the room.

The next morning Eliza filled her daughter's cup with the poor concoction that was now used as coffee. Elizabeth took a sip and grimaced. "I know the drink is poor Elizabeth but you don't have to make that sort of face. It's like when I had to give you medicine as a child."

"It's not just that, Mother. Something blew up last night. I think we can deal with it. It's just going to take some working out that's all."

"Is it Colonel Brent?"

"Yes. Mother. He's one problem. He escaped yesterday. We were hoping it would not be for a couple of weeks yet as I wanted to get Richard Clarke ready but Brent was sprung yesterday. One of the guards was off sick and another one was doing duties so our contact thought it was best to strike when the iron was hot."

"Where is he now? Here?"

"Yes. But we're getting him to the farm as quickly as possible. We'll try and do it tonight. Gabriel will forge a pass from Susan Smythe but I do not think we'll have much trouble in this weather. I can't stand anymore of this filthy stuff. " Elizabeth put her cup down on the table.

"Who is going to get him across? Harry Harper?"

"No he's too junior to be out on his own without a senior officer. Anyway he may be of more use to us later. We have got to pull Clarke out today and he can get Brent across the lines."

"Well, Elizabeth, we were going to use Clarke anyway soon. He's now experienced enough to take the Greenhow papers. It's time we stopped her game with Smithson. Washington wants to arrest him and that will give them enough. And it will kill two birds with one stone. But why do we have to pull Clarke out so suddenly?"

"Well I had heard from our source in the office that Greenhow is getting too interested in Clarke. She suspects something but not enough to arrest him. To do it now would blow part of their operation but the main reason is that Gabriel came round last night. As you know he's been saying for some time that Clarke and Susan Smythe were becoming close."

"Elizabeth, you know I never set much store by that. I never thought that Susan was such a flirt as all that. Mind you nothing surprises me at the moment with all the behaviour of these so-called respectable wives and widows. I didn't have time to tell you last night but as you know I saw Lavinia yesterday and she saw Jane Snow kissing her cousin on the railway station and she's only been a widow three months."

"Perhaps she was kissing him 'goodbye'".

"Well, she wasn't. She was kissing him 'hallo'- sort of. She told Lavinia that she and the cousin have just become engaged. Anyway Elizabeth why are you talking about Jane Snow?"

"I wasn't Mother you were. To get back to Susan Smythe and Clarke. Things have been building up for some time. Last night Susan got upset and Clarke spent a long time 'comforting' her – according to Gabriel. They didn't take it further but it can't be that far off."

"Well you're right there's nothing like a love affair to spill secrets. Are you going to use the servant idea?"

Elizabeth nodded. "Well, I've tried and tried but can't think of anything better. Can you?" Her mother shook her head.

The plan that had been quickly formulated was for Brent to pretend to be Richard's English servant. Fortunately Brent had spent some time studying in England and should be able to put on some kind of English accent. Passes for both of them had been forged.

The only possible flaw would be if they passed through a checkpoint where Richard was known to one of the soldiers or officers who knew nothing about him having an English servant. The women discussed this possibility and decided that it was so remote that it was a chance that they would just have to take.

Richard as yet had no idea of the plan. He thought he would be in Richmond for some time. Brent was hidden in one of the secret rooms in the Van Lew's vast mansion. He would not be told any of the details until the last possible moment. The 'need to know' principle was sacrosanct. That is why the Van Lew's network was so successful. The Van Lew's owned a small farm out of town and it was easy to obtain passes for their Negroes who had reason to go there. Not many sentries would think of poking into the soles of muddy shoes worn by an old Negro riding a horse or inspecting a girl's basket of eggs, one of which was an empty shell containing a coded message. This farm was also used as a safe house and was where Brent would be taken from the mansion prior to the trip to freedom.

The transfer of Rose's papers to Washington would be combined with the spiriting of Brent through the Northern lines. This would make the maximum use of Richard and thus save using two agents. Richard would not be returning to Richmond. He would not be used there again. His work would be done.

Rose had been corresponding extensively with William Smithson and a considerable number of illegal deals had been uncovered. All the material that had been intercepted had been copied and then sent on to Smithson in Washington. It was these copies that Richard was to take to Washington and hand over to the authorities. Smithson would then be arrested.

William Smithson was a prominent Washington banker. He was a cultured man and dedicated to the Southern cause; both these attributes had drawn him and Rose closely together. They had known each other for many years but since hostilities had appeared probable they had worked on the upper levels of the spy ring in Washington with Michael Thompson, a lawyer from South Carolina. The three of them formed the brains behind the organisation.

Rose had been arrested in August 1861 and after her detention she managed some of her most effective espionage. Smithson was an expert at passing information through enemy lines into the South. He had contacts everywhere.

One plan which failed even involved a sister of charity from a hospital in Washington who had promised to help pass military details into the Confederacy. Smithson gave her a hollowed – out plug of tobacco which was to be taken by a man who had been released on parole. The scheme only collapsed when the man suddenly changed his mind and decided he could not violate his parole.

Eventually Smithson and Thompson were arrested around Christmas 1861. After four months in custody Smithson was naively released by the Federals when he took the oath of allegiance and pledged not to aid and abet the South.

Rose had been sent south roughly about the same time as Smithson's release and since then they had been in illegal negotiations with each other on a massive scale. Smithson was not just dealing with Rose. He had negotiated sight drafts on Richmond as well as Eight per Cent Confederate Bonds and had dealt in currency amounting to many hundreds of thousands of dollars. In many cases he had bought them from people who had come straight from Richmond. Some of these were couriers sent by Rose.

It was a troubled young man who received a note from Clara the next day. He had barely slept the previous night. He thought he ought to reproach himself but for what? It wasn't his fault that he was the only person to whom a lonely distressed woman could turn when she just needed some comfort. It probably had not meant much more to her than that but it had thrown this emotionally inexperienced young man into deep turmoil. Had he said the wrong thing to her on such and such an occasion which gave her the wrong idea? Should he have given her that present at Christmas which may have sent the wrong message? What were her feelings anyway?

Richard shivered in his heavy coat as he picked his way over the frozen rutted roads and pavements to the railway station. He was to meet Clara under the clock. During the summer meetings had usually taken place outside – usually in isolated corners of parks. He pulled his heavy beaver hat down as far as possible and pulled up his coat.

Now, meetings had to be held inside due to the intense cold which increased the risk of snippets of conversation being heard by unintended ears. Bars, hotels and restaurants were too dangerous. You never knew who was watching and listening and to move when a suspicious -looking person appeared could draw too much attention.

The railway station was a good place. It was full of people who were in transit or who were meeting or seeing off friends or family. People were there for a purpose and when that had been achieved they left. Idle loiterers were not attracted there and if they were there was too much activity for Richard's meetings with his 'handlers' to draw much attention.

Richard elbowed his way through the thickening crowd. People were now looking increasingly war-weary, haggard, tired and hungry. Children seemed pale and pinched like little crabby old men and women. Hunger, grief and worry about possible grief had taken their toll. Many children had been bereaved and anxiety and stress in parents can have the same effect on their children. Nine and ten year-olds were agonising as to how to save their mothers money on bills or how to obtain a little extra food. Malnourished children can quickly become sick children and Richard had seen far too many small coffins in funeral procession.

The wind was searing. It was the sort of cold that withers. Skins become dry and cracked; cuts widen and take a long time to heal; lips become chapped. Richard threaded through scrawny bodies huddled in to the worn and frayed clothes which flapped round them like tattered forlorn battle flags after a defeat. When these well-made clothes were new they had fitted snugly round sleek well-fed bodies.

Richard stepped quickly to the left to avoid a pair in a passionate embrace. The memory of these glued mouths and intertwining tongues would serve as a kind of insurance against the desolation ahead. He dodged a number of tearful or joyous couples depending on whether it was a parting, or an arrival.

To add to the anguish of parting were the irritations of the uncertainties and disruptions of travel. Journeys by train were constantly frustrated by a multitude of incidents. Yankees sabotaged railways by tearing up sleepers and burning them or by dislodging the rails and twisting them and leaving them standing in the middle of the track lashed together like ungainly sheaves of wheat. Battles, shortages, sudden requisitioning by the Army, inefficiency or just plain confusion which is common in war when nobody knows what they are supposed to be doing conspired to make travel by rail a lottery.

The train had been in the station for some time. It had clanked in spluttering smoke, smut and filth like a threatening and violent beast. It had screeched to a halt amidst whistles and the scream of metal rails showering sparks as though it was collapsing after massive exertion. Now it was slumbering as though regaining its strength. Whilst it slept, its coal wagons and furnaces were fed and its water tanks replenished for its' further onslaught into the unknown.

As Richard approached the clock his path was blocked by a pile of coffins which had just been unloaded to await collection by the bereaved next of kin. The sight of coffins was a sombre one – a reminder of the dangers and tragedies of that were now part of everyday life in the South but he was appalled to see soldiers sitting on them , smoking and laughing with their feet drawn up under them tailor fashion to keep warm.

'How callous and hard war can make people', thought Richard. What he could not realise until later was that it was a case of human nature falling on its innate ability to adapt to a new and harsher situation. In times of crisis, grief or catastrophe most people can draw on resources they never knew they possessed. Indeed, if that was not the case the human race would not survive unexpected hardship or disaster.

These men were regularly seeing dead bodies either killed in battle or by disease and they were often ordered to deal with them. Now they had worked hard to unload these heavy, occupied, evil-smelling coffins from the train onto the platform and now they felt they deserved a rest.

Clara was standing under the clock. She had only been there for a minute. It had been impressed on everybody in Elizabeth's network that punctual time - keeping was vital. People hanging around in public places could attract unwelcome attention. Clara had an extensive wardrobe at the start of the war and she still looked smart. A fur hat hid her dark curls save for the odd few which peeked out mischievously. Gloved hands held the fur collar of her coat over her mouth to keep out the cold. As Richard approached she kept the collar up. This gave her a kittenish, flirtatious look. Dark eyes danced merrily as she looked up at him. She pulled her collar down, stood on tiptoe and kissed him on the mouth. Richard was startled. Neither Clara nor Amelia had done that before. She then put her arms around him and started to nibble his ear."

"Pretend we're lovers for a moment." She whispered. Richard did not find that very difficult. "Now listen carefully. Be at 106 Chapel Street at ten o'clock tonight. You will be leaving Richmond for good. When you leave Mrs Smythe's don't say anything about your leaving and don't take anything with you. All your belongings will be collected and sent on. Now go. I don't see anybody I know but you can never be sure." She kissed him again and melted into the crowd.

Despite certain feelings of regret (particularly over the fact that he would probably never see Clara or Amelia again) Richard was relieved to receive this order. He had not seen Mrs Smythe since last night. She had made it known that she did not feel well and that she was not leaving her room that day save to care for her sick son. Richard ate a quiet supper which was served to him in the library. The room had that empty deserted feeling of a situation where the normal well-regulated self-control is now suddenly missing and this in itself seems to produce a sensation of dampness and coldness.

Despite Clara' instructions to take nothing with him he managed to cram whatever he could into a bag and held it under his coat. He had meticulously observed the instructions given to him by Colonel Wilmer in Washington which had been constantly repeated by

Clara and Amelia not to keep any significant papers on him or in his room at Mrs Smythe's which could be searched. Everything had to be memorised. Sudden investigations and searches were being constantly made and sudden disappearances of people were becoming increasingly frequent.

The wind drove the heavy falling snow slapping against Richard's face. Despite the fact that he walked with his head down and his hat pulled forward he constantly had to keep wiping snow from his eyes. The snow that had lain on the ground from previous falls had frozen. Every step sunk through the new snow down onto a thick, crisp crust.

It was a good night for passing unnoticed. The streets were deserted. Places of entertainment were empty with doors firmly shut. Visibility was poor comprising white ground, black shadowy buildings and a thick, heavy curtain of slanting, driving snow.

Richard eventually battled his way near to the address, opened his coat and took out his watch. Agents were advised to wear watches that did not have covers to them – it made it easier to see the time in an emergency. He looked at the watch closely in the darkness and managed to see the black hands against the white face. It was a quarter to ten. The rules that had been engrained in him were that he arrives at his appointment not more than two minutes before or two minutes after – to allow for the differences in people's watches. He walked briskly about neighbouring streets – nobody would be out on such a night unless they were about their own urgent business in which case they wouldn't be interested in his. Alleyways could not be used. Not only could they be harbouring enemy agents or police but they were fertile ground for thieves.

The door opened as he reached it and closed behind

him engulfing him in blackness. Richard heard the hiss of a light being struck, it flickered and a candle was lit. A hand cupped round the wick preventing it being extinguished by the strong current of air. The flame guttered and then burnt more strongly. A weak, flickering light gave Richard a difficult, strained vision. He could make out a dark shape which held the candle.

Chapter Twenty Three

Richmond

February 1863

From the height of the shape barely discernible in the blackness Richard deduced that it was probably a woman.

"You will now leave Richard. Everything is prepared." It was Amelia's voice. He could now see there was somebody else in the room – taller – definitely a man. He was wearing a long coat and a hat pulled down over his face. As the figure drew nearer Richard could not make out the whiteness of the face. It must be that of a Negro.

"Go with Gabriel."

"Gabriel!" exclaimed Richard.

"Yes. Richard it's me. You're surprised. That's good. We aim to keep people surprised."

Amelia drew nearer. "Gabriel will take you to your destination and give you your instructions on the way. You will be taking the Greenhow papers and escorting an escaped Federal officer from Libby prison who will masquerade as your English servant. You should be in Washington in a couple of days. Thank you for all your good work. You have been very effective. Goodbye and good luck." She leant up and kissed him lightly on the cheek. The door clicked behind her and she vanished into the heavy, snow- laden night.

"Richard, say nothing. Ask no questions. Don't speak until I speak to you. Come with me." It was 'Richard' now, no longer 'Mr Clarke'.

Richard followed the graceful figure as he padded

along with stealthy, loose-limbed, panther-like ease through the snow. Although the weather made progress difficult it was also easier to pass undetected. The ferocious conditions had excluded any passers-by who might have made a casual observance and if anybody had been pursuing them the poor visibility would have helped the fugitives.

The soft heavy thick snow muffled any sound. Although progress was difficult Gabriel moved quickly. Despite the intense cold and biting wind Richard generated heat and after a time was sweating profusely. After about an hour they stopped in an isolated area which Richard did not recognise. He looked up and saw that they seemed to be in a thick glade of trees; a dense interlacing of branches formed a canopy now roofed with snow giving the impression of a cavern.

Gabriel cupped his hand to his mouth and gave a low whistle. Standing silently with one hand on Richard's shoulder he looked at him with the index finger of the other hand to his lips as though telling him to be silent.

After a minute Richard heard an answering whistle from nearby, a few rustlings, the odd jingle and other fairly mute sounds which were just discernible. Into the glade walked a slight figure leading a horse plodding after him somewhat reluctantly with his head down. Another slightly smaller figure followed leading a second horse. The arrivals were Negro youths. They silently handed the reins of one horse to Gabriel and the other to Richard. The animals were strapped with baggage.

The young men slipped away as silently as they had arrived. They said nothing. "We'll rest for ten minutes. Then we'll make our way. The horses are carrying all your baggage."

"I thought I'd never see it again."

"We can't allow an English gentleman who is rich enough to have his own servant to try and cross the lines with just the shirt on his back. That would be bound to cause suspicion. Also things are hidden in it. You'll find out soon enough. "

Unbeknown to Richard they were just outside the farm owned by the Van Lews a few miles north of Richmond. The youths were Gabriel's sons which he had fathered by one of the Van Lews' freed slaves. They lived at the farm with their mother.

The riding was tedious and slow. The horses toiled through the heavy snow but as on the flight from Richmond the weather protected them from detection. All Richard could see was snow, blackness and Gabriel's bent back. It was tiring to keep Gabriel in sight and required concentration on that and nothing else. To lose him would have been easy. They seemed to be picking their way down small roads, lanes and tracks. They were continually turning and changing direction. Richard was totally bewildered. Not a word was spoken. The only sounds were the occasional jingling of harness and the muffled flopping of the hooves of the poor horses as they slaved through the snow.

Eventually they drudged down yet another track. The barking of dogs suggested that they might be near some habitation. Richard glanced up and again saw white branches forming a ceiling. The effect was surreal. To Richard's relief Gabriel stopped and dismounted, motioned to Richard to do the same and handed him the reins of his horse. "Hold both horses. I'll be back shortly."

Richard stood holding the tired animals. Steam was rising from their flanks despite the cold. They champed and shook their heads up and down. Richard felt lonely and uneasy in this supernatural white wonderland. It reminded him of a frightening fairy story that had been read to him as a child. One of the stencilled illustrations showed a boy clinging on to the arched back of a wolf whose mouth was open in a terrifying snarl. The wolf was running in the middle of the pack which looked equally fearsome. The story had finished there. The boy had just disappeared into the snowy, wooded wastes. Nobody knew his fate. It would have been better for Richard if he had known the child had been eaten. Instead there was this terrible uncertainty. The story had given Richard nightmares for weeks. He had never forgotten it. He thought of it now.

Richard started to become irrational. What if Gabriel was to meet with an accident or fall into the hands of the enemy? He did not know where he was or what he was supposed to do. He would be left for ever holding these horses in this snowy wilderness. He gave a heavy sigh of relief when Gabriel appeared with his usual stealth.

Holding the reins they soon emerged from the tunnel into an opening. Richard could see big blocks of black topped with white. These must be buildings of some sort. As he drew closer he could see that they were at a small farm. Richard followed Gabriel through an open door. They were in a stable. A young Negro boy was standing by the stall and took the horses. Without any word from Gabriel or the boy Richard followed Gabriel outside again round the side of the buildings and into another door.

They were now standing in a kitchen. Immediately Richard was overwhelmed by a blanket of warmth and smell. The rich aroma of thick wholesome broth and newly-made bread made him realise that the long, difficult, frozen journey combined with fear and uncertainty had made him feel very hungry.

The fire gave out a generous heat which contrasted

with the intense cold. Richard's hands -although gloved were numb and his face frozen. He felt a pain as the heat dispelled the cold which resisted as though the two sensations were fighting for control of his body. He sank down onto a chair. He looked at a clock ticking comfortably on the mantelpiece; the reassuring sound breathed some sense of reality into an otherwise unreal world. The time was a quarter-past four. He had been travelling for over six hours. A woman was busy at the stove. She put a bowl of thick broth in front of him, a mouth-watering loaf with a thick, heavy crust and a generous slab of cheese and left the room without saying a word. Richard fell on the food like a ravening wolf.

The immediate relieving of his cold and hunger had numbed Richard's other senses but after a couple of minutes he looked up at Gabriel who was sitting across the table. Although Gabriel must have been as hungry as Richard he ate (as indeed he did everything else) with grace and style, as though the food had been placed before him by one of his servants. Richard felt ashamed at his gobbling and slowed down to a more mannerly pace. Gabriel smiled at him in a fatherly way. "Better now?" Richard nodded. Gabriel said nothing else until the meal was over. The boy needed time to recover.

"This is where I leave you. Others take over now. There is just one thing I need you to do and that is to copy out and sign this letter to Mrs Smythe explaining your sudden departure. She knows your handwriting." He slid two pieces of paper across the table. One was blank. The other bore writing. Richard felt guilty. Gabriel intuitively realised this.

"Don't feel guilty. There's no need. You've been serving the Federal cause and you've been serving it well. She enjoyed your hospitality. It was freely given in the tradition of the Old South. Anyway, at the end you paid your keep. No doubt rebels are doing similar things to our people – or worse".

This intuitive man had instantly diagnosed what had been going through Richard's mind. What an appalling waste of talent that by mere virtue of race this intelligent man was enslaved to a nation a large proportion of which was intellectually much inferior. How perverse was fate! Richard remembered the immediate impression that Gabriel made on him when he first saw him- that he must be descended from a long line of kings or chieftains. The man was born to rule. But this was no time to ponder on the wider philosophical issues of life. Gabriel went into another room and returned with pen and ink.

"Have your fingers thawed out enough to write?" Richard nodded, took up the pen , dipped it into the inkstand and began to write in the copper- plate handwriting that he had first been taught by his governess , then in school (liberally aided by strokes of the cane) and finally as an articled clerk when he had to copy out legal documents. For a few minutes the only sounds were the ticking of the clock and the scratching of the pen. Paper was becoming scarce in Richmond. Many letters were now being written on butcher's paper. The letter was short and to the point. It merely said that he had received an urgent message from relatives and had to leave. It thanked her for her hospitality and expressed the hope that the two of them would meet sometime in the future and that she and her family would come out of the war safely. When he had read it over and then signed it he handed to Gabriel.

"It's a bit bald isn't it?"

"Possibly, but it's perfectly polite and conveys no information that can be checked by the authorities. It doesn't say where your relatives are – everybody will assume correctly that they are in England. Nor does it say where you are going. The assumption will probably be that you will be returning to England. Mrs Smythe was very conveniently indisposed today so you couldn't have taken your leave personally even if you wanted to. She will probably think that the letter is just a polite way of saying that you feel so awkward after last night when she collapsed on you that you just couldn't remain in the house with her."

Gabriel scraped his chair on the stone wooden floor and left the room again. A minute later he returned with a sturdy- looking grey haired man in his fifties. "This is John. He will take care of you now." Gabriel grasped both Richard's hands in his and pressed them with real meaning and sincerity. Handshakes can tell you so much about a person's character. Richard couldn't stand it when somebody's hand lay limp and lifeless like a cold dead snake. "May good luck and God go with you?" Richard stood up as Gabriel left the room without a further word. Richard suddenly felt like a child who had been left by a competent and caring parent. This feeling of desolation accentuated his exhaustion and he staggered against the chair. John caught him before he fell.

"Come on. You must get some sleep. You can't do anything now. You're exhausted. We'll talk in the morning unless the dogs alert us to patrols but I don't suppose we'll get any this weather. If we do I'll have to get you up. "

Richard awoke from a heavy dreamless sleep. The unusually pale light which managed to struggle through the frost encrusted windows emphasised the heavy, snow-encrusted world outside. John was standing by the bed with a cup of steaming liquid. It was real coffee. Richard's nostrils drew in the delicious aroma for the first time in months.

"You've had a good sleep. Now it's time to get up. It's one o'clock. We'll see you in the kitchen in about ten minutes. Lunch will be ready."

John sat at the wooden table. The same woman as last night was putting the finishing touches to a meal. Another man sat opposite John. His eyes shone like large lanterns from his pale, drawn, cadaverous face. He started to shuffle to his feet but John leaned across the table and put his hand firmly on his shoulder. "Sit down. We won't stand on ceremony today. That will start tomorrow when you start practising at being this young man's servant. Neither of you have been told the name of the other because that's the way we do things round here. But there is no point in not doing that now. Mr Richard Clarke, Englishman meet Colonel George Brent of the United States Army late guest of the Confederacy at their charming, welcoming hotel – Libby Prison."

The men shook hands. Richard looked at Brent with awe and respect. No wonder he looked ill after those sub-human conditions.

The food was placed before them. The ham was fried just as Richard liked it. Dark pink meat with the fat on the outside golden brown so that it would split easily when he cut it with his knife. Brent just sat and looked at it as though he had stepped into another world. The daily prison routine of arguing over tiny scraps of food and even rats would be in his memory for the rest of his life. Golden fried potatoes, beans and corn were heaped on the plates alongside the ham. A magnificent apple pie, thick cream and more of last night's bread and cheese completed the meal. Richard mused that the food shortages in Richmond did not seem to have found their way up here. Patrols tended to clear a farm of most of its food but happily the remoteness ensured there were few visits and the hiding places were ready as soon as the dogs started barking.

Brent ate slowly, sparingly and deliberately. His stomach had not as yet readjusted itself to proper meals. The woman whom John introduced as his wife sat down with them. She obviously knew as much about the whole operation as her husband.

For the next few days Richard and Brent were rested and fully briefed for their journey through to the Northern lines. The good deal of ciphered information including all the material concerning Rose Greenhow was hidden in the luggage in a variety of places. Brent had been shaved of the beard that he always wore and his hair had been cut short.

John had never been to England and had had little to do with English people so he left it to Richard to work on Brent's English accent. Richard started to elaborate on the different types of English accent forgetting that anybody who had never been to England would not know much about them anyway. Should Brent be London Cockney, West Country or what? In the end John put up his hand.

"Look! These sentries will probably just be stumblebum Reb farm boys who'd never been more than ten miles away from home before the war, most of them can't read. They are not going to know the difference between an English, French or German accent. There's no need to be too particular. Just make him sound not American."

As Brent had spent a year in London studying at the Middle Temple he was not unfamiliar with the middle-class accent as spoken in London so they decided to work on that. Brent had been a Wall Street lawyer before the war. The happy coincidence of them both being in the legal profession increased the mutual respect that they had quickly formed for each other. Richard's training had not left him however. He said nothing about working for Dick Jenkins in New York. That would be revealed when they had both reported to the Federal authorities. John guided them for most of the way and fortunately Brent was not unfamiliar with the territory as a result of earlier activities in the war. The ferocious weather worked to their advantage – they had not met any patrols.

The two of them threaded their way along a narrow, winding track though a thick wood in the late afternoon. It had just stopped snowing. They rounded a bend. A heavily bearded untidy horseman faced them with his rifle aimed at them.

"Just hold it right there!" Brent reached for his weapon but before he could touch it a shot rang out.

Chapter Twenty Four
Richmond

July 1863

Kate was deliriously happy. One hand held the reins whilst the other was curled in DuFresne's as they walked their horses along the wide trail through the wood. The huge trees formed a vault shielding them from the punishing sun. Flecks and beams of light struggled through the trees giving the effect of riding through a vast, silent cathedral.

DuFresne had been charming and attentive to Kate over the last two months which had been a whirlwind of balls, picnics, barbecues and rides. Shortages were still being felt by the majority – save for those who were in control of events such as Miller and DuFresne – but despite personal hardships a heady atmosphere of exhilaration intoxicated the South.

The general temperament of the South was volatile and could quickly swing from black despair to dizzy jubilation and back again. This had been the case a couple of months ago when a victory had swept away the leaden sorrow and heavy gloom which darkened the skies.

Lee had defeated Hooker at Chancellorsville and was now preparing to press heavily into the North, cross the Potomac, take Washington, threaten Philadelphia and even perhaps New York. Britain would be bound to recognise the Confederacy now and the war would end quickly with a Confederate victory.

The only factor which slightly marred Kate's happiness was that her brothers Frank and Harry were no longer out of harm's way. Harry was now riding with Jeb Stuart (how her brother Jeff,whose life had been cruelly cut short would have loved to have been there) whilst Frank was part of Lee's invasion force. News of casualties amongst people she knew never allowed her to remain easy for too long. Even the death of the odious Tyler Lloyd at Chancellorsville where a cannon ball took off his head was received by her with a certain amount of regret- he represented part of her old life which had now disappeared for ever. By all accounts he had redeemed himself in the Army and proved an effective and resourceful officer. Aggressive bullies often make brave soldiers.

Lee's first loyalty had always been to his native state of Virginia and was the reason why he was commanding the Confederate and not the Federal forces and this was determining his actions now. Virginia was war-weary and had borne the burden of men and animals fighting and trampling over it. The invasion was giving Virginia much needed relief from pressure. A few days ago news had reached Richmond that Lee was close to capturing Harrisburg the capital of Pennsylvania and only a hundred miles away from Washington. Once Harrisburg had been captured Lee could destroy the rail links with Baltimore and push towards Philadelphia.

Despite Lee's success he had made a major tactical mistake in allowing his army to become too widely dispersed and not maintaining sufficient intelligence of the movements of the enemy. He had also allowed the gallant, brave but volatile and reckless General Jeb Stuart to race off to the east of the main thrust of the Confederates with the aim of disrupting the Union Army's communications and causing confusion in its rear.

A small town deep in Pennsylvania had little reason to be a strategic target but it did possess a shoe factory.

As usual Lee's Army was desperately short of shoes and a group of Confederate infantrymen in search of shoes ran into a Union Cavalry Detachment. The little town would henceforth be famous throughout the world. Its name was Gettysburg.

Battle was commencing as Kate and DuFresne were contentedly holding hands. Kate was happily daydreaming. Lee would soon be in Washington and she would be there as well – as Mrs DuFresne. Kate was certain that DuFresne would be appointed to an important post in the newly formed government that would result from the Confederate victory. Rose Greenhow was equally certain that no such post was forthcoming and she was not nearly as optimistic about the state of the war but she had been careful not to upset Kate. It had just been decided that Rose should visit Europe; although Kate did not know yet Rose intended that she would accompany her.

The optimism of the people had not been shared by the Government. The victory at Chancellorsville had cost the South heavy losses and the heaviest loss of all was the death of General 'Stonewall' Jackson. The tide of desertions had not been stemmed, gold was scarce and there was little confidence in the Confederate currency. Some cotton and tobacco managed to sneak through the blockades but much of it finished up at the bottom of the sea.

Rose should go to Europe to have her book published in London and to solicit whatever sympathy she could for the Confederacy. She was also able to promote a new scheme of trading with England through a form of cotton certificates. The idea was to sell cotton in exchange for ships or other goods.

Rose was instructed to act as an unofficial ambassador to try to boost the flagging enthusiasm for the South in France and England; the masculine powers of Richmond had decided that it was time for a female assault on the masculine powers of those countries. After all, everything else had failed.

Douglas Southall Freeman wrote: "One cannot think of a more appealing agent for the support of the chivalrous element in Britain than this beautiful dark-haired widow, who knows every social art and had mastered the technique of winning masculine sympathy." Carl Sandburg wrote about her " gaunt beauty, education, manners and resourceful speech......
her proud loyalty to the South and her will and courage sets her apart as a woman who would welcome death from a firing squad if it would serve her cause." His prophesy was to be eerily accurate.

Rose wanted and needed Kate to go to Europe with her. The only problem was DuFresne. Unbeknown to her that problem would soon be solved.

Later that evening DuFresne knocked at Miller's door and was shown straight into his study. This had been a regular routine over the last few weeks since DuFresne had been assiduous in his courtship of Kate. Visits to Miller's office were now unnecessary and were considered undesirable as it was thought better to stress the social side of the two men's relationship and to minimise the number of people who knew they were connected in business. The pattern of the evenings was that DuFresne would call at Miller's house,discuss business and then press his suite with Kate – although it did not need a great deal of pressing .

Miller did not even look up as DuFresne was shown into his study. A third man was sitting in the corner of the room. He stood up as DuFresne held out his hand.
" Good to see you Bullingdon ", and you DuFresne.
 If one did not know Lord Bullingdon was an English aristocrat this fact would have been guessed by

anybody who had spent much time in England. He was tall, fair , handsome and distinguished –looking with an arrogant air that gave the impression that he was from a superior race that was born to rule.

"DuFresne, we can now start moving. I heard today from our British agents that the financial aspects are now agreed and the money is sitting in the specified accounts in Lombard's Bank- Bullingdon has seen to that." Bullingdon nodded.
. You should marry right away. As you know the plan to get Rose Greenhow to England and away from here has worked. The right seeds sown in the right places have achieved wonders. Kate can still work for Rose in England even if you are there."

"So Bullingdon, Greenhow,Kate and I are to travel to England together?" DuFresne grimaced. "Greenhow doesn't like me."

Miller folded his hands and leaned forward on his desk looking at DuFresne intently. "Well, not everybody can like you DuFresne. You'll just have to be adult and make the best of it. When you reach England I don't suppose there will be that much for Kate to do for Rose so you won't have to be together that much. And you will be married and Kate should be much more forthcoming – pillow talk and all that."

DuFresne proposed to Kate that night and she accepted in a mixture of rapture and excitement. They were to be married two days later in Miller's house. "But he's not in the Army. He's not going to be sent to the front. What's the rush? wailed Miller's wife Henrietta. She was totally disregarded and she looked very cross indeed on the morning of the wedding.

Two days gave no time for elaborate preparations for the wedding but in any event wild and conflicting rumours about Gettysburg rendered planning impossible. What should have been a day filled with happiness for Kate had been reduced to one of terror. Worry and anguish had invaded her stomach with those dreadful feelings of tightness, butterflies and sickness.

Frank was with Lee in the theatre of danger. Kate then realised that Harry was also there. Her first thought had been of Frank and her other brother had ranked a very poor second. Guilt was now combined with worry and fear which made her wretched during the wedding service. This should have been the happiest day of her life and the dreadful uncertainty caused by the battle was heightened by the fact that those she cared about most were absent – her father, mother and brothers. She was only just able to withhold tears and seemed very uncertain when voicing her responses a fact that did not go unnoticed in the small congregation – not least by her husband.

Immediately after the ceremony (if such a paltry occasion was worthy of that name) the party was withdrawing to the dining room for refreshments. As they crossed the hall Kate heard a knock at the front door. As they were about to take their seats the butler whispered something in Miller's ear. Miller left without a word. On his return concerned faces looked up at him in frightened anticipation.

"I'm afraid we have been defeated with massive casualties." Women raised their hands to their mouths in shock to the sounds of gasps and the odd sob.

"What about casualties?"asked Kate in what was somewhere between a whisper and a croak.

"Lists are coming in at the moment and are being posted outside the offices of 'The Richmond Dispatch' and 'The Richmond Daily Examiner'."

"I must get down there." Kate jumped up. DuFresne put a heavy hand on her shoulder.

"Sit down and have some of your wedding

breakfast. There'll be crowds of people milling around there."

"How can I? When my brothers might be dead. GET OFF ME." She screamed as the grip became vice-like. She twisted round and dragged herself away. She made for the door and before anybody could stop her she was out of the front door racing towards the offices of the 'Dispatch' followed by the wedding party. Not only was Kate oblivious of the fact that she was still in her wedding-dress which had been produced from the scanty materials that were available at two days notice but so was everybody else in the streets.

Panic- stricken people stampeded their way through the streets trying to make their way to the newspaper offices. As Kate drew nearer she became wedged in a solid mass of surging humanity which ebbed backwards and forwards like a tide. Faces were grey and taught with anguish.

Every time a list was posted on the front of the building it was greeting with shouts of " where's the 4th Virginia ?." or " what about the 6th South Carolina ?" and- when the lists of the appropriate regiments were available- " are the ' Fs' out yet or " when are we going to get the 'Ms' . Anguish was intensified because the lists were high up on the wall and people without exceptional sight could not see them. Eventually as the telegraph juddered out the endless lists of names the paper's printing press churned out further copies which were handed out to the clawing, grasping hands which quickly became stained with the printers' ink. Miraculously not many were torn and were handed backwards when it was realised that the name of the loved one was not on it.

All too often Kate heard piercing cries of "no" or Oh my God no."or bursts of hysterical sobbing. Mothers stood weeping in the arms of their husbands. Often couples wept together. Frightened, bewildered children asked after their fathers or elder brothers "what about Danny? is he alright?". Where there was not yet news their petrified parents tried to reassure them in flat toneless voices.

People stifled under the dark, brooding, heavy threatening sky. The oppressive atmosphere stoked up by uncertainty and terror combined with the crushing throng made the situation unbearable for many in the crowd. Some began to faint; as there was no room to lay them on the ground they sagged against their neighbours the pressure of whom kept them in a kind of collapsed standing position. Eventually gaps were made and the victim could be stretched out and the frayed collars of worn dresses and shirts could be loosened.

By eight o' clock Kate still had no news. The crowd was thinning. DuFresne was still by her side despite her repeated requests for him to go home. She would take months trying to analyse why she didn't want him there. She should have done. His presence should have been her most important and treasured support.

For some reason Kate of Richard Clarke. Why?. She had more or less dismissed him from her mind when she met DuFresne but when he suddenly disappeared without any explanation she had suddenly found him interesting. Now a web of mystery had woven about him in Kate's mind although she should not have found it that unusual; at the moment people were disappearing from view without any explanation .At one of the few social gatherings Kate attended with Rose she had asked Susan Smythe only to receive a curt " oh, he had to sort out some problem about relatives I think" with an immediate change of subject.

Kate subsequently discussed the matter with Rose. "Well I don't know but I did hear that there may have been some romantic entanglement which went wrong. I could tell from the way Susan looked at him that she liked him." The fact that Richard had awakened the interest of an attractive older woman now made him seem more desirable to Kate. It would have been too much to say she found him fascinating but the man whom she had previously considered as an inexperienced youth had now acquired a sexuality and sophistication. This was only increased when Rose that experienced femme fatale and judge of male attributes added "I'm not surprised. He's a handsome, charming young man. I always told you that you could do worse."

Kate was now brought back to stark reality when she heard more screams. New casualty lists were being handed back. She looked on in pity at a little boy of about six with fair curly hair. His big blue eyes were uncomprehending. He was wearing a smart blue velvet suit with a white lace collar and brass buttons. The suit was unfrayed – probably a hand-me-down from an elder brother who had grown out of it when it was in good condition; such a suit would be unavailable now.

Tears streamed down the child's face. He was standing with his father and mother and had obviously been told that his elder brother had been killed. "But Johnny must come home. He promised. He asked me to look after Fido and I have. I kept my promise. Why couldn't he keep his?" His devastated parents were trying to gulp out some words of comfort through their own tears but their constricted throats would not allow many. Kate wondered pointlessly as to whether Johnny had been the previous wearer of the blue suit.

Eventually the list that Kate had been both dreading and praying for appeared – that of Frank's regiment. She had to wait eternally,first for the 'T's' then the Turners. As to be expected in such a common surname there were a number. She half-closed her eyes as she looked at the initials and reached the 'F's. 'Turner. Francis G. Lieut.; Turner Francis J. Pte. Turner Francis N. Pte. Turner Fredk. L. Capt.' No Franklin! He wasn't there. She felt numb with relief and emotional exhaustion.

A few minutes later the list for Harry's regiment was handed out. Two Harolds, five Henrys but no Hereward. Harry couldn't stand his proper name. As a boy Colonel Turner had devoured the tales of the Saxon hero Hereward the Wake who had bravely fought guerrilla actions against the Normans after England had been defeated by William the Conqueror. Harry had no problem with that but he could not see why that meant he should be lumbered with that liability of a name and from a very early age had insisted on 'Harry'. Kate was glad of her father's whim now. With such a distinctive name she was certain that her brother was safe. Again the wave of guilt that she was more concerned for Frank than for Harry ; also the fact that her Turners were alive did not detract from the fact that the families of the other Turners would be grief-stricken.

The momentary relief dispelled for a short time the doubts that would return. The names could be on the next list or the one after that. Many corpses could not be identified and there was the ever-present threat of disease and the risk of dying in prison camp from malnutrition was greater than dying on the battlefield.

Kate didn't argue as DuFresne steered her home. The streets were emptying. Kate passed faces racked by grief or uncertainty – tear-stained, grey, haggard and gaunt. As they turned a street corner she saw a woman sobbing in the arms of her husband. His eyes stared blankly over her head. Kate recognised the white face. It was the father of the hapless Michael Wilson whom she had so churlishly spurned when Henrietta had intervened during her first meeting with DuFresne.

Kate felt guilty now and regretted her unwarranted and capricious behaviour. All the poor boy wanted was a woman to smile on him kindly before he rushed to submit himself to needless slaughter. In his youthful patriotism this chubby faced child saw himself winning honours and promotions and wearing his lady's favours in his cap like a chivalrous knight-not agonisingly screaming his life away in a field-dressing station whilst the surgeon sawed off the leg which had been shattered by a Federal shell.

Soon the Confederate Government began to grasp the grim consequences of Gettysburg. The Confederacy had now lost the only expectation of military success which was the only hope she had amongst the shortages of almost everything, spiralling prices, pending economic disaster and worry about relatives in the field. The possibility of recognition by Britain and France as an independent power was growing fainter by the day. Any possible straws had to be grasped such as diplomacy and individual wheedling by those with charm such as Rose Greenhow who had been so effective at manipulating the Yankee officers. Four weeks later Rose Greenhow, Lord Bullingdon and Mr and Mrs Philip DuFresne left for England.

Chapter Twenty Five

South Carolina

July 1863

For no real identifiable reason Solange had been feeling better over the last two to three days . She had been drinking less and had not felt in so much need of laudanum. She had received a letter from the Colonel in England and although it had been written some six weeks earlier any letter was welcome. The terrible news of Gettysburg very quickly followed by the loss of Vicksburg on the Mississippi had been tempered by the relief that neither of her sons had been on the casualty lists; some of her wider family and friends had not been so lucky.

This morning Solange had felt a new awareness and sharpness . She walked round the room on the ground floor and ran her finger along surfaces. Dust lay where it shouldn't , items had been shifted without her approval and some things appeared to be missing altogether-a silver cigar-case of the Colonel's , a silver paper-knife with a mother-of- pearl handle and a number of other items. She descended to the kitchens – a sloppy disorder reined; things were not in their proper place and everything was cloaked in a thick grey film of grime. As for the store- rooms they were chaotic . She opened the door of one of them and everything tumbled over her . Rachel was not up to the job . The girl had had her chance . Solange would now have to find a proper housekeeper.

Solange now decided to inspect the plantation. She must look smart. She had let herself go in the past few weeks- disgusting! "Pull yourself together Girl", she upbraided herself. She had her hair dressed and sent word to Matthew to bring Jack round to the front door at three o'clock. Jack hadn't had nearly enough exercise since Kate had left. Matthew was the only groom left now. Still, there were less horses and mules. Beaumont was, however, better off then most plantations. The guile of the Colonel in the skilful hiding of the livestock and stores coupled with Miller's influence had blunted the inroads of the Commissary.

Now that all-important part of a woman's toilette – her hair was in a reasonable state Solange felt much better. Her not quite black hair was now shining and there were not that many grey hairs.

Solange then gave orders to Susie the maid to lay out her best riding-habit. She was the mistress of Beaumont and she was going to look it today – not like some poor old drab of the 'cracker' class. After Susie had finished fussing around Solange looked at herself in the cheval mirror and smoothed down her skirt. It had been well-cut and fitted snugly round her waist and thighs.

An integral part of the hat was a buckle in synthetic diamonds. Solange decided to match it with the genuine diamond brooch that the Colonel had given her when he brought her to Beaumont as a young bride of seventeen. She pinned it on just below the collar of her habit. She looked at herself again. Not bad for forty - five. She felt proud of herself today. She had allowed her self-respect to slip. That had to stop. She had to take control once again.

Solange had spent two hours riding round some of the plantation and what she saw was satisfactory bearing in mind the straitened circumstances in which they were operating. She had to admit that Harrison was a good manager despite the fact that she found him opinionated and lacking in the deference to which she was accustomed. She was trotting from the plantation when she saw Schneider riding away from Harrison's quarters. She wheeled Jack round; Harrison, hearing the sound of hooves cantering up, stepped on to his veranda.

"Harrison, what is that man doing here?" As Solange looked down at him from her saddle he saw an image which personified everything he found repellent about Southern society. When most people were suffering from a lack of food and clothing here was a well-dressed, bejewelled lady sitting side-saddle on a thoroughbred horse imperiously addressing him by his surname. He had been used to people addressing him as 'Mr. Harrison' in the North and would never adapt back to the old ways in which he had grown up.

"Ma'am" – he stressed the word so as to convey sarcasm but he thought that Solange was too stupid to realise it – "I have just sold him some cotton".

"But I told him I wouldn't deal with him."

"Well, I didn't know that and in any event I have dealt with him before when Miss Kate was present." Solange tried to calm the fidgeting Jack. Her concentration was being diverted which undermined her confidence. Had she been wearing normal relatively casual clothes for riding the plantation she would have been able to dismount without difficulty but the tight riding- habit restricted her movements.

"Look Harrison, I can't carry on a conversation like this. Help me dismount please." Harrison helped her down holding her far too closely round the waist for Solange's liking. Harrison motioned to her to come into his quarters and tied Jack to the hitching – post. Solange shook her head; it was unthinkable for the mistress to enter into the living accommodation of the manager.

"You say that Miss Kate knows about this?" Harrison nodded. Solange did not want to accuse him of lying outright so she chose her words carefully. "You must be mistaken. Miss Kate knows that I won't be able to deal with that man."

"Well, she didn't mention it to me Ma'am. She was with us when some of the deals were made." Solange had to think before she replied. All she could think of was.

"Harrison. I don't want you dealing with him again. Do you hear?"

"May I ask why?" Solange now really did lose her temper. She had never been addressed by a subordinate like that before. Moreover, she couldn't stand his arrogant supercilious manner. She thrashed her whip against the rail."

"NO." She screamed. "You may NOT ask why. But since you have the impertinence to question my orders I will tell you. I don't trust that man and I think that some of the cotton may end up with the Yankees." Harrison stood unmoved looking at her without expression.

"So. Does that matter as long as we get a good price and keep our plantation running?" Solange was now white.

"It is not 'our' plantation. It is 'my' plantation. That means it belongs to me and my family and you are our servant and you will do as I tell you. Do you understand?" She hissed the words through gritted teeth.

"No." Before Solange could expostulate Harrison continued. "Ma'am I was employed by your husband to run this plantation to the best of my ability during his absence and that I will do. If I consider it right to deal with Mr Schneider then I will deal with Mr Schneider. Anyway Mr Preston Miller knows all about it and he agrees."

They stared speechlessly at each other for a few moments. Solange could not believe that Miller would be party to such treachery. "I am sure that my brother doesn't know all about it and that he doesn't agree."

"Why don't you ask him?" Solange realised there was no way out of this impasse but would just have to withdraw without appearing as helpless as she felt. She had to overcome the immediate practical difficulty of mounting with as much dignity as she could muster in her restrictive habit. She certainly wasn't going to ask Harrison for help. She untied Jack but Harrison held the bridle. She mounted at the mounting block carefully and expertly. Once more in the saddle she felt some of her confidence and self-control return.

"I will ask my brother to come over here. There must be some misunderstanding." She refrained from saying that Harrison had spent several years up North and was probably a Yankee sympathiser. Before Harrison could reply she galloped back to the house. Harrison, smiling quietly to himself withdrew into his quarters.

"Married!" Solange sank down on the settee in Miller's drawing room. She had just appeared unannounced to seek her brother's help with regard to the situation at Beaumont. Her journey by rail car had been terrible. Three times all the passengers had to leave the train when it was commandeered by the Army. She had been jostled by all sorts of horrid, common people. When she could find a seat it was always hard and uncomfortable. A woman like her was just not used to travelling like that. She was used to first class travel, servants and deference. She arrived exhausted to resolve one problem only to be confronted with shattering news about a totally different matter. "Who to?" She whined.

Miller explained in a few short sentences. "You said you gave your consent. You had no right."

"I had every right. I'm her only male relative."

"What about her father and brothers? They are not dead yet".

"There wasn't time. We could not contact them. William is in England and the boys are at the front."

"Well, you should have all waited until William could have been contacted. Any why wasn't I consulted. I wasn't even informed. I'm her mother!"

"There wasn't time."

"You keep saying there wasn't time. Why not?"Solange suddenly put her hand to her mouth. "Oh my God. She's not …..."

"No. Of course not."

"What do we know about this man? Where does he come from? Who are his people?"

"I know him very well. I have done a great deal of business with him and the war has put a great deal of pressure on things replied Miller evasively." Eventually he went on to explain as much as he felt inclined. Miller never explained more than he felt inclined.

Solange retired to bed for three days. Harrison, the reason for her visit had been displaced from her mind by the other devastating news. When she eventually mentioned him to Miller he didn't even raise an eyebrow. He knew about Schneider. He just said that Harrison was doing a good job and that nobody should interfere. He didn't seem to care that some of the cotton could finish up with the enemy. The war seemed to have driven everybody mad! Miller had always been a very good brother but he now seemed to care for nothing but business and as for Kate's actions in

357

marrying a man without her mother's knowledge , let alone her consent and then departing for England !. It was unspeakable!"

Solange returned to Belmont after a week, a very sad, crushed woman. She went about her tasks in an expressionless and mechanical way. She fell back on her old crutches of laudanum and alcohol. Harrison did not of course expect any remonstration from Solange and just proceeded as though there had never been any confrontation between them.

Rachel lay in Harrison's arms the night of Solange's return in his quarters. Whilst their mistress had been away they had slept in her bed; they now had sufficient control over the other servants for them to be too frightened to tell her.

Harrison had saved the good news until just after they had climaxed. Rachel loved to talk then – it enhanced the aftermath of their love making.

"Things are really going our way. First Gettysburg, then Vicksburg and now this".

"What darling?" murmured Rachel as she nuzzled against his chest.

"Today I learnt that the Negro regiment under Robert Gould Shaw have just taken part in their first action for the North at James Island. We are getting closer and closer."

She kissed him and they made love again.

Chapter Twenty Six

Somewhere in Virginia near the Union Lines February 1863

The heavily bearded untidy horseman fell from his saddle. Brent and Richard dismounted and dropped to the ground motionless. Then an English voice rang out from the undergrowth. "It's alright Richard you can get up now. There's nothing to worry about. It's me. Harry Harper."

Richard heaved a sigh of relief. "Oh. Hallo Harry. Aren't I glad to see you? How are you?" Brent somewhat bemused by this exchange between two Englishmen which could have been a chance meeting on Lords Cricket Ground inquired "You two know each other?"

"Yes, replied Richard we were at school together."

"Well. I always knew that you Limeys weren't easily rattled but this takes the biscuit." Richard stood up and took his horse's bridle.

"How did you know I was here Harry and how did you get here?" Brent shuffled to his feet.

"Never mind how he got here let's just concentrate on getting the hell out."

Harry indicated the way as they led the horses into the wood. "It's alright. I'll guide you to the Union lines. You're very close now. Just help me get this body out of sight." They lugged the body into the undergrowth and concealed it a few hundred yards away from the track. Harry brushed himself down. "That's fine. Nobody will find him for ages – if ever."

Harry went on to give them a few words of explanation. He had been informed of their whereabouts and was asked if he could engineer matters so that he could keep an eye on them. What he didn't know was that the request had originated from Elizabeth Van Lew whose existence was unknown to him. Richard had now heard of her from his time in Richmond but only as ' that eccentric old bat'who dresses like a scarecrow and is sympathetic to the Union'.

Harry had volunteered for a scouting assignment with just one other man who was an experienced scout who had heard the fugitives and told Harry to remain in the wood. The scout now lay dead. There was no time for much conversation and Harry left them with mutual expressions of hope that they would all meet up soon in more agreeable circumstances.

Later that evening Richard and Brent were safely behind Union lines. The weather had continued to help them. They encountered nobody else. Two tired, cold and bored sentries looked at them without interest. They were going off duty in ten minutes and they were not going to waste their rest period interrogating two harmless – looking Englishmen. They pored over the forged papers laboriously as though they were translating the Bible from Medieval Latin. John had been right. They were semi- literate and were just going through the motions. The papers were handed back without expression.

It would take some weeks for Brent to stop marvelling how his escape had been aided by two Englishmen who were at school together and whose paths had crossed again by a mysterious quirk of fate.

Four days later Richard had been rested and was in Washington for a debriefing by Colonel Wilmer and Alan Pinkerton.

Chapter Twenty Seven

New York

July 1863

Richard sat in Dick Jenkins's office and closed the file. He had just been checking a contract for one of Dick's clients who were supplying footwear to the Government. He stacked the papers neatly to one side on the desk. He was going out for the evening. He felt he deserved it.

Due partly to Richard's work Smithson the banker had been arrested in May. His papers had been seized which contained a mass of incriminating evidence ; among them was found a certificate of one hundred and twenty dollars of railroad stock in Rose Greenhow's name. Richard had undergone a thorough debriefing from Colonel Wilmer and Pinkerton which had lasted several days; every aspect of his time since leaving Washington for Richmond had been covered.

At the end of the final day when it was clear that Richard had given all possible information Wilmer stood up. "I expect you've been thinking about your future?" Richard had. Wilmer went over to a cabinet and pulled out a small piece of paper. He slid it across the table. "This is something for you to be going on with and with our grateful thanks." Richard opened it up. It was a draft for a thousand dollars. He looked at it in disbelief.

"Its no more than you deserve Richard. You put your life in danger doing dangerous work and you did it skilfully and well. We won't use you for a while; but at sometime in the future – who knows."

After a further discussion of about half an hour Richard left the office. He was satisfied but drained. The debriefing had been exhausting and he still had not recovered from the period in Richmond when he could never relax. He'd had to be careful about what he said to everybody and the final journey home had been particularly taxing. When he and Colonel Brent passed the final sentries he was taut like a violin string until they were long out of sight. It was always possible that a Confederate detachment could come galloping after them. Eventually they met a Union picket. Brent heaved a sigh of relief. "O. K. You can relax now."

After a brief meal the two men parted. Richard had to leave for Washington and Brent had to be medically checked and rested before undergoing his own debriefing. Brent held out his hand. "Thank you Richard. I owe you a lot."

"I was only doing my job."

"Maybe. But there are various ways of doing one's job. There is just doing it and there is excelling in it. And you excelled in it. I shall never forget what you have done. And I shall see to it that we will meet again."

The various options for the future discussed between Wilmer, Pinkerton and Richard included a number of possibilities. As Richard had enough money to keep him for a couple of years they included doing nothing for a while , returning to England, returning to Dick Jenkins's office (or another lawyer's office), enrolling for a law course at one of the universities , or following his original idea of joining the Army.

The first two options were ruled out immediately. Doing nothing was not in Richard's nature and returning to England was unthinkable. He could not return to his old life after all his experiences. Although he had been away for just under two years it seemed like ten and he felt about thirty- five instead of twenty – one . In any event he loved this young vibrant, exciting country where everything seemed possible. English society seemed boring and stagnant by comparison. It was far more difficult to break out of the strata of society in which one was born.

University seemed interesting but the time was not right for Richard. He had experienced too much recently to settle down to study now. Anyway young men were out there doing things. Momentous events were happening and horizons were constantly changing and Richard wanted to be part of them.

That just left a legal office and the Army. Richard thought he would probably do both. He did not want the Army just yet. He felt he wanted to calm himself down after living on tenterhooks over the last few months. He would go back to the law for a time and perhaps join the Army later. Wilmer approved this choice.

"Lawyers are still crying out for staff. Commerce is still booming. And Dick Jenkins thought very highly of you." Richard now knew of course that the purpose of his initial employment by Jenkins at the suggestion of Dr Matthews was that he could be observed for security work. Both men were involved in the Government and security in some way but Richard did not know in what capacity and would never know.

"If you join the Army you will have to enlist as a private in the usual way and be trained. We may be able to use you again in intelligence – either in uniform or out." Wilmer pulled out his hip flask, took a long gulp, sighed with satisfaction and wiped his mouth with the back of his hand in a very unofficer-like manner. He offered the flask to Richard who shook his head. "But if it is to be military intelligence you will have to undergo the normal training as a soldier. We will know through the usual channels if you enlist but when you do please drop me a note as the administrative machinery can be rather slow. We will have means of monitoring your progress."

Richard was gratified with the interest that was being shown in him. He had proved his worth and now there were people who really seemed to care about his future and took into account his own wishes. His father had never given the appearance of showing interest in what Richard wanted. . He had just told Richard what to do. When Richard heard from his sister Laura his views were confirmed.

Richard returned to the Matthews household at their insistence. He intended to obtain his own lodgings but accommodation in New York was in very short supply. He accepted their offer but on condition that he paid his keep. He had received no letters from his father or Laura during his absence. He had written to them before he left New York saying that 'he was going away, they were not to worry and he would contact them as soon as he was able.'

Laura had replied immediately to the first letter he had written on leaving the ship. She was hurt that he had not been able to confide in her but in a way she understood. George had refused to discuss Richard at all and forbade his name to be mentioned in the house. Although Richard was not that surprised by this reaction he was still hurt by it- the negative feelings of anger had overridden the positive ones of care and love which any normal father should have for his son.

Richard had resumed work in Dick Jenkins's office. They had got on well before, the work was interesting and he saw no need to change to another firm.

Meanwhile social life continued to fascinate Richard. Dr Matthews had given a vague explanation of

Richard's absence to his children - Dick Jenkins had sent him away on business. The children did not believe that for one minute they knew that both their father and Dick Jenkins were connected with the Government in some way but they knew better than to probe. Foster, now a Surgeon Lieutenant stationed locally in one of the big military hospitals visited frequently – resplendent in his smart uniform. His sisters Susannah and Ann continued to be good company and a fruitful source of new introductions. Constant topics of conversation were the probability of the Draft being introduced and the fate of mutual friends who had enlisted. A disturbing number of these had been killed, wounded or taken prisoner.

Northern morale was now very low. The defeat at Fredericksburg just before Christmas had added to the enormous losses of the previous months. A strong groundswell of public opinion was now urging Lincoln to end the war and come to terms with the South.This was due mainly to the new inventions of telegraph, railways, photography and reporting by newspapers which meant that disasters now hit the population with immediate effect. Battlefields were no longer distant places which did not embroil the population in the horrors of war. Now the reality and suffering was brought immediately to the American people fuelling the pressure on Lincoln to compromise.

Telegraph transmitted news of defeats as well as victories and casualty lists were produced quickly although they were often inaccurate. Families had the frightening experience of checking lists pinned outside public buildings or printed in newspapers. Direct notification was haphazard and depended on the conscientiousness (and in some cases the literacy) of the officers of a man's regiment. After a battle with heavy losses systematic notification was impossible.

Railways rushed wounded troops to hospitals in and around towns and cities where local women tended their smashed –up bodies, listened to their dying words and sometimes wrote letters to wives and mothers describing their loved one's last moments.

After Richard had been back in New York a week he came into contact with the invention which had done more than anything to transform the impact of the war from imagination to stark reality – photography. Matthew Brady's gallery was crammed with the study of corpses taken some months earlier after the Battle of Antietam Creek. Some five thousand men had died on the battlefield and eighteen thousand others had been seriously wounded of whom some three thousand were also to die. Most towns in the North held exhibitions of these photographs.

Richard gaped at these pictures – fascinated but appalled. This was the first time that Americans had seen the effects of battle stripped of the glorious panoply of war. Troops had paraded in towns all over America before they had departed with crowds cheering, drums beating and girls following them blowing kisses and throwing flowers.

Americans had sent off healthy , handsome , young men in splendid new uniforms bedecked with sparkling buttons and accoutrements , waving gleaming sabres and sitting astride well-fed prancing horses arching glossy, well-groomed necks.

These same Americans now saw bloated corpses , jagged severed limbs, gaping holes in bodies, mangled slabs of flesh where faces had been , staring eyes , open mouths and faces which bore dreadful grins or expressions such as terror or just surprise. Hundreds of thousands of Northerners had flocked to see these photographs. Mothers, sweethearts, wives and sisters were constant visitors and the enthusiasm which had whipped them into goading their men to enlist quickly evaporated. Just before Christmas the defeat at Fredericksburg had dealt a further body-blow with twelve and a half thousand dead and seriously wounded.

Not surprisingly the North was now racked with a severe crisis of recruitment exacerbated by losses and desertions and the fact that volunteers who had joined for two years at the outset of the war (encouraged by a bounty of three hundred dollars) were coming to the end of their term. Everywhere Richard saw recruitment posters, stalls and centres, exhortations by uniformed soldiers, impassioned pleas at public meetings and rallying cries in newspapers but this was not sufficient to assuage the Army's insatiable appetite for men.

Only one solution now remained – the Draft. This was anathema to free-thinking Americans who had won their independence many of whom were immigrants or descendants of immigrants who had left oppressive regimes to come to America.

Richard was undecided now as to whether he should enlist. He thought he would eventually but the work with Dick Jenkins was interesting and he was having a good social life; for the time being he would wait and see. He was made to feel awkward by the aggressive heckling from recruiting officers and taunts from complete strangers in the street but Richard Clarke was not a man to be frightened or brow-beaten into doing anything against his will. Besides, he had done his 'bit' already although nobody would know about it. He probably would enlist but in his own time and nobody else's.

The Draft had finally been introduced a couple of months ago in May to mixed reaction. Every able-bodied man aged between twenty and forty-five was liable to be conscripted. The day after the Act had been passed Richard, Foster and a number of other friends had gone to a restaurant after a visit to the theatre. Everybody was familiar with the terms of the Act which had been anticipated well in advance. Richard was not one to take an instant dislike to people but he made an exception to one young man whom he had never met before and who had been merely introduced as 'Hal who worked on Wall Street'.

Hal had a loud and overbearing manner and during the short time that Richard had known him had managed to have arguments with a theatre attendant, a waiter in the restaurant and the escort of one of the young ladies in the party to whom he made offensive and suggestive comments. When during the meal somebody mentioned the Draft Hal plonked his glass down slopping red wine over the table.

"Well I'm not going to put my butt on the line. There's a whole pile of money to be made in this war and I'm sure as hell going to make it." He forked a heavy load of meat, cabbage and mashed potatoes into his mouth and with bulging cheeks masticated noisily. Richard could not let this pass.

"What will you do if you're drafted?" Richard asked and immediately regretted it. He knew what the answer would be.

"Pay somebody else to do it stoopid," Hal replied scornfully with his mouth full, liberally spraying the table. Richard saw to his satisfaction that a number of the company were as unimpressed as himself. "The Army's only for dummies, and if I can't find anybody to pay to do it I can buy my exemption for three hundred bucks. I can make that in a couple of days. It's a damn liberty that they've brought the Draft in at all. I'm a free-born American but if I have to pay my way out I will."

Although Richard was appalled he didn't feel like

furthering an argument with somebody he hardly knew during what was otherwise a convivial evening. He was further bewildered by the apparent equanimity with which Hal's unpatriotic views had been received by the other people in the group. Despite a few disapproving expressions nobody voiced disagreement. If such views had been expressed in Richmond the speaker would have been forced to leave the room – at the very least.

As they walked home Richard expressed his surprise to Foster at the lack of interest in a war which was killing so many of the group's fellow countrymen. "Well. You shouldn't be that surprised. You know that people are sick to death of the casualties, the financial burden of the war is crippling and people want rid of Lincoln. This war is taking us nowhere. You know people are calling for an armistice." Richard knew all this to be true but Foster's apparent acceptance of Hal's views seemed to reflect the war-fatigue of the nation.

Instinctively realising that he had spoken rather abruptly to his friend Foster put his hand on his shoulder and smiled. "Look, I know Hal's a jerk. I can't stand him neither can my sisters; he's always touching them up and making obnoxious remarks but he only said what a lot of people are saying and thinking. And Lincoln's freeing all the slaves in January didn't help either. He probably had to do it to keep the support of Europe but Negroes are filling the jobs of men that are going to be drafted. Lincoln pleased the abolitionists but few else- save the blacks of course. I see trouble. Tell you what! The next time I come home let's go to a Draft meeting."

It was not until the middle of June that Foster came home next. The Draft had been in operation for some weeks; the uncertainty and unfairness of it were causing much controversy with the increasingly lengthy casualty lists and there was talk of riots. "No wonder",said Foster. "If you're rich you can buy your way out of it and if you're poor you risk having your bloody head blown off." It was common knowledge that the Scottish-born industrialist Andrew Carnegie, Roosevelt the businessman and the banker J. Pierrepoint Morgan had all been drafted and had paid substitutes.

Richard handed to Foster the New York Times which he had been reading and pointed to an article. "Read that. It's about the Irish again." Foster picked it up and read it.

"Yes. There's been lots of talk about that as well as articles. They are saying the Draft is fixed so as to get them out of the way. There may be truth in that. After all, somebody has to choose the names to put in the barrel in the first place. Anyway, we'll see for ourselves this afternoon.

Although there were large numbers of Irish who fought voluntarily on each side (each Army had Irish brigades a number of which ended up fighting each other) there was also a sizeable section of the Irish community who felt they were expected to take part in a war to free the slaves who would then become a threat to their jobs. Matters were not helped by the suspicion that the Draft was rigged against them. This antipathy between the Negroes and the Irish would be a bitter legacy of the war.

The hall was packed with apprehensive people. Many were pale and tight-lipped. Some were making jokes and laughing unconvincingly. On the platform at the front of the building stood the drafting wheel -a large barrel with a handle. Several nervous-looking officials sat at a table. A number of soldiers were standing around the hall watching the crowd carefully, trying to identify potential trouble- makers. Although there had not as yet been major trouble at a Draft meeting-mainly small disruptions,it appeared only a matter of time before a serious outbreak of violence erupted.

One of the officials stood in front of the wheel and was securely blindfolded. He cranked round the handle and put his hand into a hole in the wooden structure. He pulled out a piece of paper and handed it to another official. A young woman sitting in front of Richard gripped her husband's hand until her knuckles whitened.

"Whelan – Joseph. P. 37 White Street. Date of birth 14th July 1842. There was no sound. Presumably neither Whelan – Joseph.P. nor any of his relatives had seen fit to attend the meeting.

"Well, that's the first name and that's Irish," whispered Richard to Foster who nodded in agreement." The meeting progressed and names were quickly pulled out and read out to occasional cries of dismay, screams or even outbreaks of sobbing. The young woman in front of Richard now had her arms round her husband and was gripping on to him as though somebody was about to snatch him away from her . A substantial number of names were Irish.

"Doyle- Daniel. 1130 Richmond Street. Date of birth 3rd June 1829. Richard heard a yell behind him. A huge dirty –looking man in rough clothes had leapt to his feet pushing over his chair.

"Oi don't believe it. Oi don't bloody believe it." The accent was strong Southern Irish. Richard had now heard so many different forms of Irish accent that he could tell the part of Ireland from which the speaker originated and sometimes even the county. "The bloody English hanged my father at the gates of Dublin. And drove me, my mother and my brothers from our home and forced us onto a coffin ship here. Now the bloody Protestant American bastards are trying to kill me.

Well, I won't go and that's that. They'll have to bloody shoot me first."

Doyle barged his way out of the hall to mixed rumbles of approval and disapproval and shouts such as 'Long live the sons of Erin', 'they won't get me either', 'Traitor' or 'Shirking Irish bastard.'

Then the last name was read out. "O' Sullivan – Michael 107 Brook Street. Date of birth 15th January 1843." Richard heard a scream from just behind him. "You're not taking my boy. He's only just twenty. You bastards have fixed it against us Irish." A large woman rushed up to the platform waving her umbrella but the soldiers were too quick for her; screaming and sobbing she was removed but now the shouts of support seemed to outnumber the cries of disapproval.

The meeting finished. Save for the relieved young woman in front of Richard who was folded in her husband's arms in a passionate embrace the mood of the meeting was ugly. Foster turned to Richard as they shuffled their way out. "It's a miracle there was no violence. But there will be soon. The authorities are building up trouble for themselves".

Now, as Richard stepped into the street he sensed unusual tension. New York had always been a busy, vibrant place but this evening a feeling of panic and frenzy filled the air. People were running, cab and carriage drivers were swearing at each other. Even the horses seemed to sense unease. They were restless in the solid jam of traffic, their whinnies mingled with the shouts.

A very fat overdressed man puffed along and stopped just by Richard to catch his breath. He leant down and put his hands on his knees and breathed in heavily. Eventually, he stood up and removed his hat; sweat coursed down his large, flabby face in rivulets.

Richard put his hand on the man's shoulder. "Are you alright? What's up?"

"I'm going to the Telegraph office. They say there's a terrible battle taking place. Come with me." Richard walked with his hefty companion who was now wheezing along with his fists stuck into his sides to ease the stitches.

A solid mass of humanity jammed round the Telegraph office. Richard and his unfit friend couldn't reach nearer than a hundred yards or so. They asked others what was happening and received a number of different answers but Richard managed to glean three consistencies – a terrible battle was taking place, the location was a small town in Pennsylvania called Gettysburg and the generals in command were Meade for the North and Lee for the South.

During the next four days Richard scarcely saw the Matthews family. Foster had been recalled to his military hospital and there was no prospect of his having any leave in the near future. Dr Matthews and his daughters were constantly at the hospitals dealing with the huge wailing cargoes of railway wagons which constantly rattled into the city. Mrs Matthews was preoccupied with committees and fund- rising.

New York was a bewildering cauldron of apprehension, excitement, jubilation and despair. Conflicting rumours swirled around and were superimposed on each other. "A great victory has taken place and Lee has surrendered and the war is over." ------- " Meade has been whipped , our losses have been catastrophic . Lee is now pushing North and East. He will be in Washington shortly dictating the terms of peace. We are finished." ------ "Haven't you heard? Britain will now have to recognise the Confederacy and the rest of Europe will have to follow. Our blockade of the Confederate coast will be broken."

Opinions and moods swung backwards and forwards. Views were optimistic or pessimistic depending on the disposition of the bearer. Gradually the swirling flood of rumours subsided leaving a thick turgid slime of certainty. Yes, a victory had been won by the North but in a sense it had been a pyrrhic victory. The financial and human cost was enormous. The casualties took weeks to quantify but eventually those of the South were estimated at some twenty – eight thousand men. This fact did not console the bereaved families of the North which lost twenty- three thousand.

Both sides would agree on one thing – that the lives of over fifty – one thousand men most of whom were in their early manhood were a terrible and unnecessary price to pay for a difference of political opinion.

The news of the 'victory' became certain on July 4 – exactly fifty-seven years after the Declaration of Independence. As the days flashed by it appeared that this was yet another case where the victors failed to consolidate their victory. Meade could have crushed Lee when he was crossing the Potomac but failed to do so.

Pennsylvania was in turmoil. Gettysburg and surrounding towns of a great radius were in chaos resulting not only from the confusion and destruction caused by conflicting armies but from the deluge of wounded troops.

Stricken men lay everywhere and remained helpless on the ground until they were eventually relieved or died. Here,-as indeed throughout the war- local women (known as ' angels of the battlefield')flocked to the battlefield and tried to provide what comfort and help they could – such as dippers of water but nobody on either side had foreseen the terrible carnage and the organisation (such as it was) was completely inadequate to deal with it.

Once the wounded had been collected they were then transported by wagon, boats and rail. The journeys were often very rough (particularly in carts jolting over uneven ground) exacerbating the injuries that had been received. The suffering were then dumped where they could be treated. Every public building in the vicinity which had four walls and a roof was converted to an improvised hospital and sometimes men had to be tended on open ground.

Citizens who had no medical skills found themselves caring for the wounded. Shirts, sheets and any other form of linen were used as bandages. Many people of Pennsylvania would not sleep between sheets for a considerable time to come.

The wounded streamed into New York in clattering rail cars. Some died on the way, some were conscious, some were crying, some were delirious and some were groaning. All were suffering.

On Monday July 13th 1863 Richard was walking in the upper part of the city on his way to a meeting when he saw a knot of angry people outside a building. His good sense told him to cross to the other side of the street and walk as fast as he could in the opposite direction but curiosity overcame good sense and he stopped to see what was happening.

Suddenly, a Negro came racing round the corner at a speed that Richard had never seen anybody run before. The man was near exhaustion, his upper lip was drawn back laying bare his teeth. His hands were flapping and his breath was rasping. He was followed by a crowd carrying sticks, clubs and any other kind of weapon. Most of the mob consisted of roughly dressed working men although there were a few women. Richard leapt into a doorway to prevent himself being knocked over. A number of people in the crowd which Richard had joined attached themselves to the pursuers. The air was rife with angry shouts and violent threats such as "get the goddamn black sonofabitch" or "let's tree the coon." Somebody reacted to this last comment.

"There ain't no goddamn trees man."

"We'll drive him up a goddamn building then and spike him."

Demonstrating crowds always contain two elements – the perpetrators and the onlookers. The former always orchestrate and participate whilst the latter tend to have little else to do but find idle amusement for themselves. They appear to support the protagonists and are always on the fringes of activity but are quick to melt away once they think that there may be any chance of their being hurt or singled out for detection and punishment . The loafer lounging against the wall clearly fell into the category of onlooker. He was tall, cadaverous, unshaven and wore a battered top-hat tilted to one side. A grubby red handkerchief was knotted round his neck. His filthy trousers were tied round with string at the knees leaving a space of about three inches long of bare leg above the battered boots whose uppers peeped up cheekily from the soles. He was chewing on a quid of tobacco.

"Why are they chasing that man?" Asked Richard.

"Because, man, he's a coon. That's why."

"Why should they chase him just because he's a Negro?" Richard immediately realised that his question was naïve and regretted it. He was well aware of the amount of anti- Negro feeling which had escalated since Emancipation and the introduction of the Draft.

Loafer raised his eyes to Heaven in the way that is done when trying to explain something to a child who is being particularly obtuse. "Man, you don't know nothin". He then paused. Something had occurred to him. "Say- you limey?" Richard nodded. Loafer smiled slyly as though some great revelation had been made to him uncovering decayed, brown, tobacco-stained uneven teeth like the posts of a rotten fence.

"We-ell. That explains it. You limeys don't know nothin". Then in a slow and deliberate manner Loafer continued. "We fight this war over the goddamned coons. Right?" The statement was over simplistic and Richard was about not to agree but Loafer was not to be thwarted.

" Abe then goes and frees every goddamn coon and they all come and take our boys' jobs when they're fightin' for them and now so many of our boys are getting' killed they are draftin'." Richard had heard and read these sentiments a number of times although expressed somewhat more eloquently.

Many northerners were against slavery but were opposed to total emancipation and saw Negroes as a threat to their jobs. Few regarded Negroes as an equal and favoured deportation to countries such as Liberia. Anti-Negro feeling was also fuelled by the heavy losses in battle and by the fact that employers had used Negroes as strike-breakers in recent strikes.

Richard's reflections were interrupted by screams such as he had never heard before. These screams were of a person in real terror as well as pain. They pierced through the sounds of running, shouting and traffic. Then suddenly the screams stopped. 'They've killed him'. He thought.

Now Richard became concerned for his own safety as a huge tide of maniacal activity surged towards him. Before he was able to move his feet in any direction they left the ground as he was swept through the door of a building. He could now see that he was in a drafting hall. The promised Draft Riots had begun and due to his own stupid curiosity he had been caught up in them. How ridiculous it would be when he had accomplished dangerous and difficult work in the South and arrived back safely in the North only to be trampled to death by an unruly mob!.

The Draft was in progress and the drafting wheel was being turned by officials. Lists and records lay on the table before them and observing the procedure was a crowd of people consisting of mainly potential draftees or their relatives who were not part of the riot.

Richard felt himself being carried forward as helplessly as a paper boat being swept along by a raging stream. He saw a narrow gap between a cupboard and corner of the room. He managed to plonk his feet on the ground and gradually inched his way through the tide of pushing, shoving and cursing humanity and eventually managed to wedge himself in the gap. He now became more of a terrified observer than a mere object being thrown about. .

Many rioters were armed with sticks, clubs, the odd sword and pistols. A heavily-built unkempt youth grabbed the drafting wheel and smashed it against the wall and now he and others were pulling it apart. Books and records were being thrown about.

Children were crying in the way that children do when they are frightened but not in pain. Then Richard heard a different kind of child's cry. This was a piercing scream, full of panic and terror. A little boy had been cut from eye to chin by a huge piece of splintered chair. Now the distraught mother was trying to comfort the child and at the same time staunch the flow of blood that was welling from the wound and flowing down her hands and covering her dress. A first glance would indicate that she was the victim.

Richard now heard heavily shod feet clunking up the stairs. The rabble was now taking over the entire building. The windows were dark with men outside trying to climb in. One clung to the outside of the window frame with one hand and awkwardly swung a club with the other against the window. There was a cracking sound and with another two ungainly swings the smashing glass showered those on the inside. Mobsters were now jumping into the room on top of those who were trapped near the window and their screams and cries added to the din.

Richard looked on in futile horror at the demoniac scene and thought for the second time in ten minutes that he was going to be killed. Would his father regret his coldness and indifference? Kate came into his thoughts again. Why was he thinking of her? Would she be upset to learn of his death (if she ever did) or would it leave her unmoved? What about Susan Smythe about whom he still felt guilty? Would she think he had got what he deserved? She almost certainly would if she ever learnt that he had been spying for the North.

There was now no movement at all in the room. The vandals who were trying to force their way into the building were wedged up against the innocent people who were previously in the building and now trying to make their exit. The result was an impasse.

Suddenly, to his horror Richard saw a lighted torch tossed through the window. Shouts of 'Fire' added to the frenzy. Richard's brain was now playing funny tricks and he remembered likening the chaos around him to illustrations from Dante's Inferno that he had seen as a child. The only difference was that nineteenth century dress had been substituted for medieval.

Now some idiot had thrown a bottle of whisky onto the flames causing them to flare with a brilliant white light. The flames spread to a desk and suddenly the impasse was transformed into a wild stampede towards the street. Screams rose to a crescendo .Richard now panic-stricken was clawing, snatching, punching and choking his way to the door. His smoke- laden lungs were agonisingly painful and the smell of smoke would be with him for weeks. After what seemed like five hours but were probably only a couple of minutes he reached the door and tumbled down the steps in a jumble of people and flopped onto the ground gasping.

Richard never quite lost consciousness as he lay on the ground but the whole scene was viewed by him as through a blurred telescope. Later he would recall seeing people lying on the street with others attending them and more assisting those who were still falling out of the building no longer violent, vengeful rioters but poor pathetic victims glad of help. Eventually Richard felt kind gentle arms around him.

"Come on old fellow can you stand?" A man and a woman helped him to his feet and draped his arms round them either side. The trio then hobbled and shuffled to a neighbouring street. A cab was stopped and Richard half lay half sat on the back seat with the other two leaning forward holding him so that he would not fall on the floor.

Eventually they stopped at a house and the couple with the aid of the cab driver assisted Richard up the steps took him inside and laid him onto a sofa. After some discussion most of which was lost on him in his blurred consciousness save for "he had better stay here for the time being" he felt himself being carried upstairs and then lost consciousness. When he awoke he saw a good-looking middle – aged woman sitting by his bed. He moaned, he felt sick and choked with smoke.

"You are alright – no bones broken – just very badly battered, bruised and smoke-filled."

Richard tried to move and winced. The woman smiled. "It will be a day or two before you will be able to do that without pain."

"Where am I? How long have I been here?"

"You're in my house. You've been here for about six hours. When you were brought in I gave you a sedative and examined you." That information was too much for Richard to absorb and he slipped back into oblivion.

When he awoke he was alone and was able to gather his thoughts and piece together what had happened. About half an hour later the woman returned to the room. "Well, you are looking much better now- I have brought you tea. I'll get you some food soon. You should be able to return to Dr Matthews in a few days. I found his address in your pocket. I know him well."

Richard painfully raised himself on one elbow so that he could take the tea and drink it without spilling it. After he had taken a few sips. "I think I heard you said that you examined me."

"That's right."

"You mean like a doctor- you took all my clothes off?" exclaimed Richard horrified. The woman laughed.

"No, not like a doctor, but as a doctor and yes I did take your clothes off – with the help of my assistant. When we heard the noise we thought there would be casualties so we went to see whether we could be of any assistance. He was with me when we found you in that sorry state on the street. I have seen a good many naked men and expect to see a good many more before my time is over- so don't look so embarrassed but I suppose I should have expected that reaction from an Englishman - Dr Matthews has told me all about you . Female doctors are unknown in England – fortunately we do exist in America although there aren't nearly enough of us."

Richard learnt that the streets were still unsafe. The riots were still raging and would continue for some days. During the time that Richard had been in bed over one hundred people had been killed, thousands injured and many buildings looted and burned. Negroes had been the focal point for attack and the most despicable act had been the destruction of the Orphan Asylum for Coloured Children; this beautiful building had been regarded as one of New York's finest architectural achievements.

The mob swept banshee-like into the building and carried off whatever they could seize – beds, bedding , carpets, furniture and the very clothing from the backs of the terrified children . These items were passed through to the street in a chain-like method to the women and children in the street who spirited them away. Some of the Negro children were killed, many of them were driven onto the streets to wander and be picked off by further predators. The orphanage was burnt to the ground. Nobody was surprised to learn that many of the accents of the rioters were Irish.

Richard stayed in bed for the next two days. The Matthews sent notes expressing concern and best wishes but were too busy to visit but Richard would be fit enough to go to them in a few days. Richard came to like his hostess Mrs McGuire and although she mentioned her husband ' The Senator' on a number of occasions it was clear that each lived their separate lives- she preferring to devote herself to her medical practice rather than be a 'political wife' accompanying him to political and social functions.

On the morning of the third day Richard's eyes flickered open . A man was sitting by his bed . Richard thought he was still asleep and dreaming but then he heard a voice. " Good morning Richard." He was now wide awake. The man was his father.

Epilogue

England

Present Day

Roger put aside the pile of papers. Much against his will he now had to leave for the college. He could see that he had several more nights reading. What had happened to Richard Clarke and Kate Turner? Did they finish up together? There must be some reason why there was so much material about the two of them in one place. Above all why had all these papers been lying in his uncle's loft for over seventy years?

Bibliography

Judith W. McGuire – Diary of a Southern Refugee during the War.

Donald E. Markle – Spies & Spymasters of the Civil War.

Ishbel Ross – Rebel Rose – Life of Rose O'Neal Greenhow, Confederate Spy.

Ann Blackman- Wild Rose – The True Story of a Civil War Spy.

Donald E. Markle – Spies & Spymasters of the Civil War.

Rosemary Agonito – Miss Lizzie's War – The Double Life of Southern Belle Spy Elizabeth Van Lew.

Elizabeth R. Varon – Southern Lady , Yankee Spy- The True Story of Elizabeth Van Lew , A Union Agent in the Heart of the Confederacy.

Edward Ball – Slaves in the Family.

Walter Johnson – Soul by Soul- Life inside the Antebellum Slave Market.

Adam Rothman – Slave Country – American Expansion and the Origins of the Deep South.

Sally Jenkins – The State of Jones .

Elizabeth Fox – Genovese – Within the Plantation

Household – Black & White Women of the Old South.

John D. Bennett – The London Confederates – The Officials, Clergy. Businessmen and Journalists of London Who Backed the American South during the Civil War.

James Marten- The Children's Civil War.

Anne. E. Beidler – The Addiction of Mary Todd Lincoln.

Maggi M Morehouse & Zoe Troda – Civil War America- A Social & Cultural History .

Reid Mitchell- Civil War Soldiers – Their Expectations and Their Experiences.

The Civil War Letters of Charles Harvey Brewster – When this Cruel War is over.

Chandra Manning – What this Cruel War was Over – Soldiers, Slavery and The Civil War.

E.C. Murdock- One Million Men – The Civil War Draft in the North.

Catherine Clinton – The Plantation Mistress – The Woman's World in The Old South.

Mark Dunkelman – Brothers One and All.

David .C. Rankin- Diary of a Christian Soldier – Rufus Kinsley and the Civil War.

Sarah Morgan – The Civil War Diary of a Southern

Woman.

Bell Irvin Wiley – The Life of Billy Yank – The Common Soldier of the Union.

Bell Irvin Wiley – The Life of Johnny Reb- The Common Soldier of the Confederacy.

Ernest B . Furgurson – Ashes of Glory – Richmond at War.